# My Own World

Mike Holmes

:01

First Second
New York

**First Second**

Published by First Second
First Second is an imprint of Roaring Brook Press,
a division of Holtzbrinck Publishing Holdings Limited Partnership
120 Broadway, New York, NY 10271
firstsecondbooks.com
mackids.com

Library of Congress Control Number: 2020919548

Our books may be purchased in bulk for promotional, educational, or business
use. Please contact your local bookseller or the Macmillan Corporate
and Premium Sales Department at (800) 221-7945 ext. 5442 or by email
at MacmillanSpecialMarkets@macmillan.com.

First edition, 2021
Edited by Mark Siegel and Jill Freshney
Cover design by Kirk Benshoff
Interior book design by Molly Johanson
Color assistance by Jason Fischer
Printed in China by 1010 Printing International Limited, North Point, Hong Kong

Penciled, inked, and colored digitally in Photoshop CC 2014
using a Cintiq 22HD display on a 2015 iMac.

ISBN 978-1-250-20828-6 (paperback)
1 3 5 7 9 10 8 6 4 2

ISBN 978-1-250-20827-9 (hardcover)
1 3 5 7 9 10 8 6 4 2

Don't miss your next favorite book from First Second! For the latest
updates go to firstsecondnewsletter.com and sign up for our enewsletter.

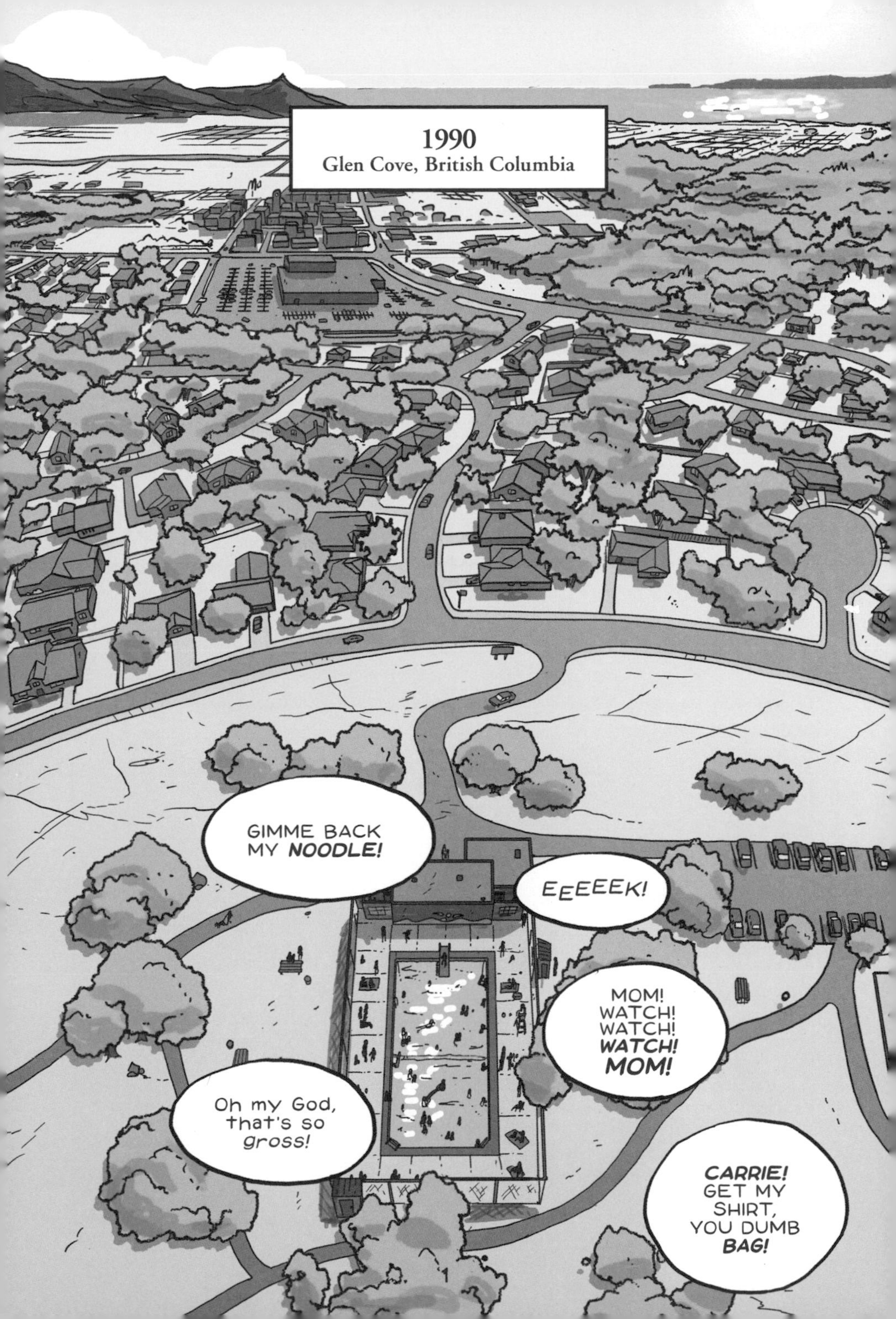
1990
Glen Cove, British Columbia
GIMME BACK MY NOODLE!
EEEEEK!
MOM! WATCH! WATCH! WATCH! MOM!
Oh my God, that's so gross!
CARRIE! GET MY SHIRT, YOU DUMB BAG!

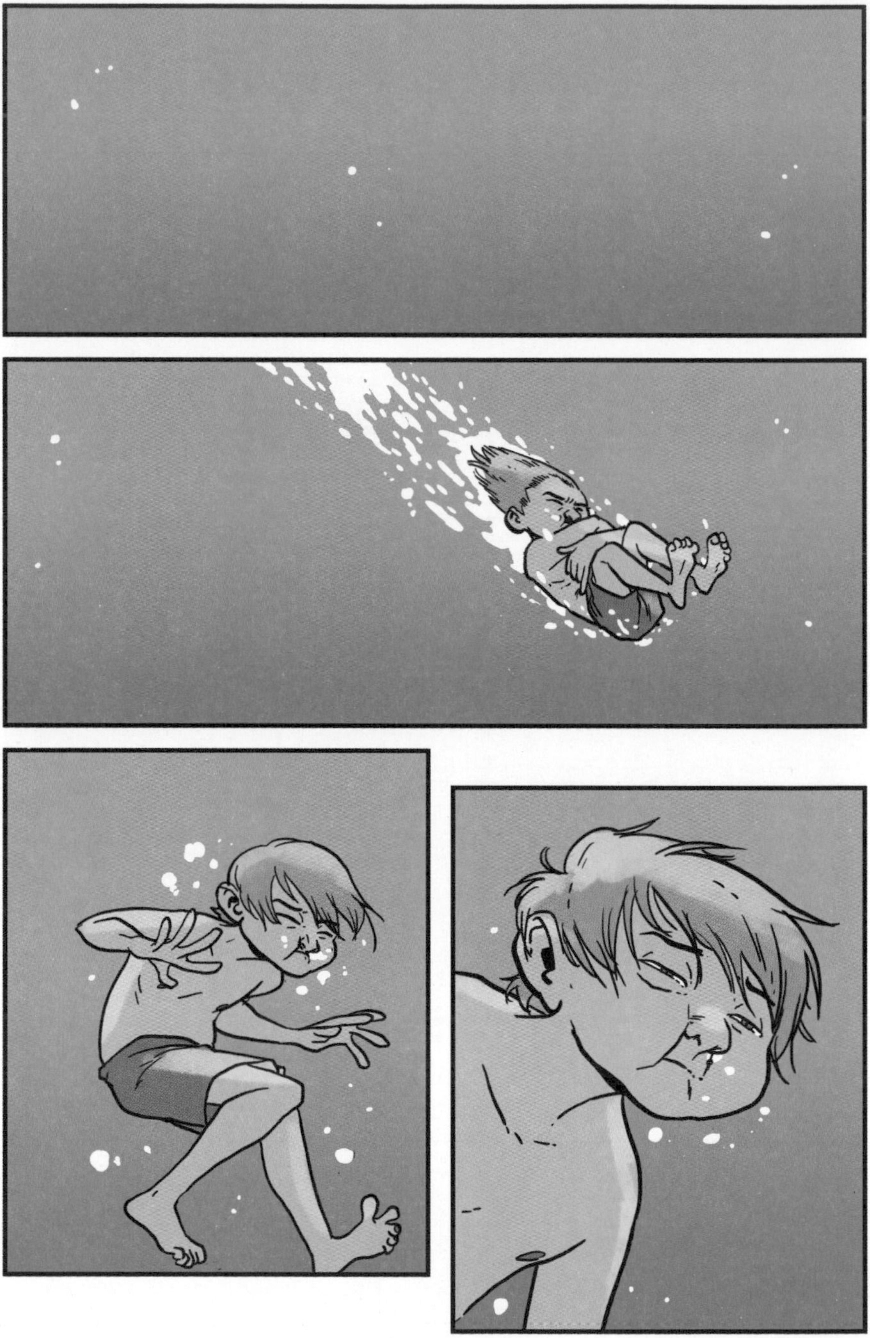

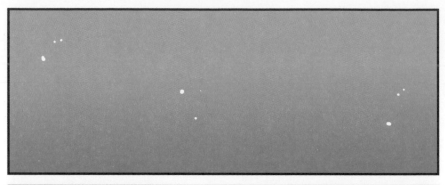

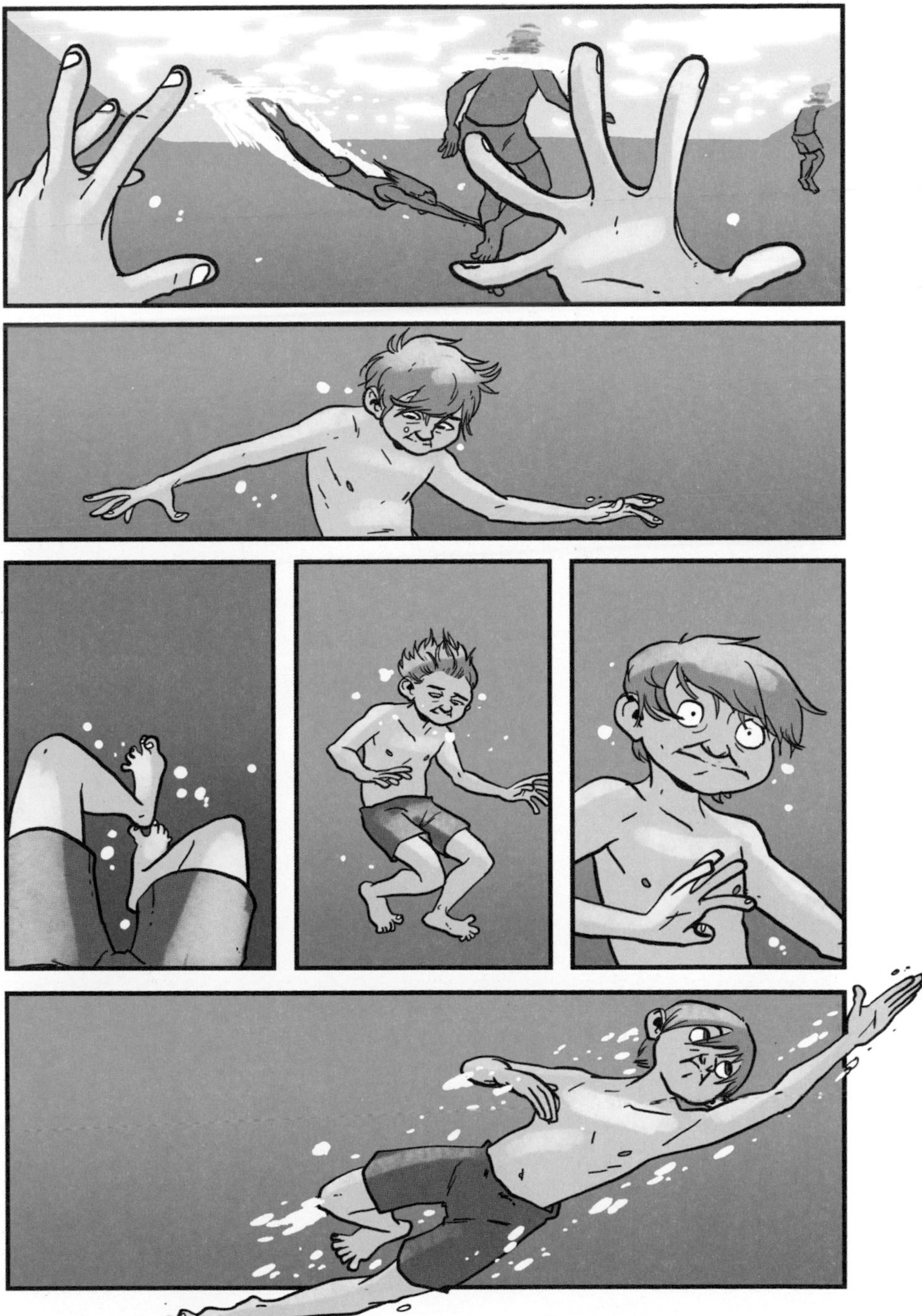

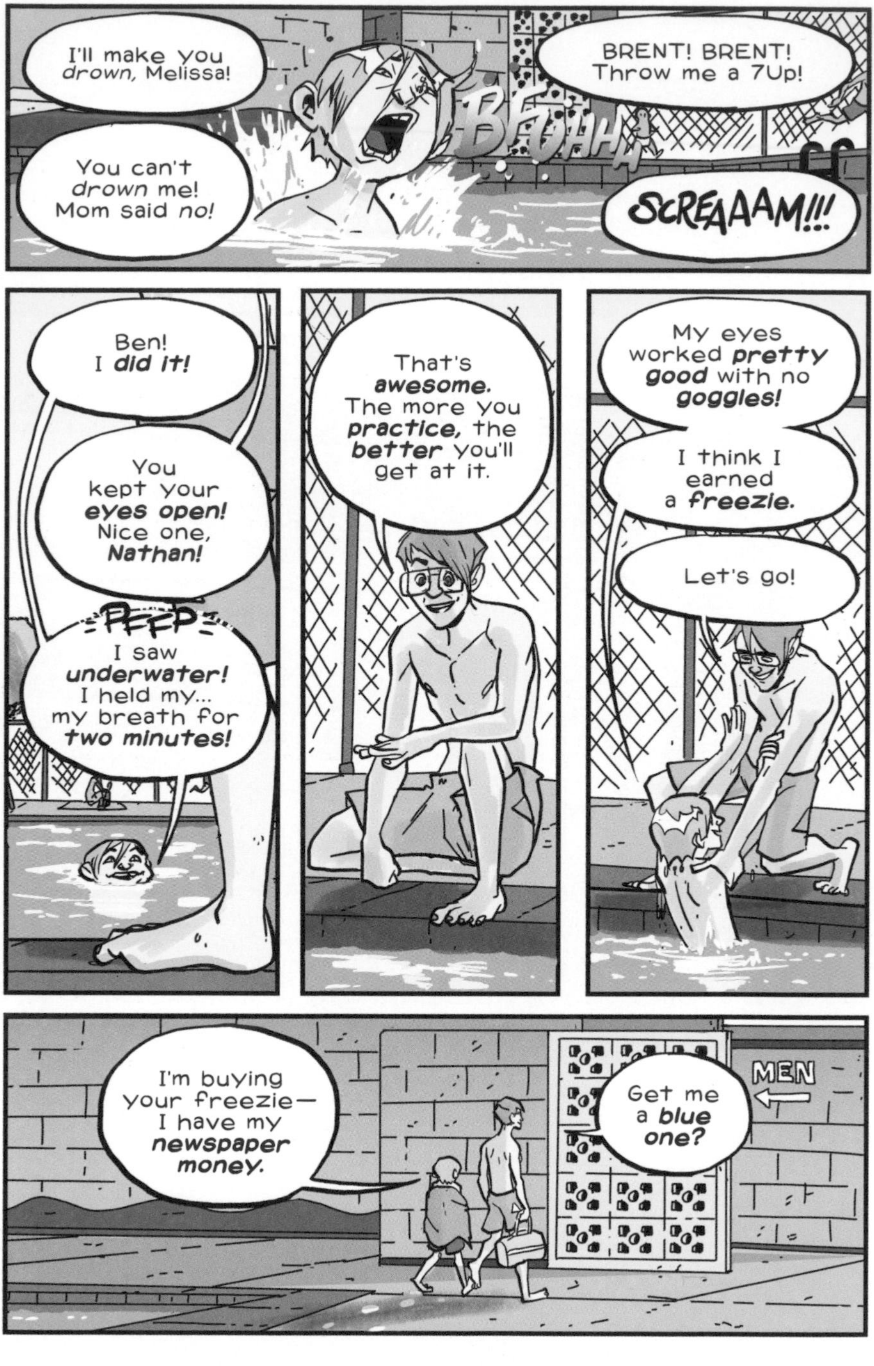
I'll make you *drown*, Melissa!
You can't *drown* me! Mom said *no!*
BFOHHH
BRENT! BRENT! Throw me a 7Up!
SCREAAAM!!!
Ben! I ***did it!***
You kept your ***eyes open!*** Nice one, ***Nathan!***
PFFP
I saw ***underwater!*** I held my... my breath for ***two minutes!***
That's ***awesome.*** The more you ***practice,*** the ***better*** you'll get at it.
My eyes worked ***pretty good*** with no ***goggles!***
I think I earned a ***freezie.***
Let's go!
I'm buying your freezie— I have my ***newspaper money.***
Get me a ***blue one?***
MEN

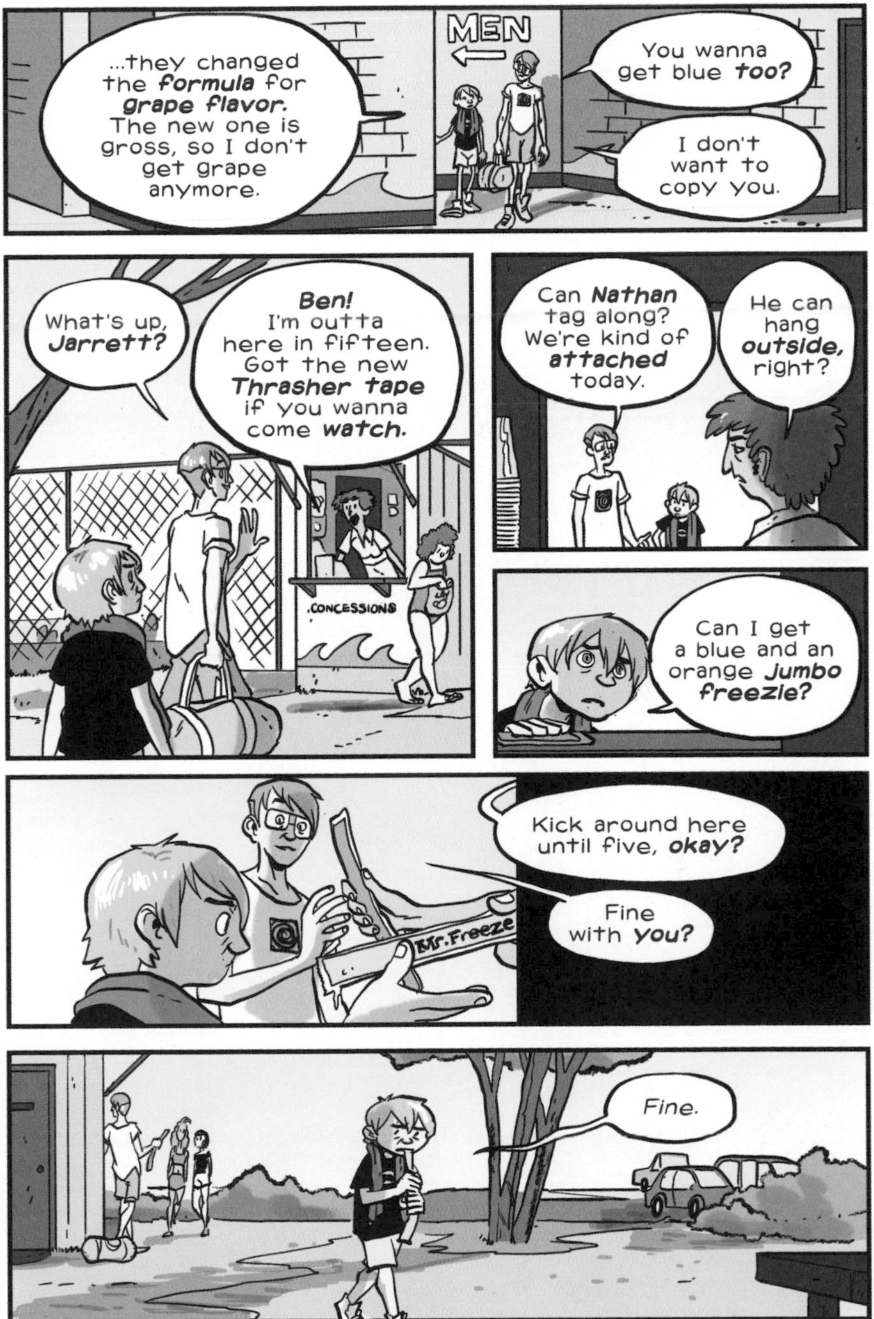
...they changed the formula for grape flavor. The new one is gross, so I don't get grape anymore.
MEN
You wanna get blue too?
I don't want to copy you.
What's up, Jarrett?
Ben! I'm outta here in fifteen. Got the new Thrasher tape if you wanna come watch.
CONCESSIONS
Can Nathan tag along? We're kind of attached today.
He can hang outside, right?
Can I get a blue and an orange jumbo freezie?
Kick around here until five, okay?
Fine with you?
Mr. Freeze
Fine.

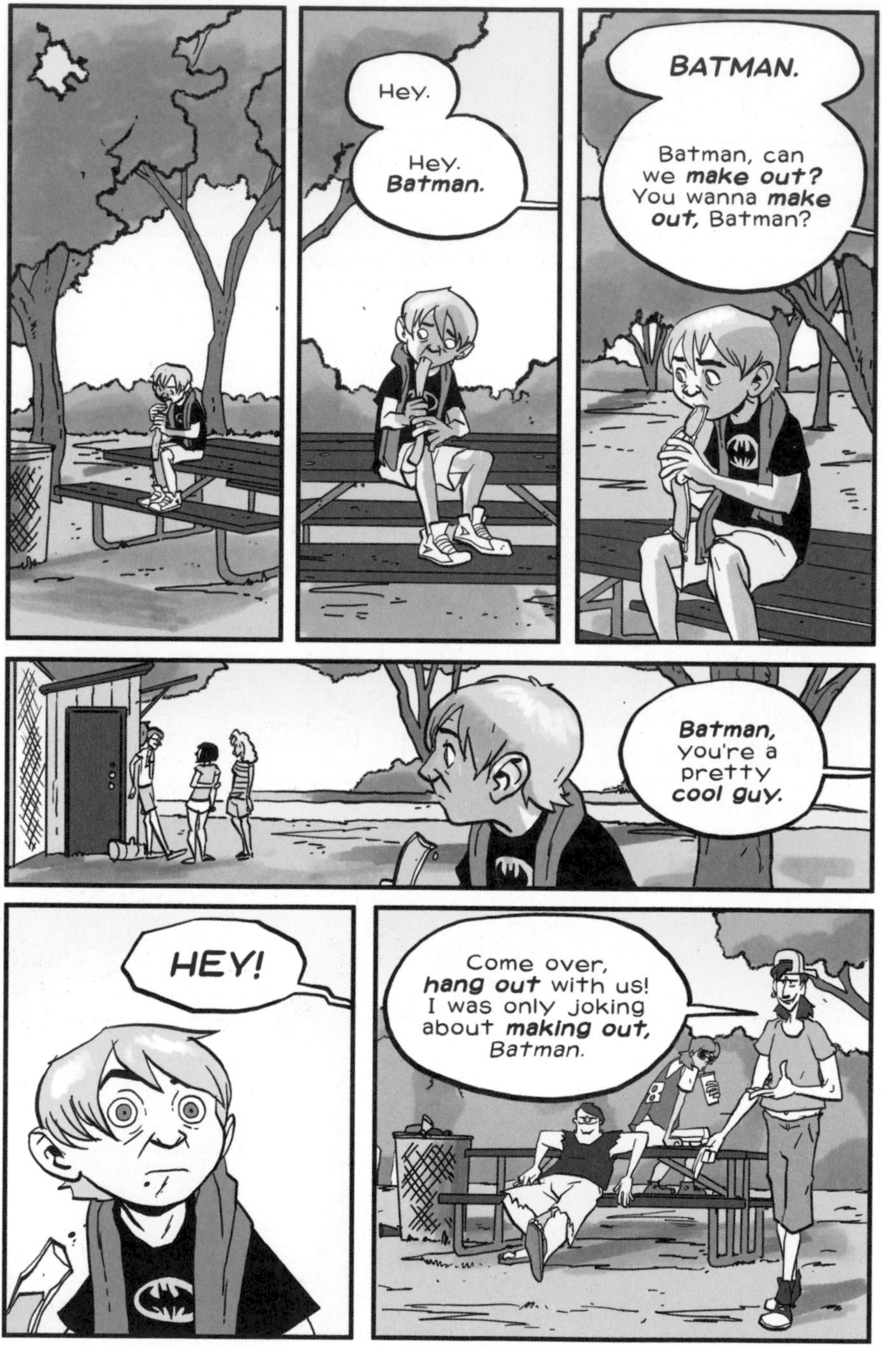
Hey.
Hey. **Batman.**
**BATMAN.**
Batman, can we ***make out?*** You wanna ***make out,*** Batman?
***Batman,*** You're a pretty ***cool guy.***
***HEY!***
Come over, ***hang out*** with us! I was only joking about ***making out,*** Batman.

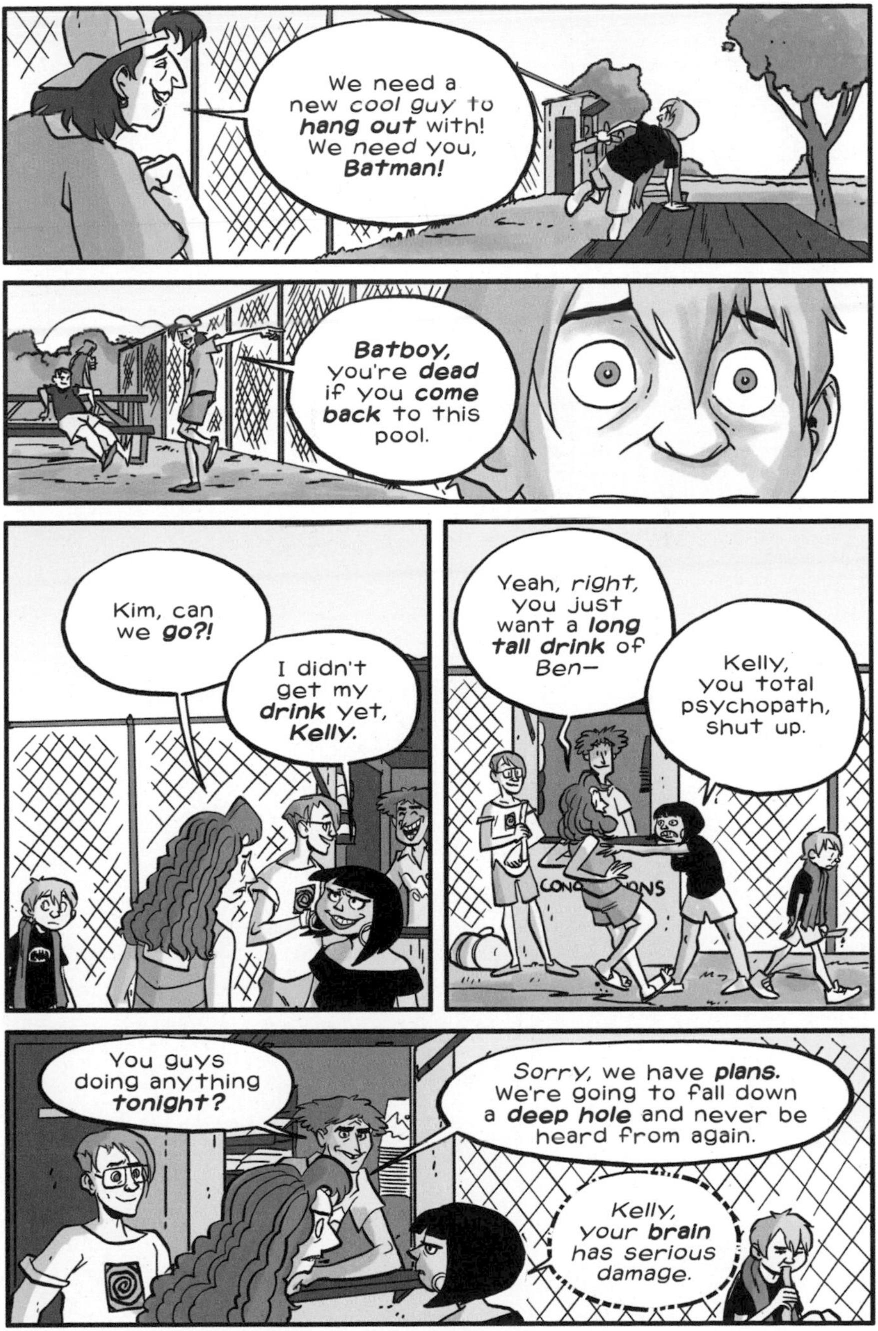
We need a new *cool guy* to **hang out** with! We *need* you, **Batman!**
**Batboy,** you're **dead** if you **come back** to this pool.
Kim, can we **go?!**
I didn't get my **drink** yet, **Kelly.**
Yeah, *right,* you just want a **long tall drink** of *Ben—*
Kelly, you total psychopath, shut up.
You guys doing anything **tonight?**
*Sorry,* we have **plans.** We're going to fall down a **deep hole** and never be heard from again.
Kelly, your **brain** has serious damage.

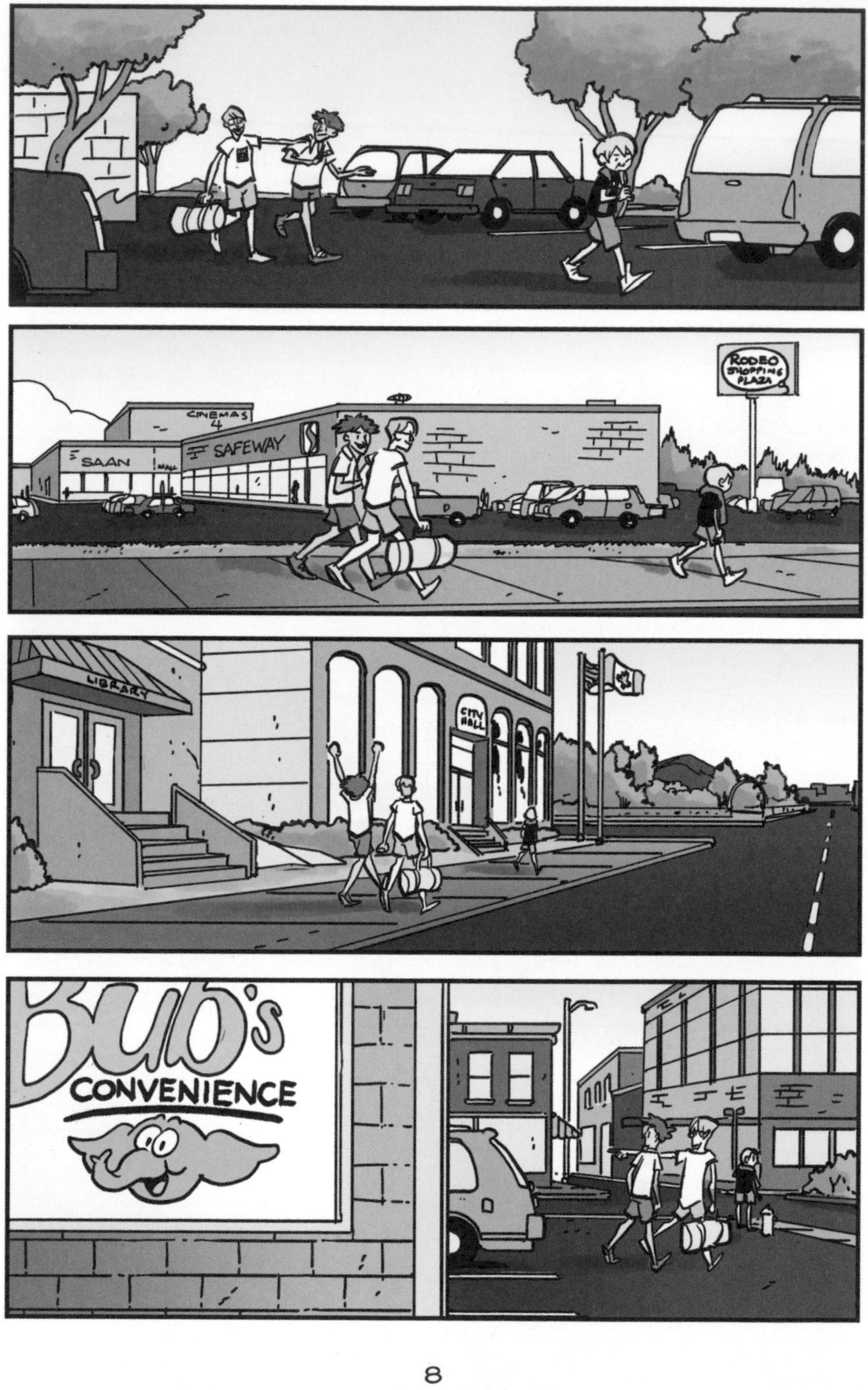
CINEMAS
4
SAAN
SAFEWAY
RODEO
SHOPPING
PLAZA
LIBRARY
CITY
HALL
Bub's
CONVENIENCE

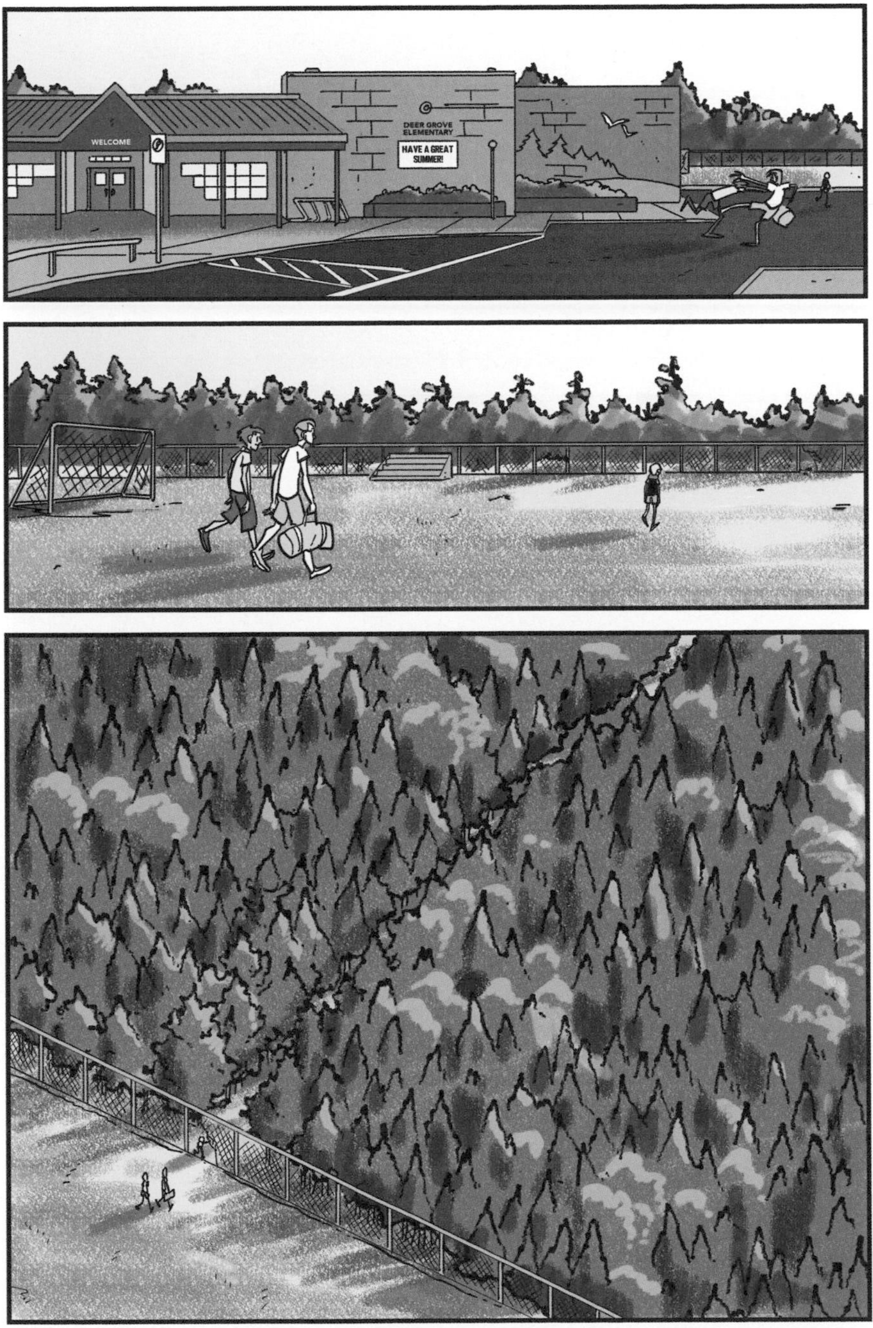
WELCOME
DEER GROVE ELEMENTARY
HAVE A GREAT SUMMER!

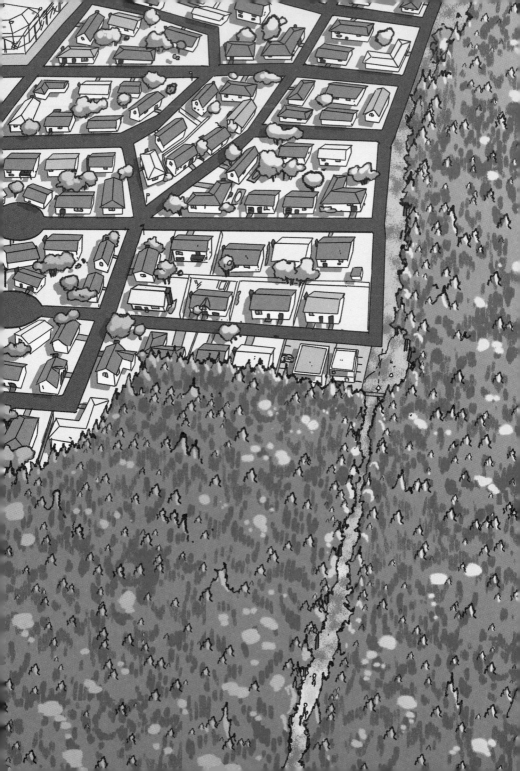

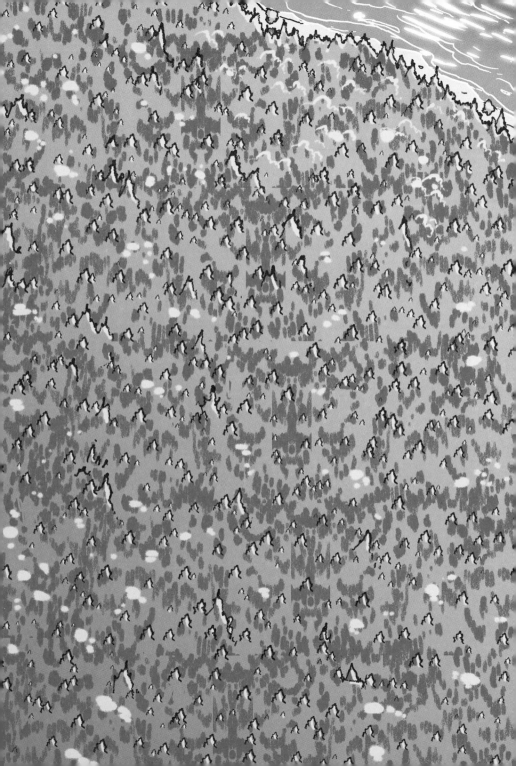

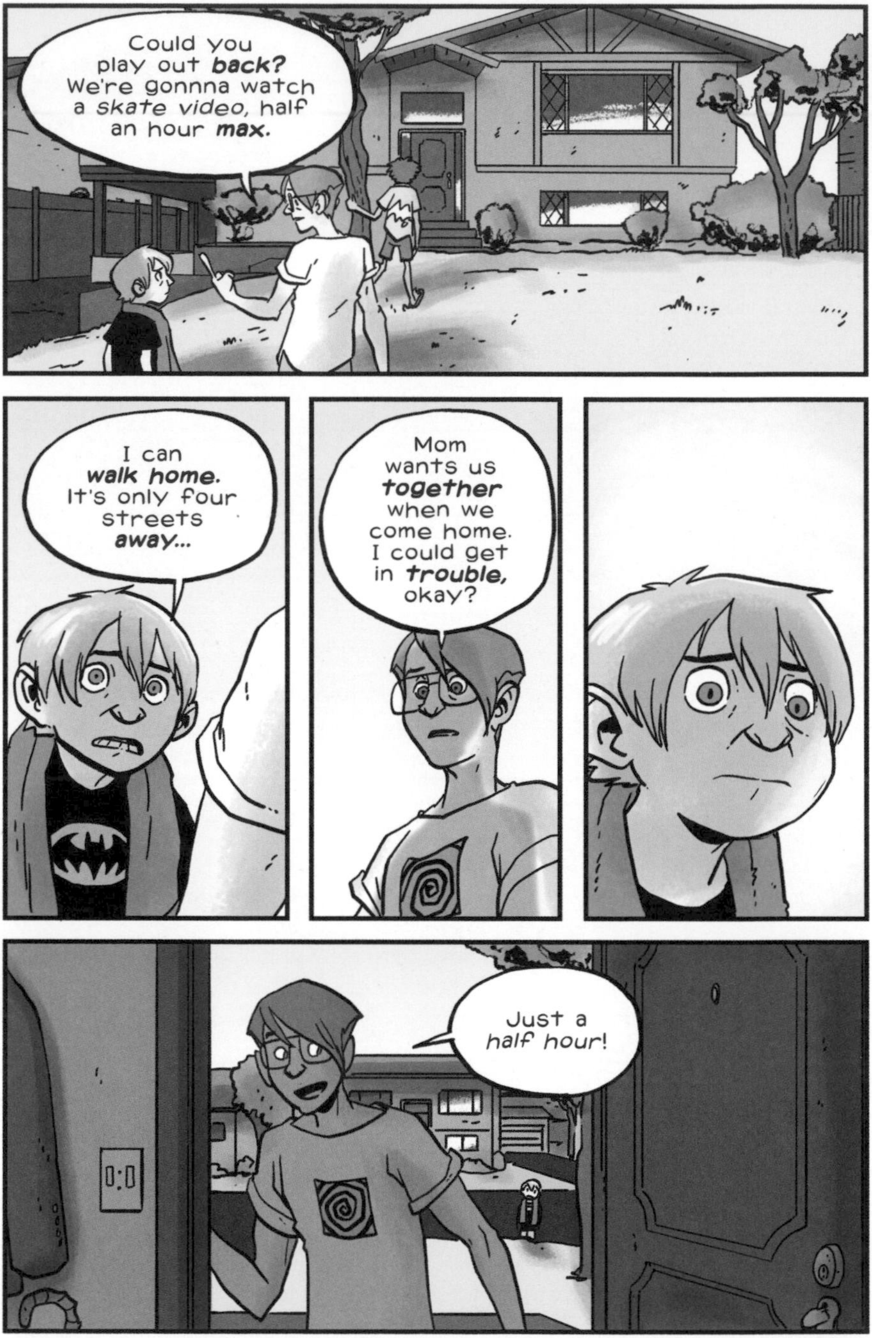
Could you play out back? We're gonna watch a skate video, half an hour max.
I can walk home. It's only four streets away...
Mom wants us together when we come home. I could get in trouble, okay?
Just a half hour!

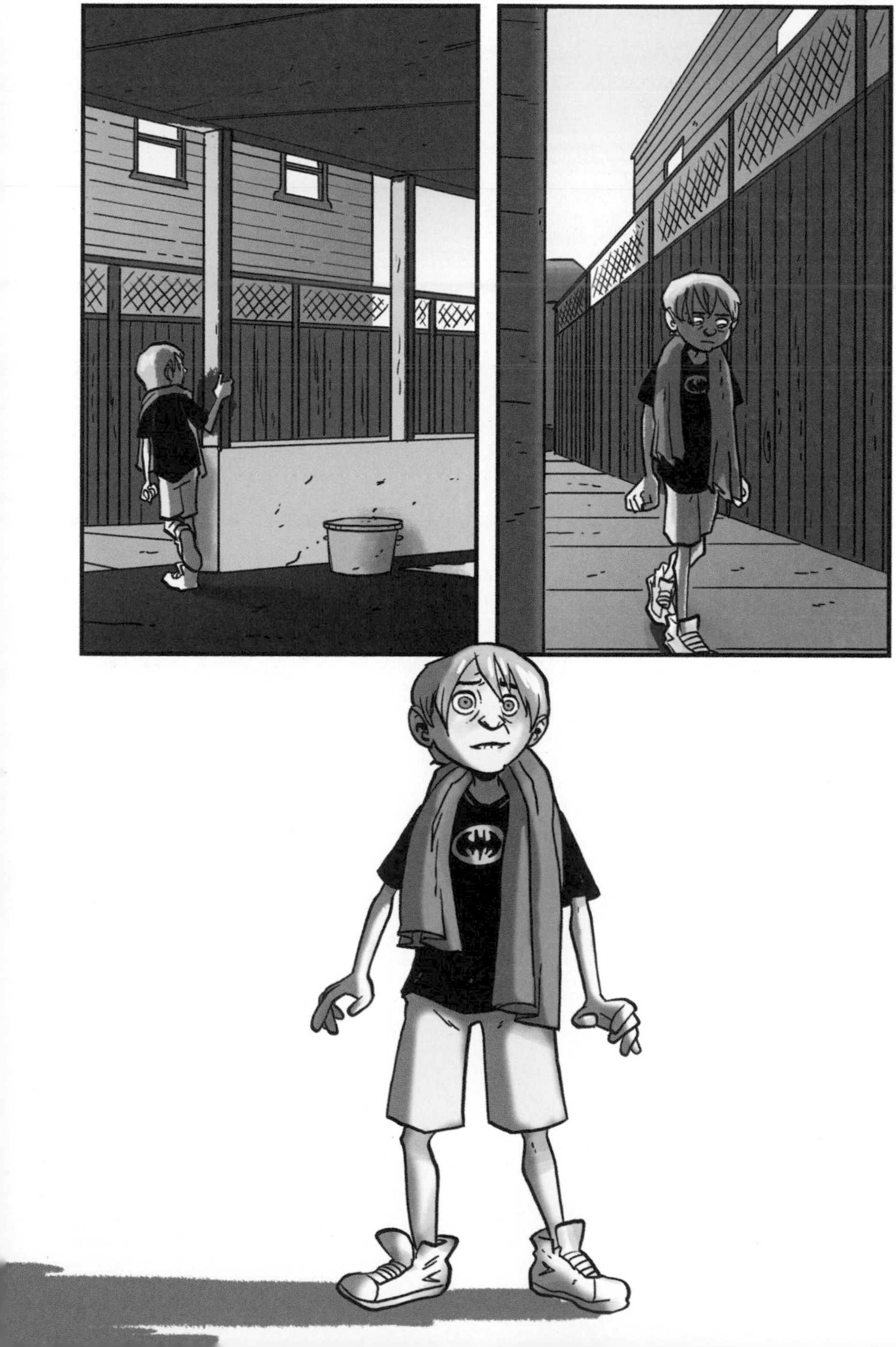

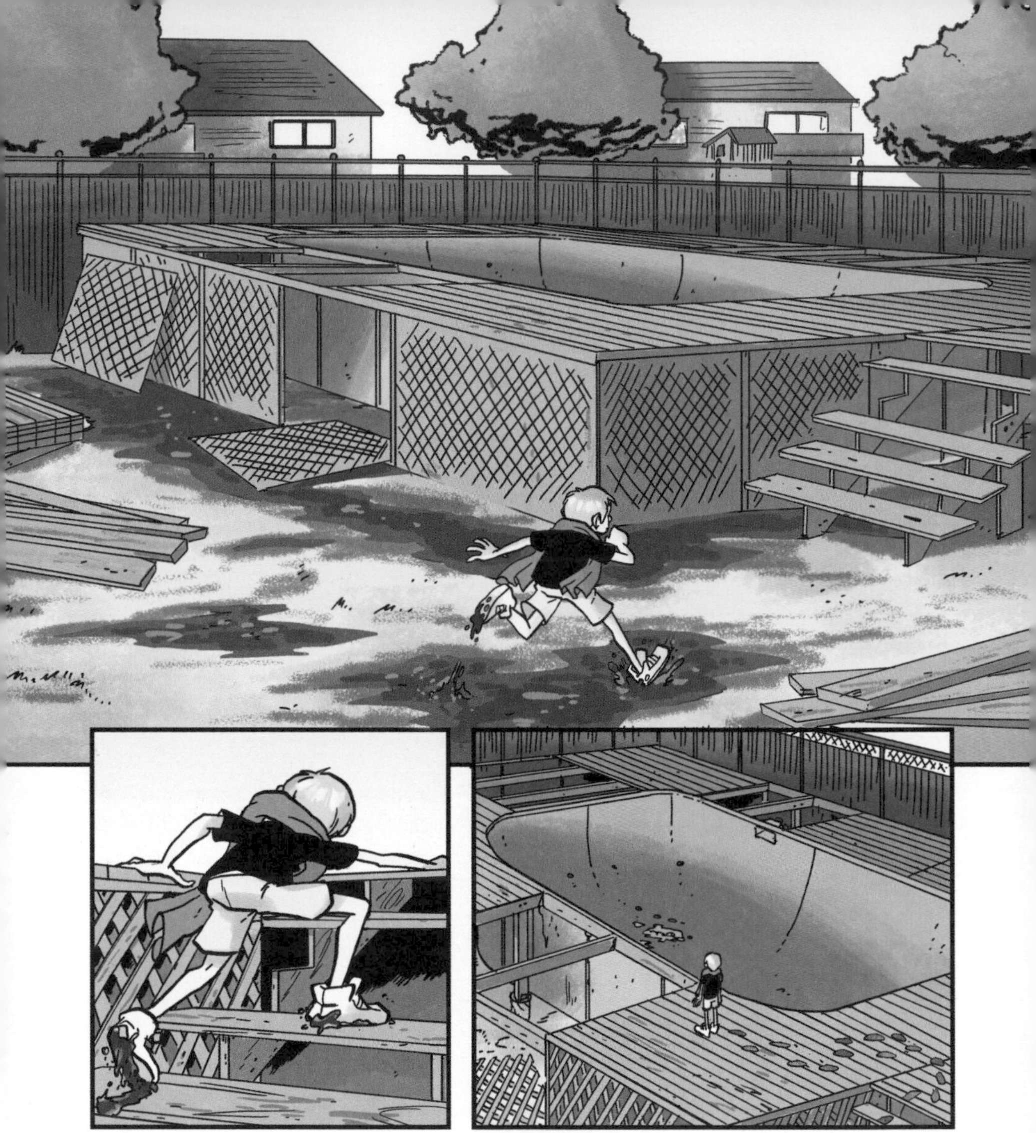

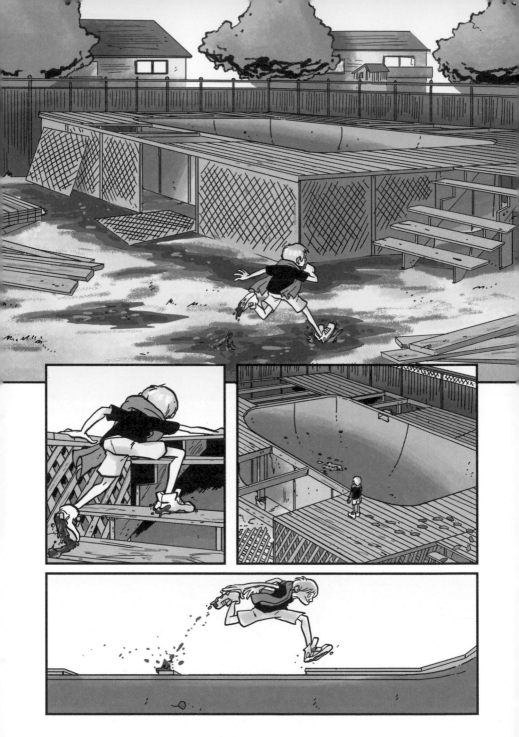

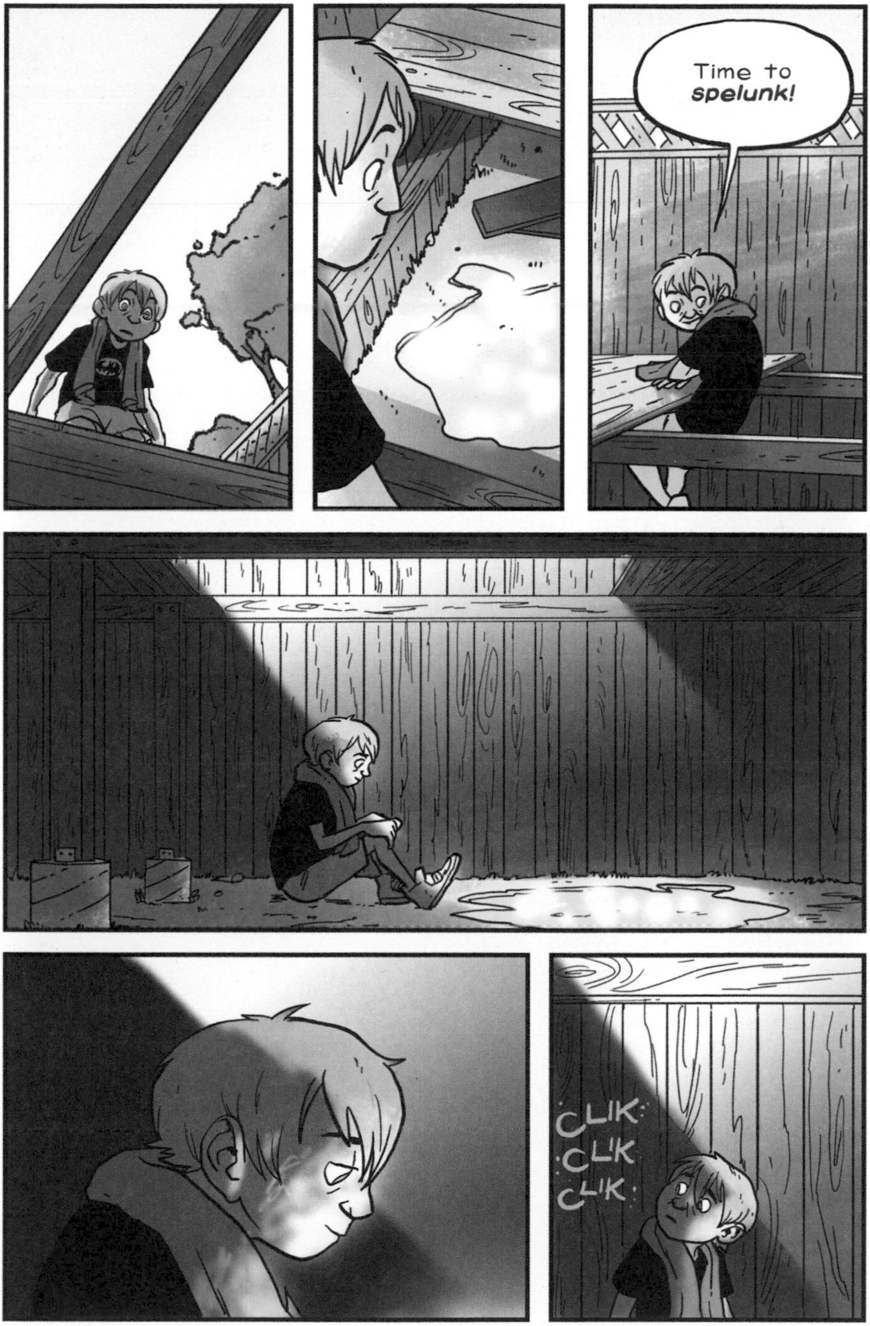
Time to spelunk!
CLIK
CLIK
CLIK

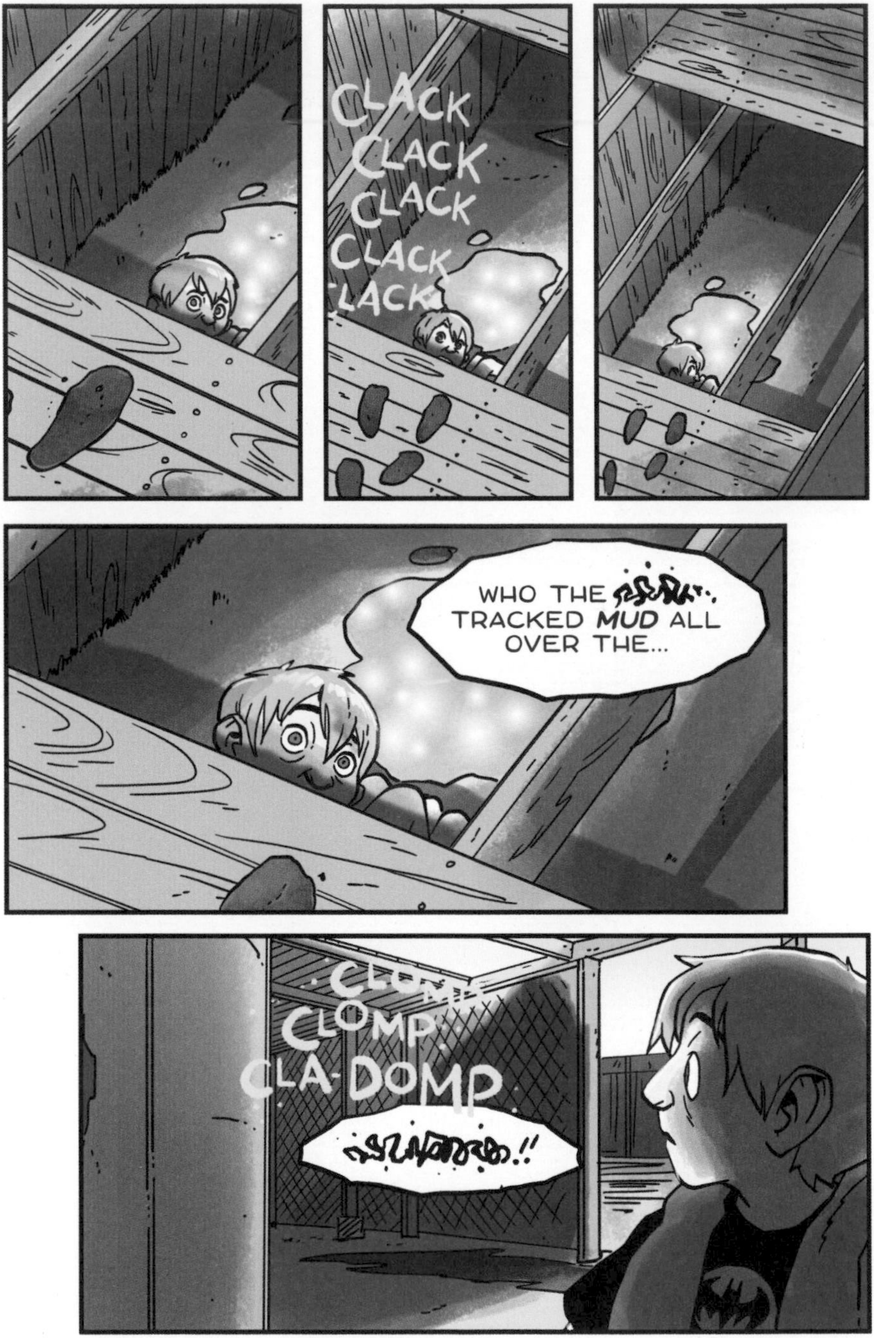
CLACK
CLACK
CLACK
CLACK
LACK
WHO THE TRACKED MUD ALL OVER THE...
CLOMP
CLA-DOMP

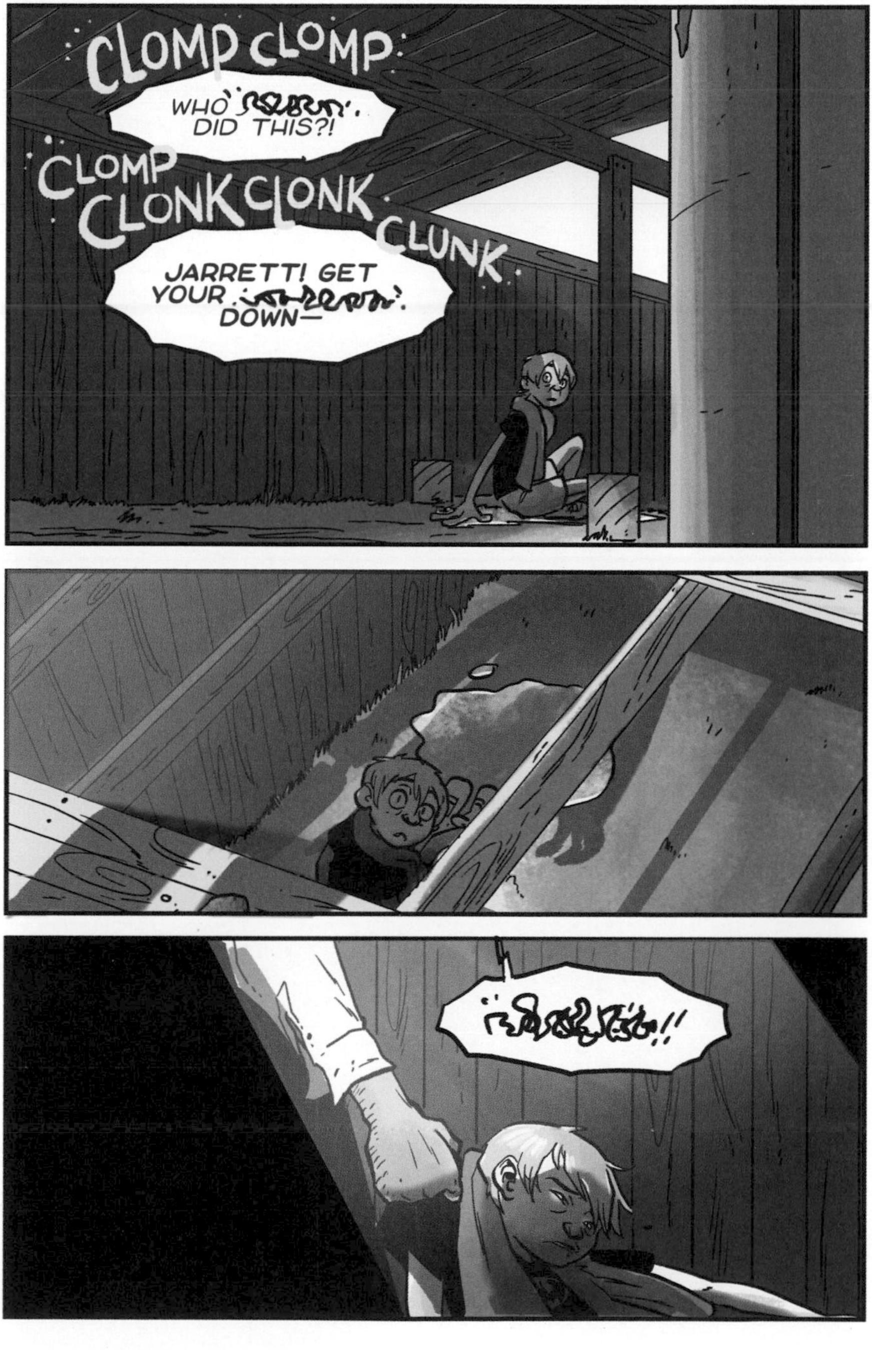
CLOMP CLOMP
WHO [grawlix] DID THIS?!
CLOMP
CLONK CLONK
CLUNK
JARRETT! GET YOUR [grawlix] DOWN—
[grawlix]!!

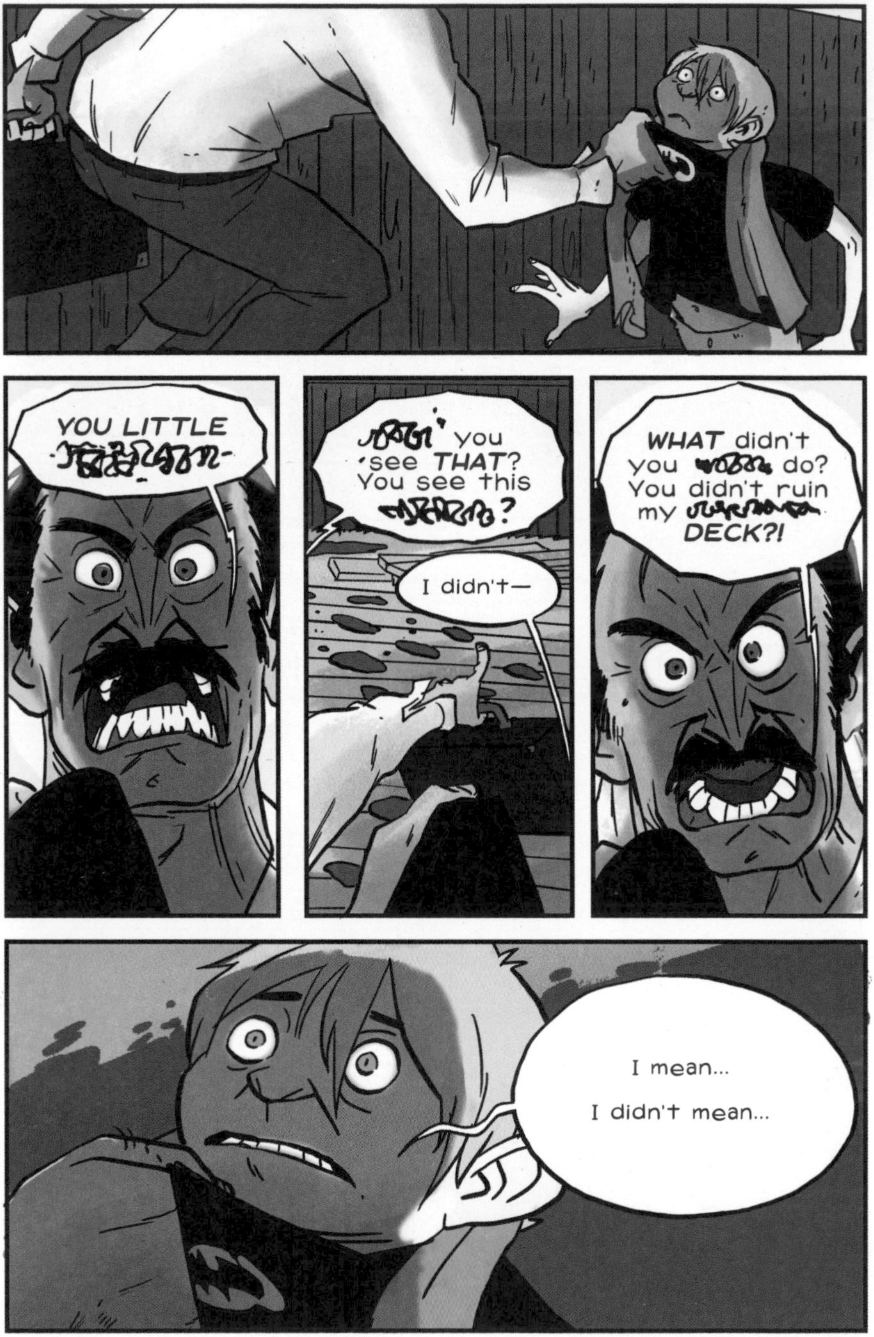
YOU LITTLE
you see THAT? You see this ?
I didn't—
WHAT didn't you do? You didn't ruin my DECK?!
I mean...
I didn't mean...

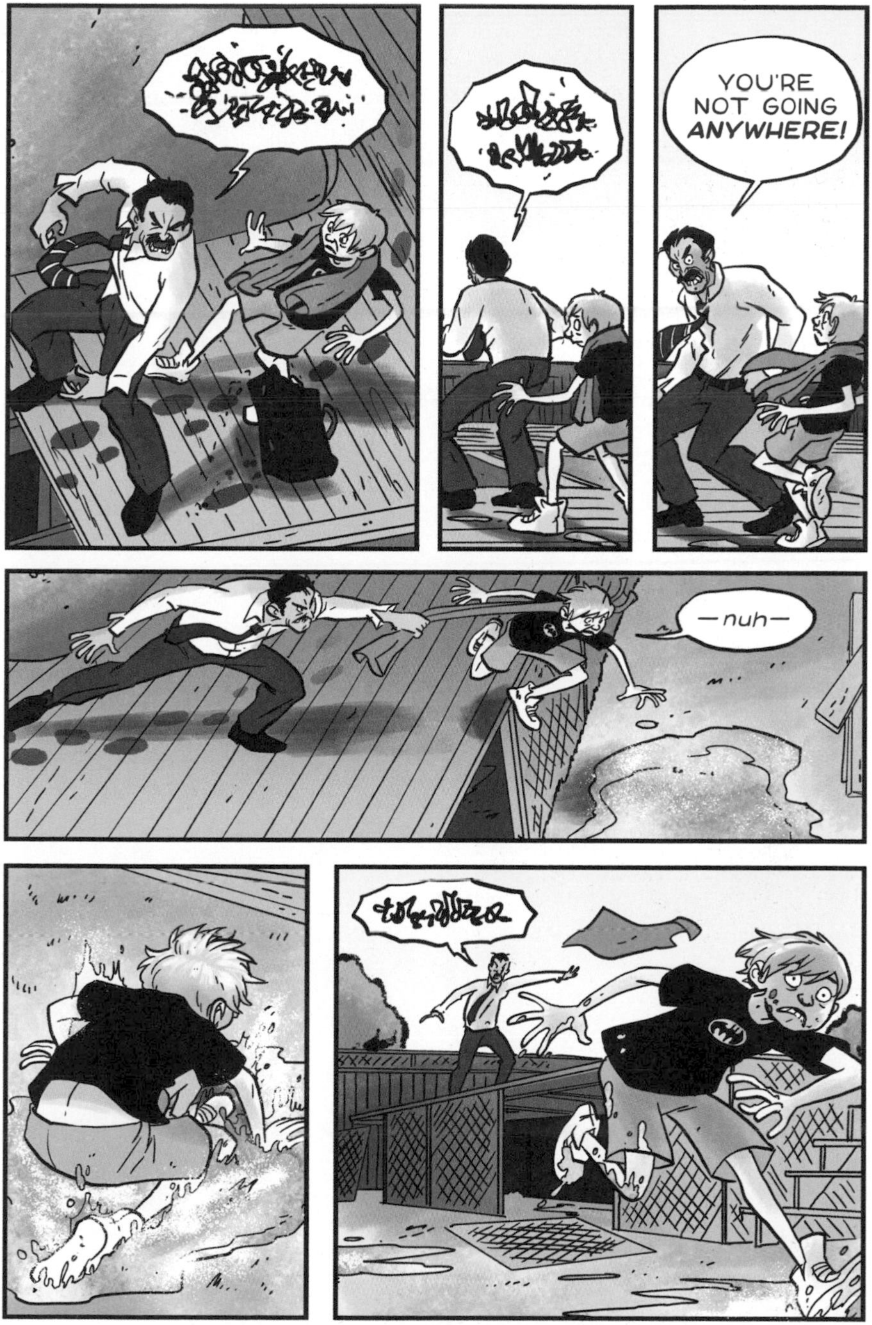
YOU'RE NOT GOING ANYWHERE!
—nuh—

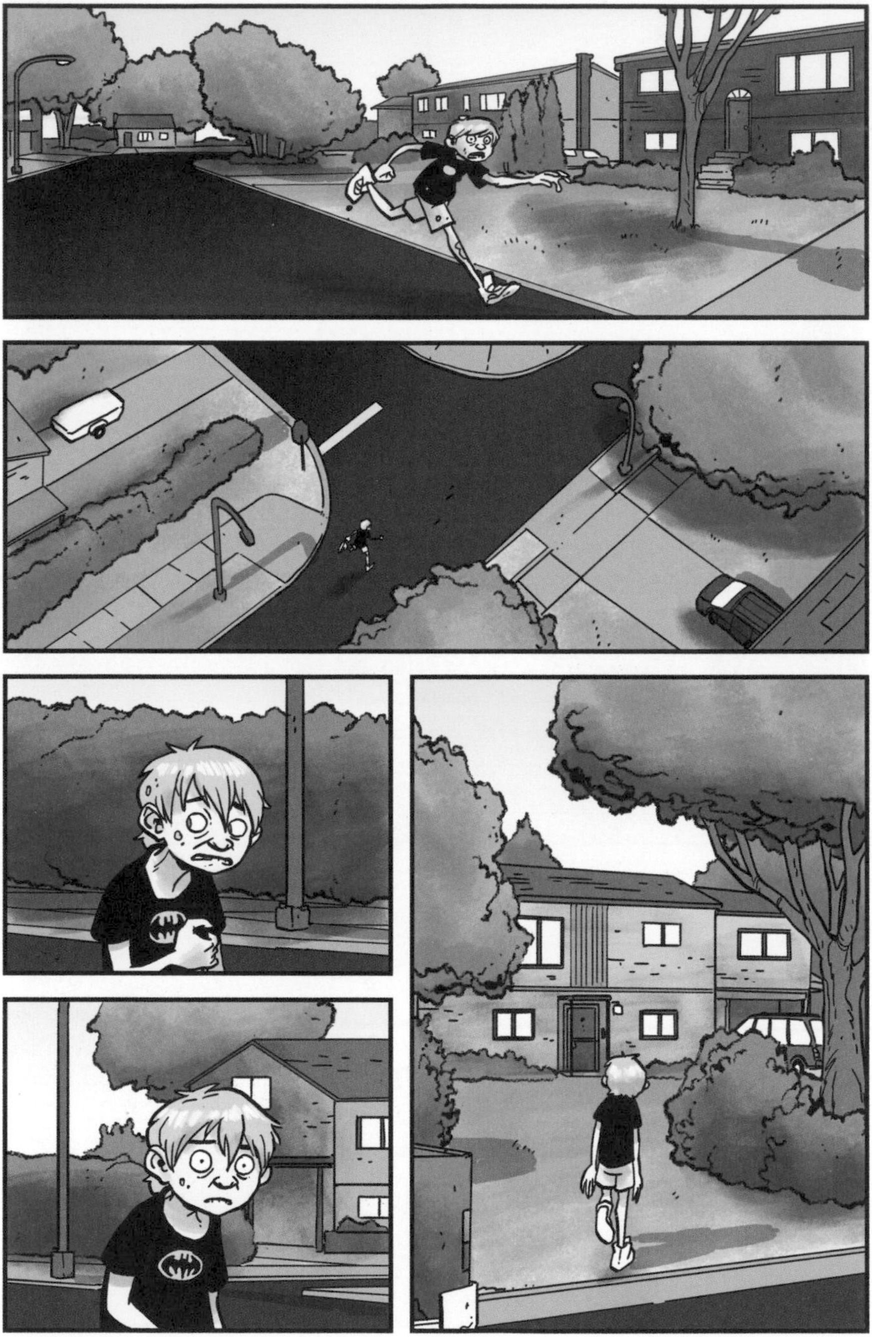

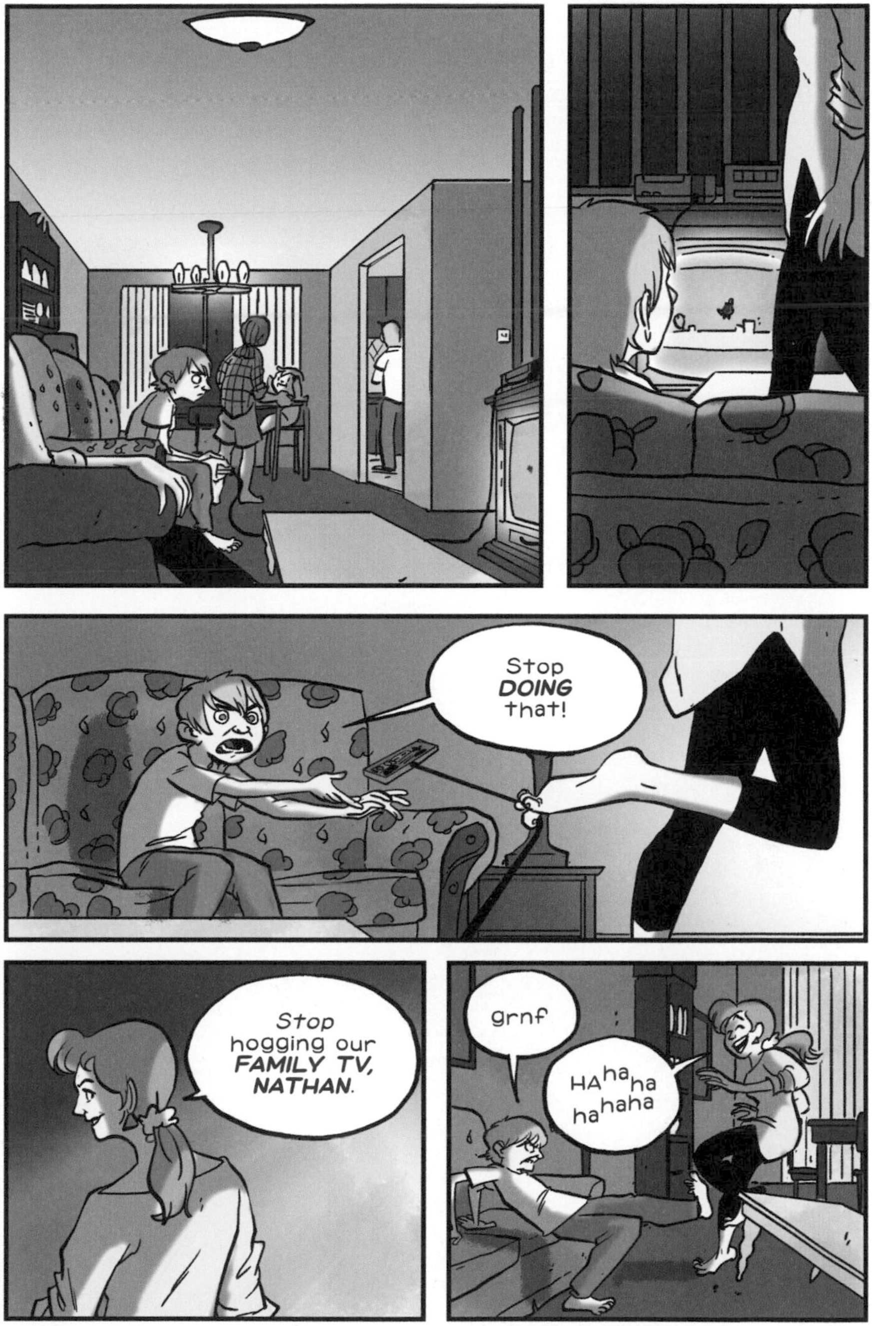
Stop DOING that!
Stop hogging our FAMILY TV, NATHAN.
grnf
HAhaha hahaha

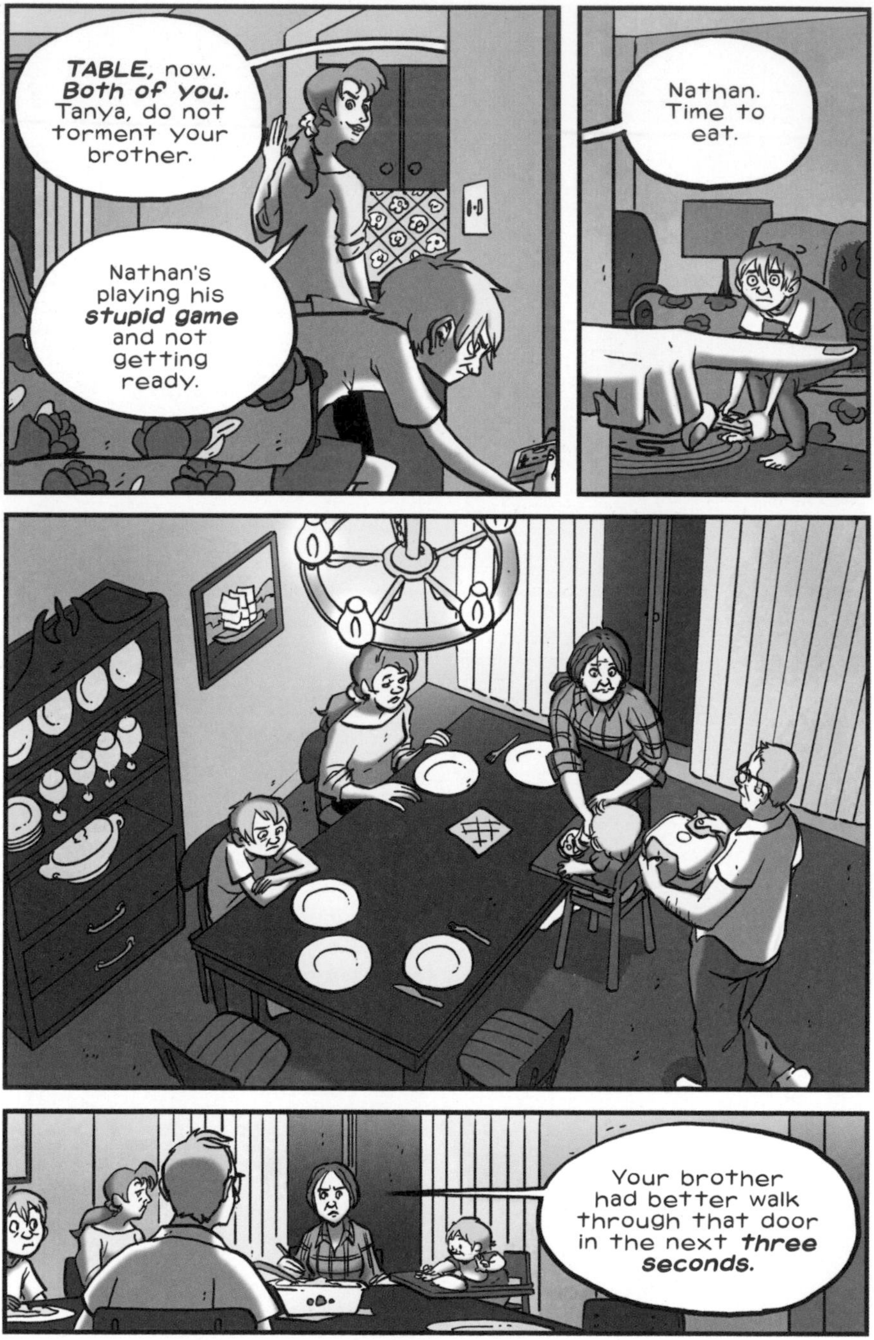
TABLE, now. Both of you. Tanya, do not torment your brother.
Nathan's playing his stupid game and not getting ready.
Nathan. Time to eat.
Your brother had better walk through that door in the next three seconds.

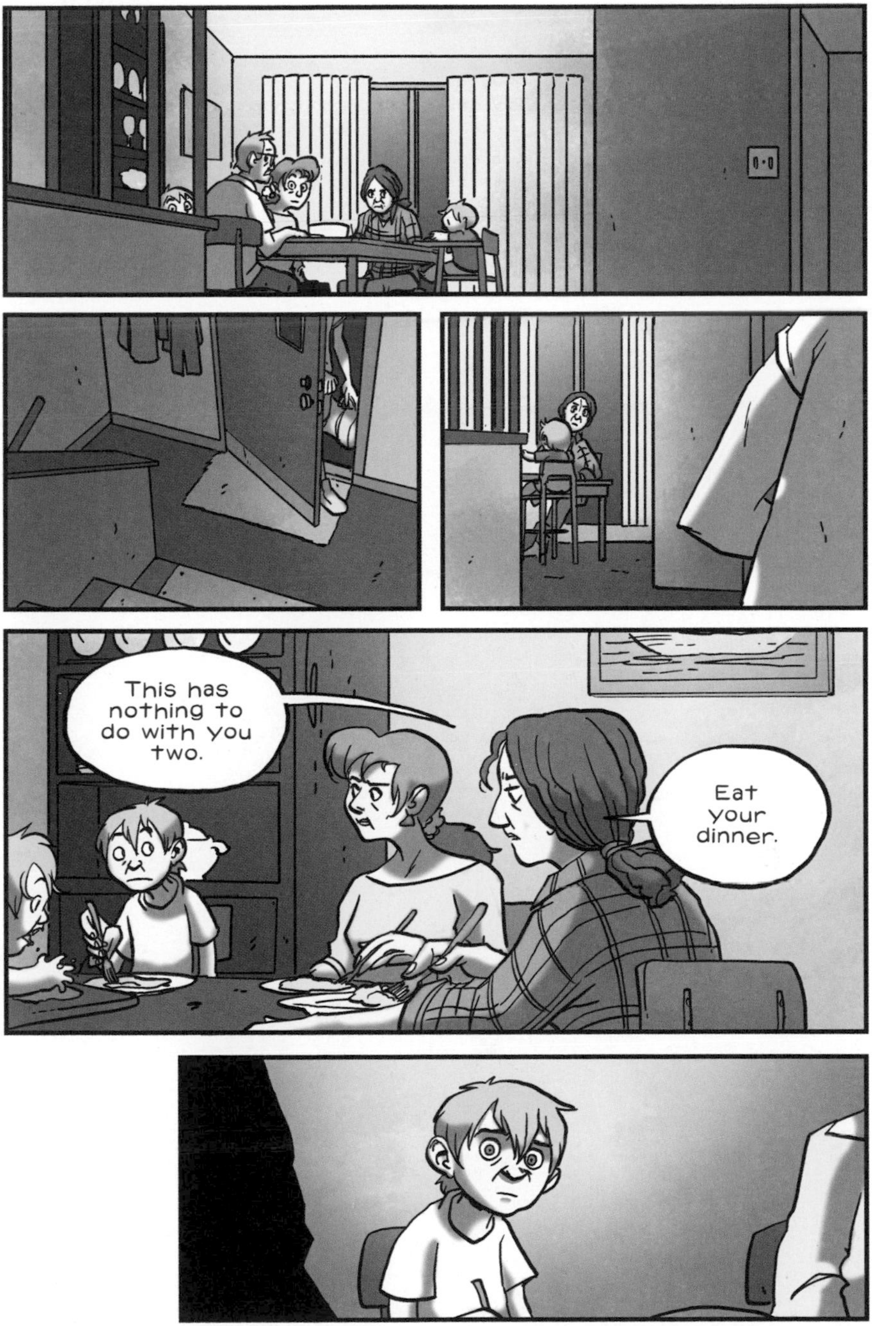
This has nothing to do with you two.
Eat your dinner.

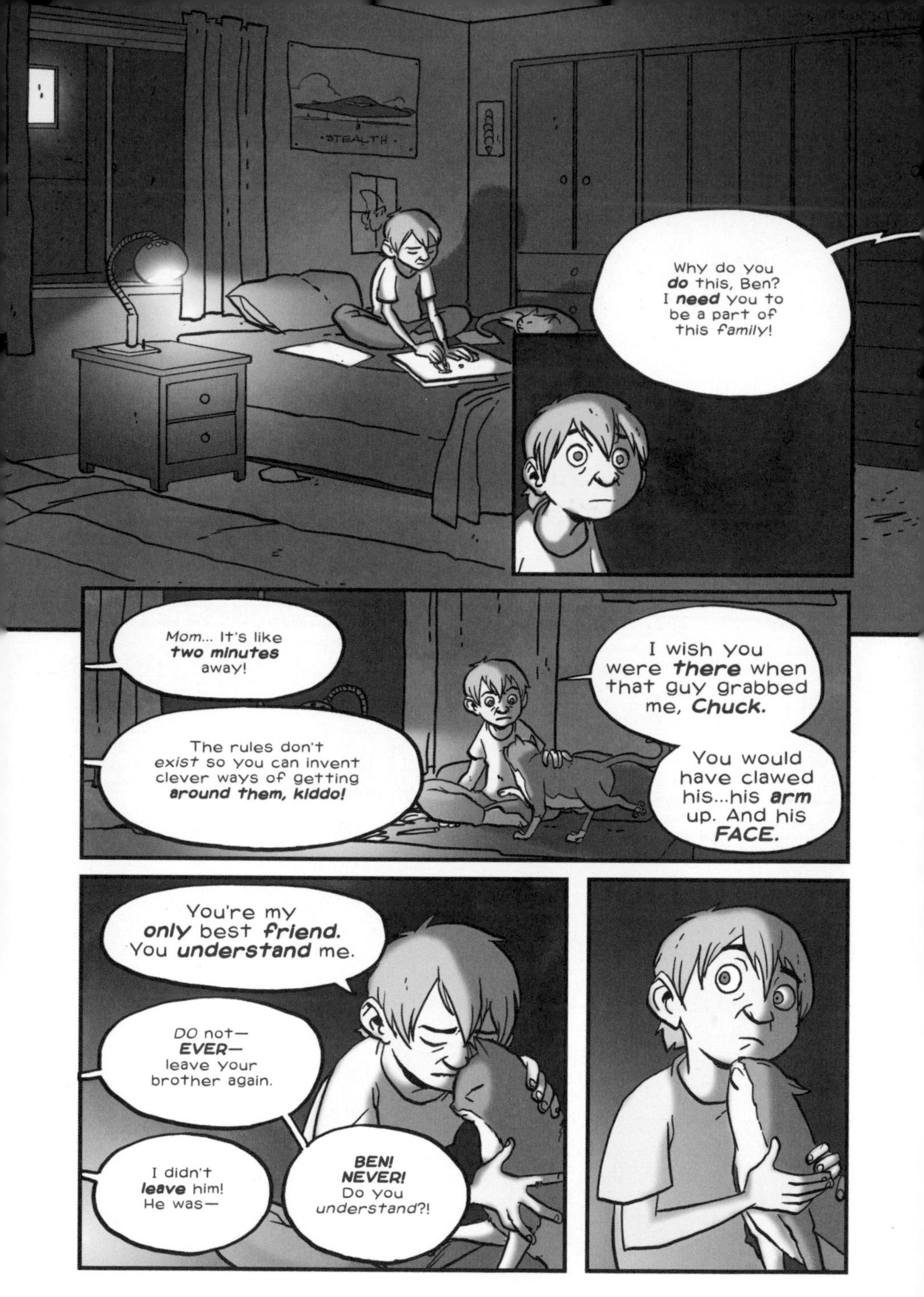

STEALTH
Why do you **do** this, Ben? I **need** you to be a part of this *family*!
*Mom*... It's like **two minutes** away!
I wish you were **there** when that guy grabbed me, **Chuck.**
The rules don't *exist* so you can invent clever ways of getting **around them, kiddo!**
You would have clawed his...his **arm** up. And his **FACE.**
You're my **only** best **friend.** You **understand** me.
*DO* not— **EVER—** leave your brother again.
I didn't **leave** him! He was—
**BEN! NEVER!** Do you *understand*?!

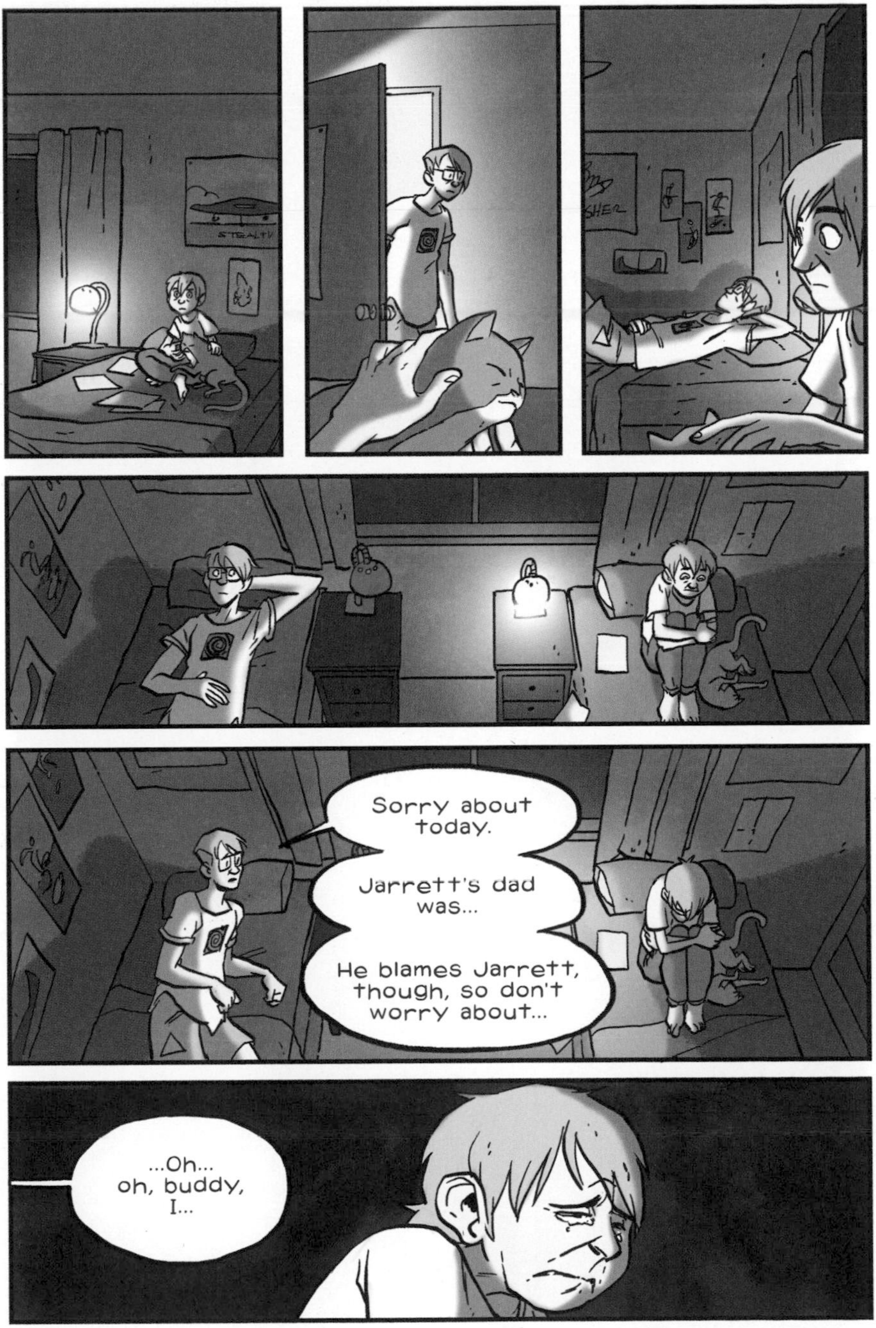
STEALTH
Sorry about today.
Jarrett's dad was...
He blames Jarrett, though, so don't worry about...
...Oh... oh, buddy, I...

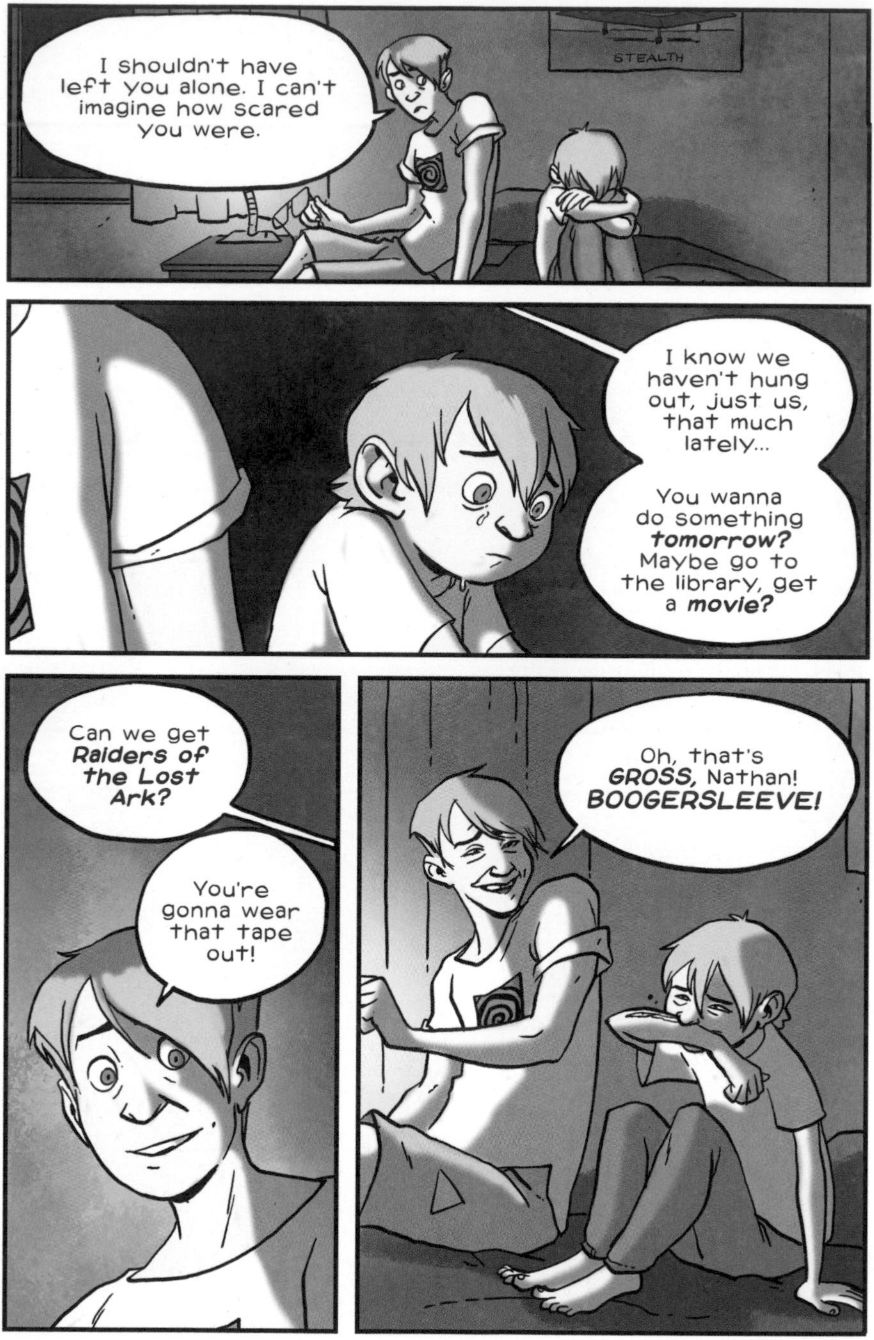
STEALTH
I shouldn't have left you alone. I can't imagine how scared you were.
I know we haven't hung out, just us, that much lately...
You wanna do something **tomorrow?** Maybe go to the library, get a **movie?**
Can we get ***Raiders of the Lost Ark?***
You're gonna wear that tape out!
Oh, that's ***GROSS,*** Nathan! ***BOOGERSLEEVE!***

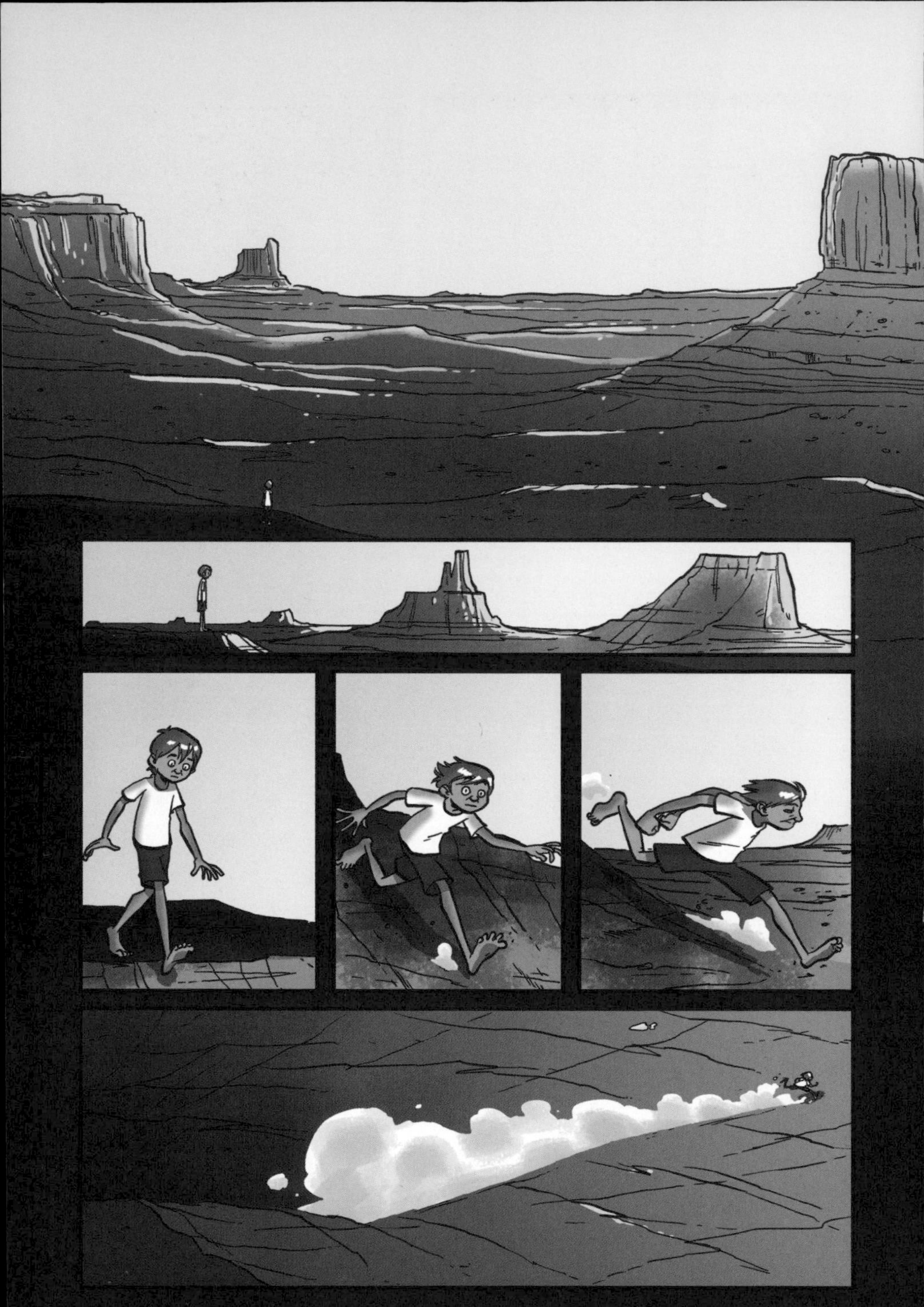

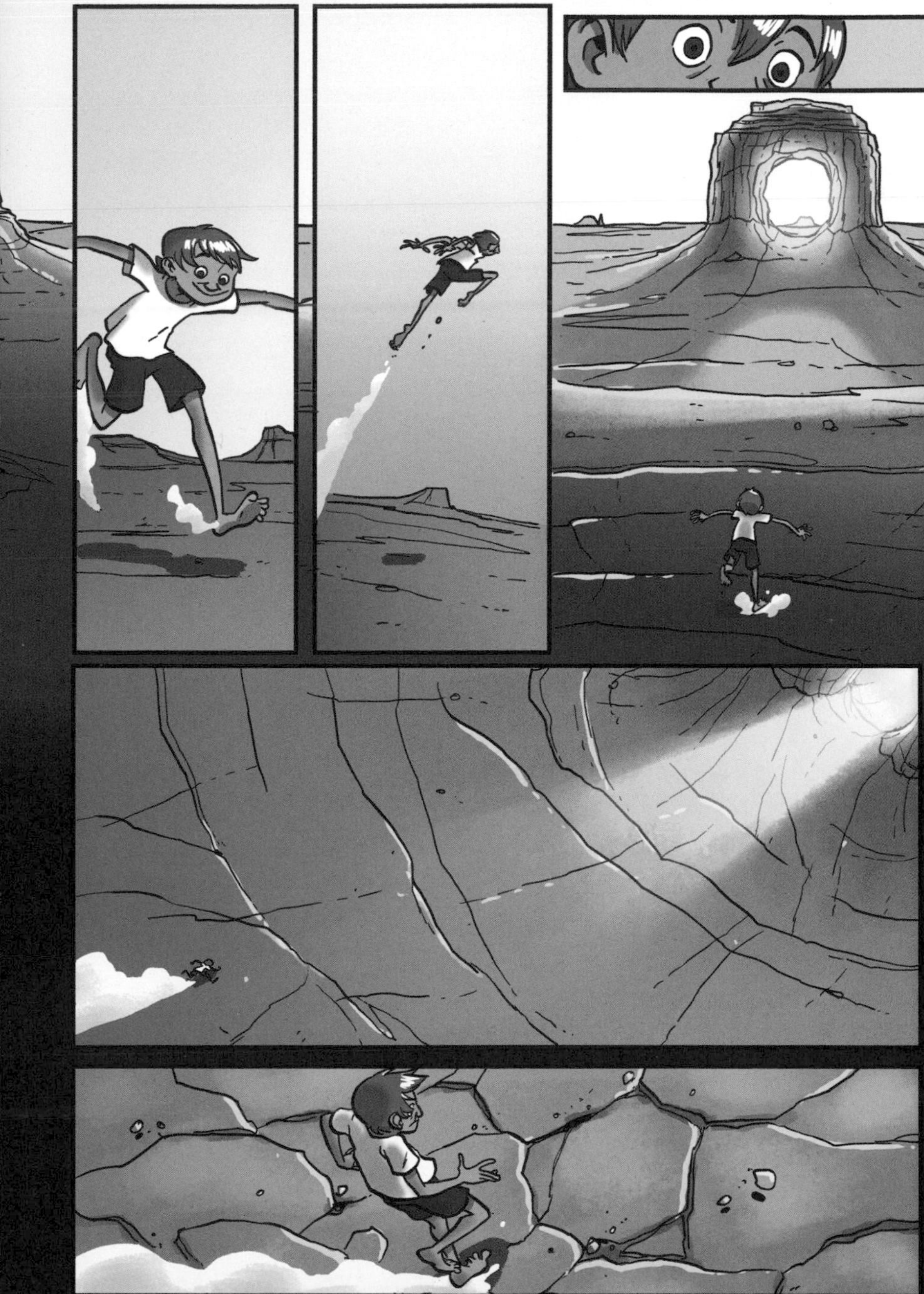

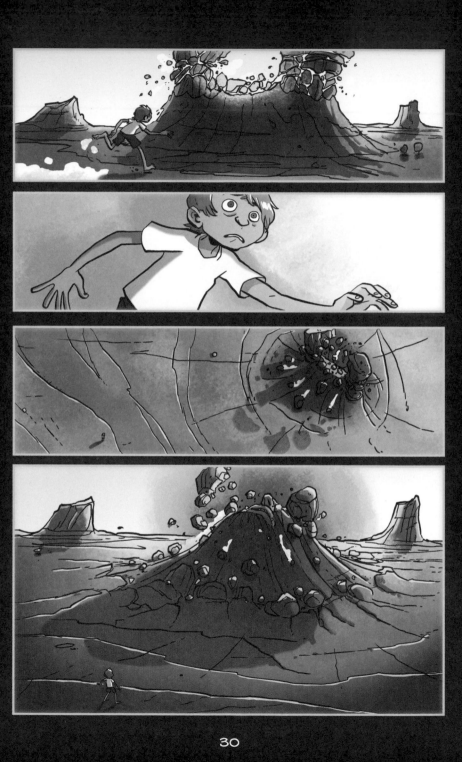

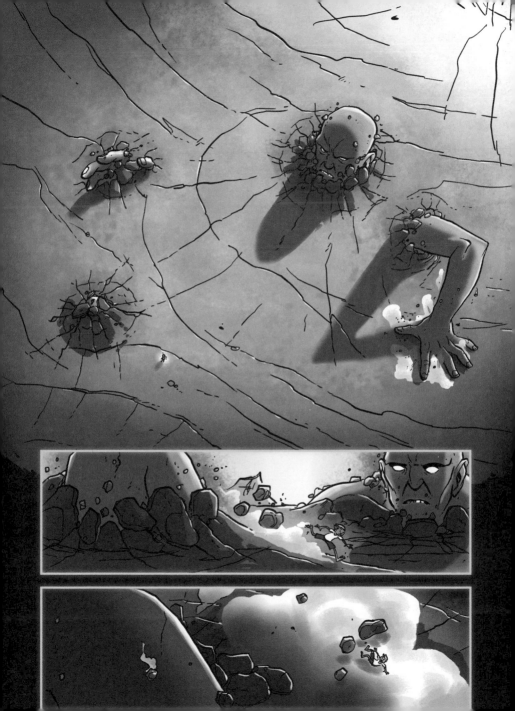

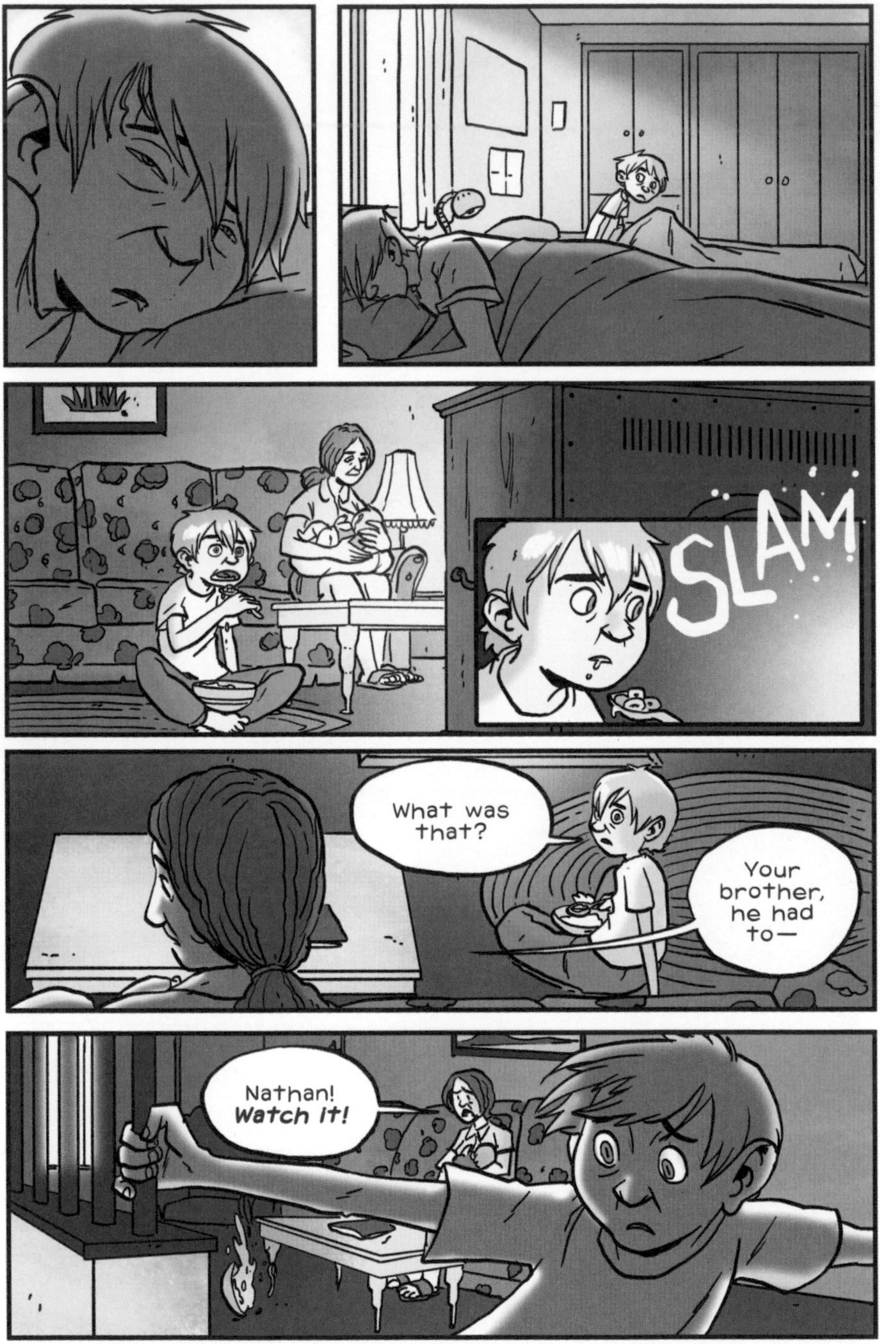
SLAM
What was that?
Your brother, he had to—
Nathan! **Watch it!**

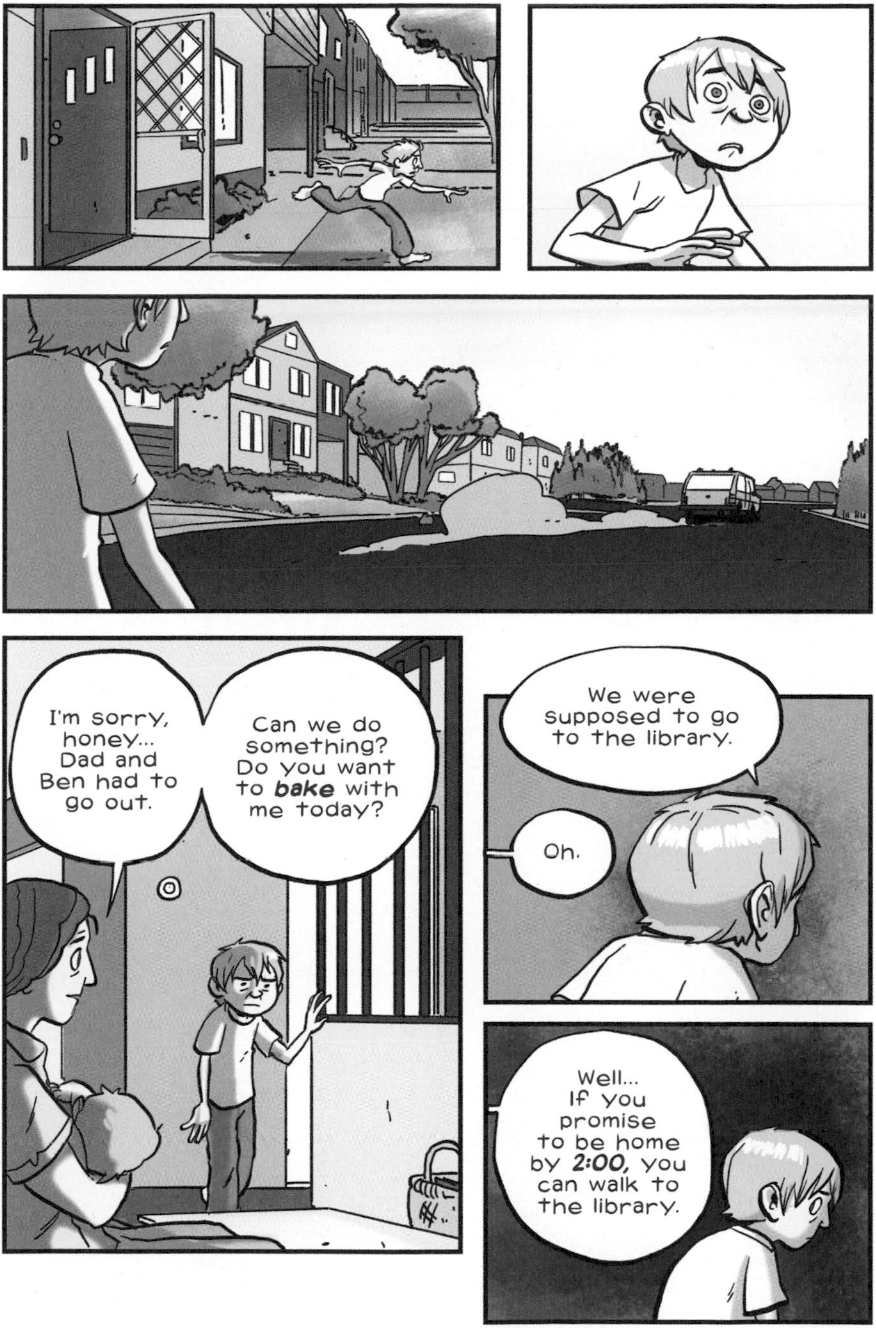
I'm sorry, honey... Dad and Ben had to go out.
Can we do something? Do you want to **bake** with me today?
We were supposed to go to the library.
Oh.
Well... If you promise to be home by **2:00,** you can walk to the library.

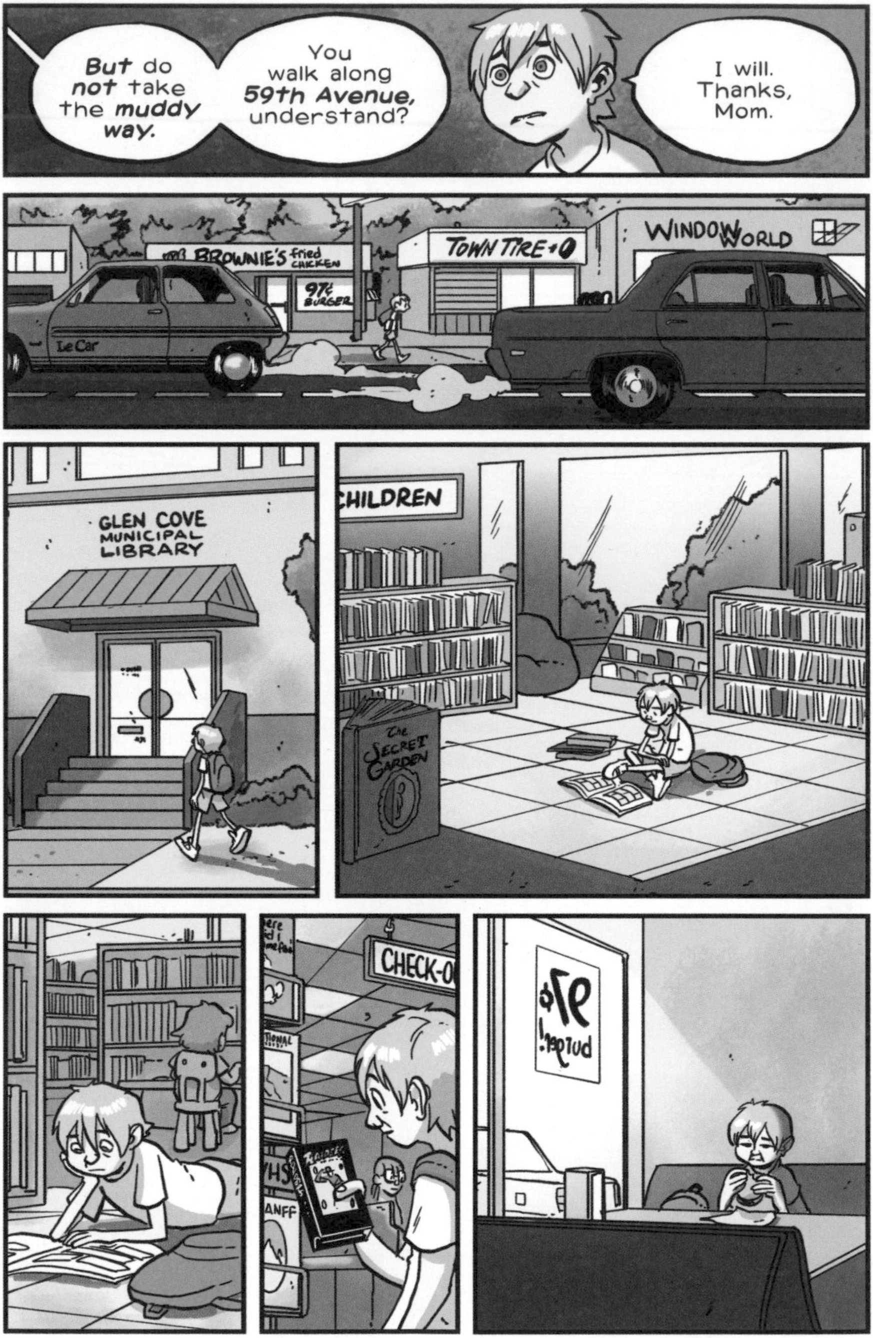

*But* do *not* take the *muddy way.*
You walk along ***59th Avenue,*** understand?
I will. Thanks, Mom.
BROWNIE'S fried CHICKEN
97¢ BURGER
TOWN TIRE
WINDOW WORLD
Le Car
GLEN COVE MUNICIPAL LIBRARY
CHILDREN
The SECRET GARDEN

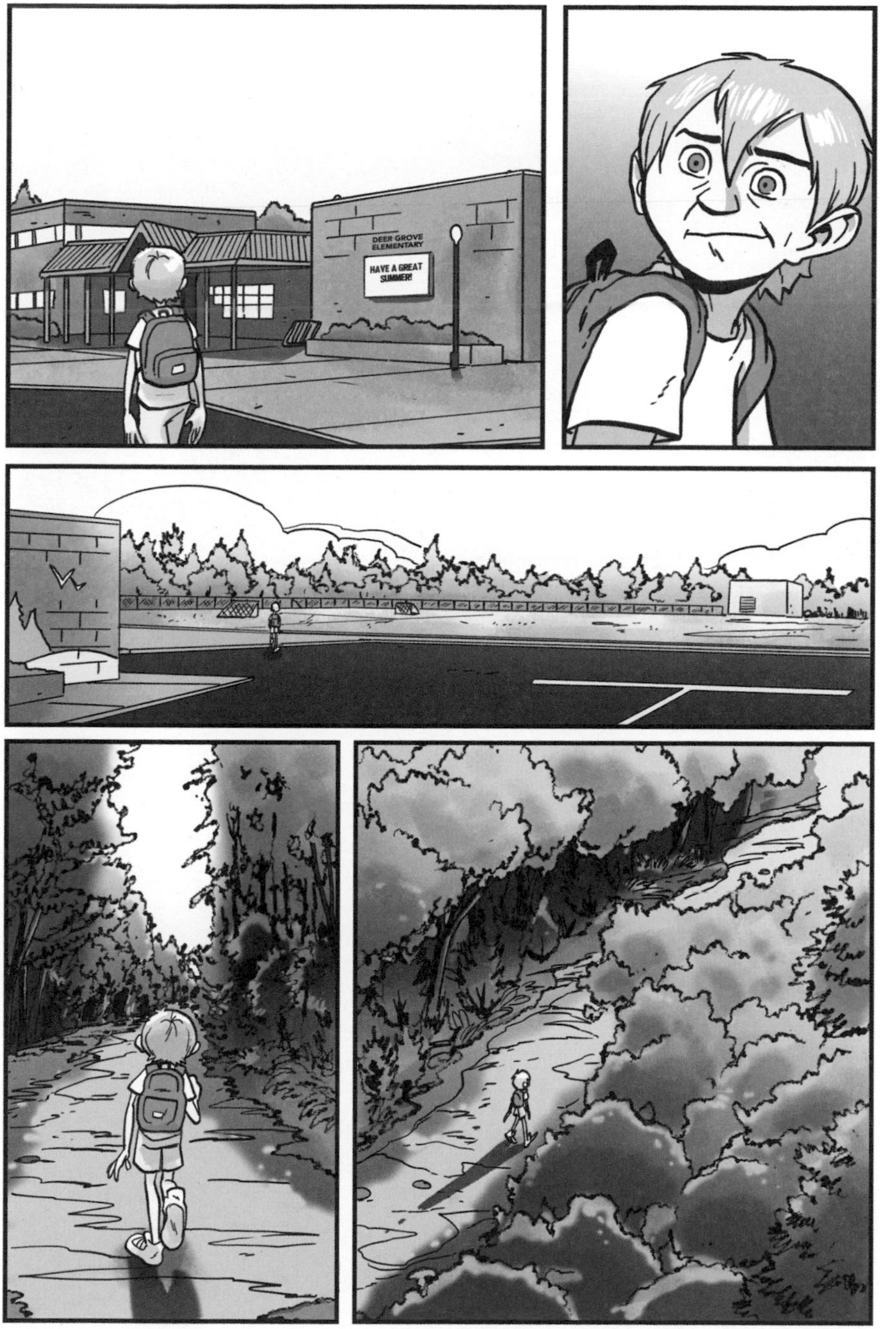
DEER GROVE ELEMENTARY
HAVE A GREAT SUMMER!

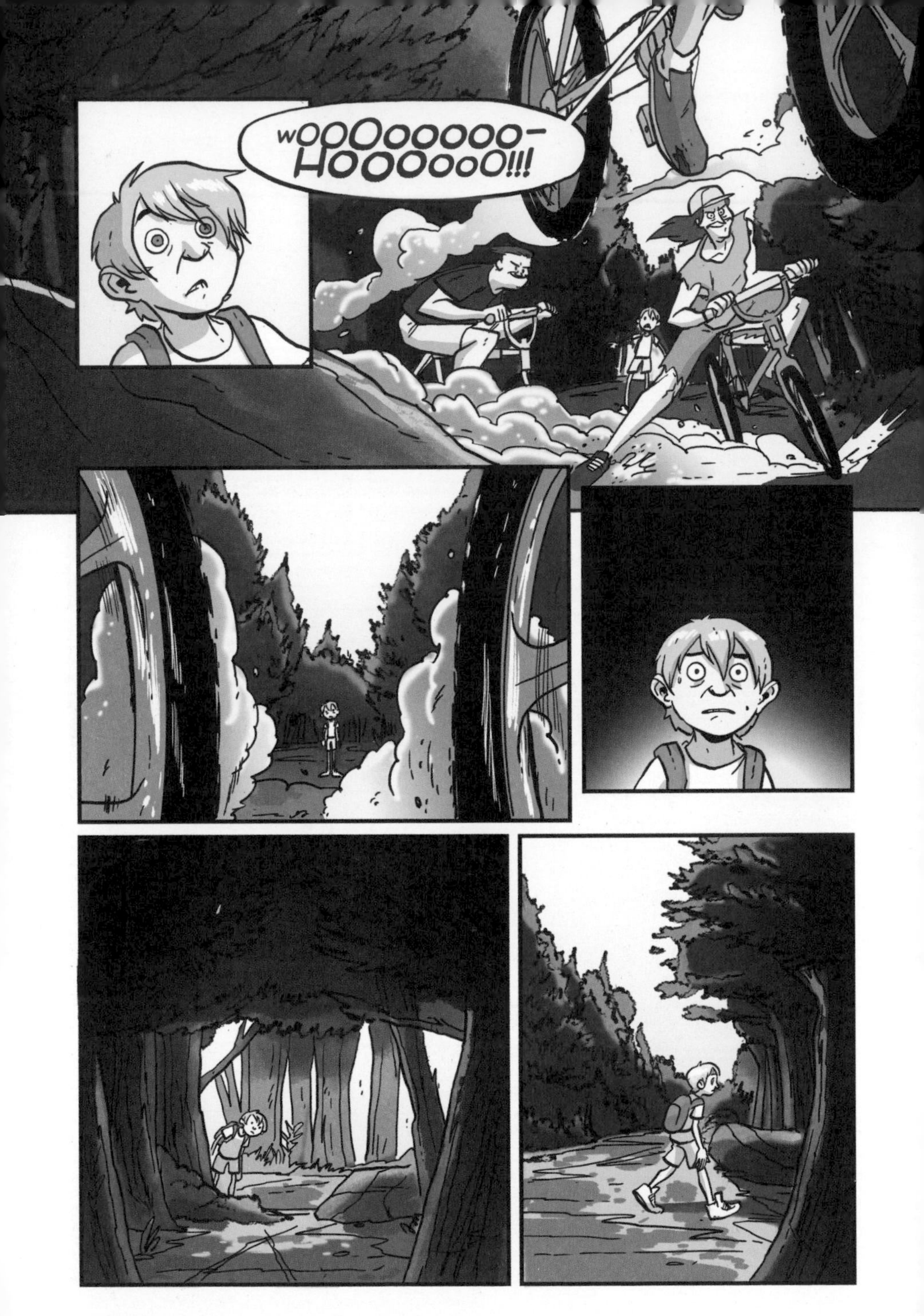
wOOOoooooo-HOOOooO!!!

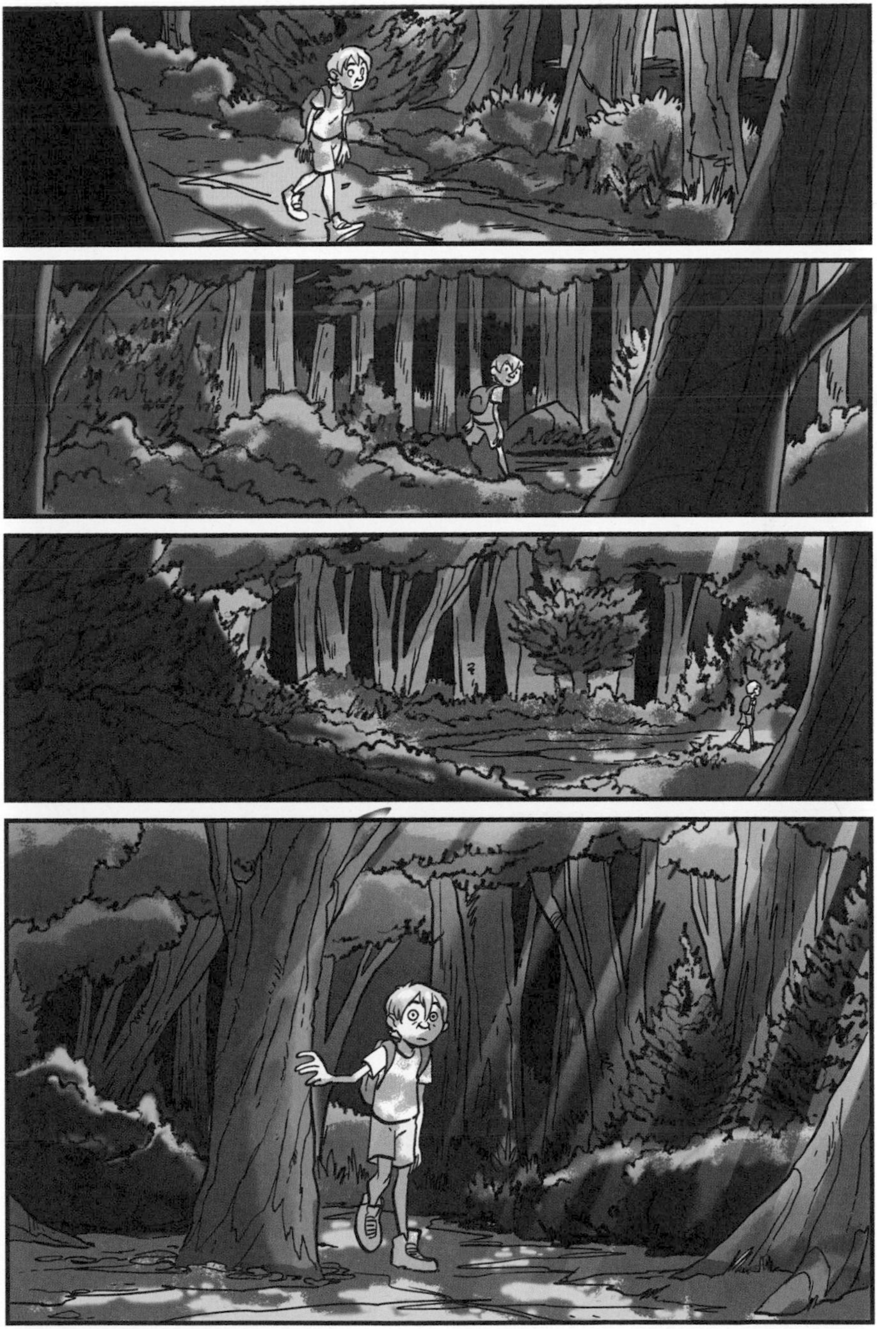

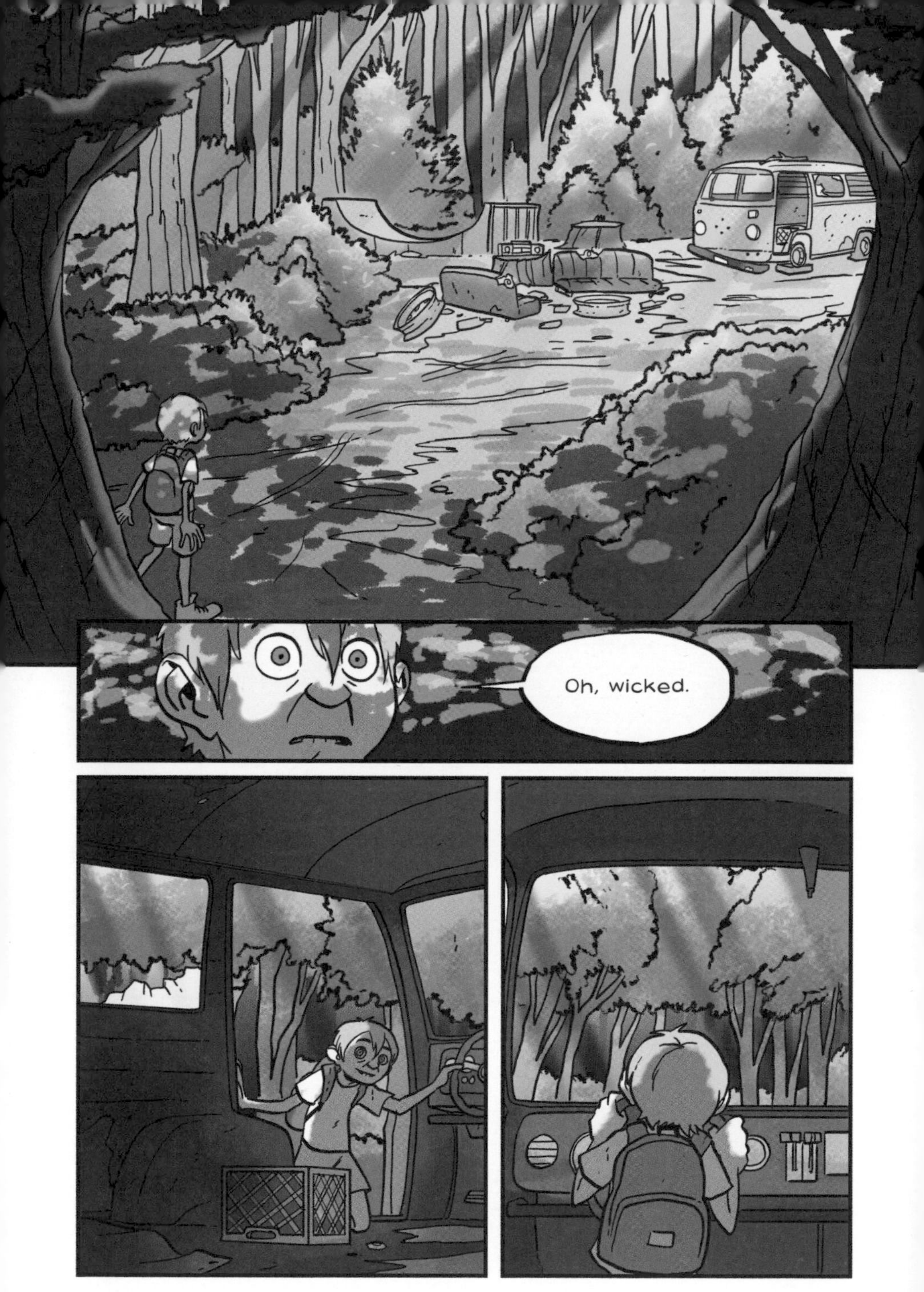
Oh, wicked.

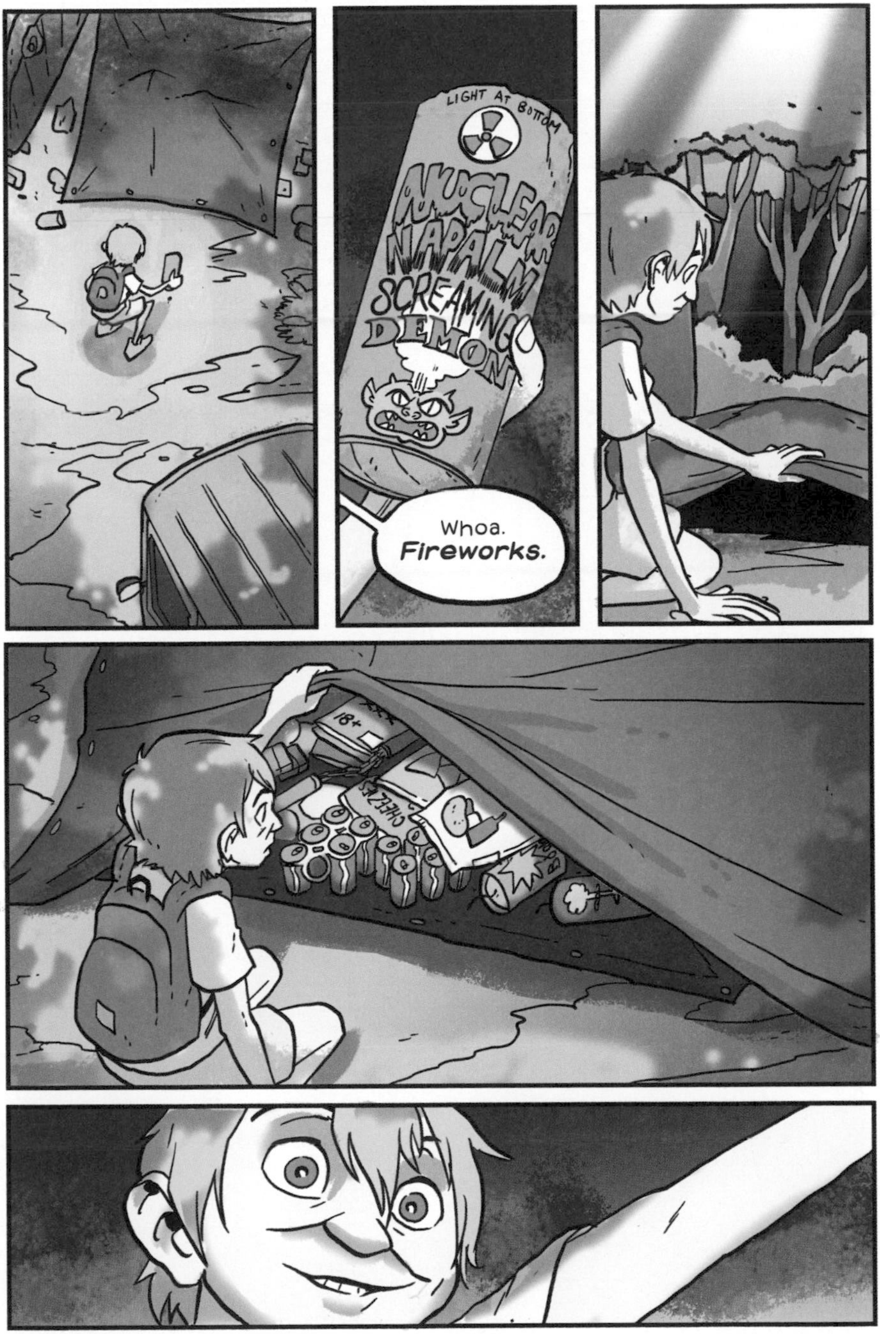
LIGHT AT BOTTOM
NUCLEAR NAPALM SCREAMING DEMON
Whoa. **Fireworks.**
18+

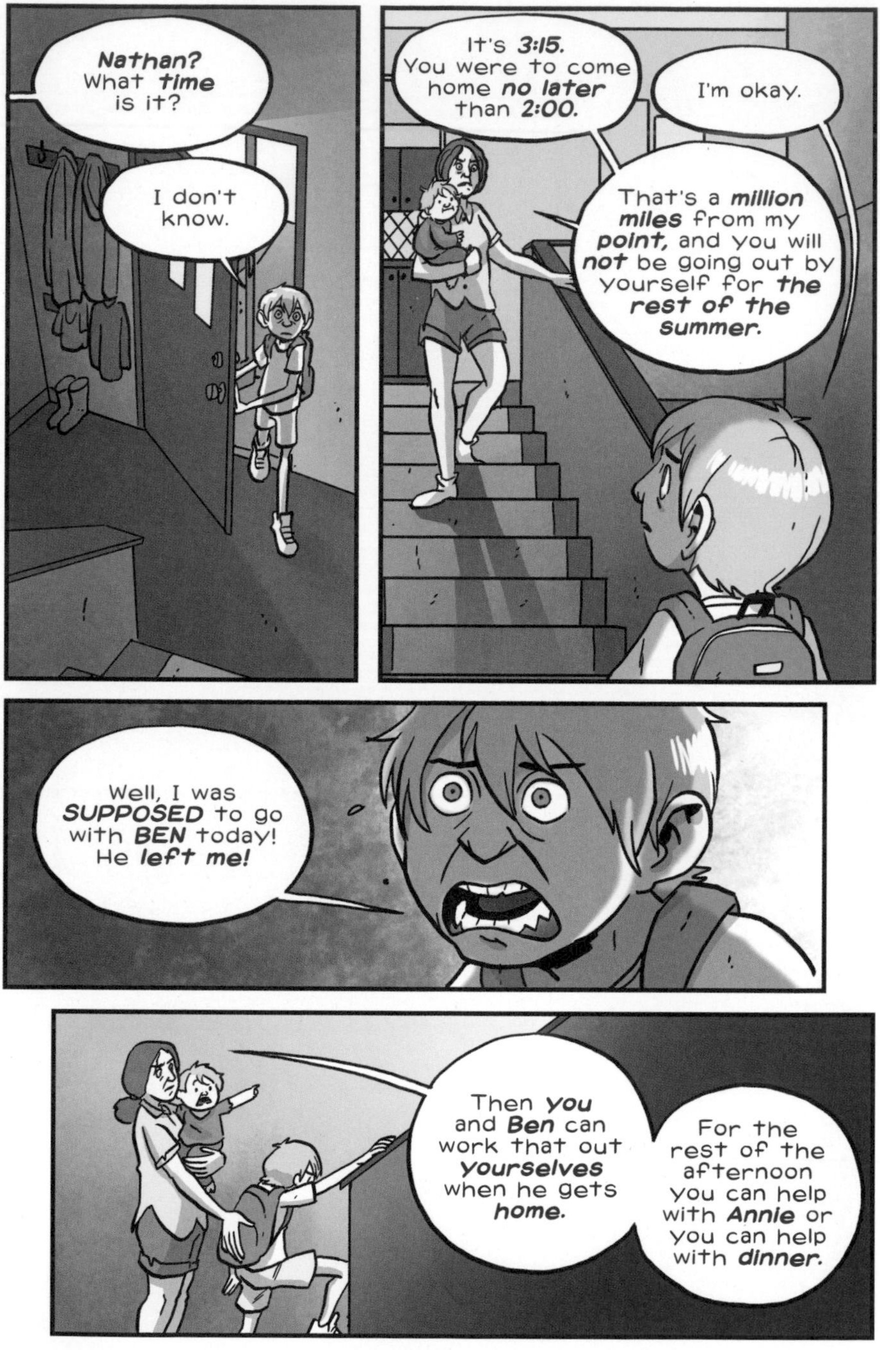
Nathan? What time is it?
I don't know.
It's 3:15. You were to come home no later than 2:00.
I'm okay.
That's a million miles from my point, and you will not be going out by yourself for the rest of the summer.
Well, I was SUPPOSED to go with BEN today! He left me!
Then you and Ben can work that out yourselves when he gets home.
For the rest of the afternoon you can help with Annie or you can help with dinner.

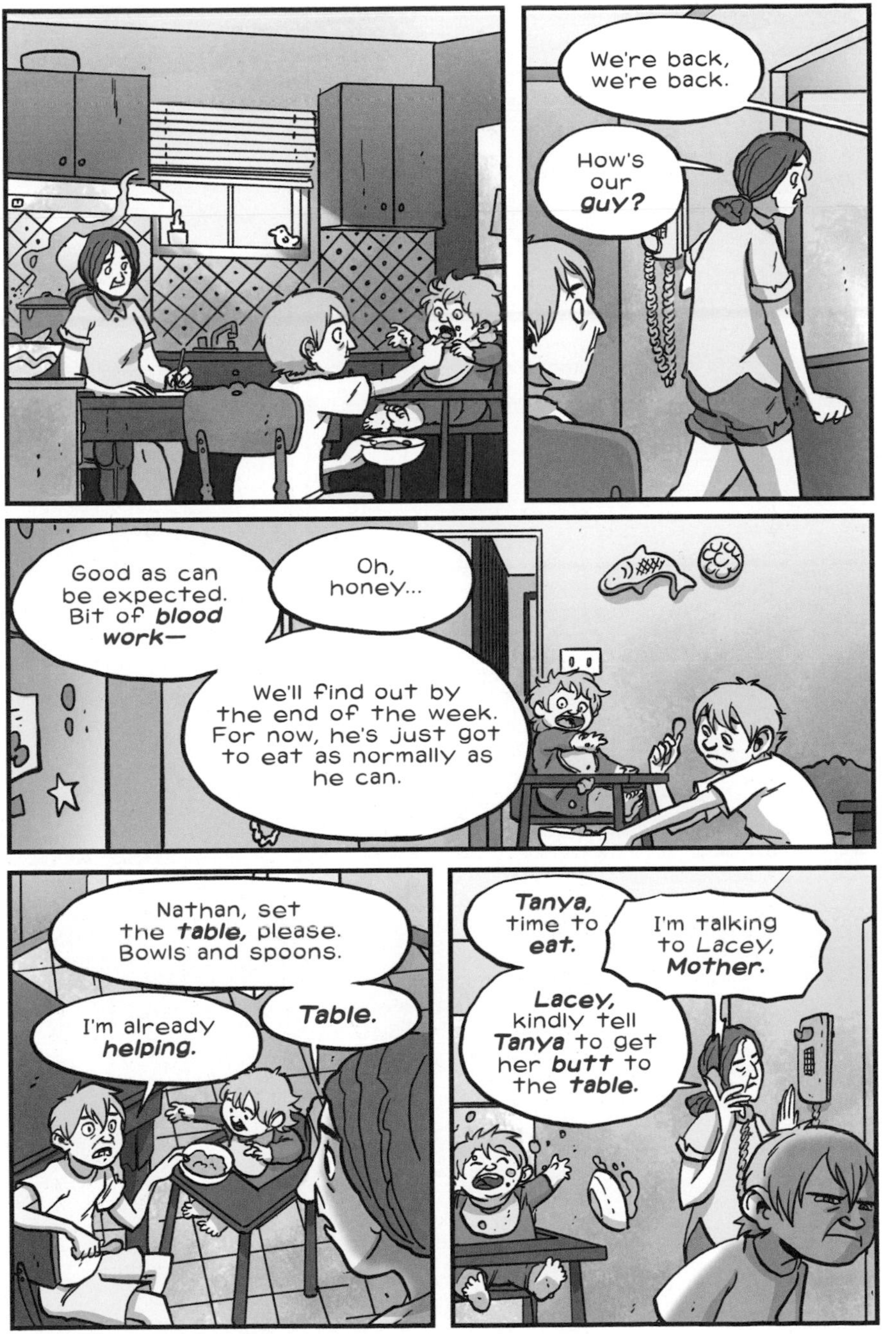
We're back, we're back.
How's our **guy?**
Good as can be expected. Bit of **blood work**—
Oh, honey...
We'll find out by the end of the week. For now, he's just got to eat as normally as he can.
Nathan, set the **table,** please. Bowls and spoons.
I'm already **helping.**
**Table.**
**Tanya,** time to **eat.**
I'm talking to Lacey, **Mother.**
**Lacey,** kindly tell **Tanya** to get her **butt** to the **table.**

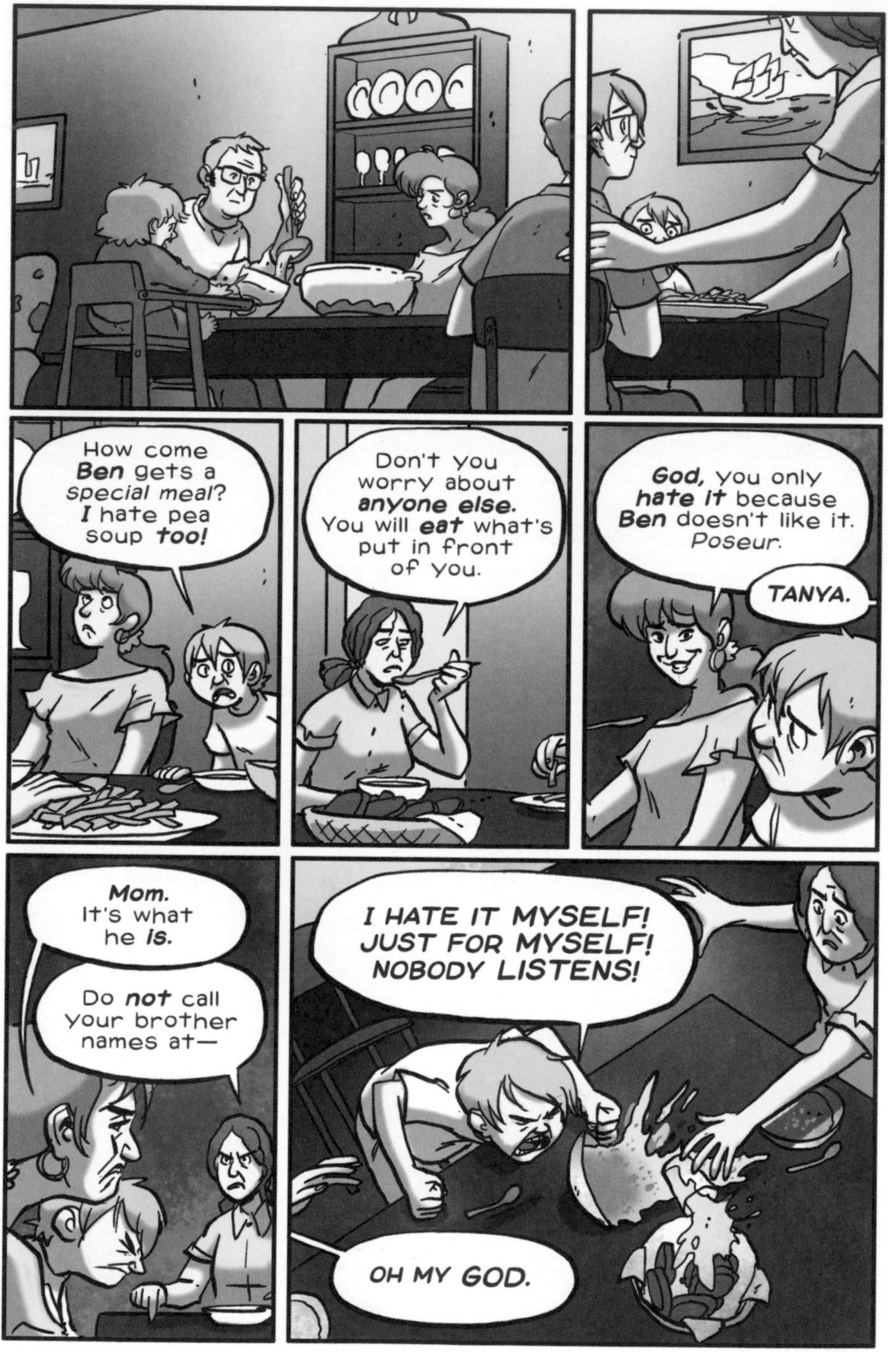
How come **Ben** gets a *special meal*? *I* hate pea soup ***too!***
Don't you worry about ***anyone else.*** You will ***eat*** what's put in front of you.
***God,*** you only ***hate it*** because **Ben** doesn't like it. *Poseur.*
***TANYA.***
***Mom.*** It's what he ***is.***
Do ***not*** call your brother names at—
*I HATE IT MYSELF! JUST FOR MYSELF! NOBODY LISTENS!*
*OH MY GOD.*

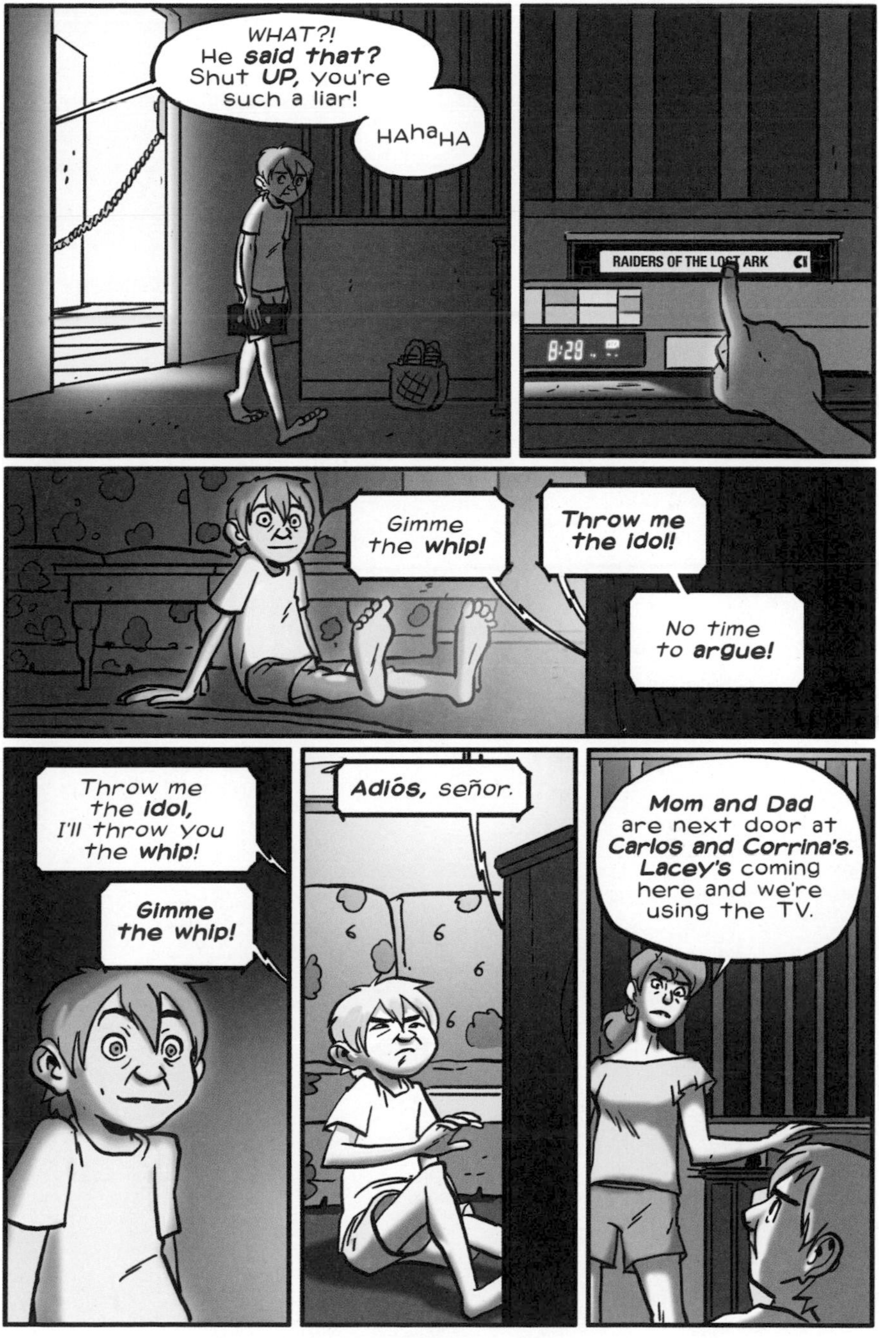

WHAT?! He said that? Shut UP, you're such a liar!
HAhaHA
RAIDERS OF THE LOST ARK
8:28
Gimme the whip!
Throw me the idol!
No time to argue!
Throw me the idol, I'll throw you the whip!
Gimme the whip!
Adiós, señor.
Mom and Dad are next door at Carlos and Corrina's. Lacey's coming here and we're using the TV.

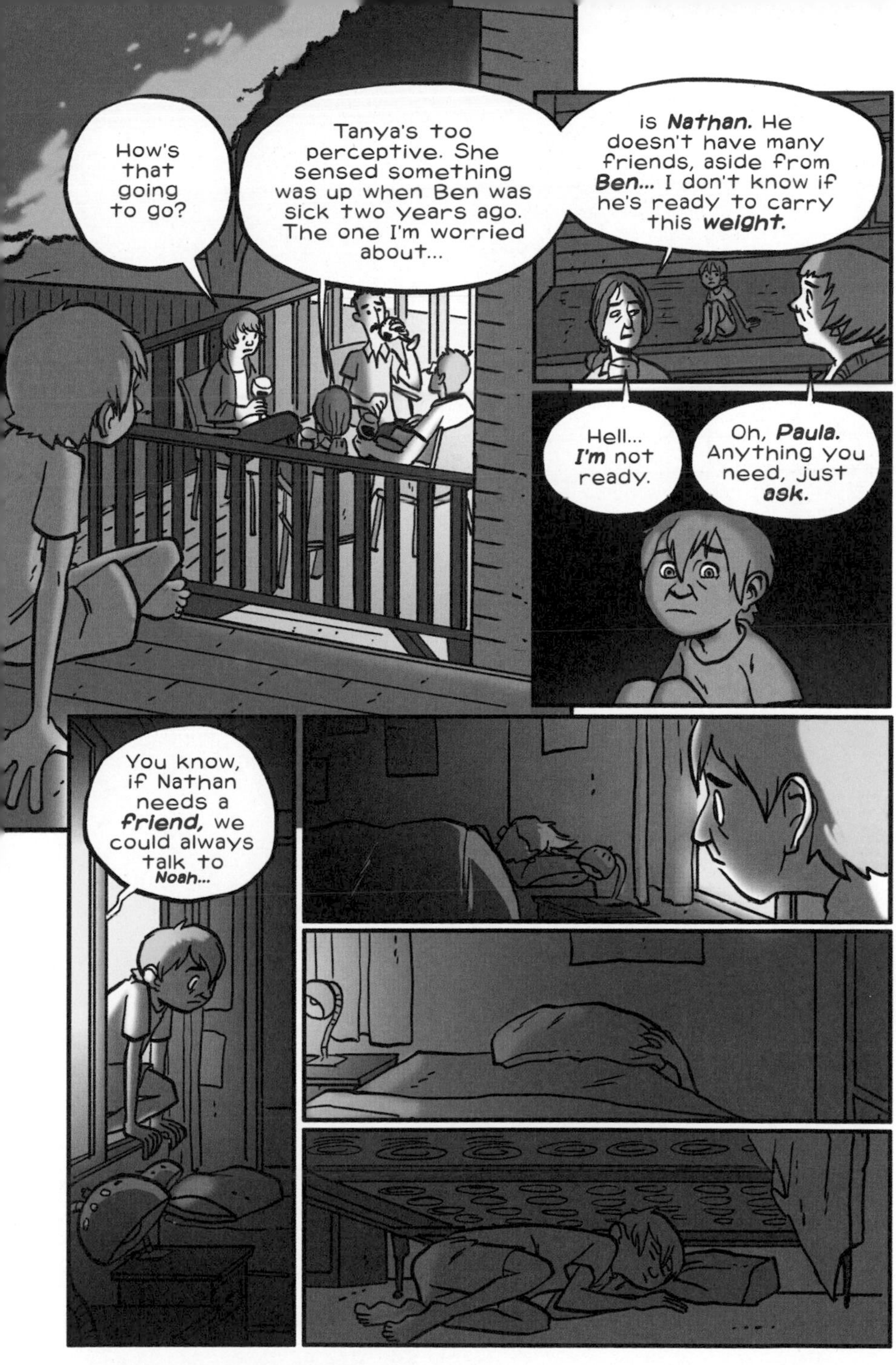
How's that going to go?
Tanya's too perceptive. She sensed something was up when Ben was sick two years ago. The one I'm worried about...
is Nathan. He doesn't have many friends, aside from Ben... I don't know if he's ready to carry this weight.
Hell... I'm not ready.
Oh, Paula. Anything you need, just ask.
You know, if Nathan needs a friend, we could always talk to Noah...

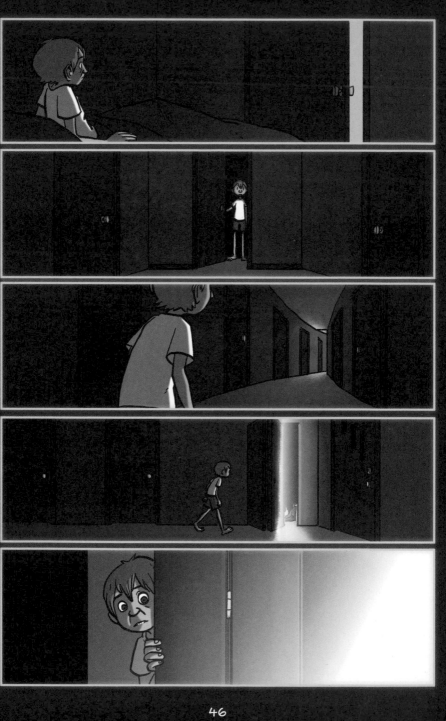

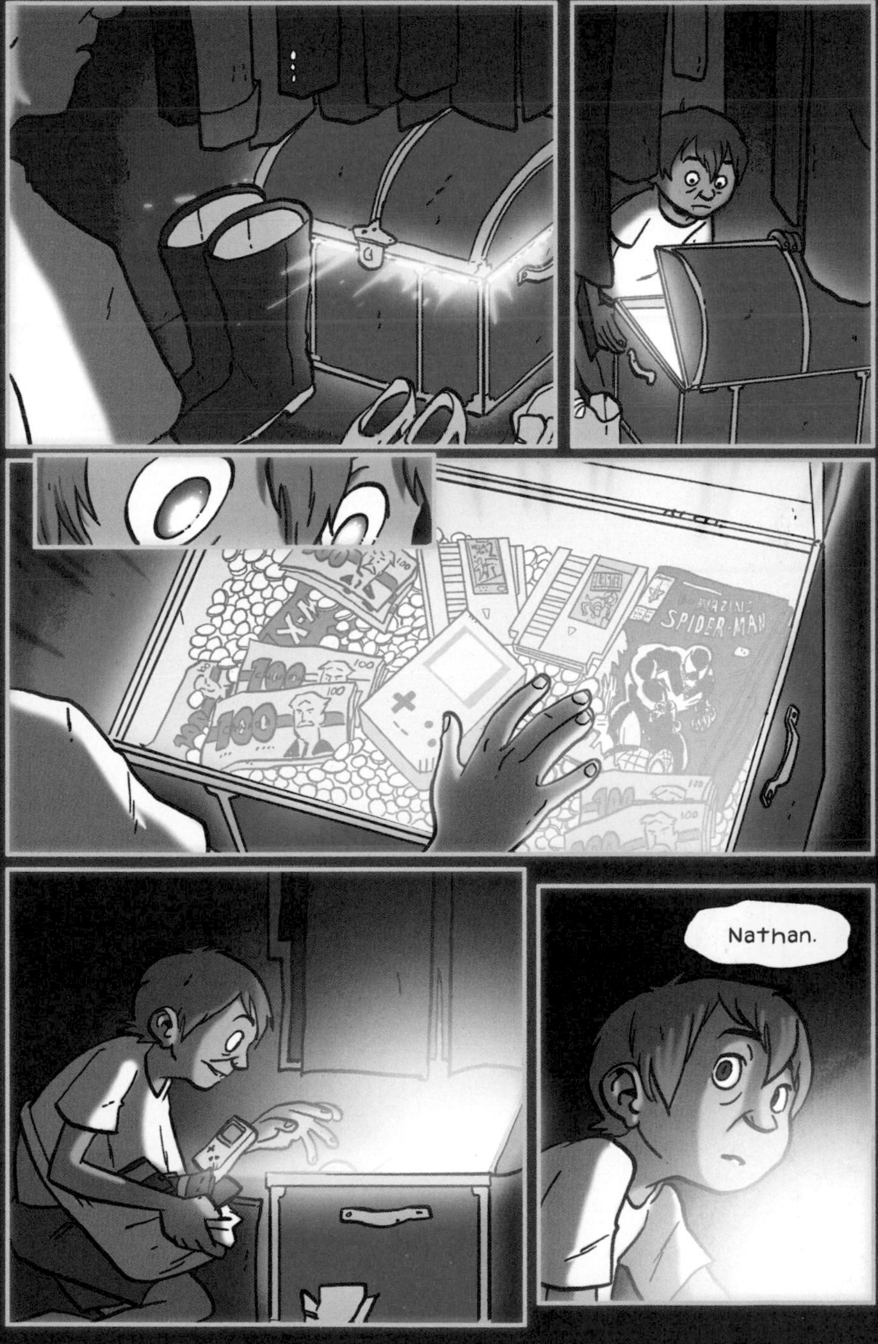

X-MEN
AMAZING SPIDER-MAN
Nathan.

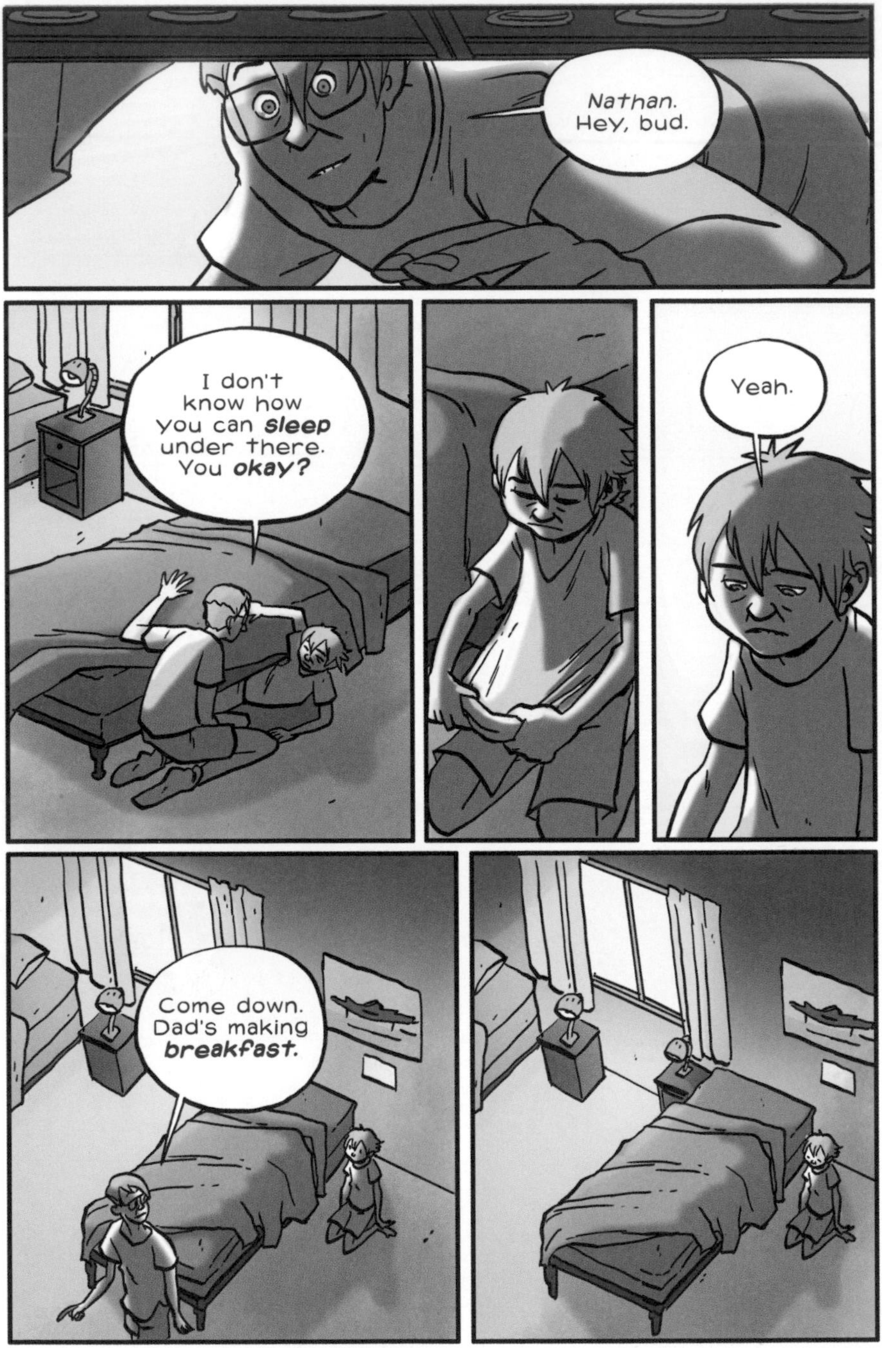
Nathan. Hey, bud.
I don't know how you can **sleep** under there. You **okay?**
Yeah.
Come down. Dad's making **breakfast**.

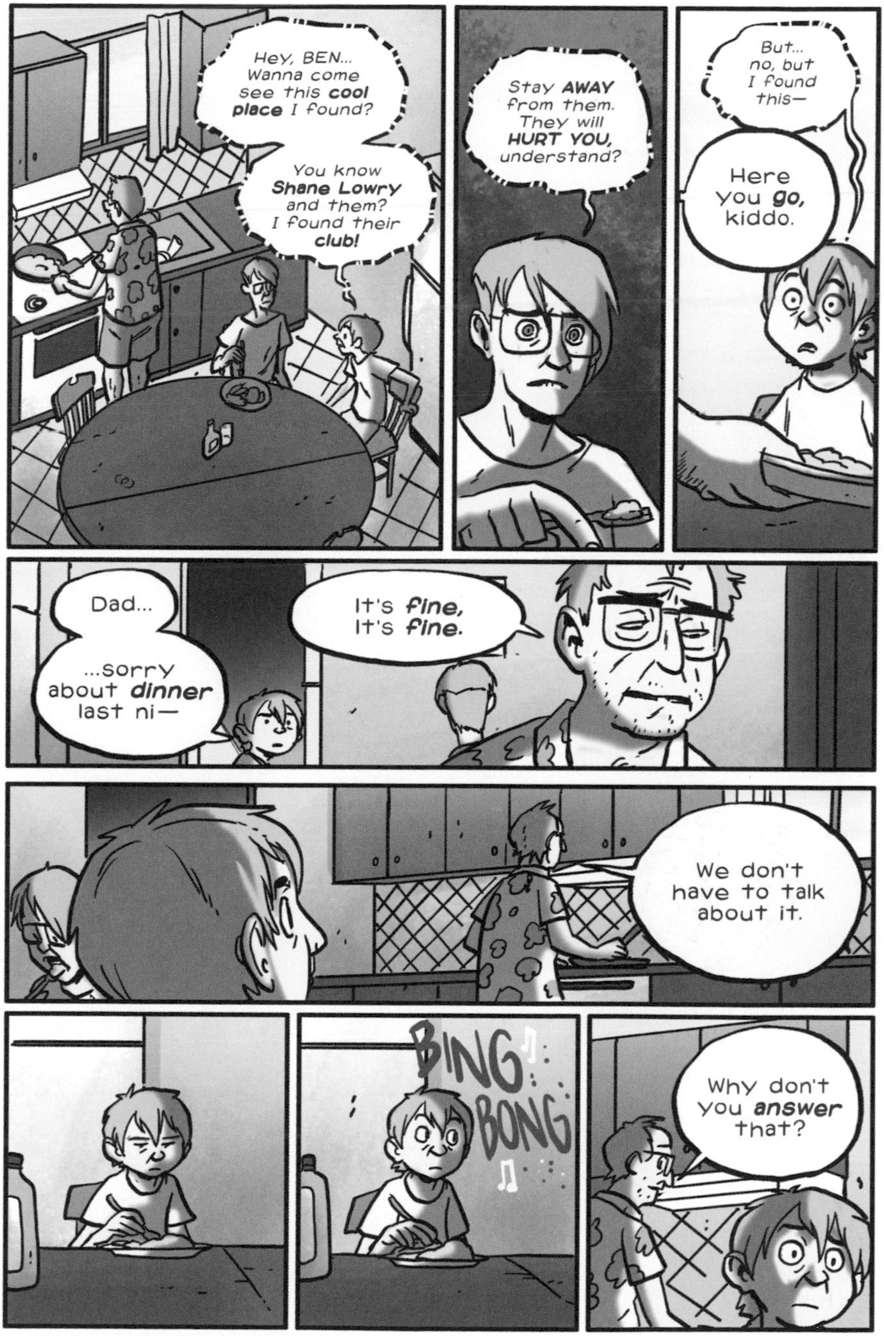
Hey, BEN... Wanna come see this **cool place** I found?
You know **Shane Lowry** and them? I found their **club!**
Stay **AWAY** from them. They will **HURT YOU,** understand?
But... no, but I found this—
Here you **go,** kiddo.
Dad...
...sorry about **dinner** last ni—
It's **fine,** It's **fine.**
We don't have to talk about it.
BING
BONG
Why don't you **answer** that?

50

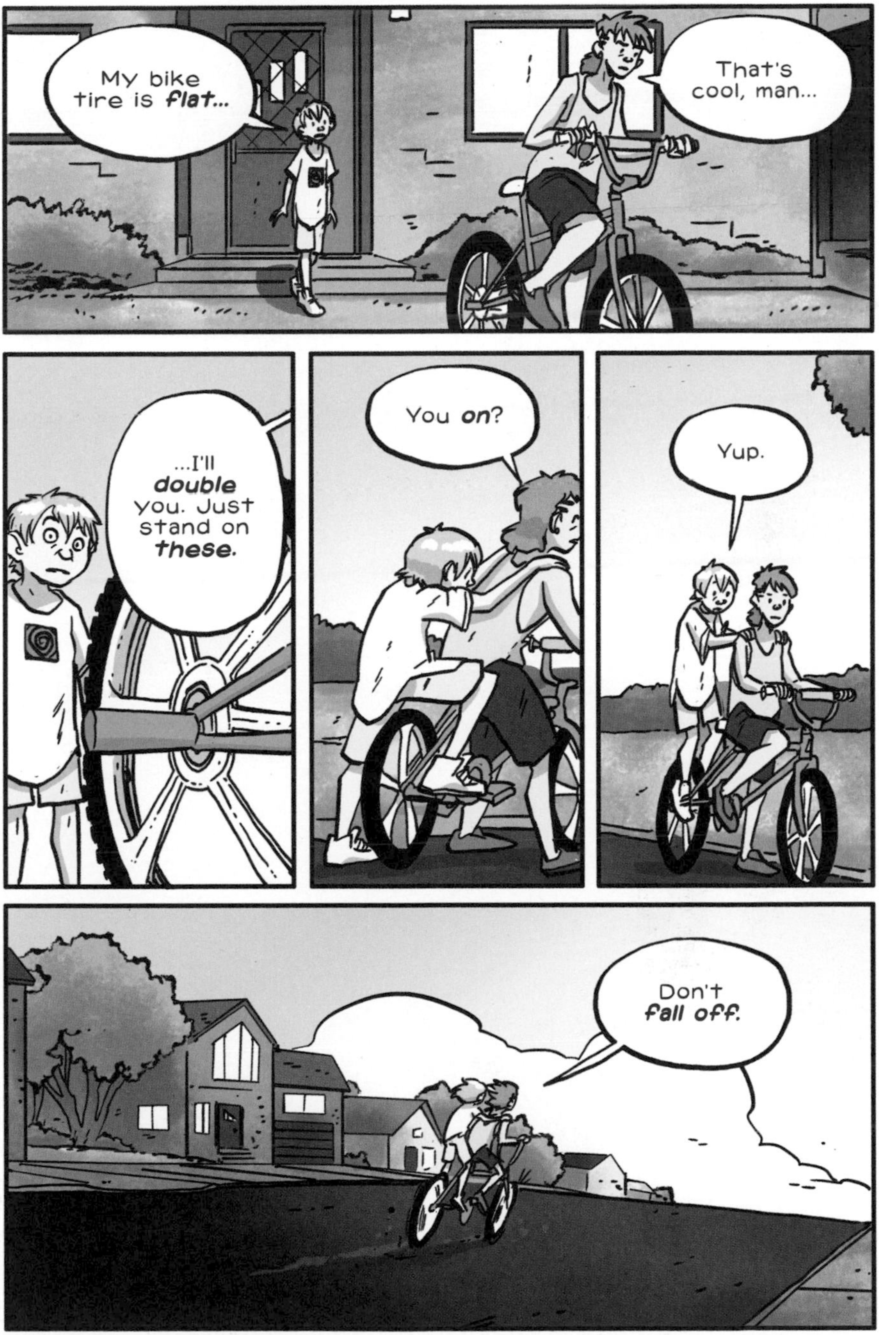
My bike tire is *flat*...
That's cool, man...
...I'll *double* you. Just stand on *these.*
You *on*?
Yup.
Don't *fall off.*

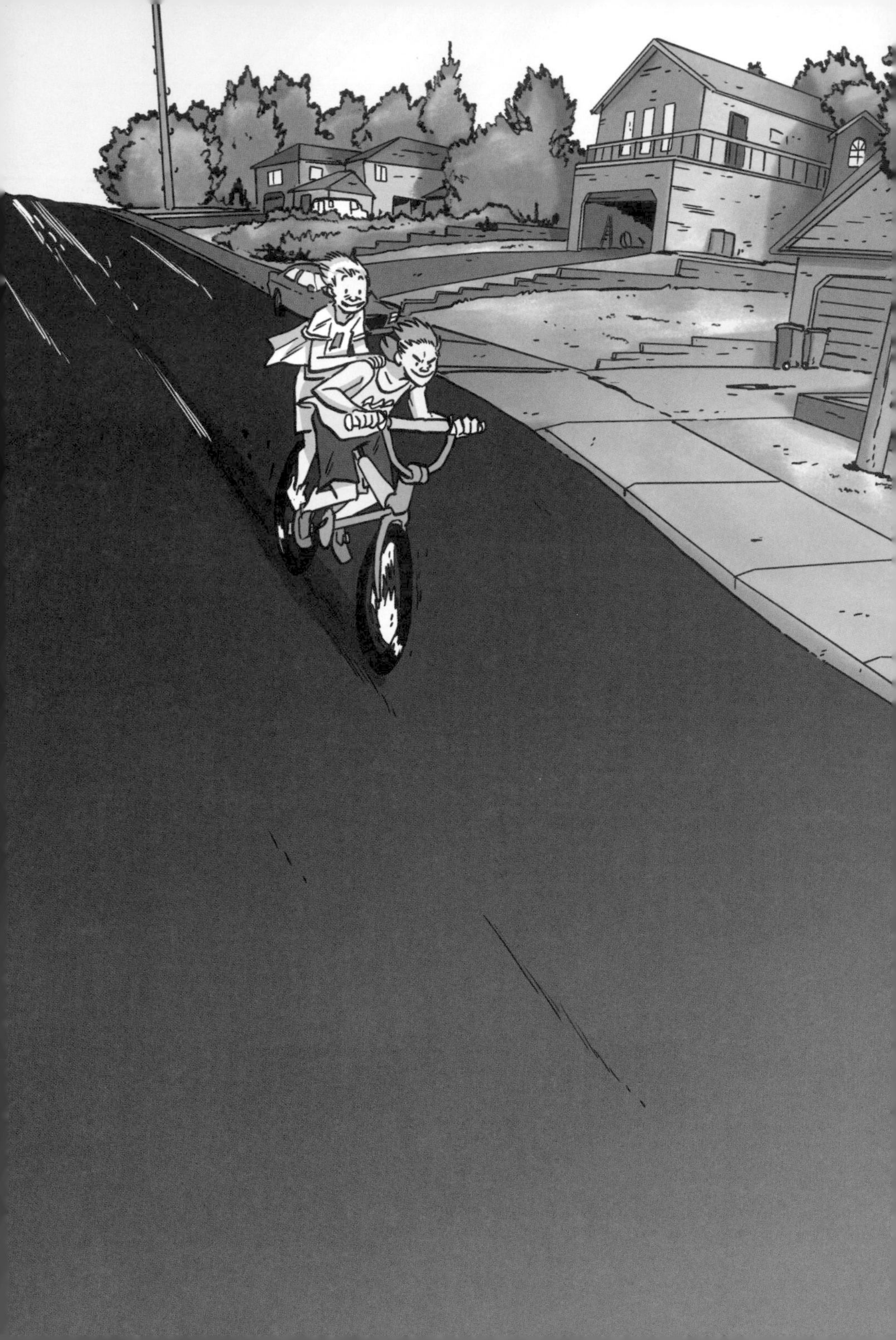

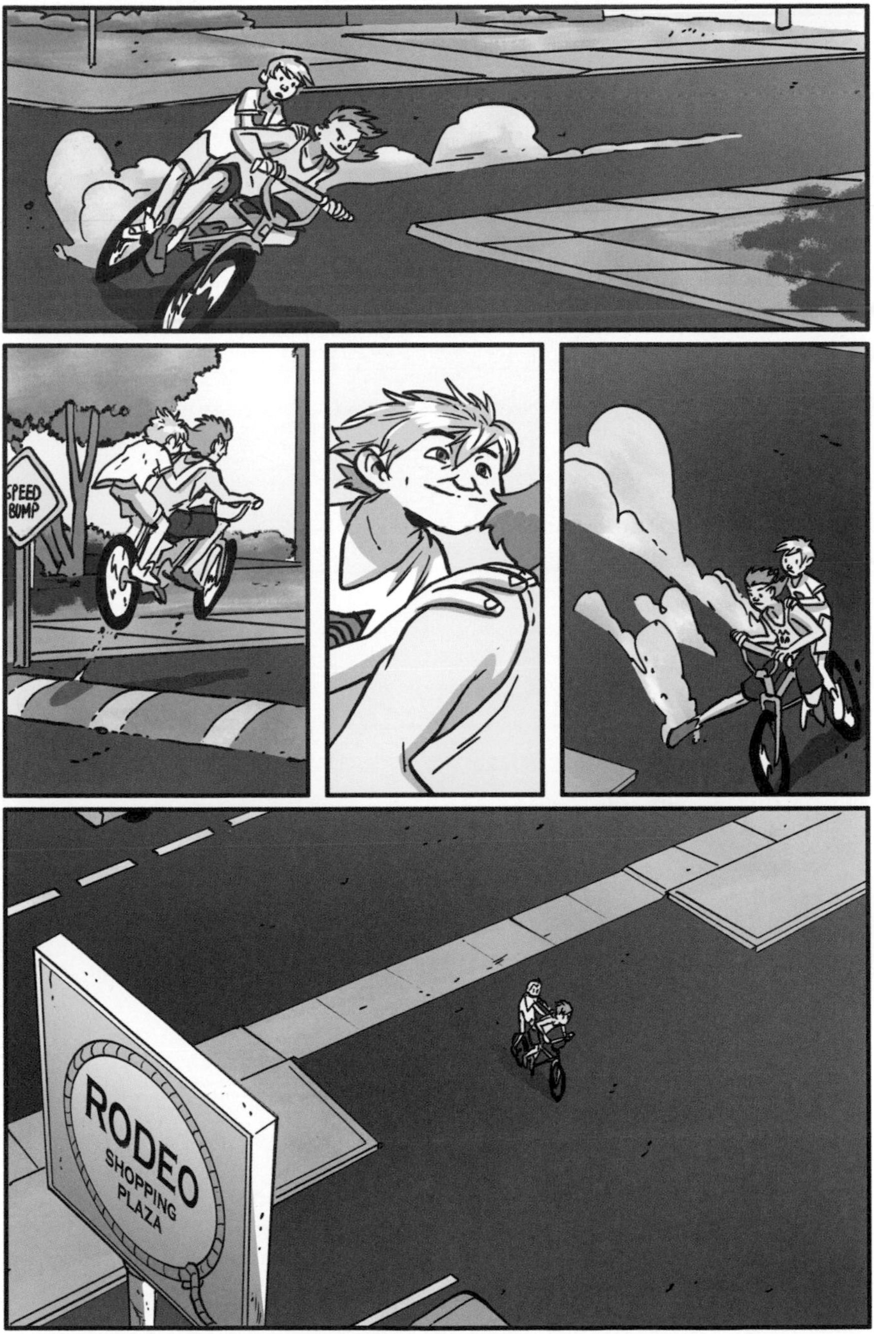
SPEED BUMP
RODEO
SHOPPING
PLAZA

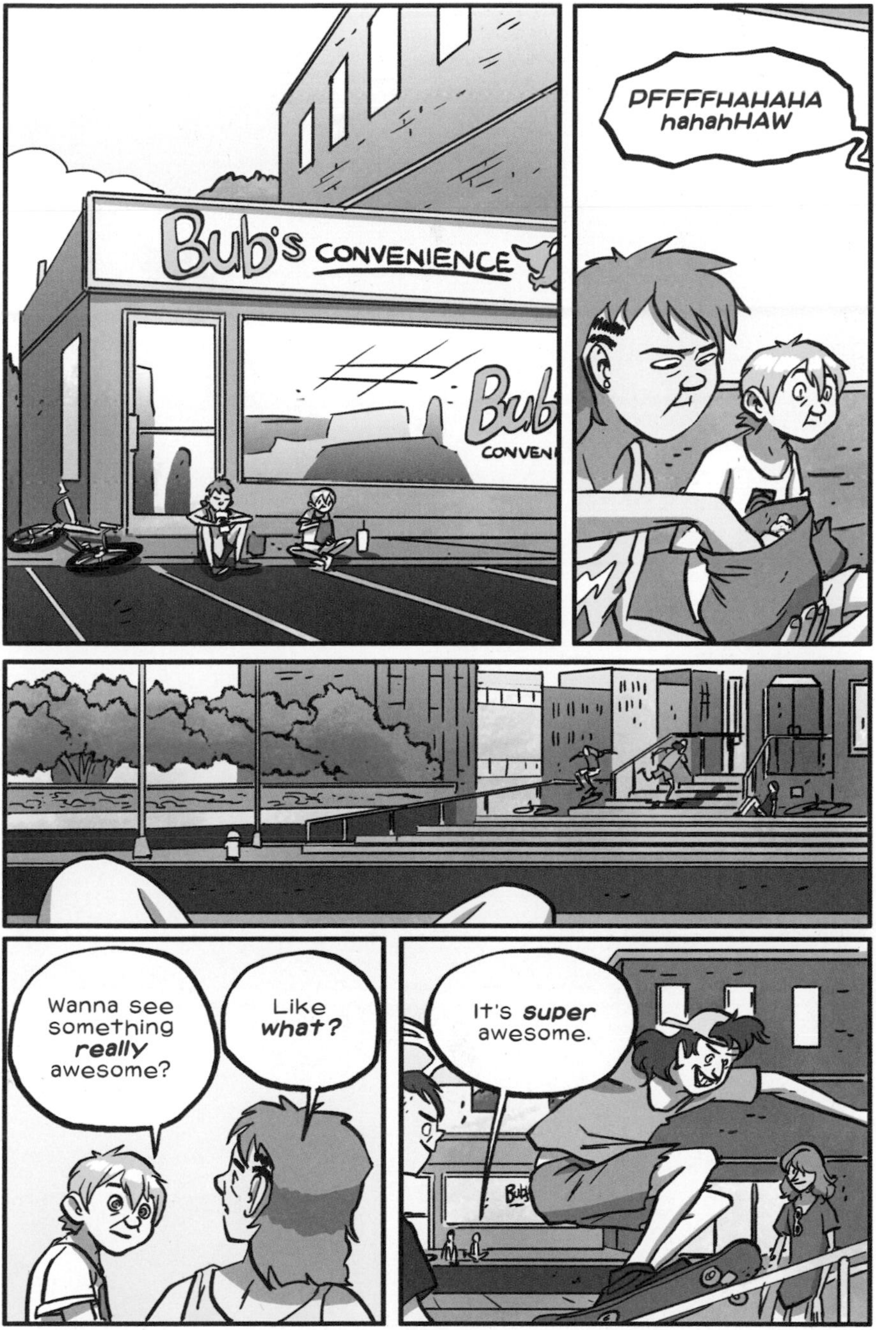
Bub's CONVENIENCE
Bub's CONVENI
PFFFFHAHAHA hahahHAW
Wanna see something *really* awesome?
Like *what?*
It's *super* awesome.

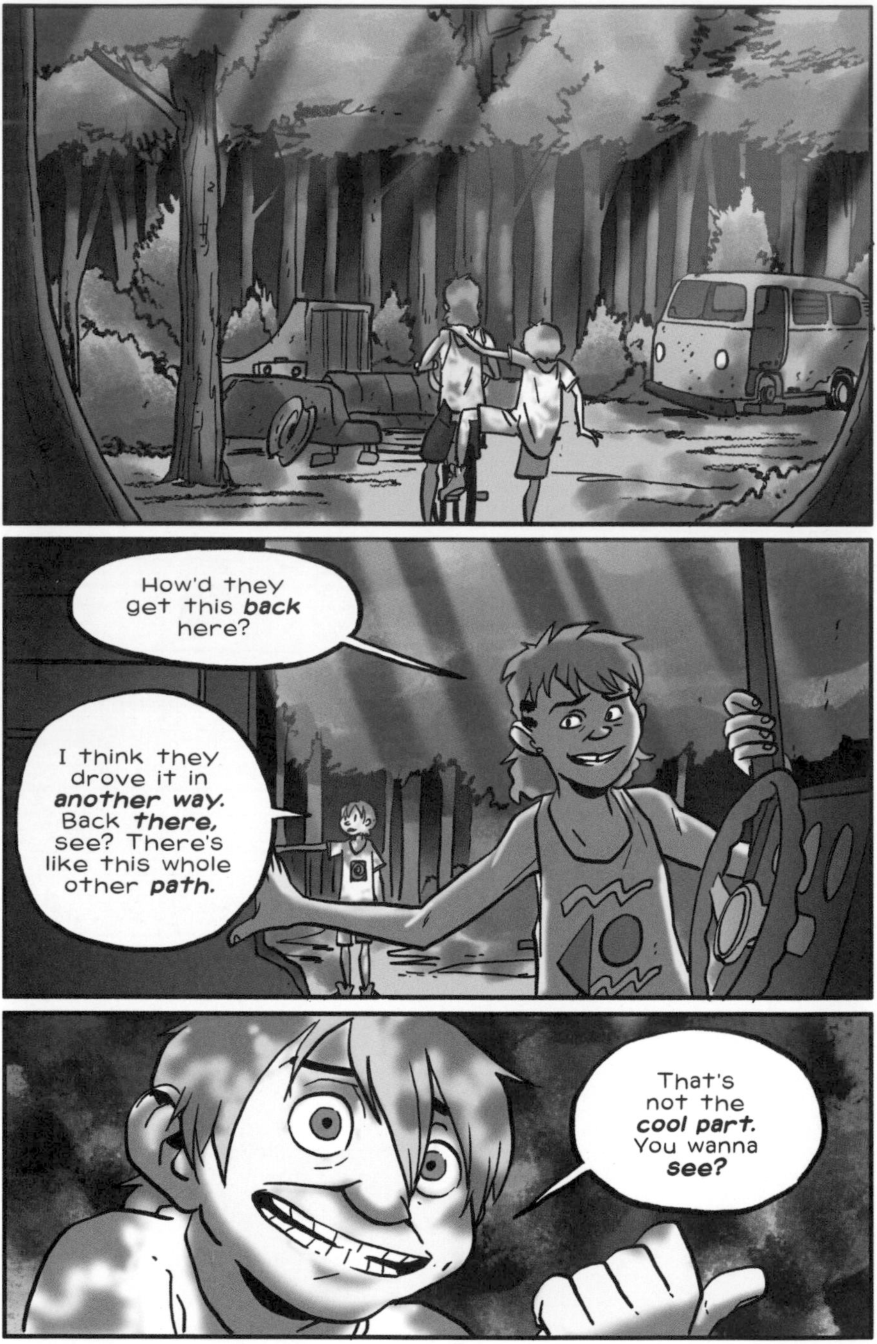

How'd they get this back here?
I think they drove it in another way. Back there, see? There's like this whole other path.
That's not the cool part. You wanna see?

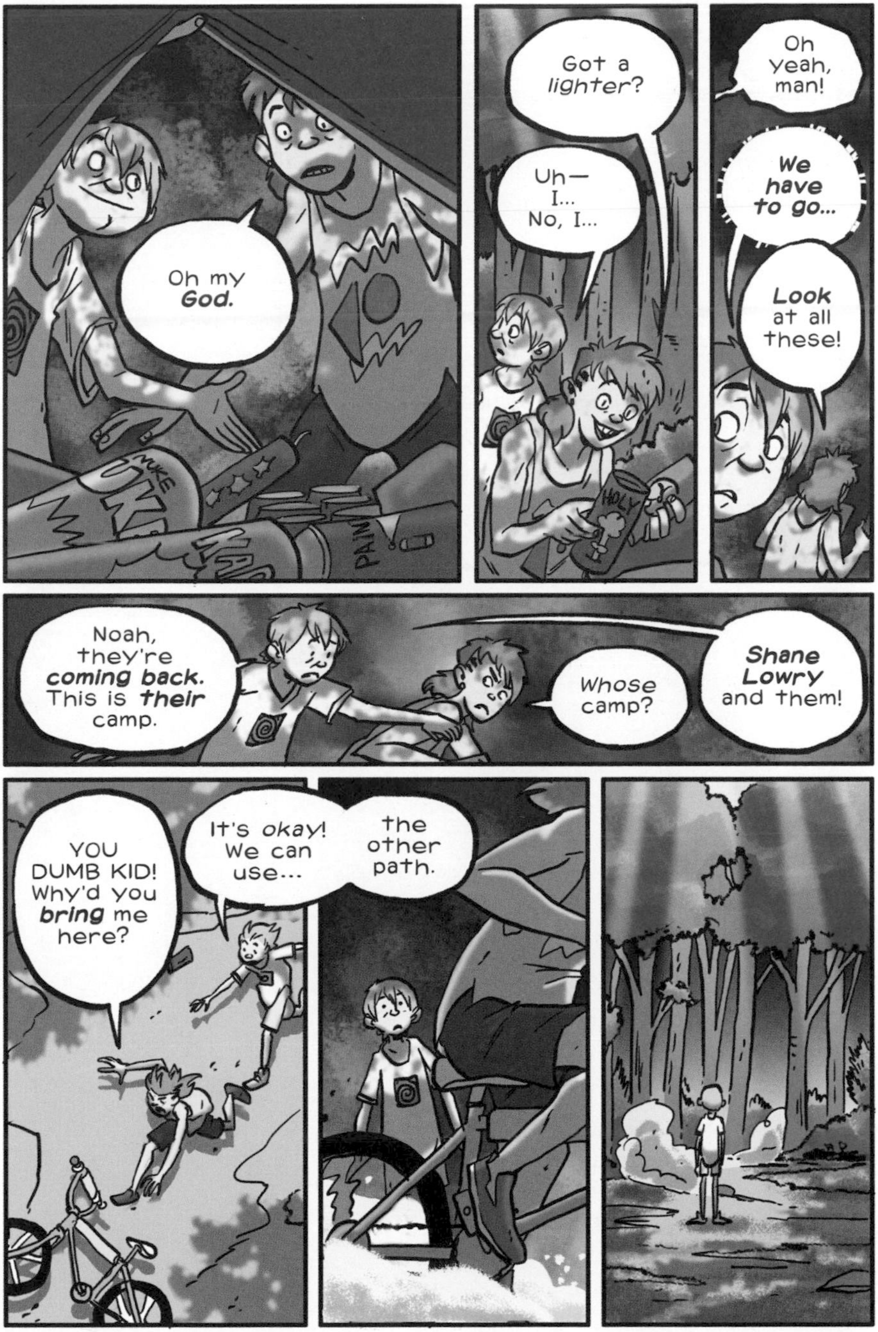
Oh my *God.*
Got a *lighter*?
Uh—
I...
No, I...
Oh yeah, man!
***We have to go...***
***Look*** at all these!
Noah, they're ***coming back.*** This is ***their*** camp.
*Whose* camp?
***Shane Lowry*** and them!
YOU DUMB KID! Why'd you ***bring*** me here?
It's *okay*! We can use...
the other path.

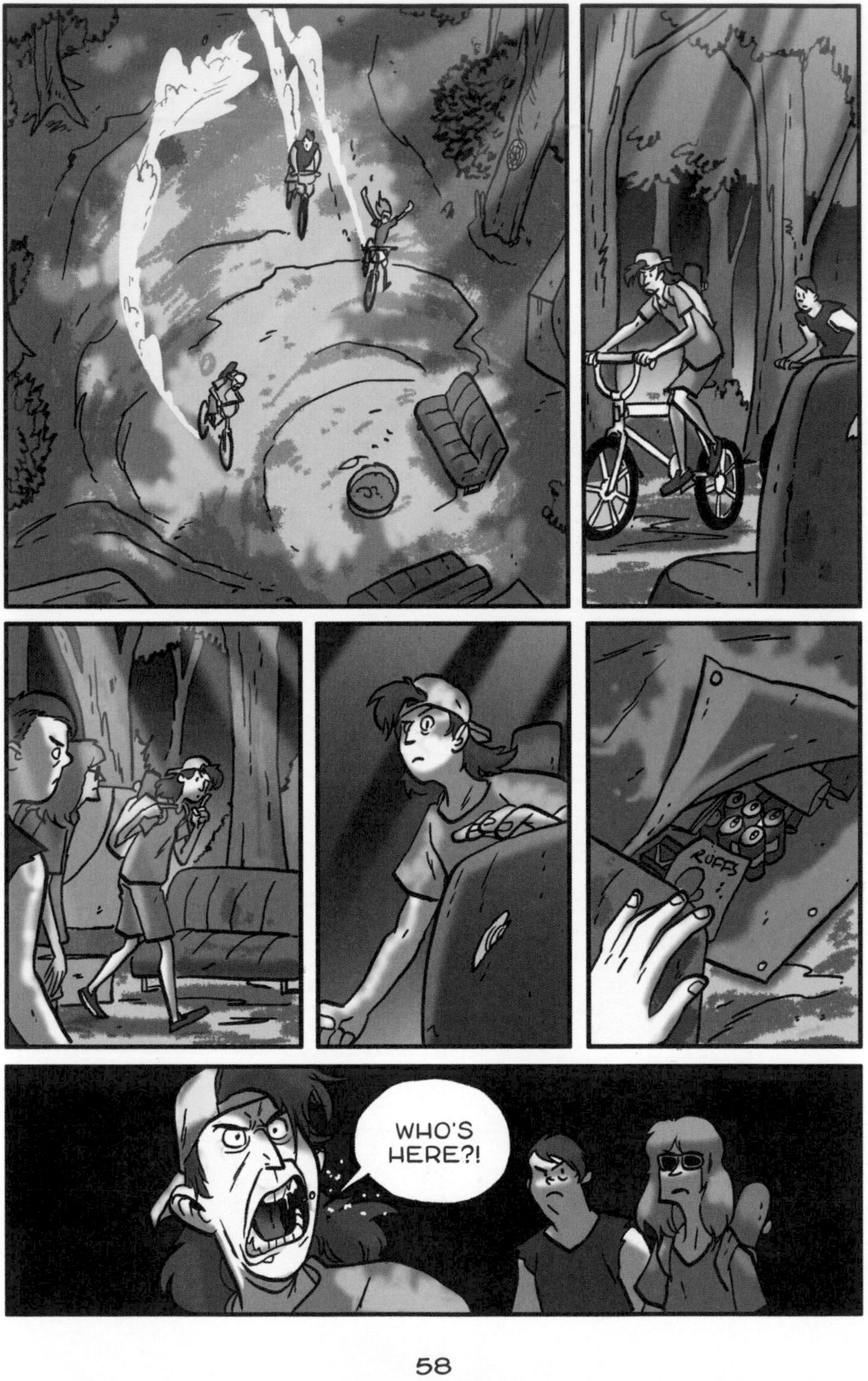
RUFFS
WHO'S HERE?!

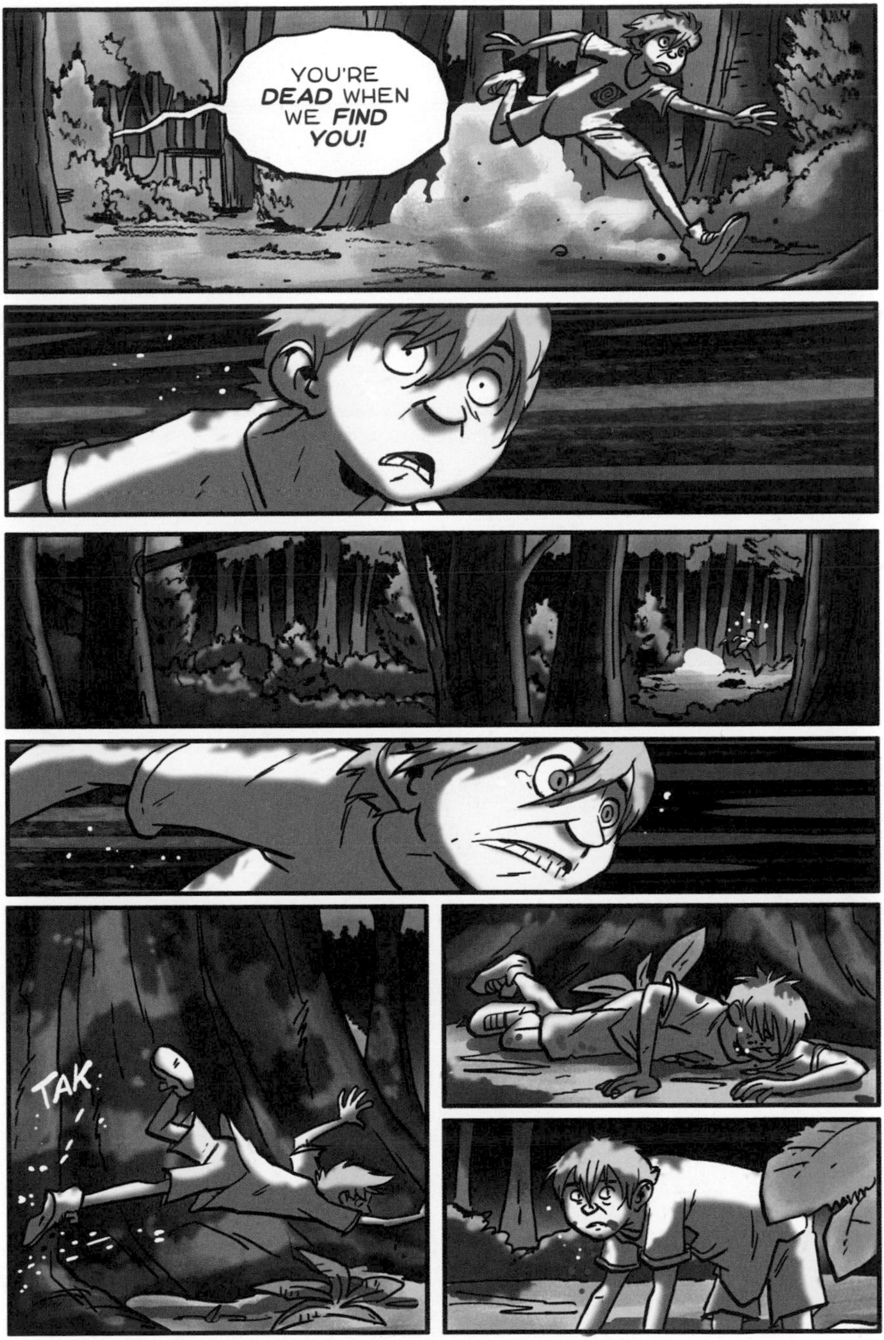
YOU'RE **DEAD** WHEN WE **FIND YOU!**
TAK

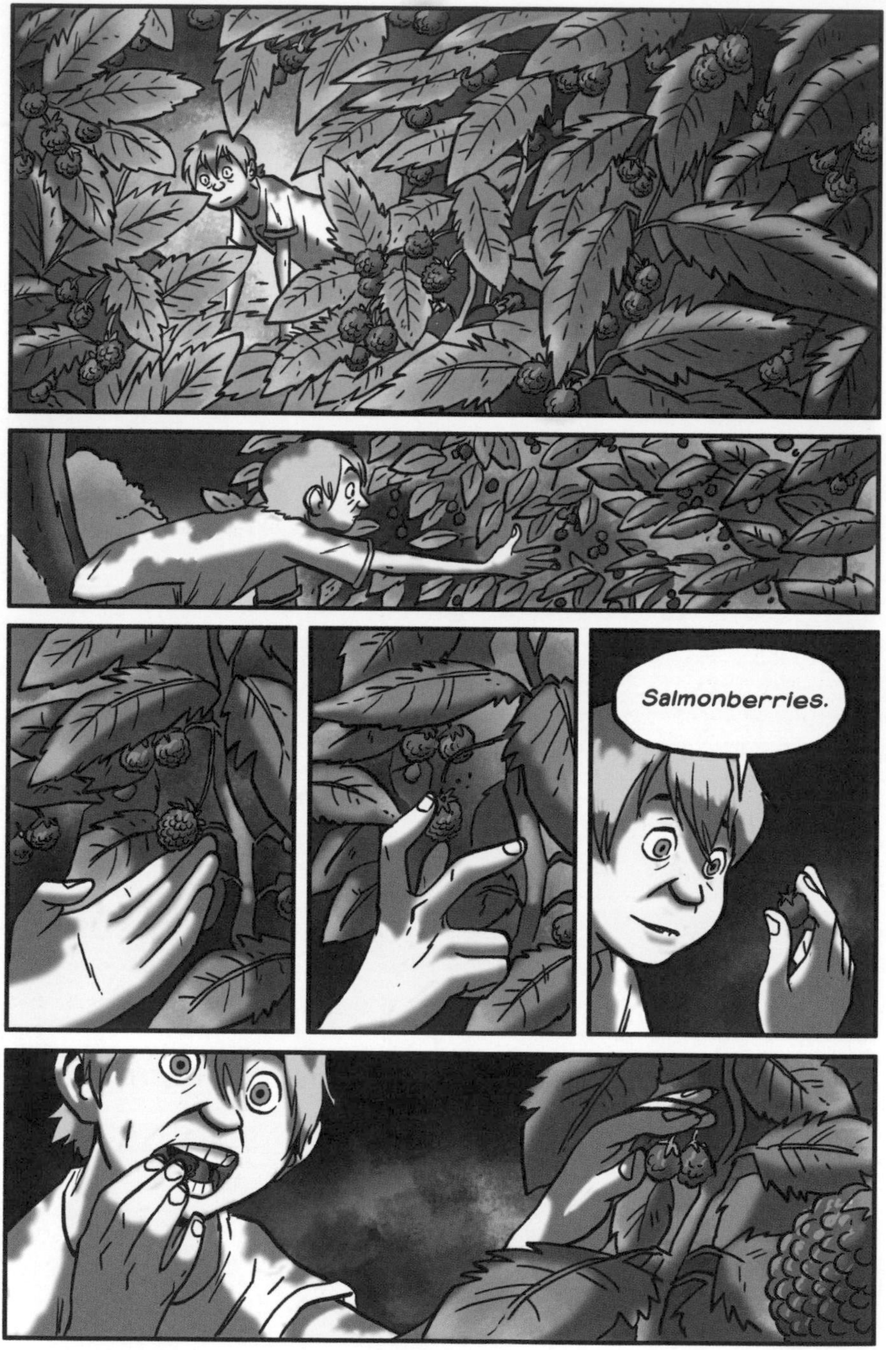
Salmonberries.

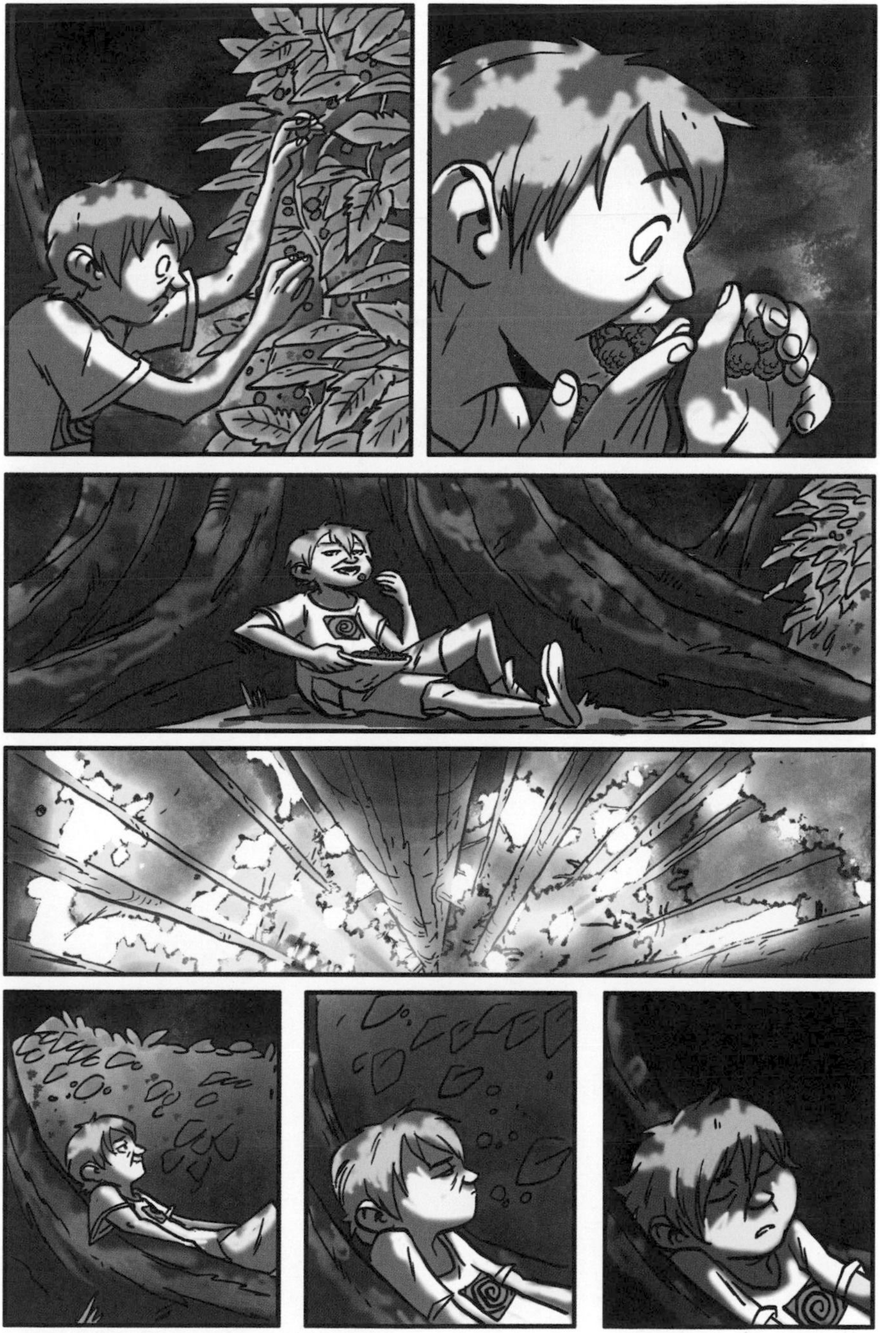

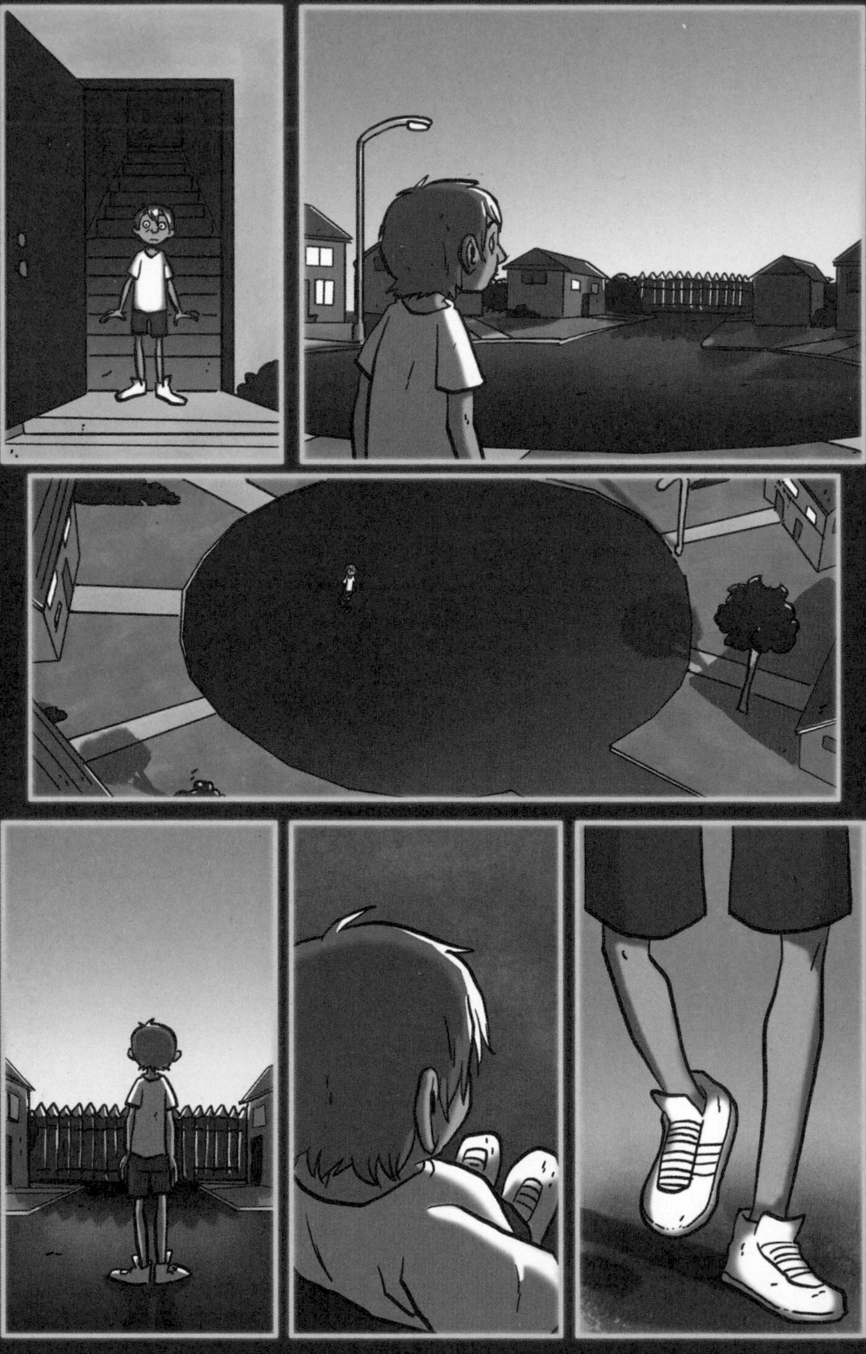

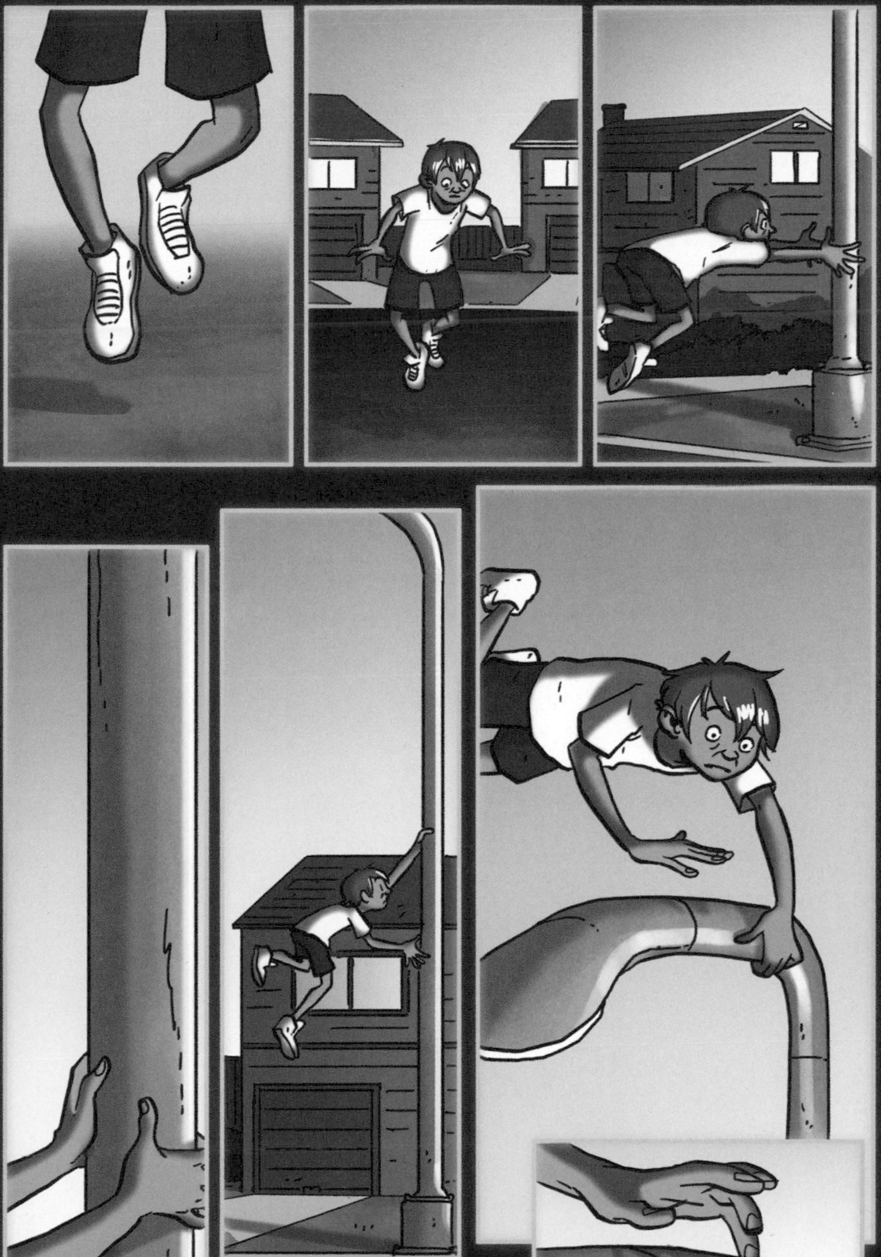

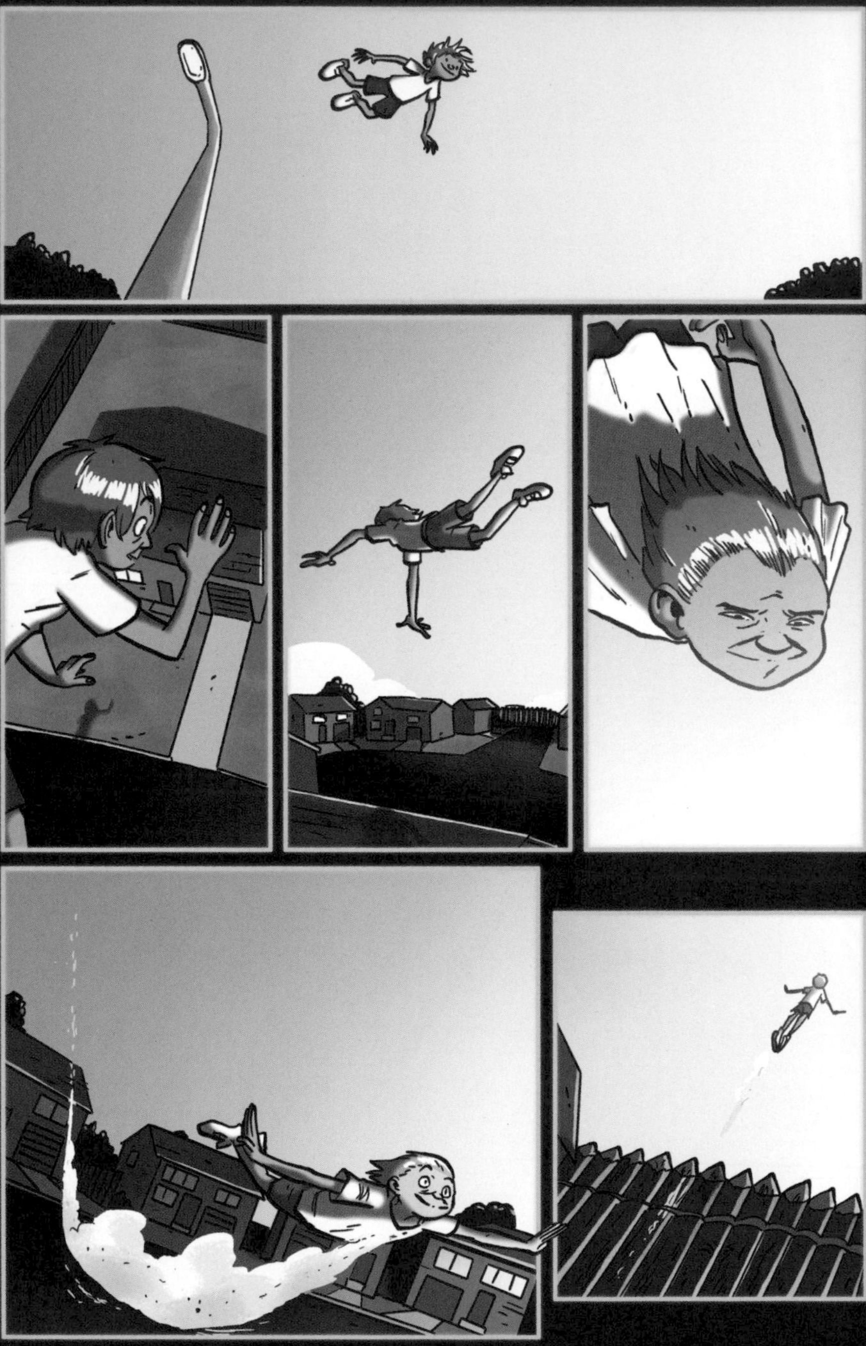

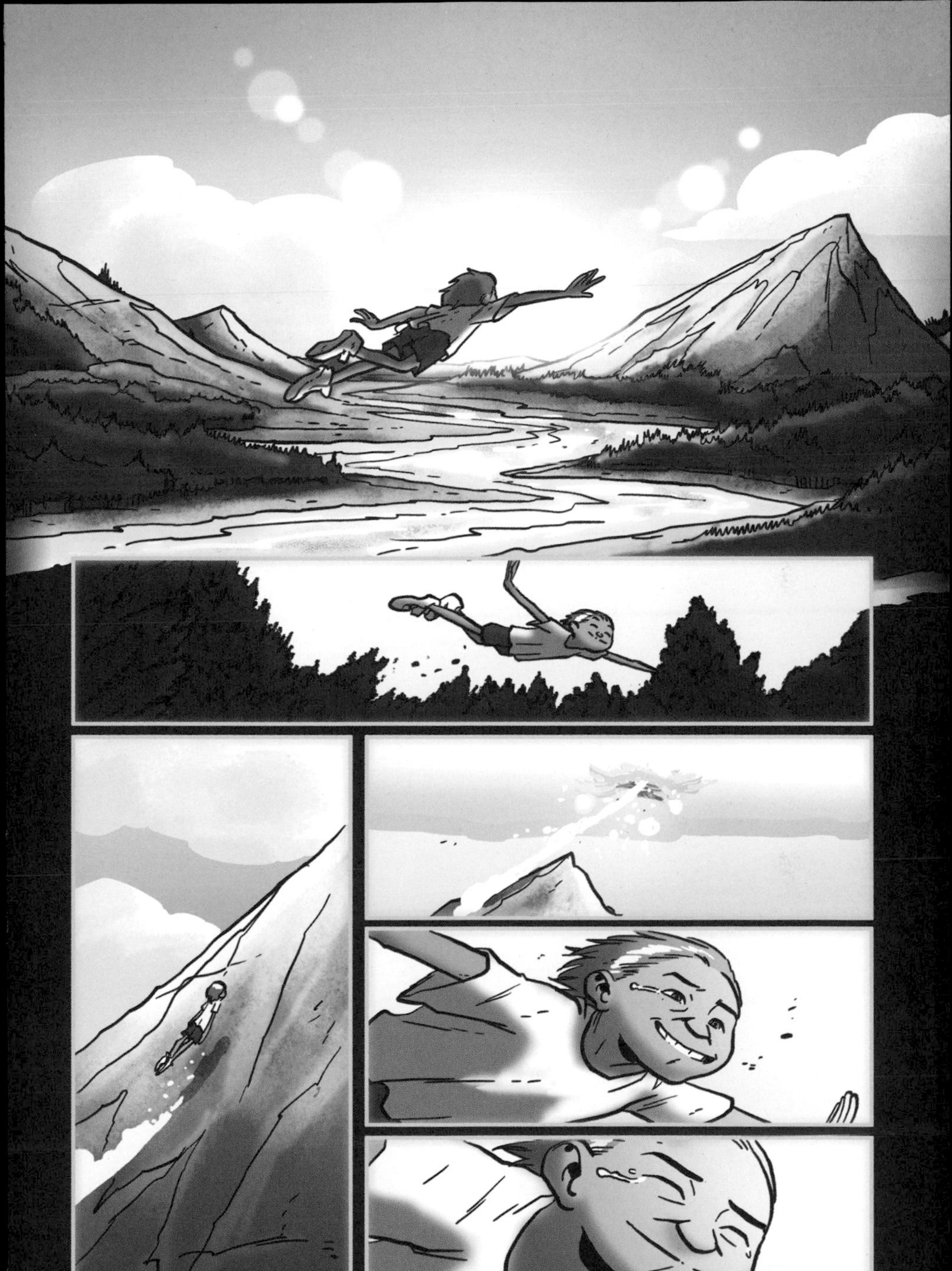

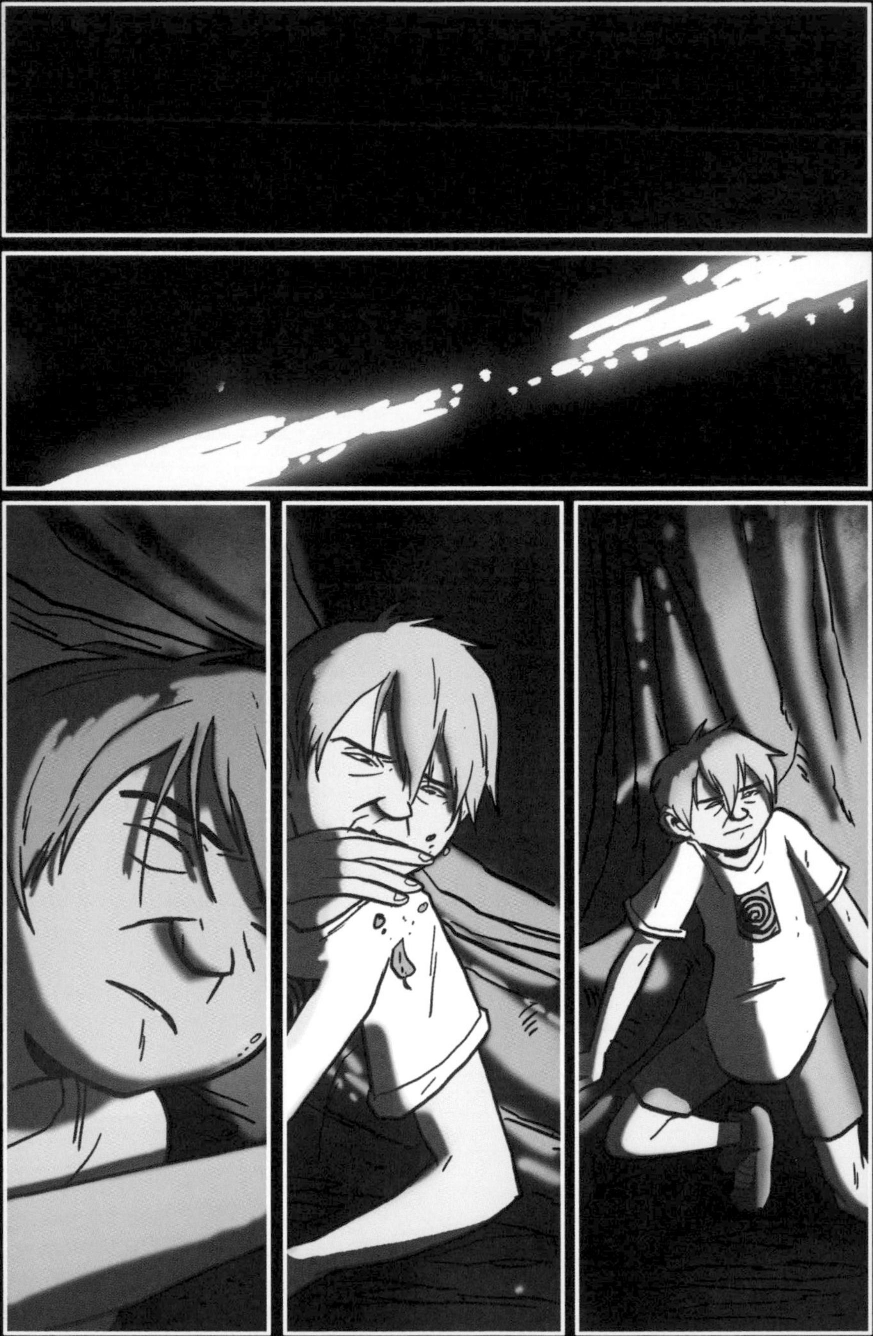

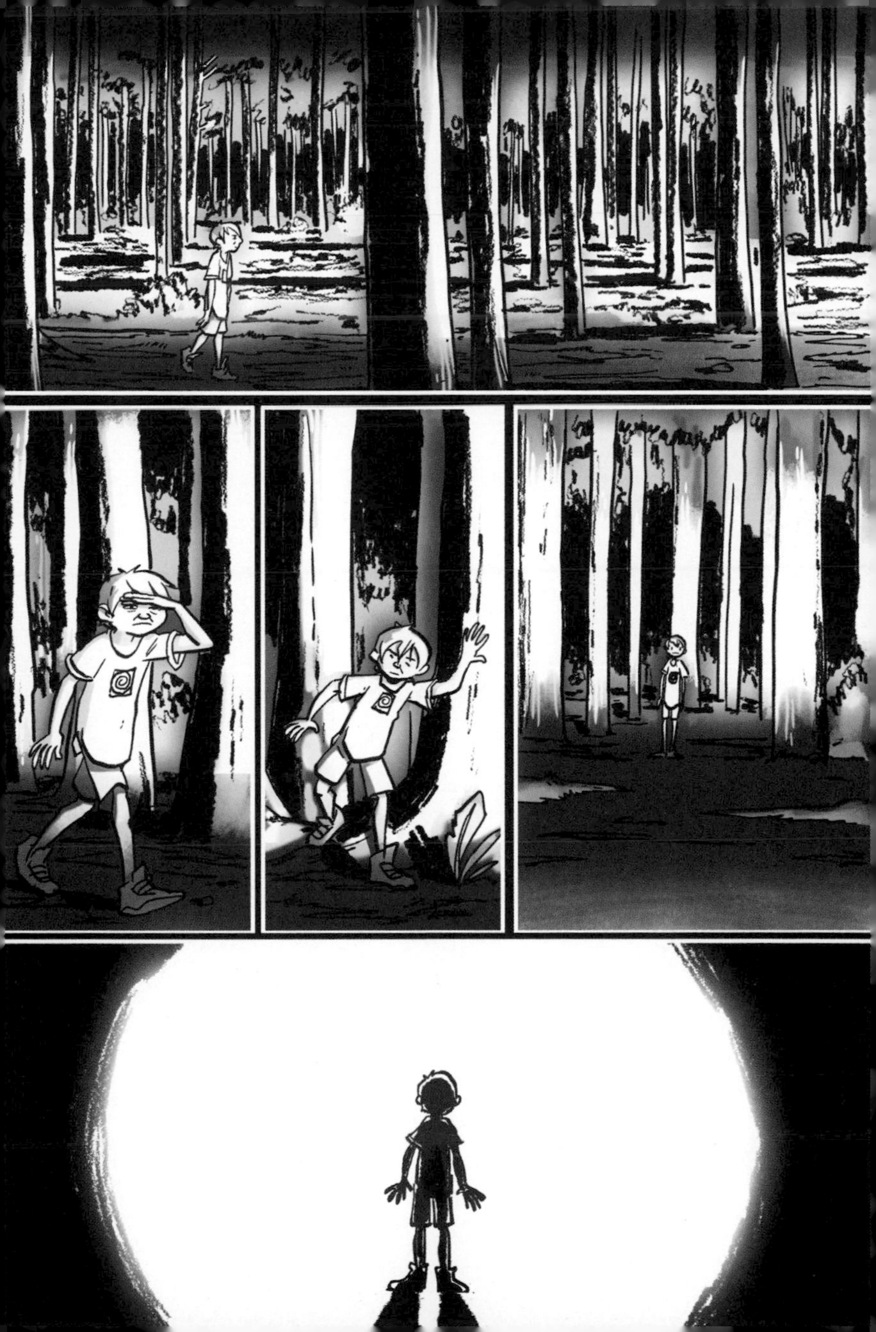

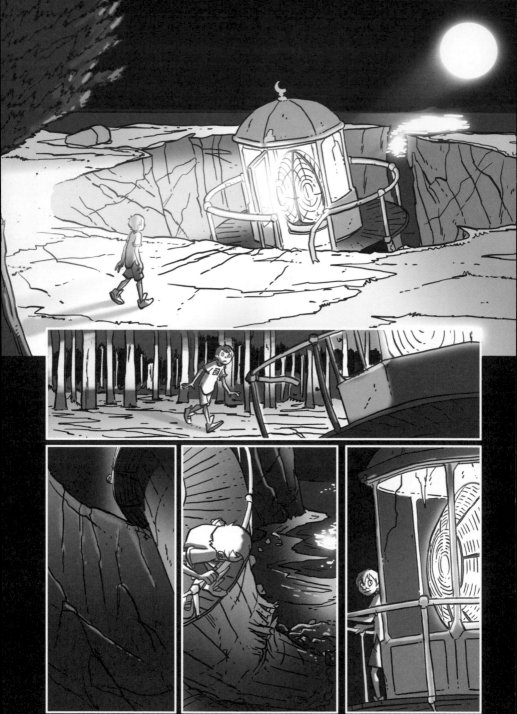

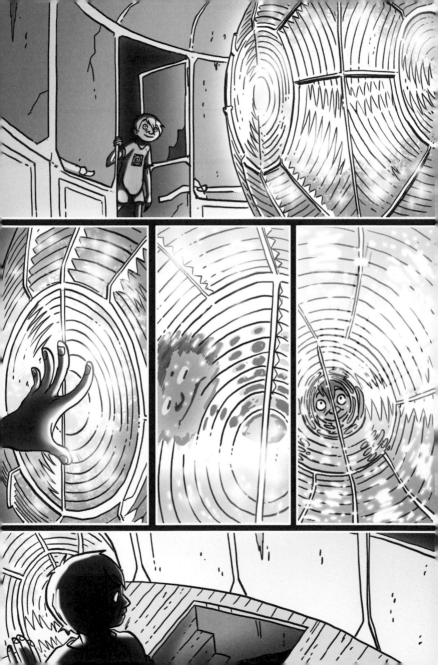

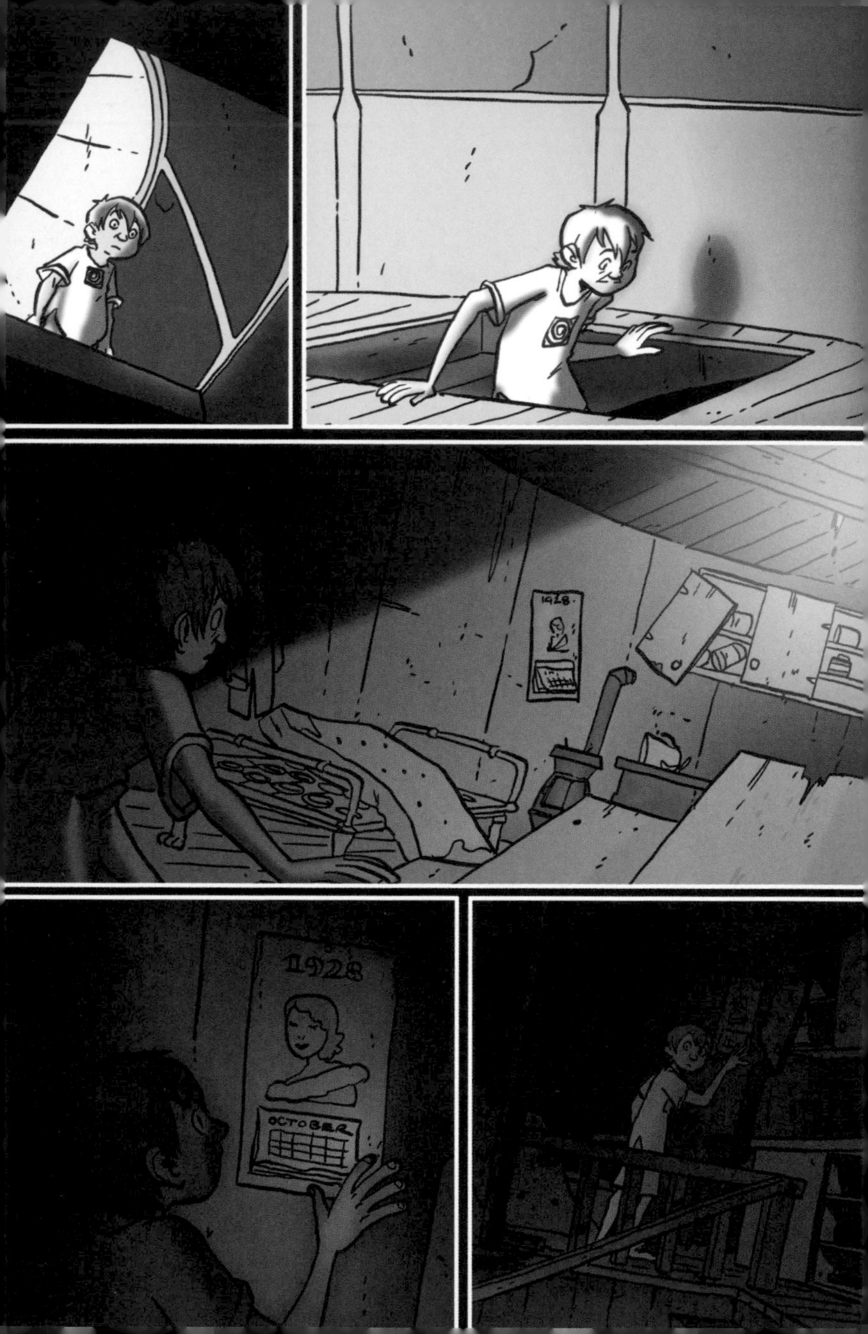
1928
1928
OCTOBER

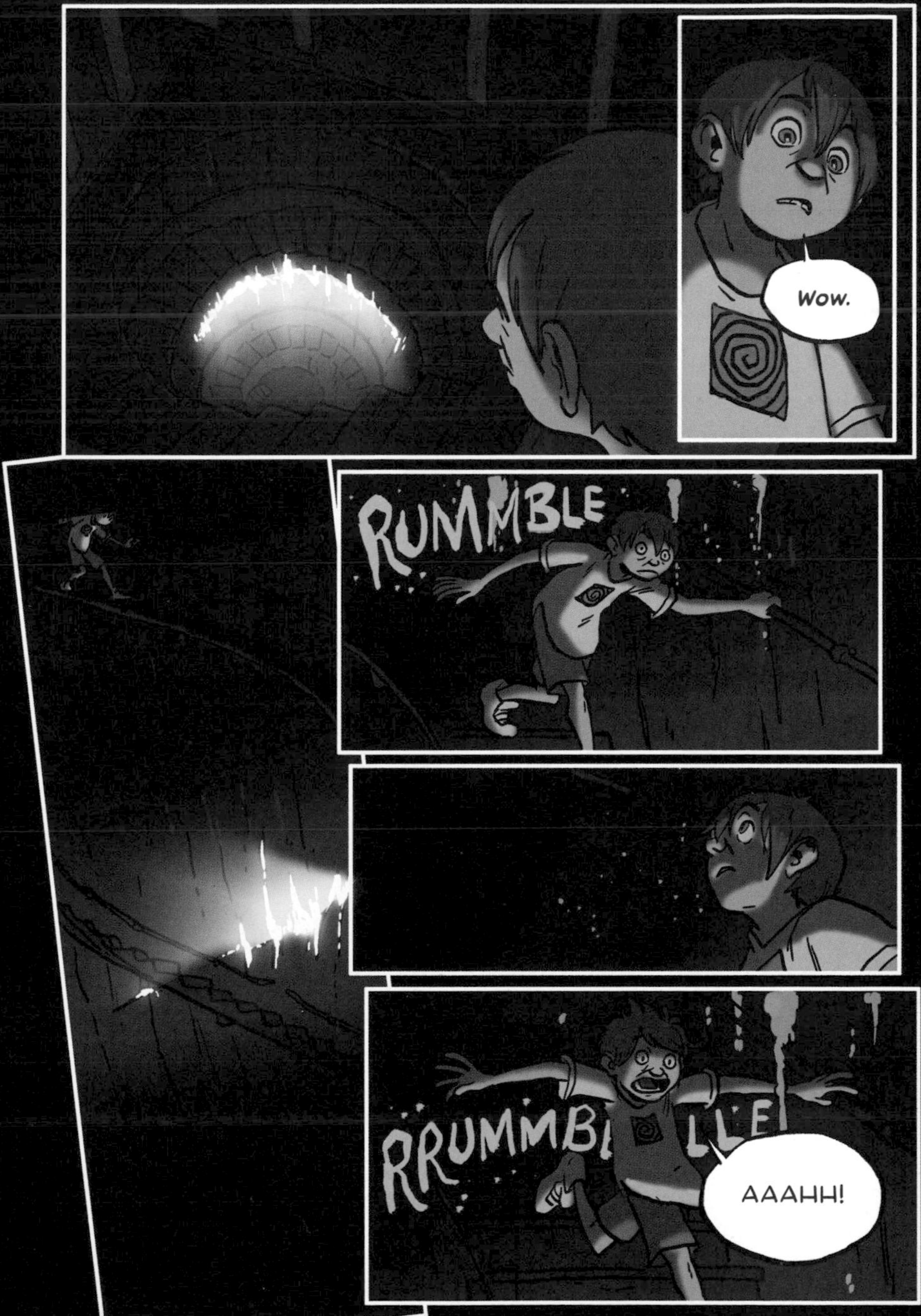
Wow.
RUMMBLE
RRUMMBLLE
AAAHH!

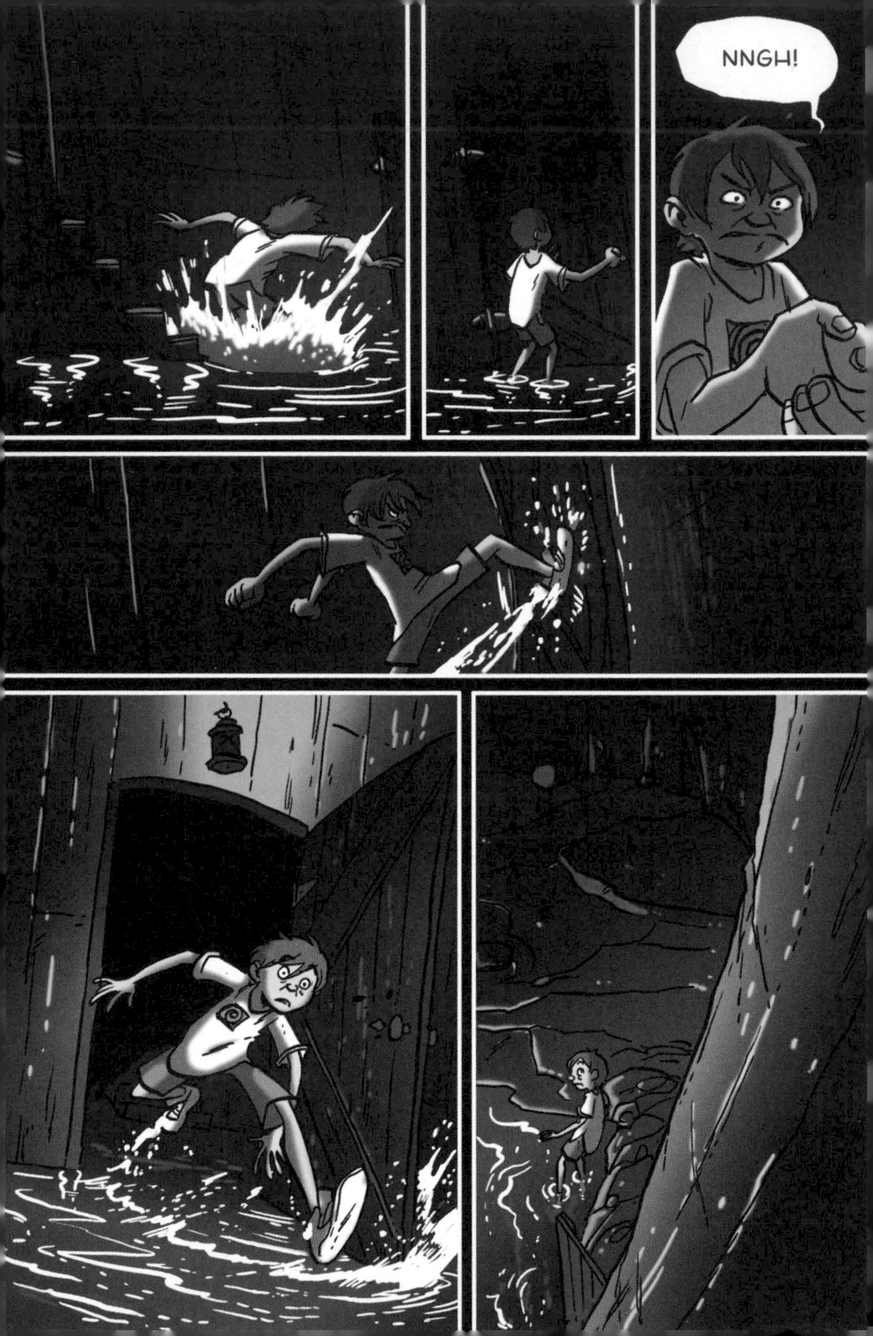
NNGH!

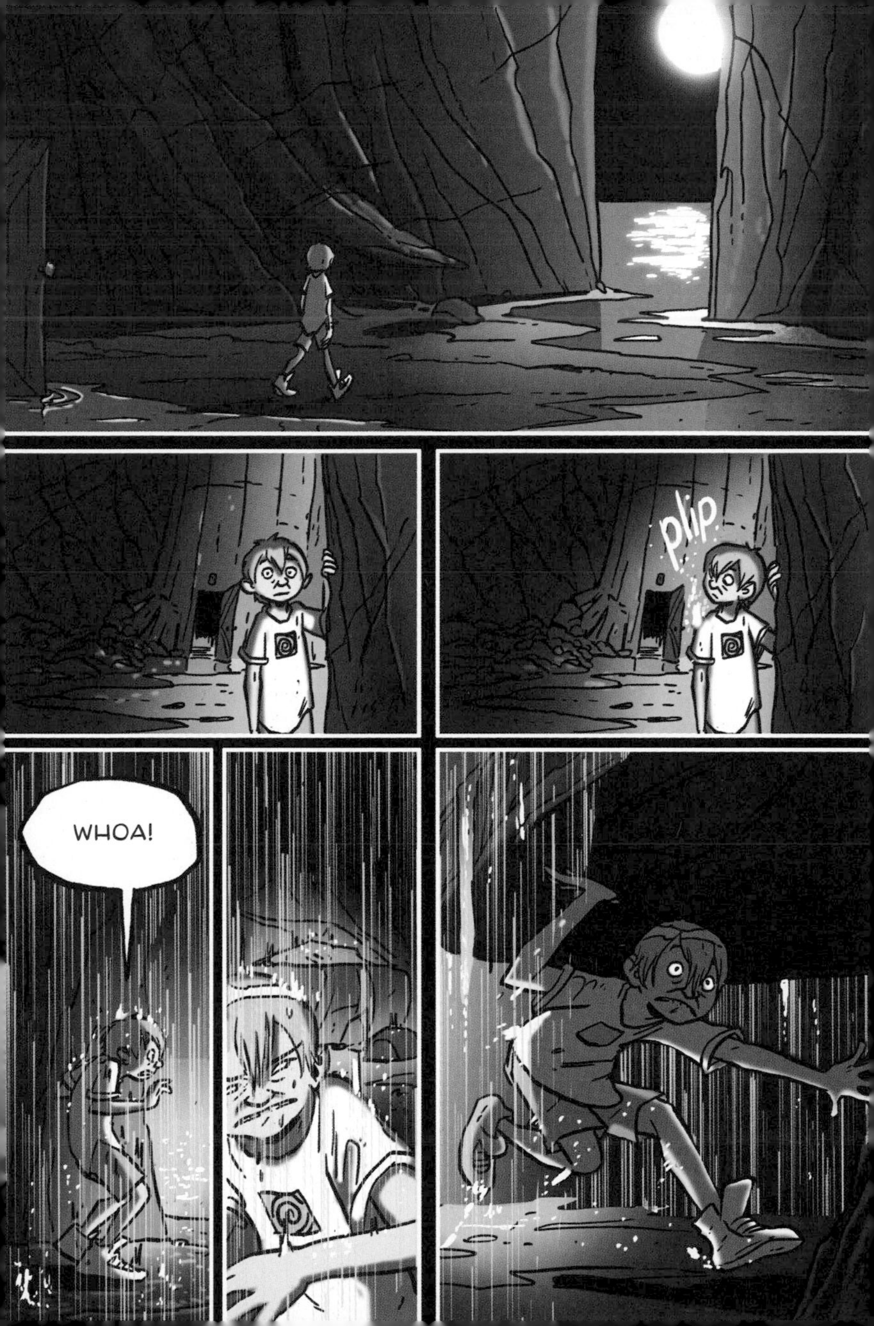
plip
WHOA!

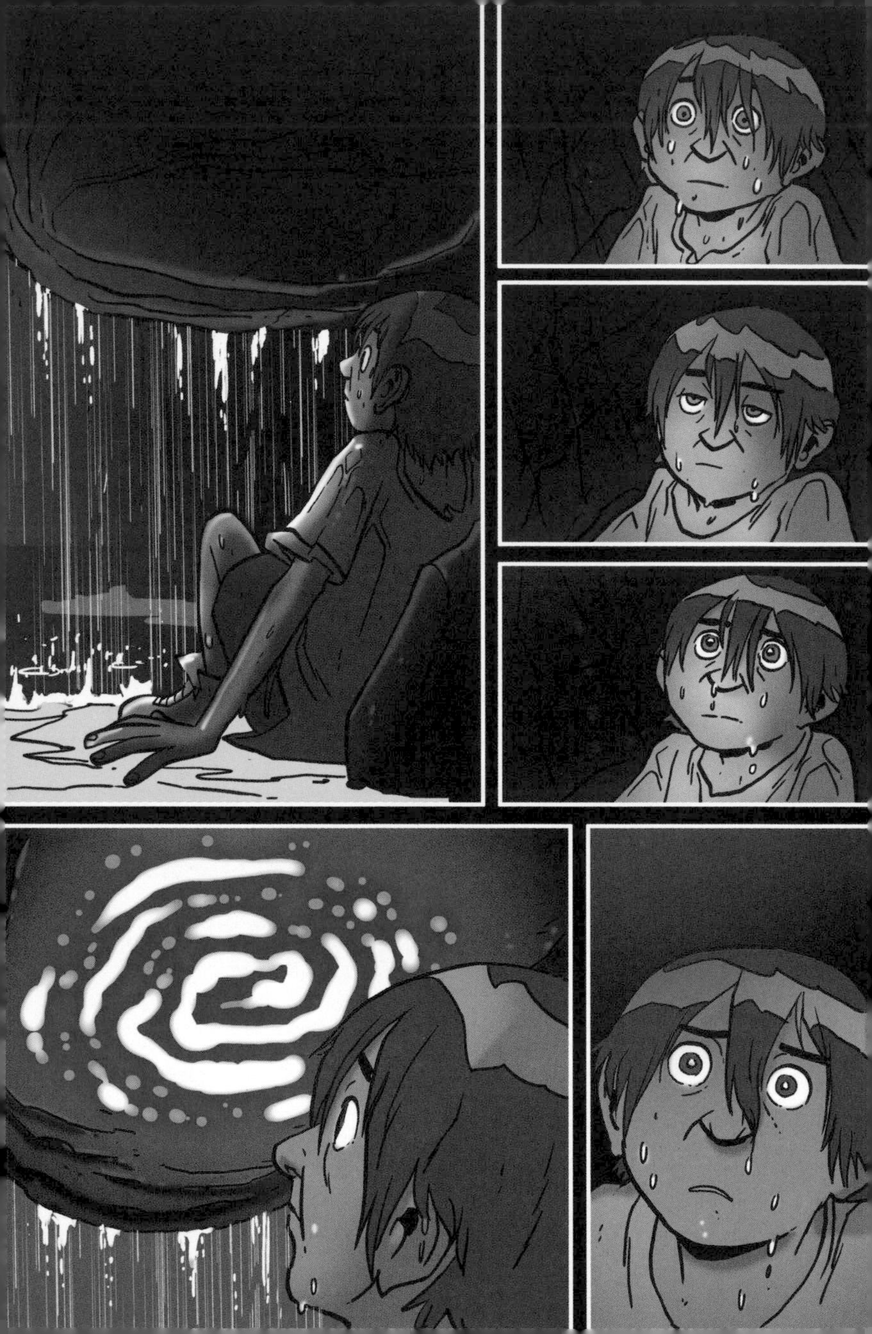

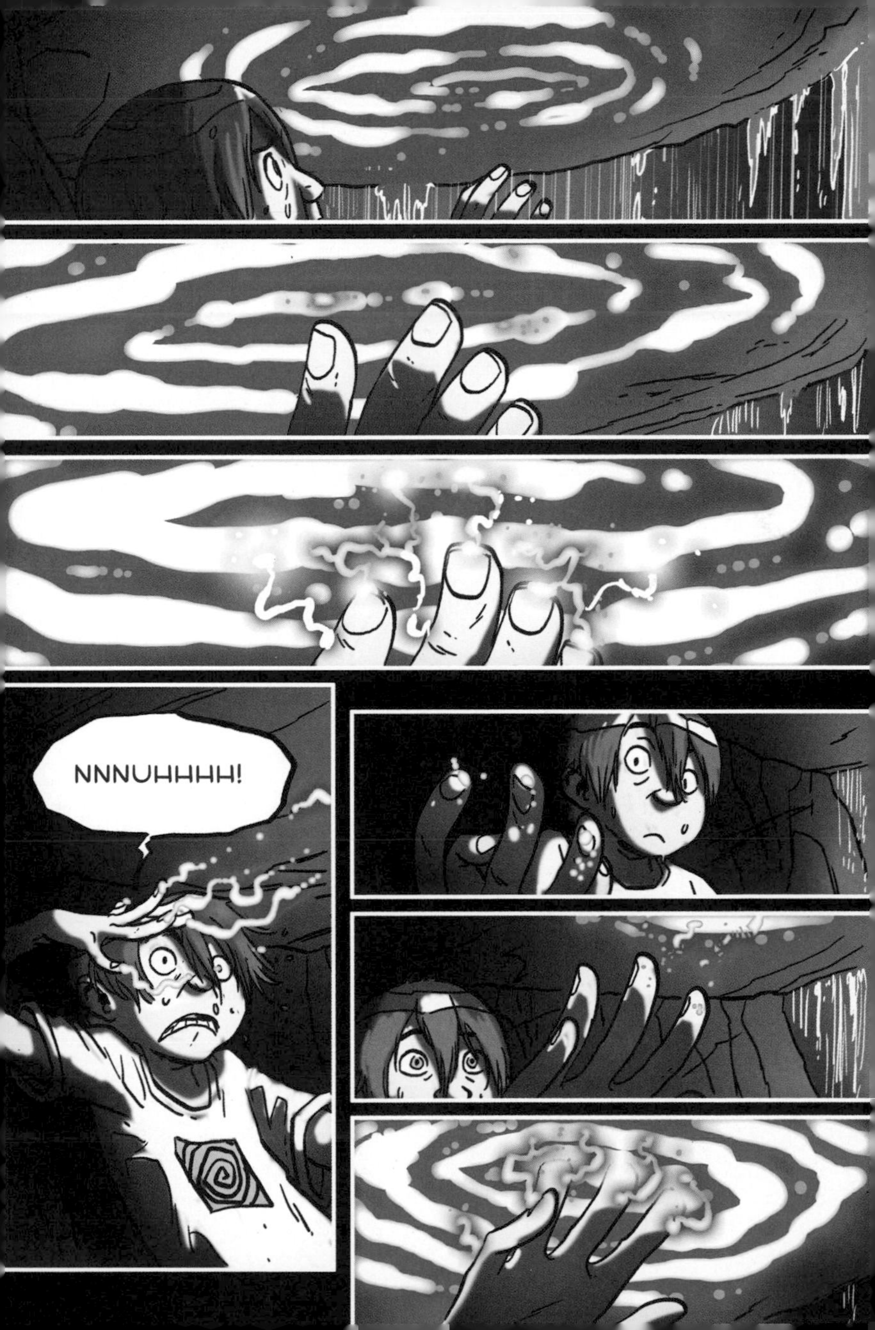
NNNUHHHH!

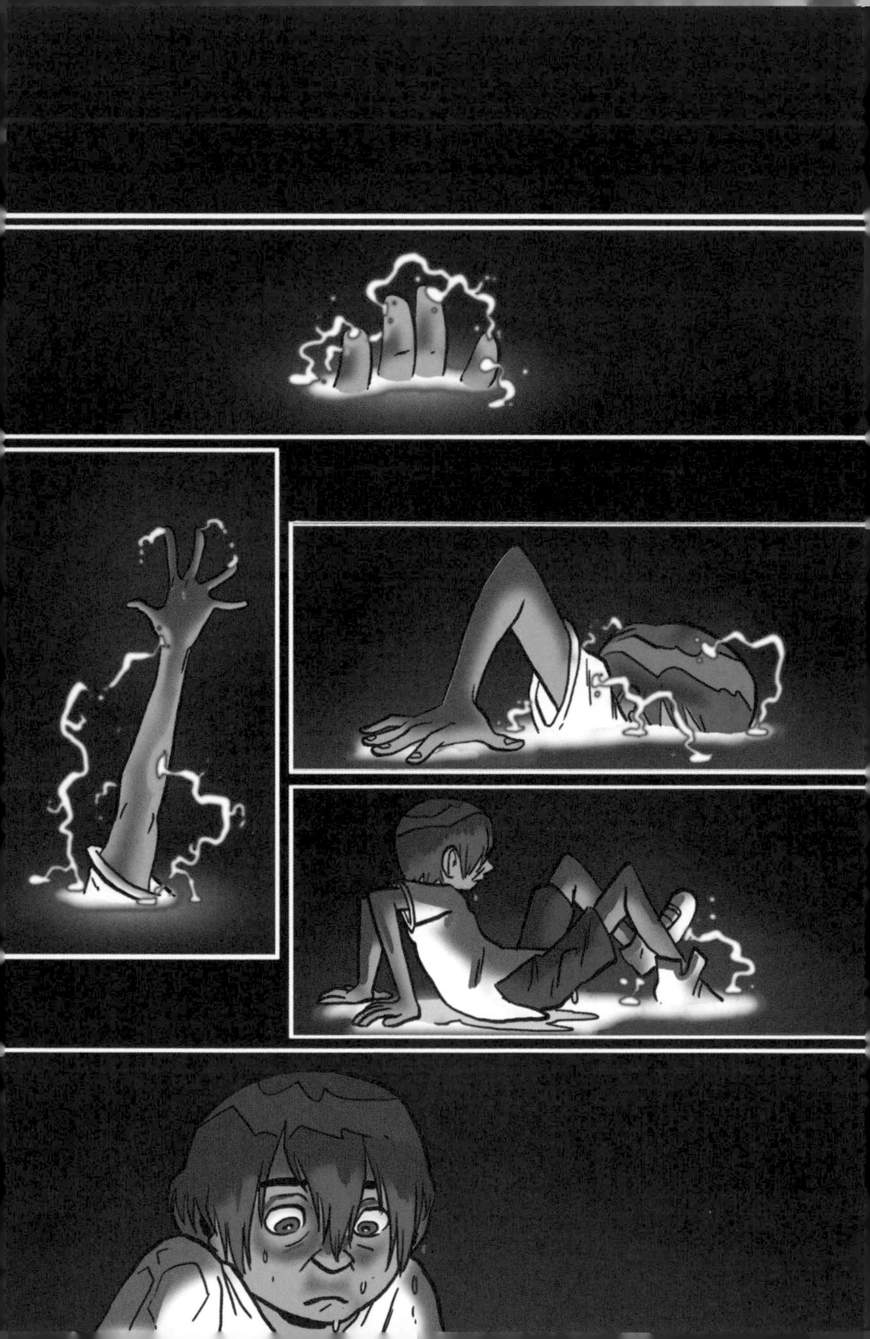

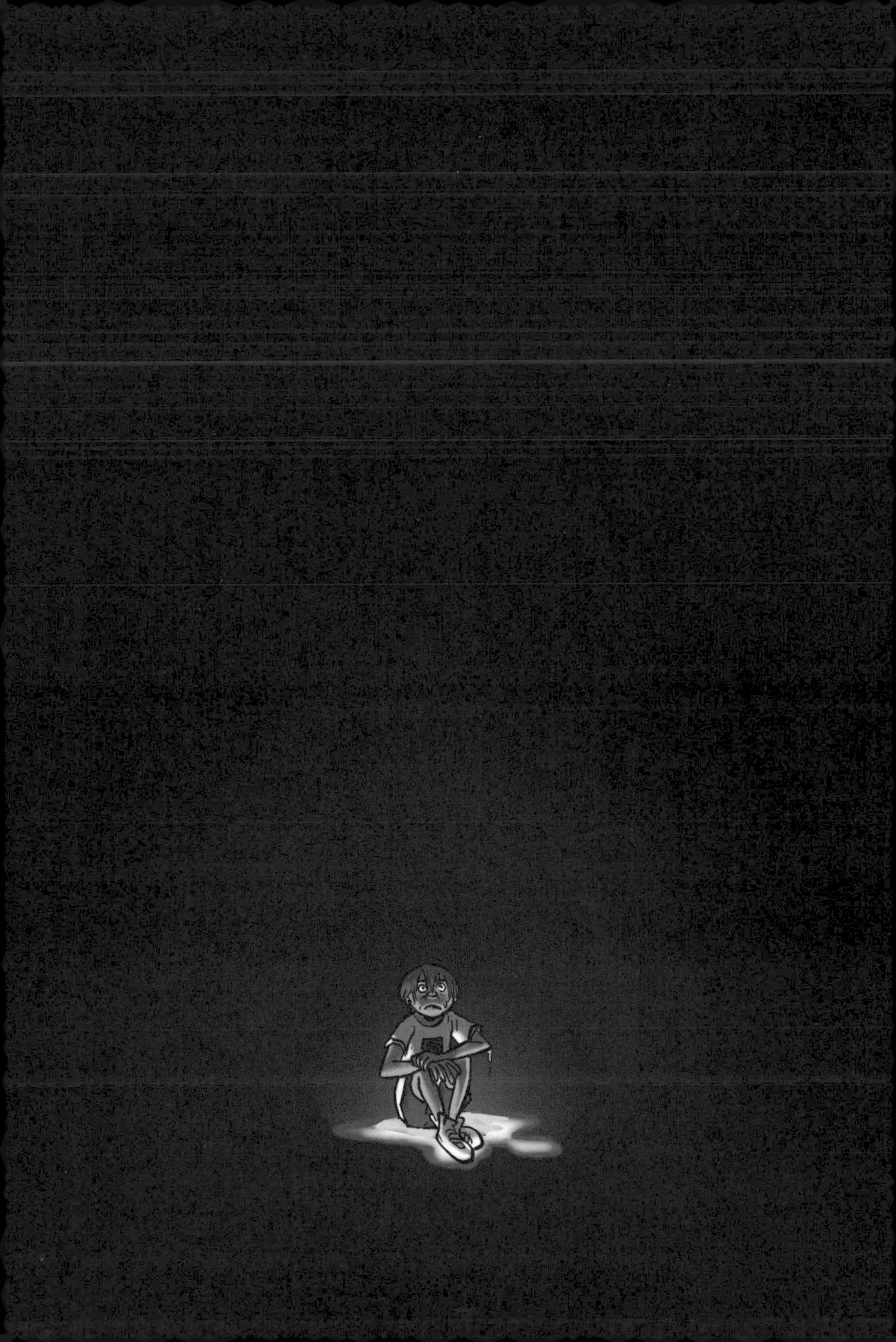

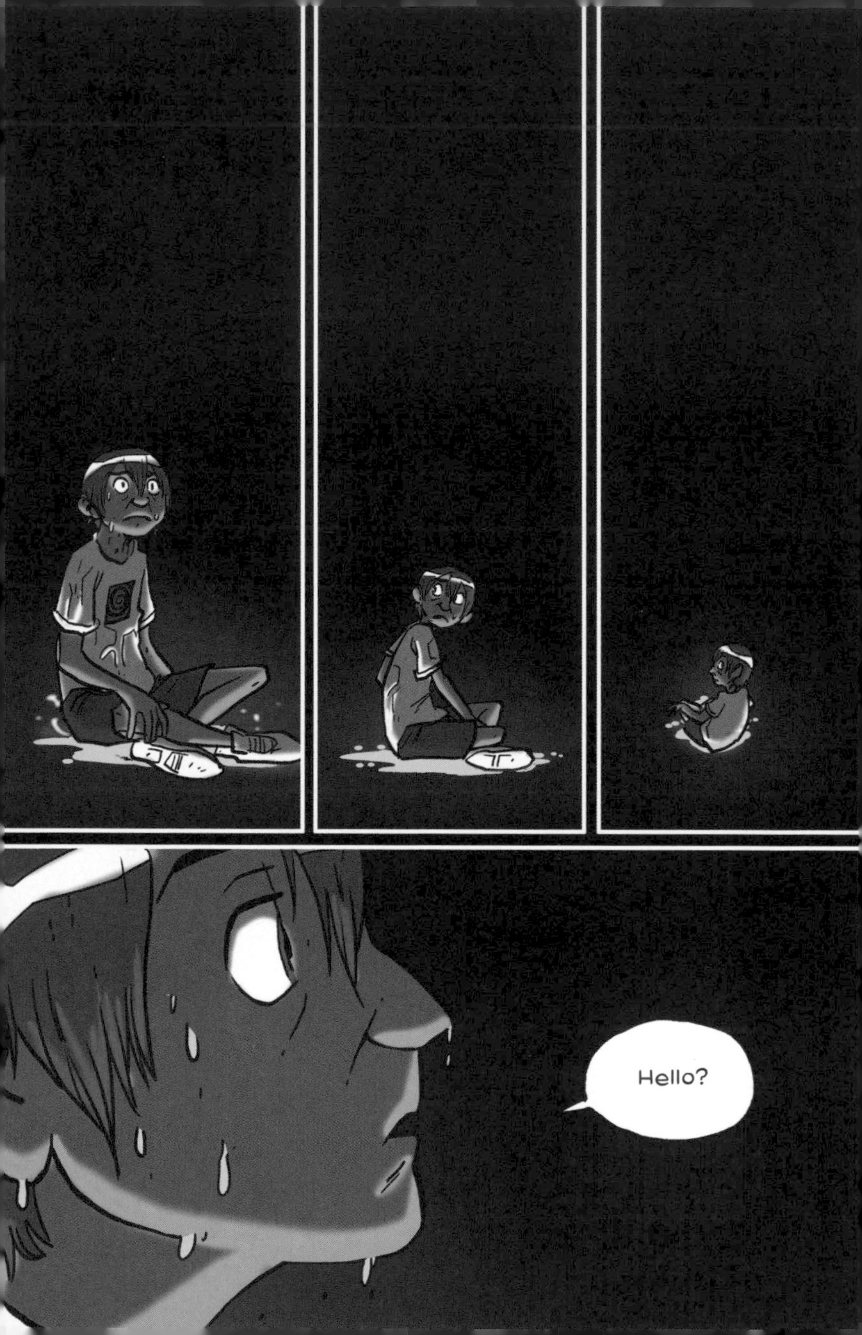
Hello?

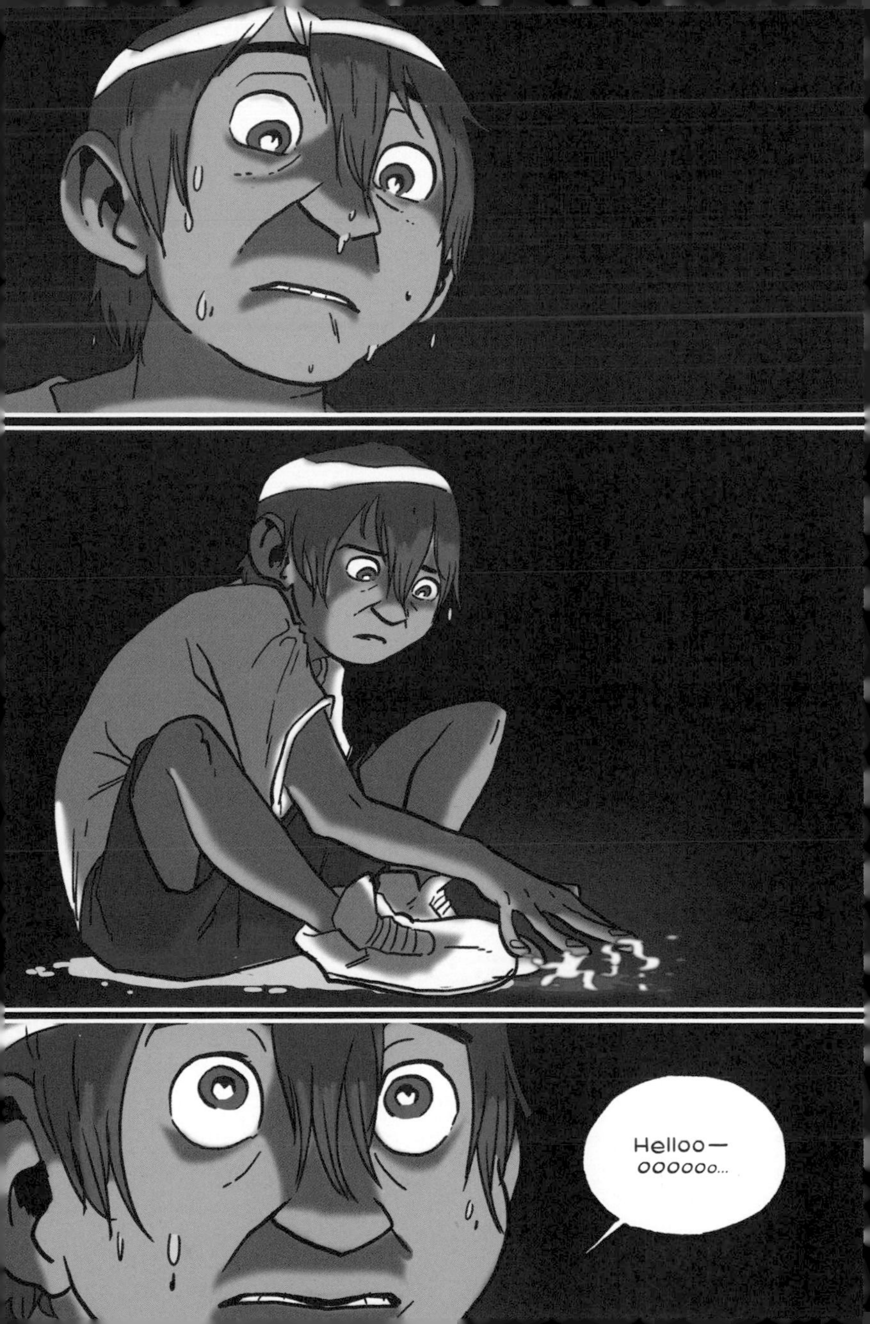
Helloo—
oooooo...

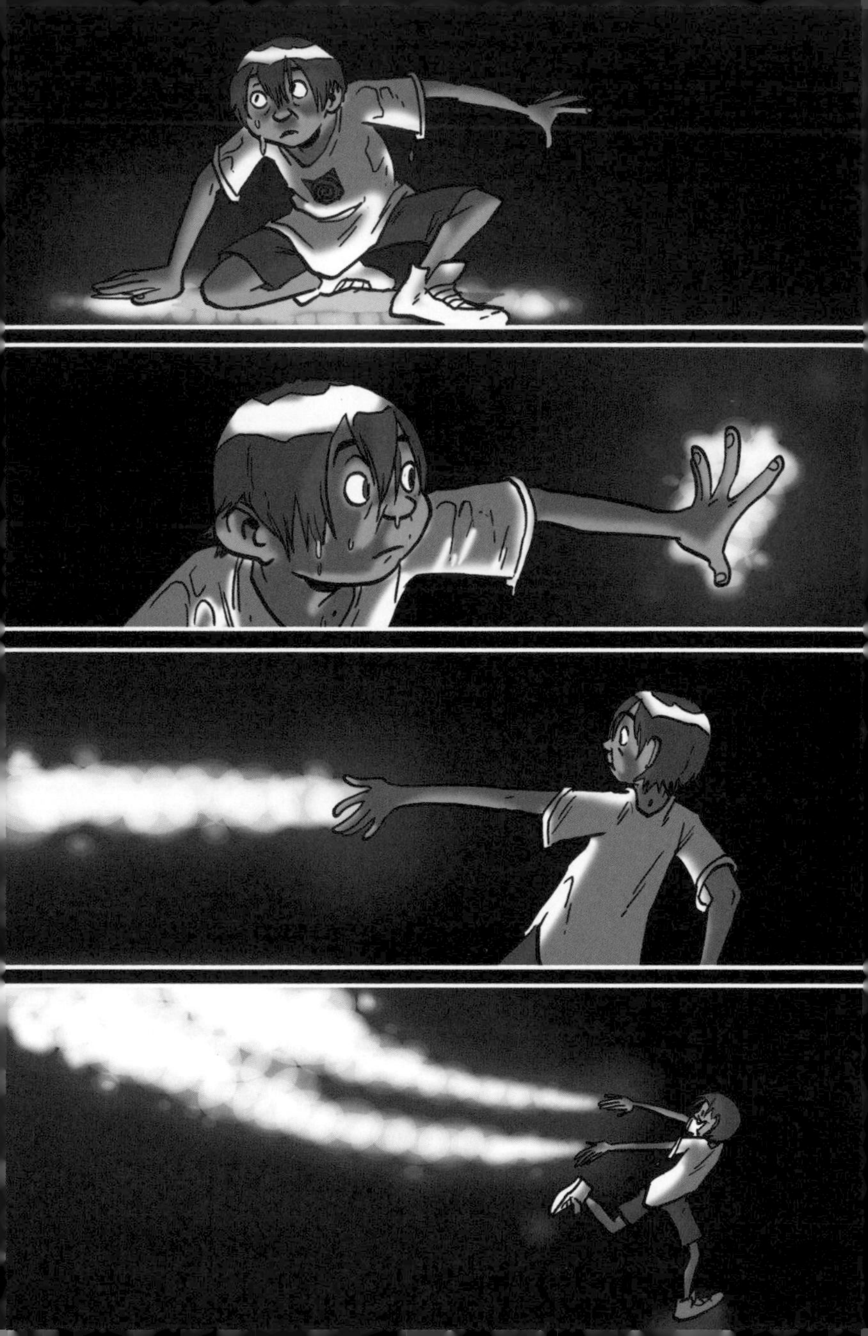

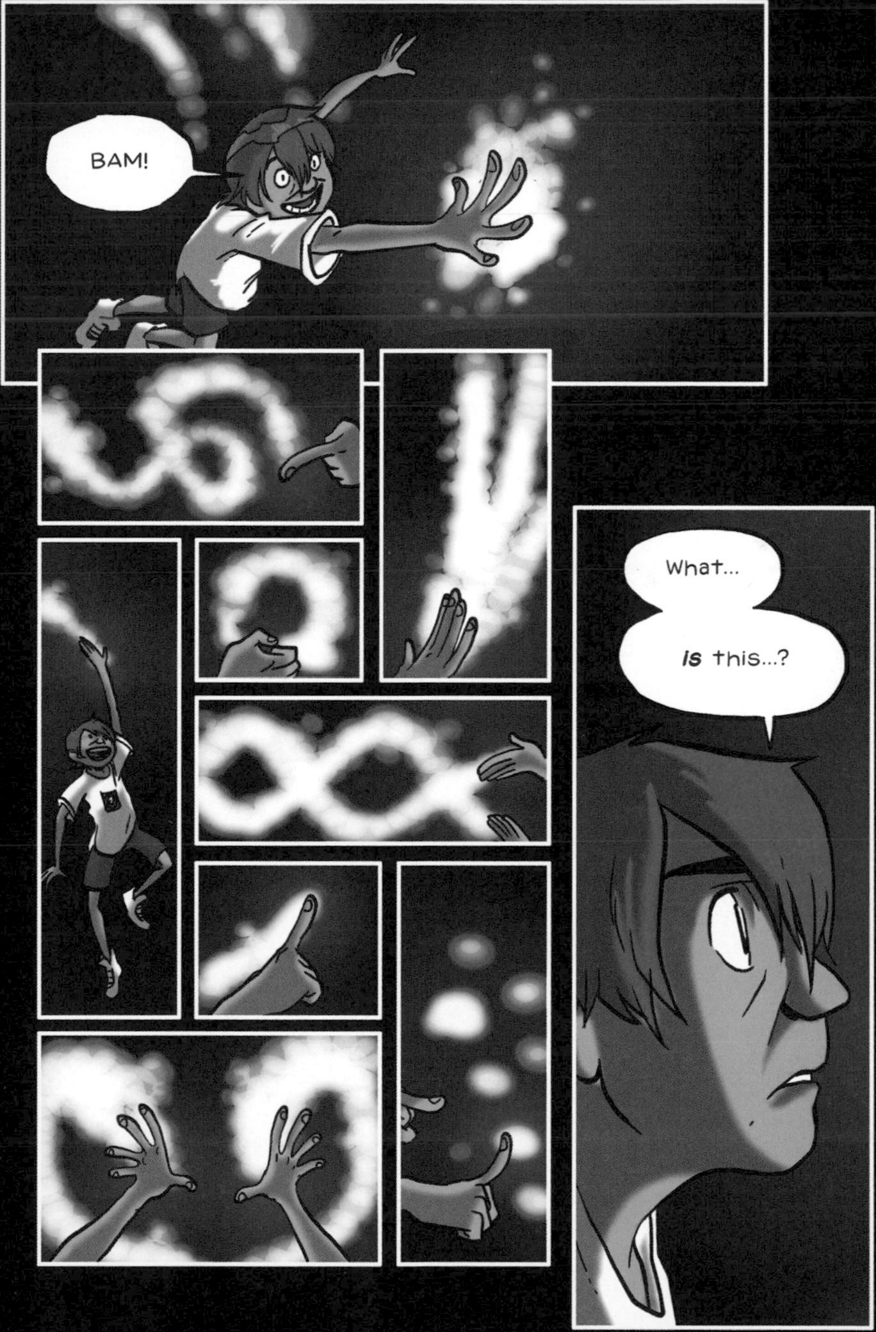
BAM!
What...
*is* this...?

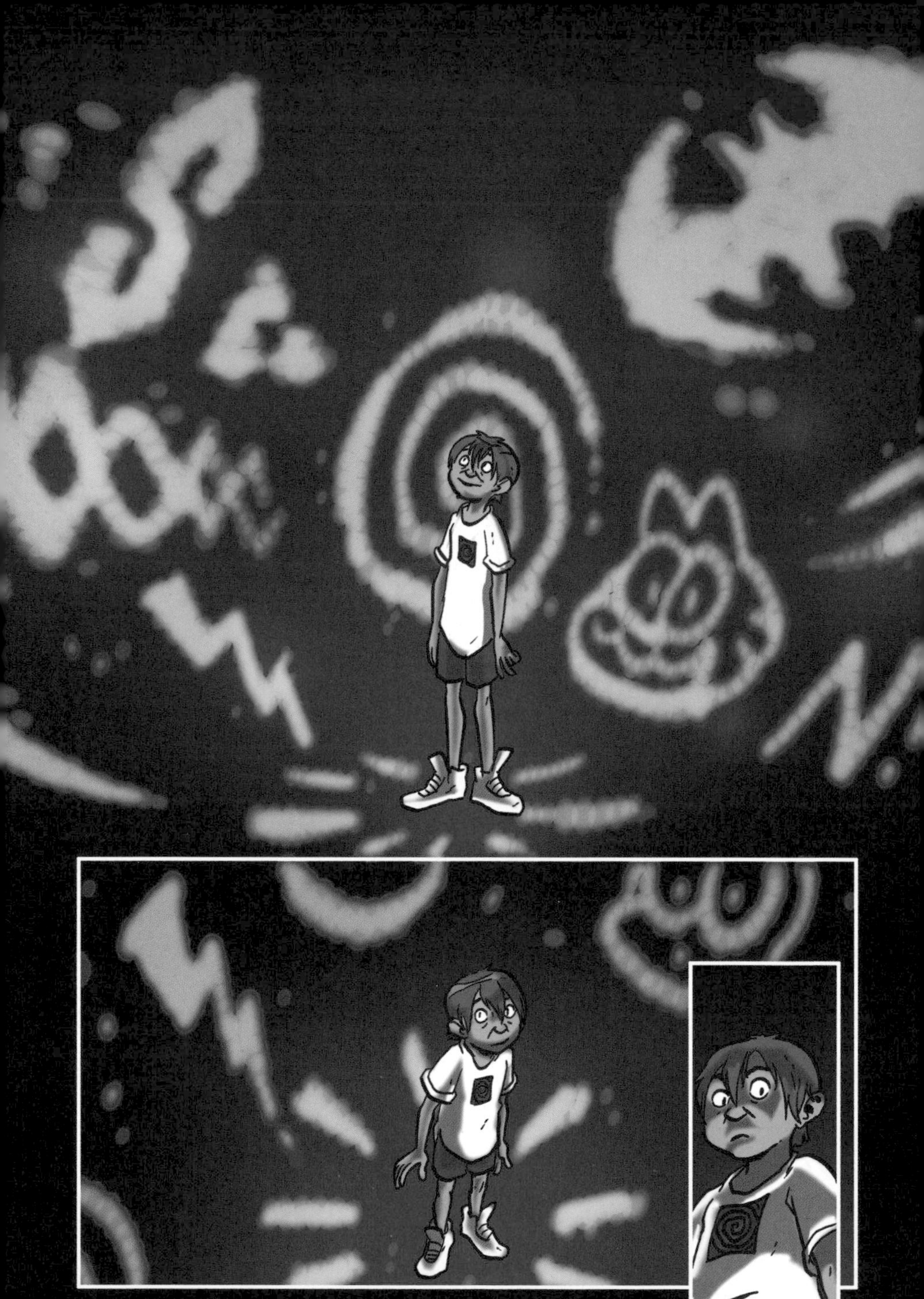

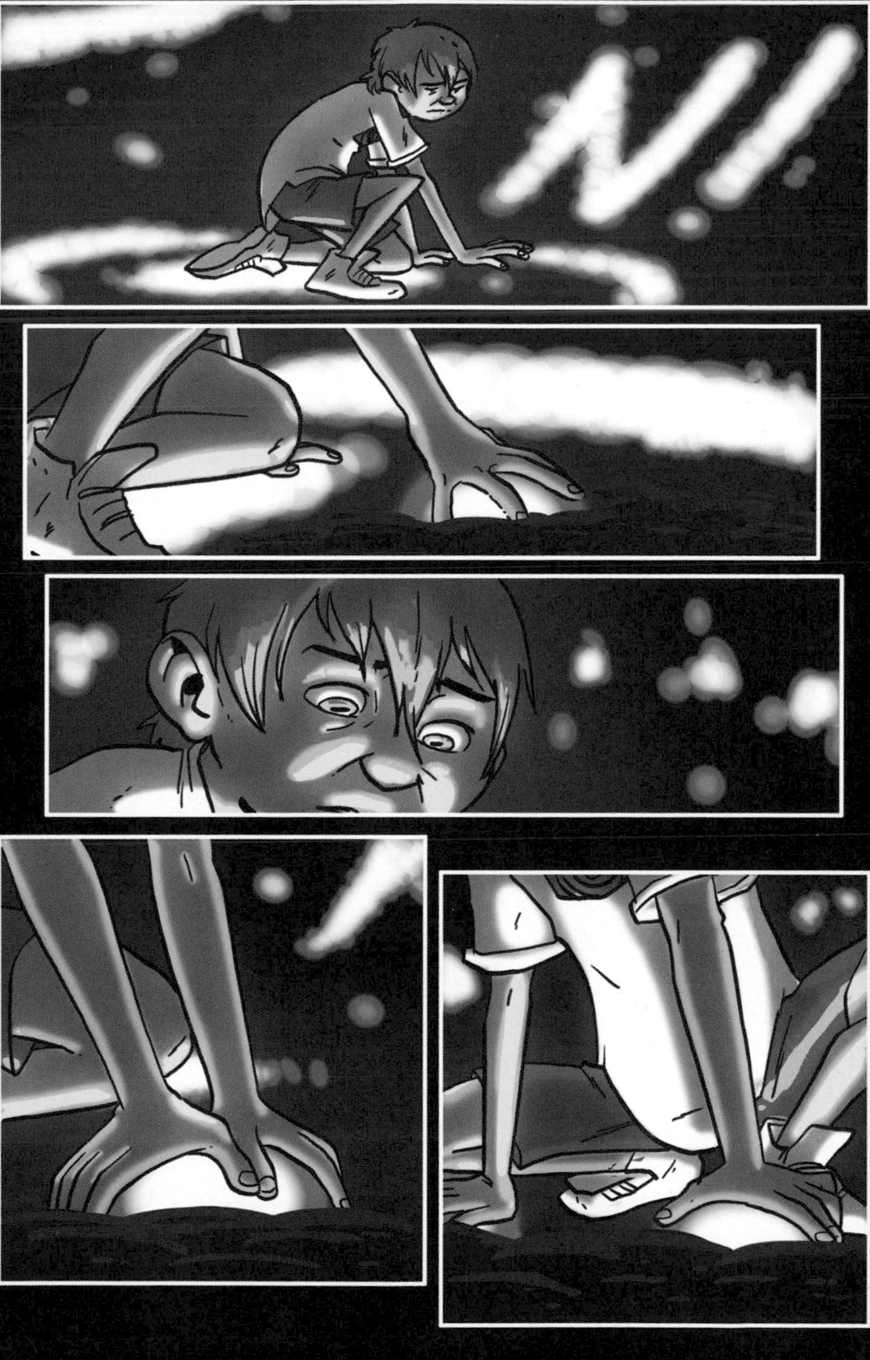

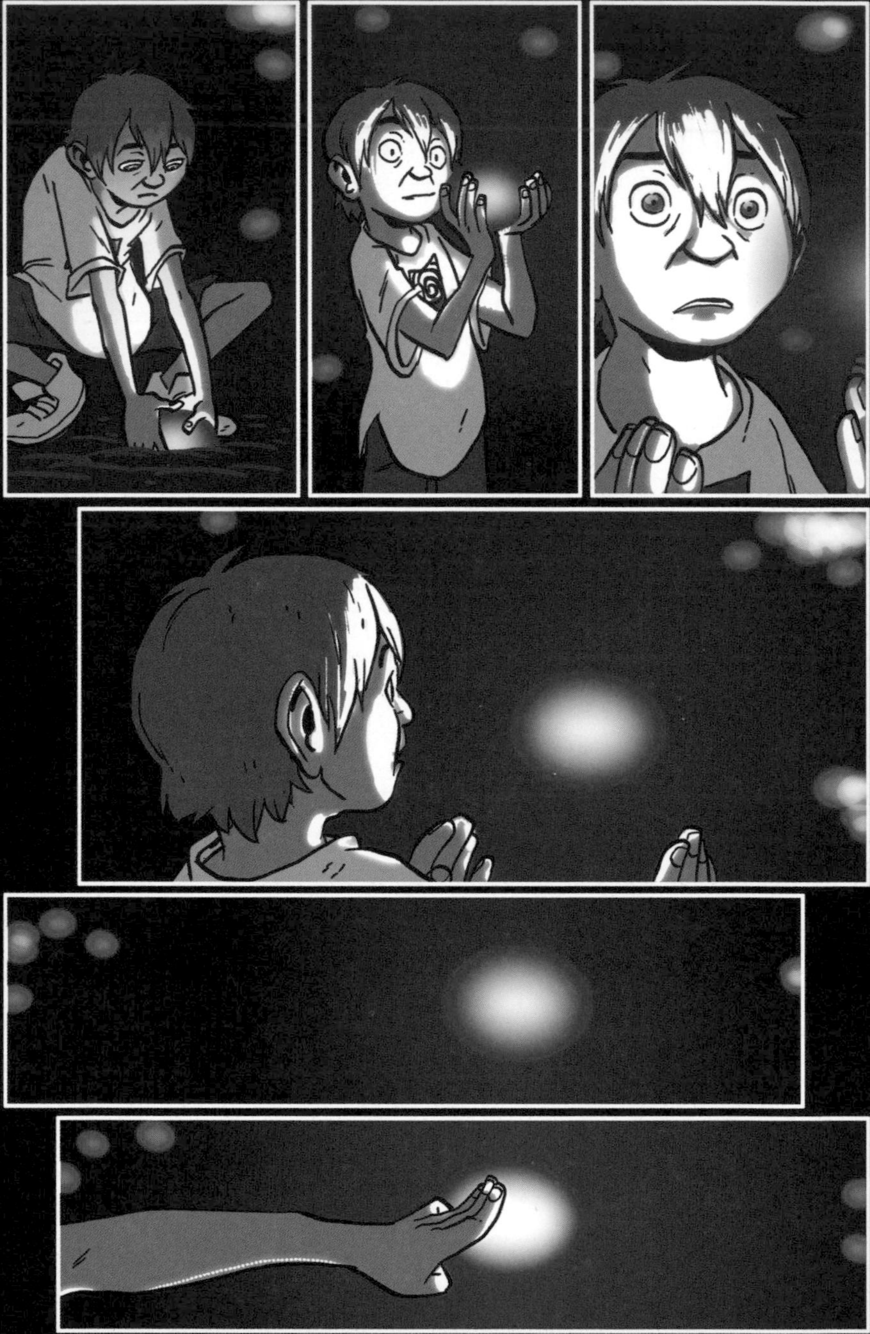

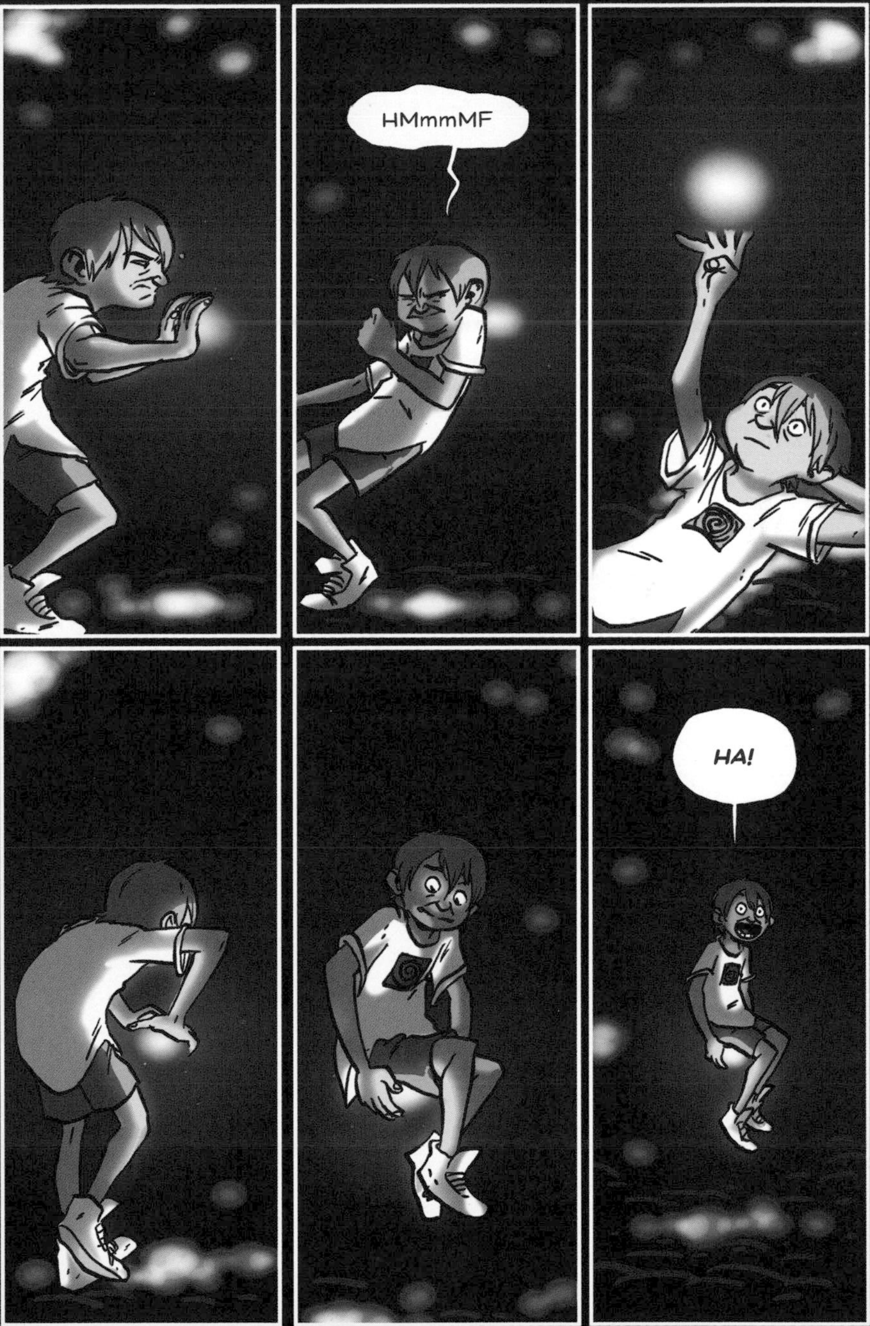
HMmmMF
HA!

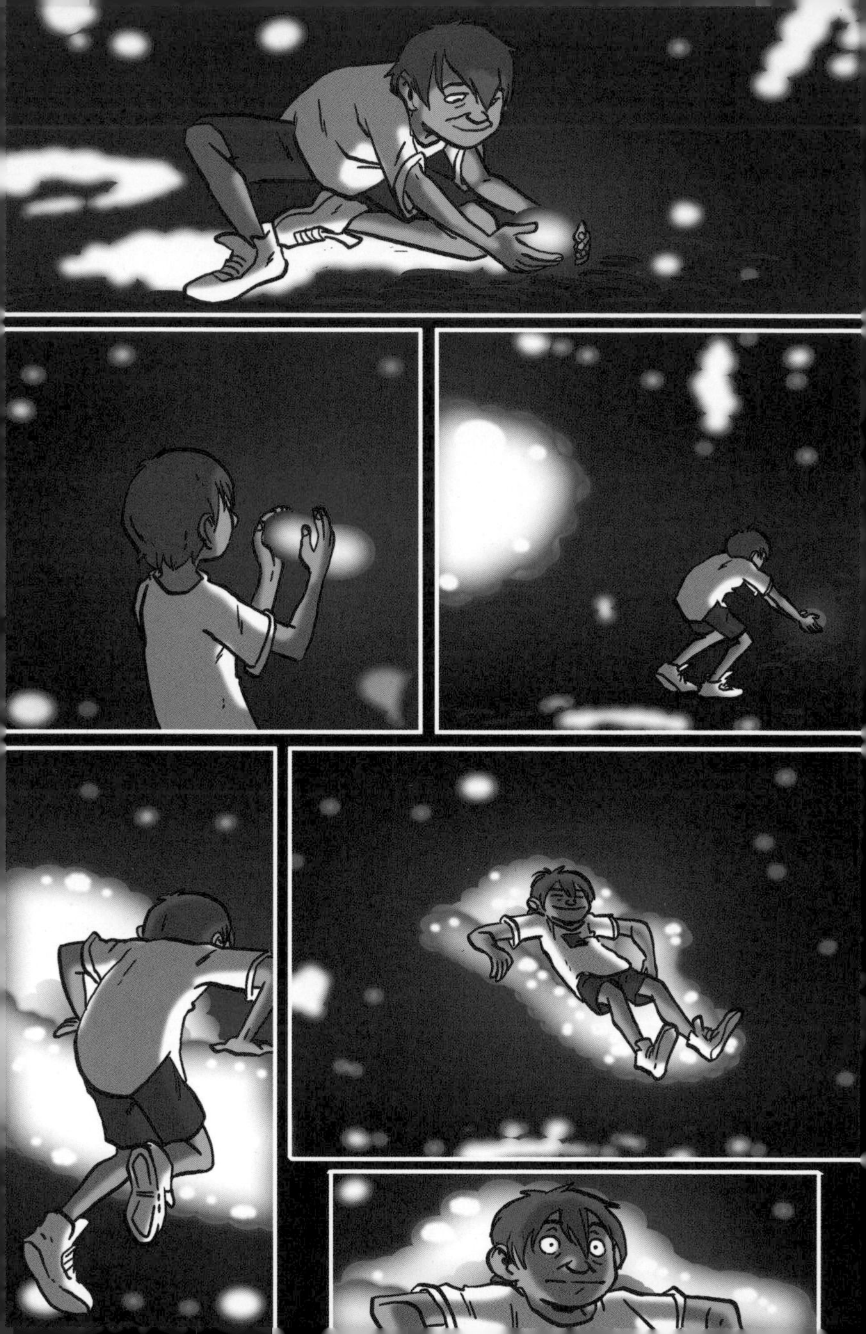

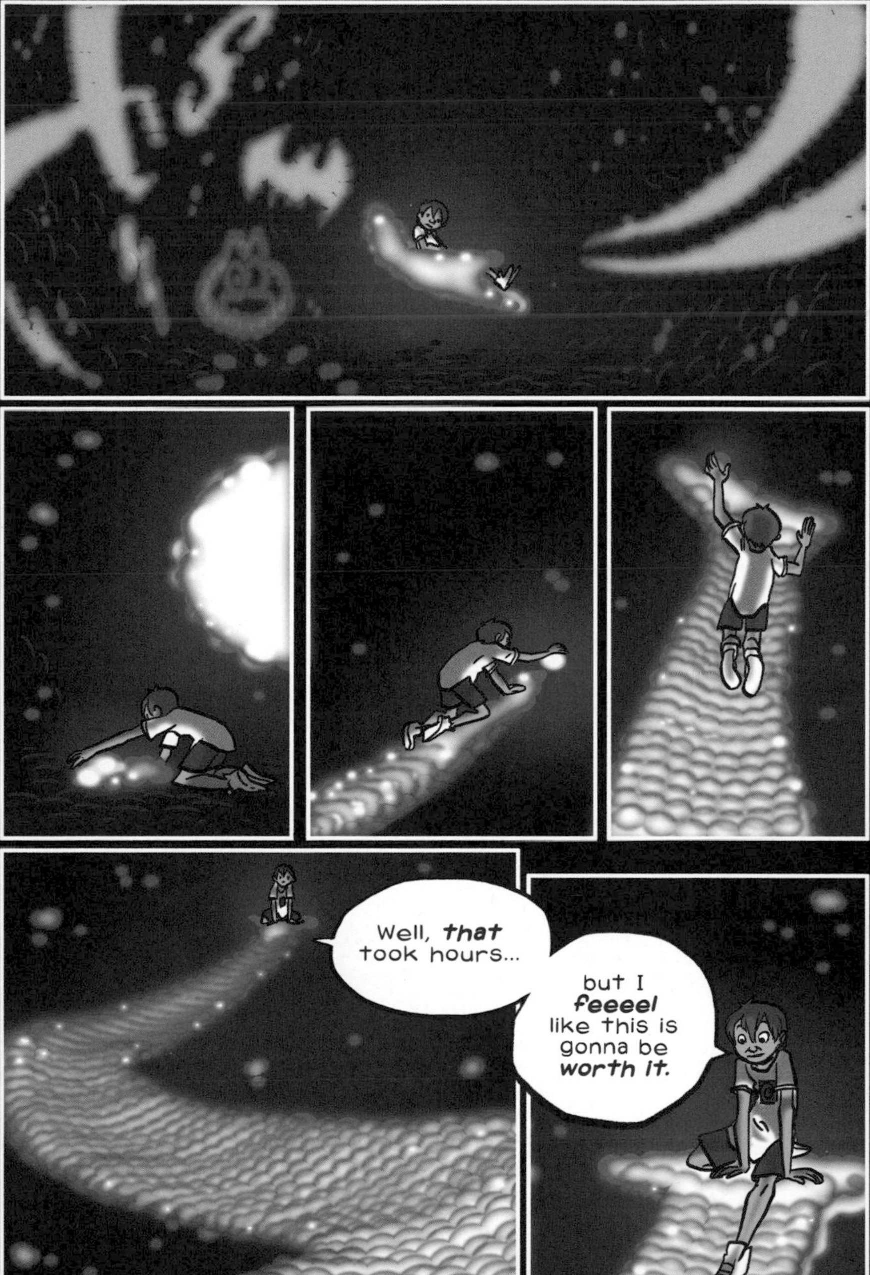
Well, *that* took hours...
but I *feeeel* like this is gonna be *worth it.*

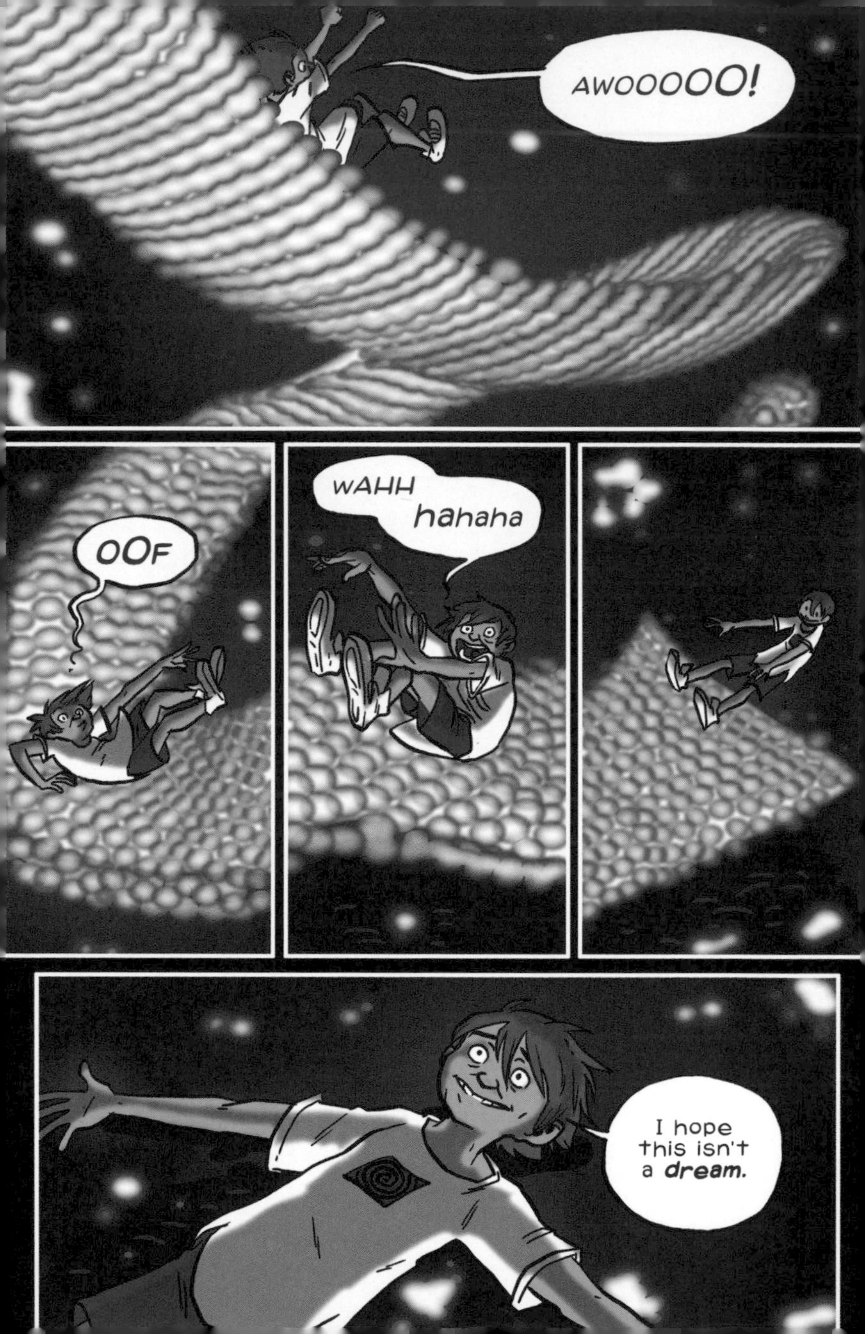
AWOOOOO!
OOF
WAHH hahaha
I hope this isn't a *dream.*

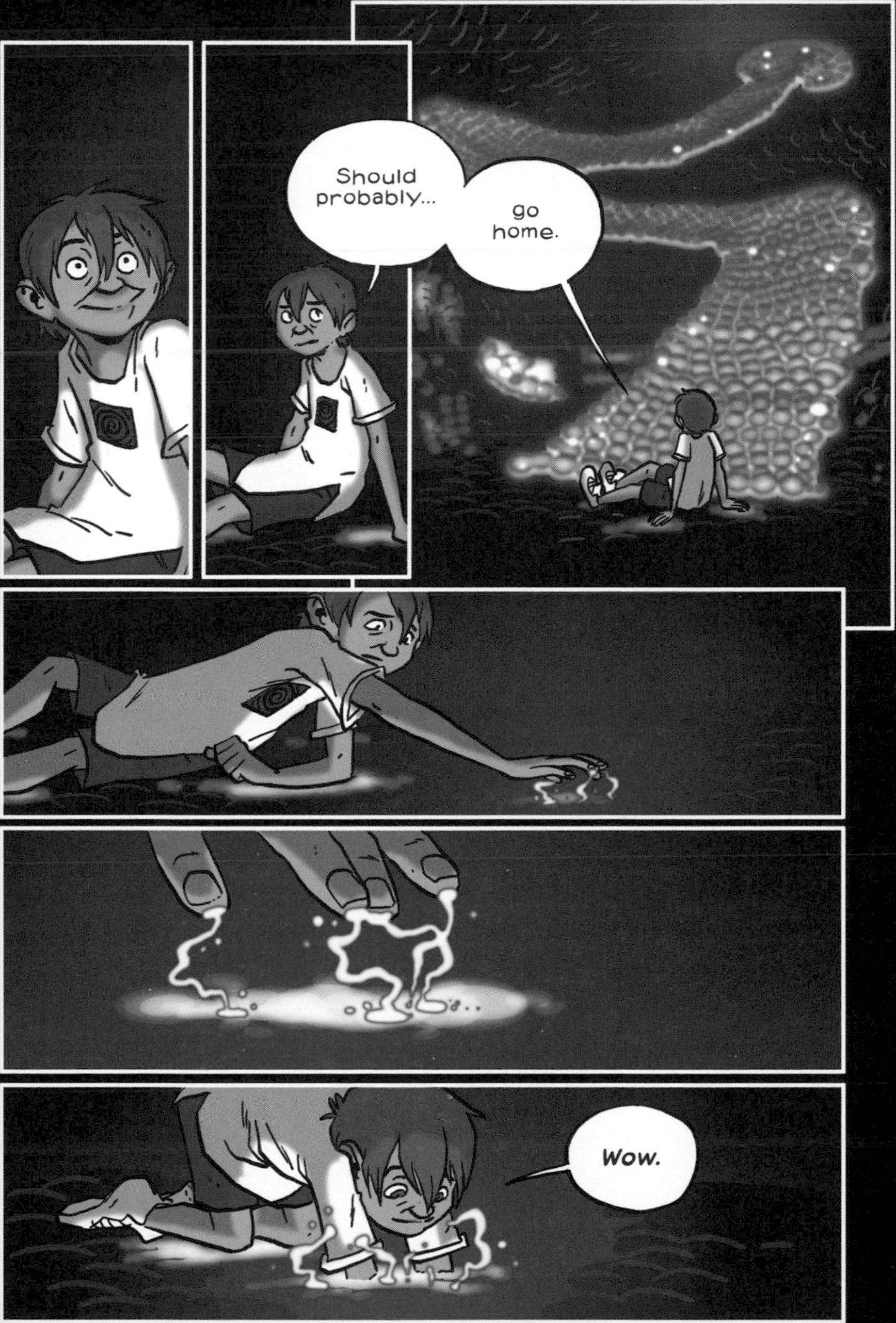
Should probably...
go home.
Wow.

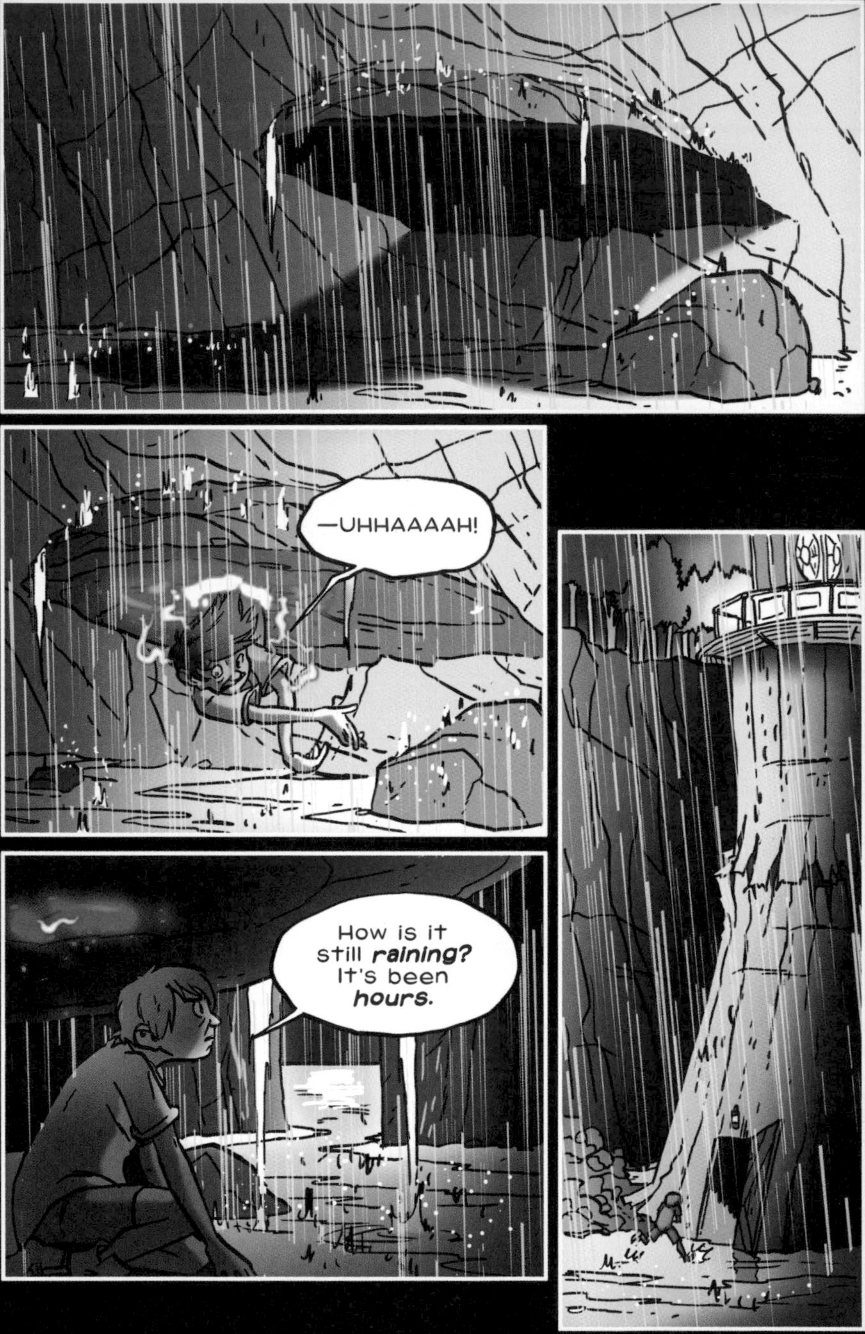
—UHHAAAAH!
How is it still *raining?* It's been *hours.*

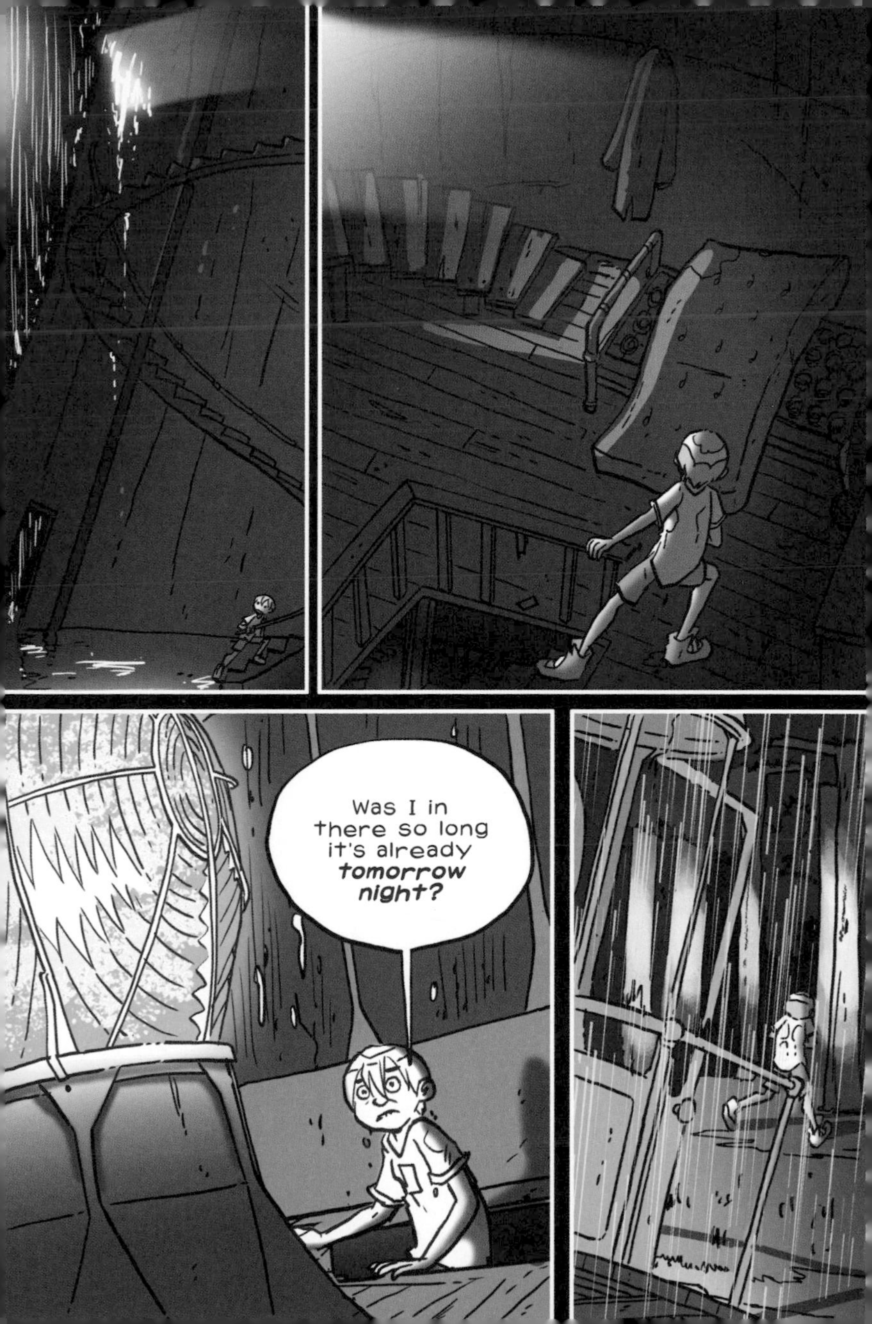
Was I in there so long it's already *tomorrow night?*

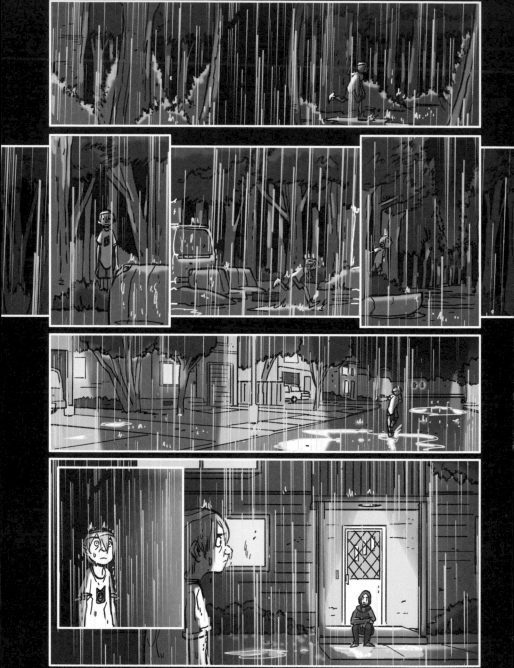

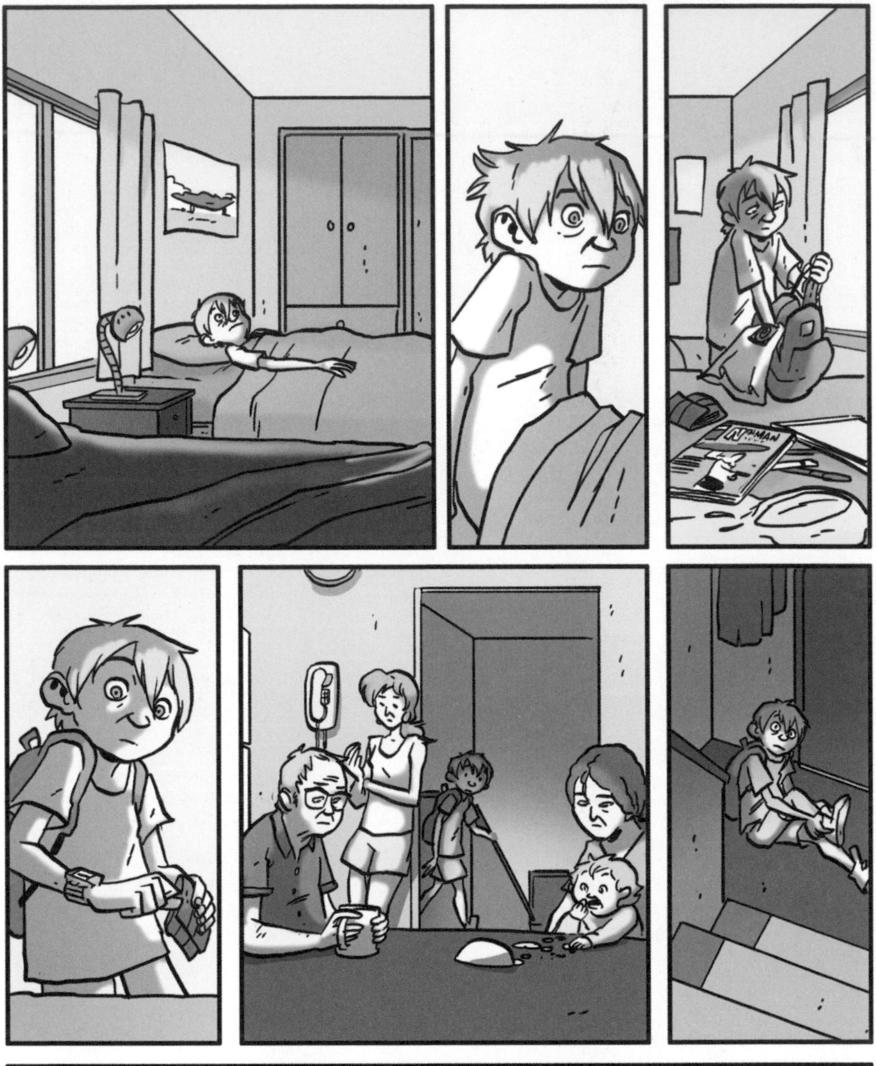

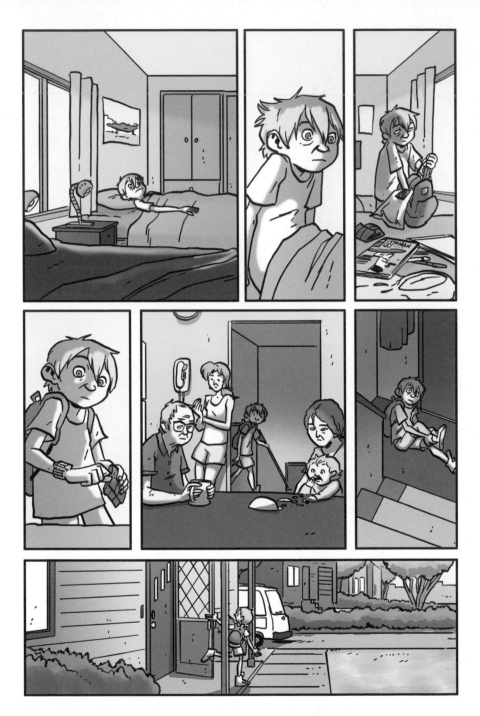

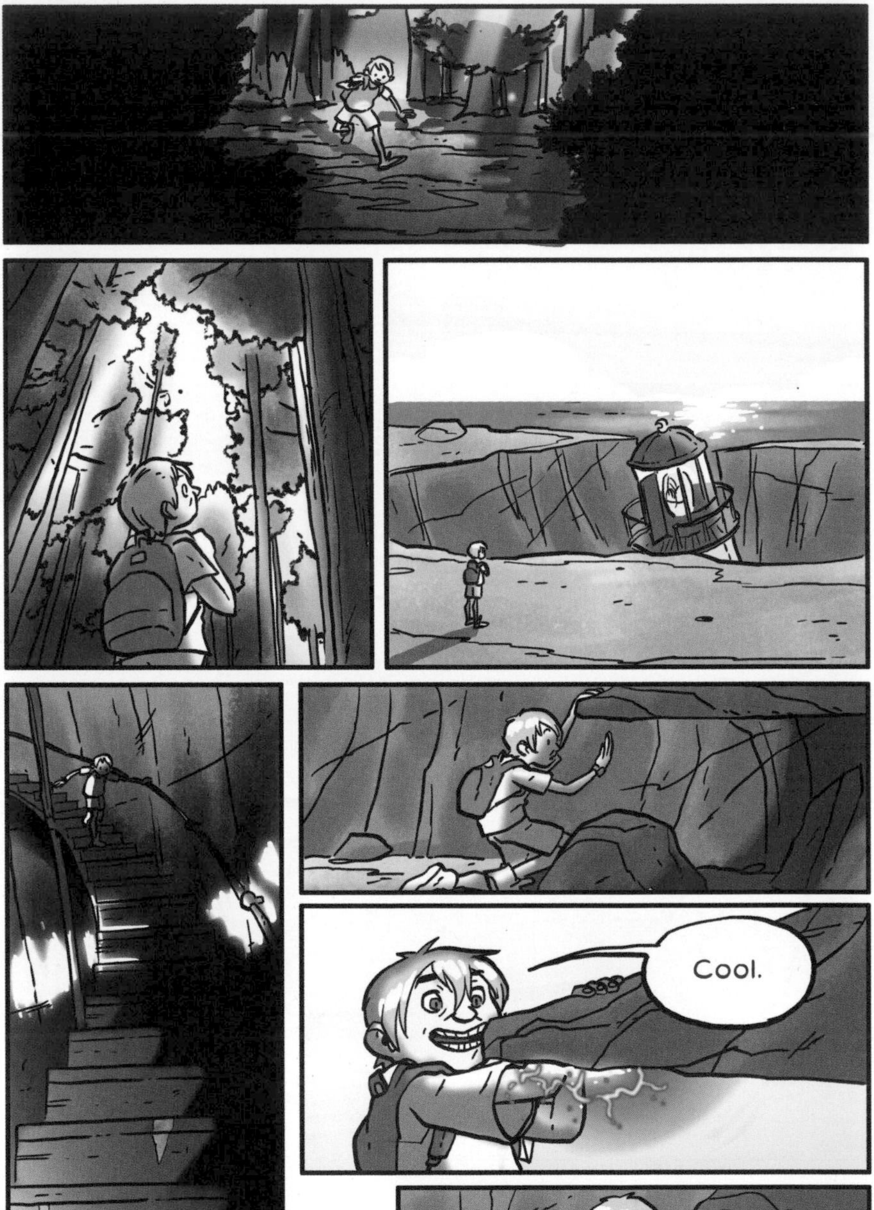
Cool.

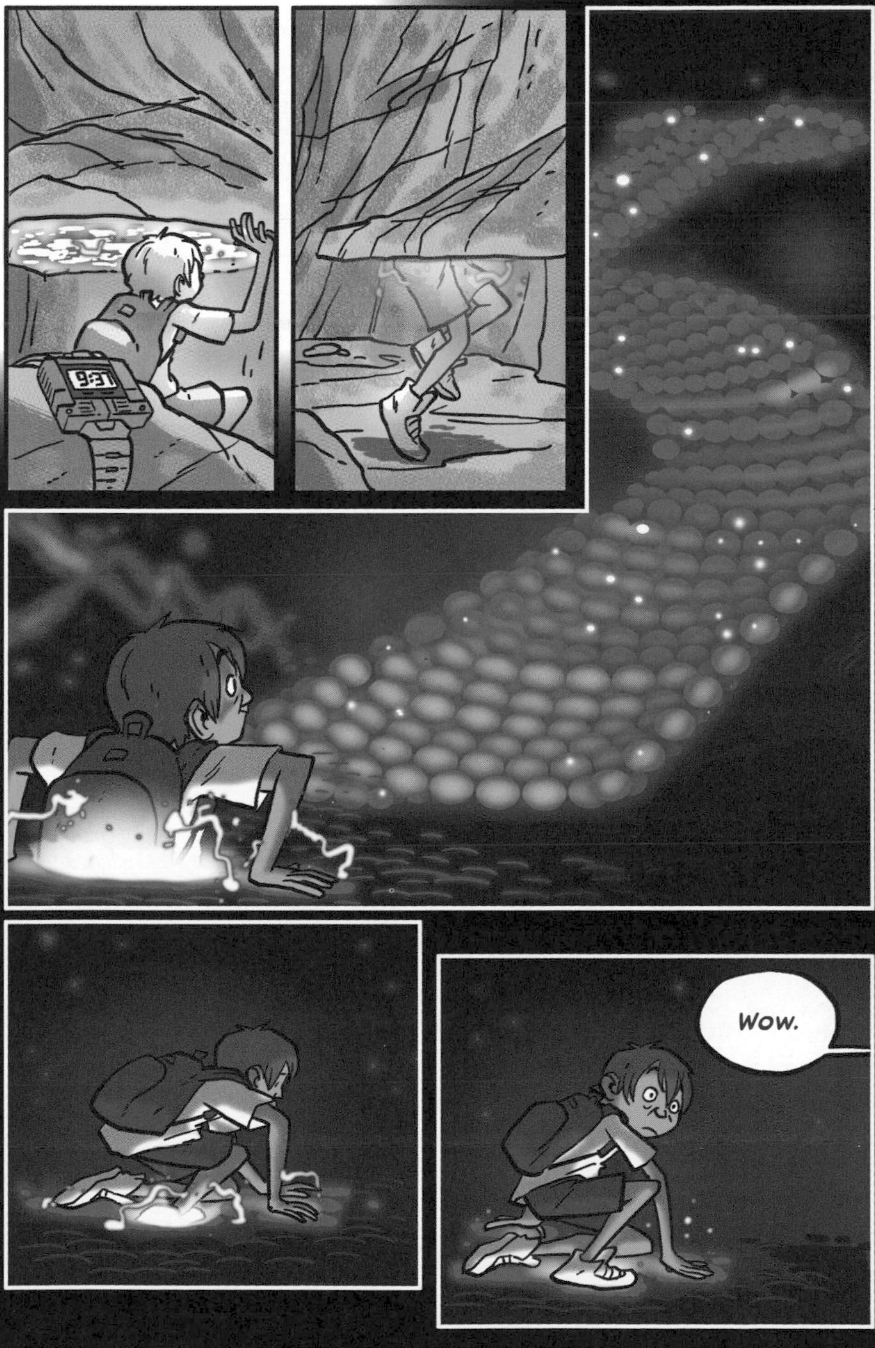
9:37
Wow.

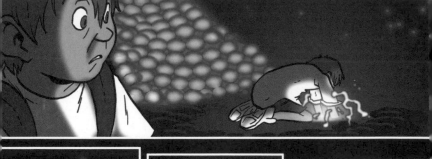

...but...

...*me.*

Huh.

Full of **surprises,** aren't you?

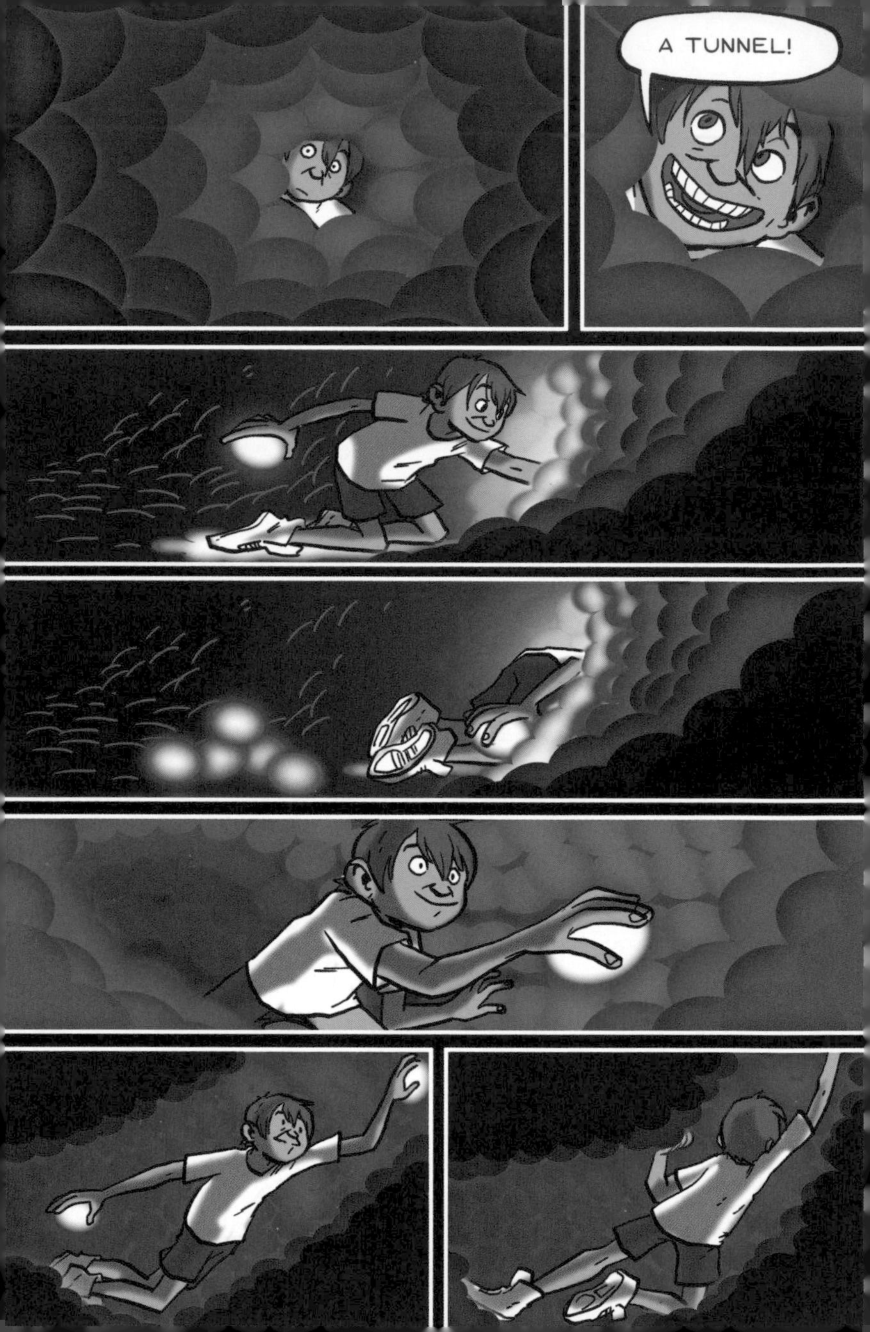
A TUNNEL!

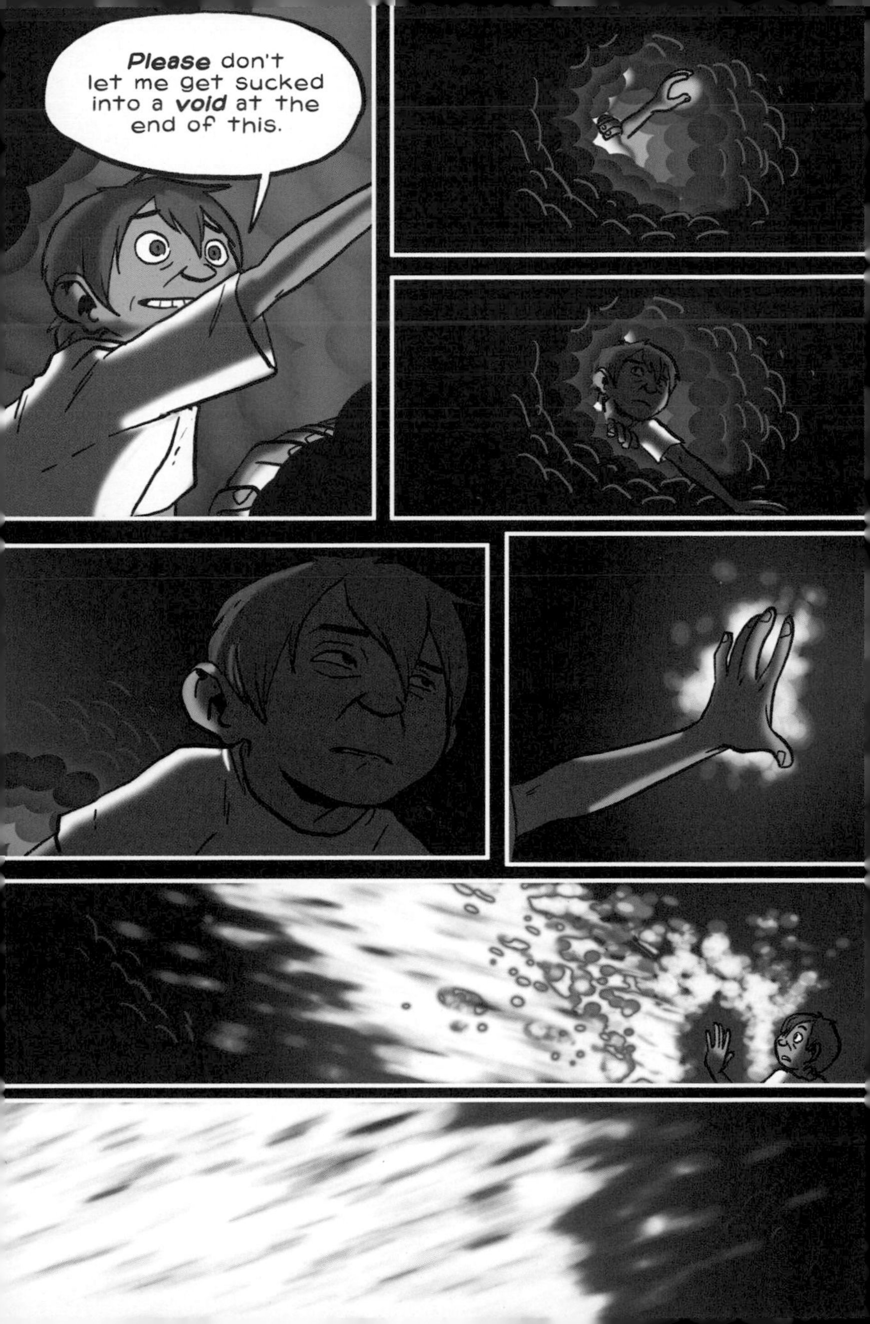
Please don't let me get sucked into a void at the end of this.

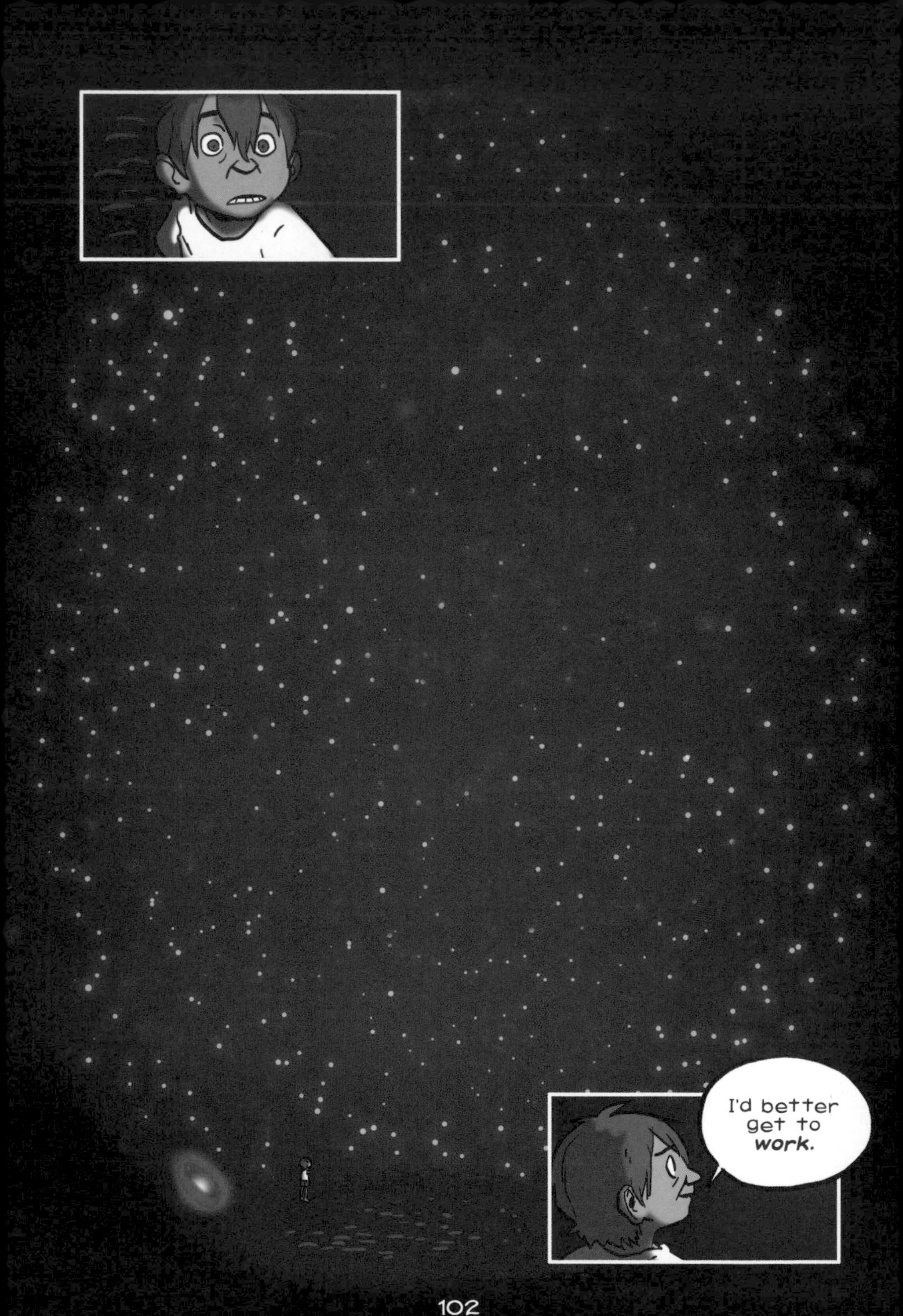
I'd better get to **work.**

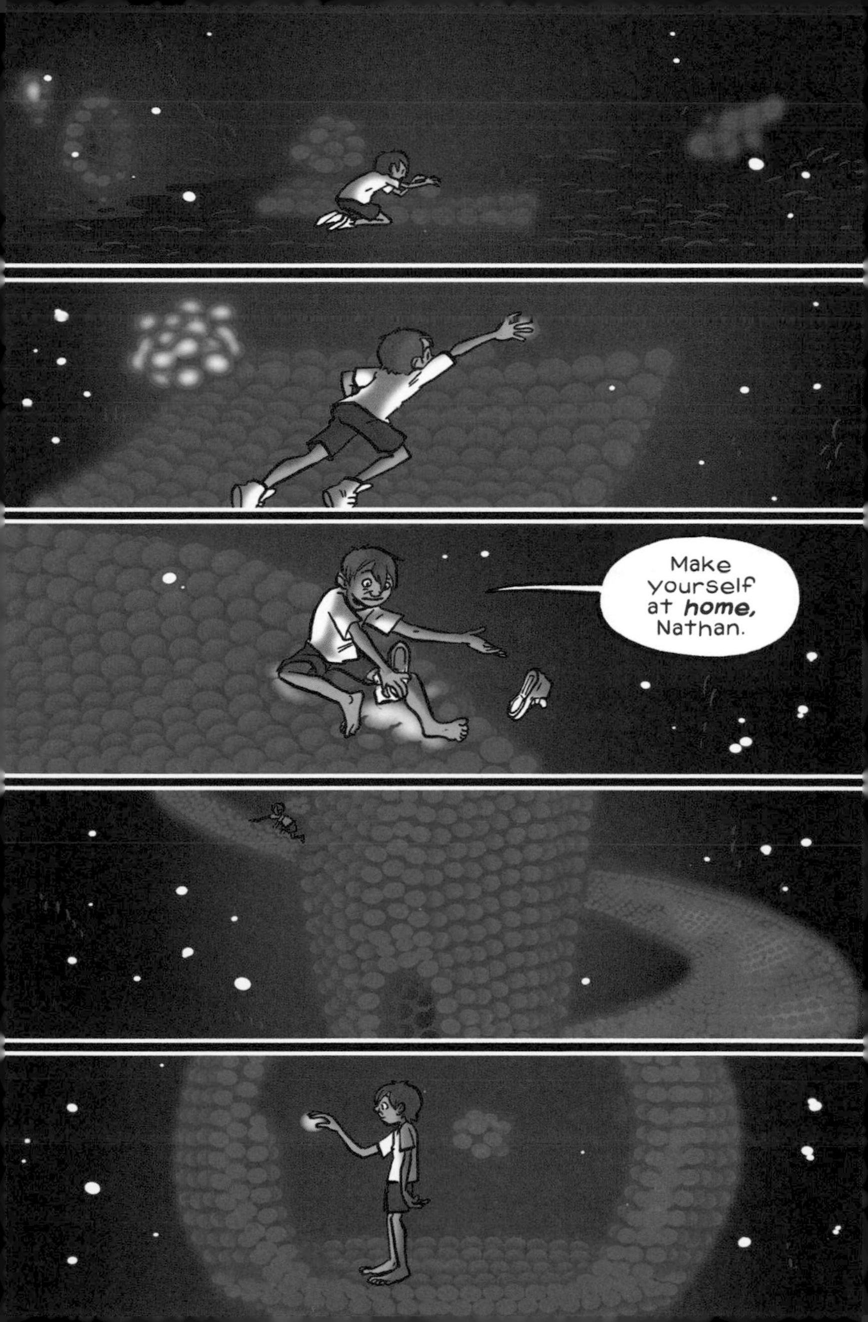
Make yourself at *home,* Nathan.

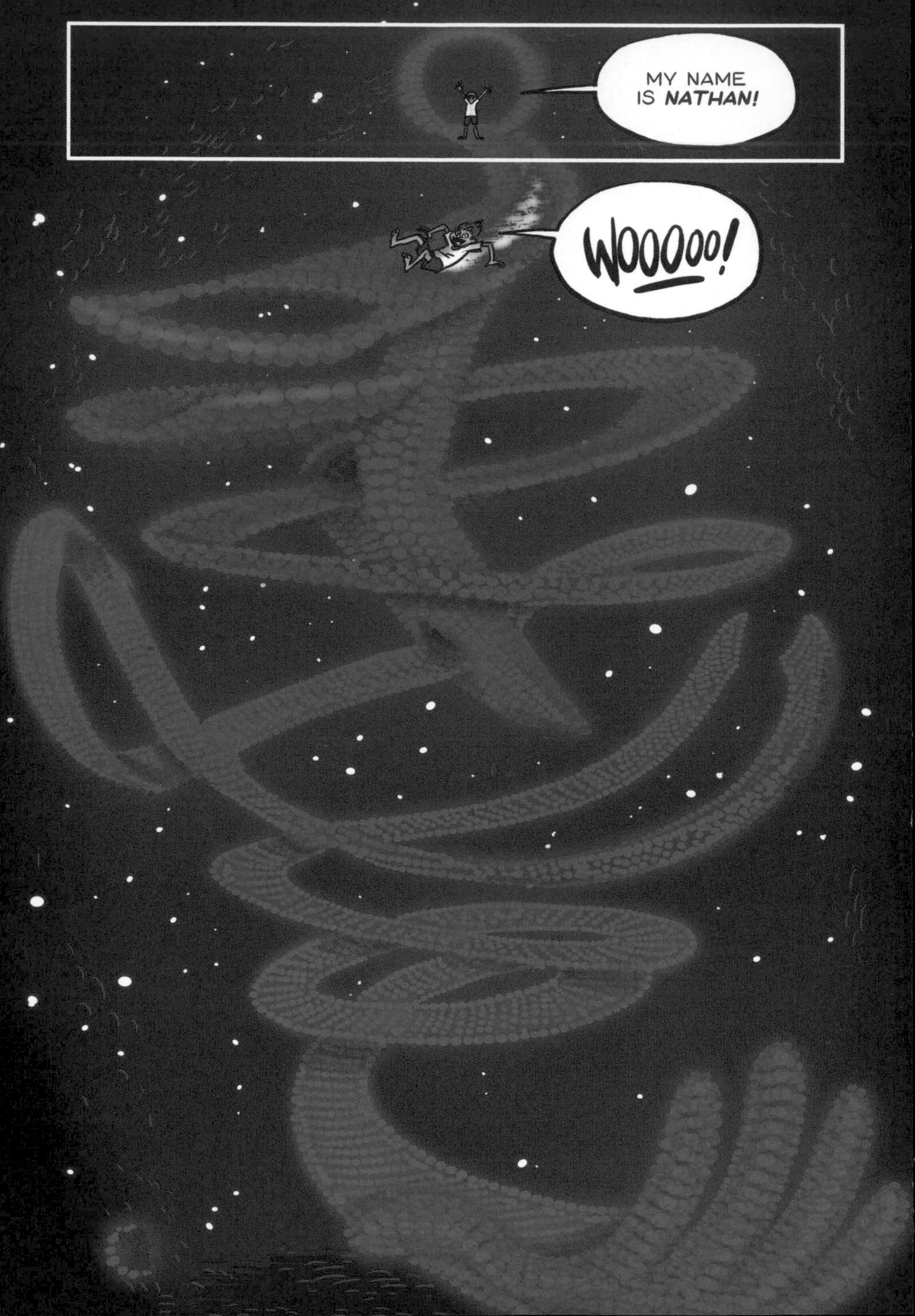
MY NAME IS NATHAN!
WOOOOO!

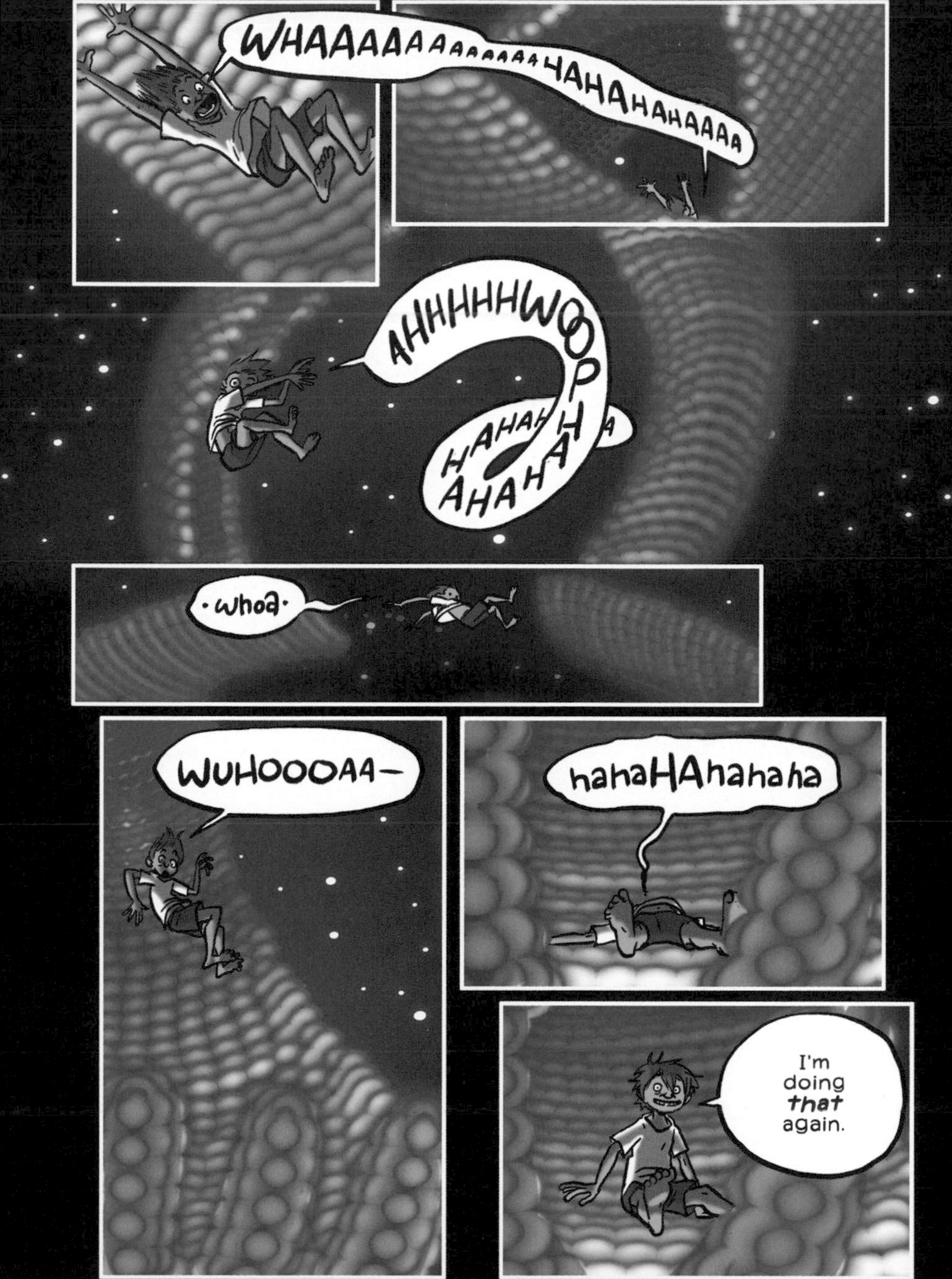
WHAAAAAAAAAAAAAHAHAHAHAAAA
AHHHHHWOOPHAHAHAHAHAHa
·whoa·
WUHOOOAA—
hahaHAhahaha
I'm doing ***that*** again.

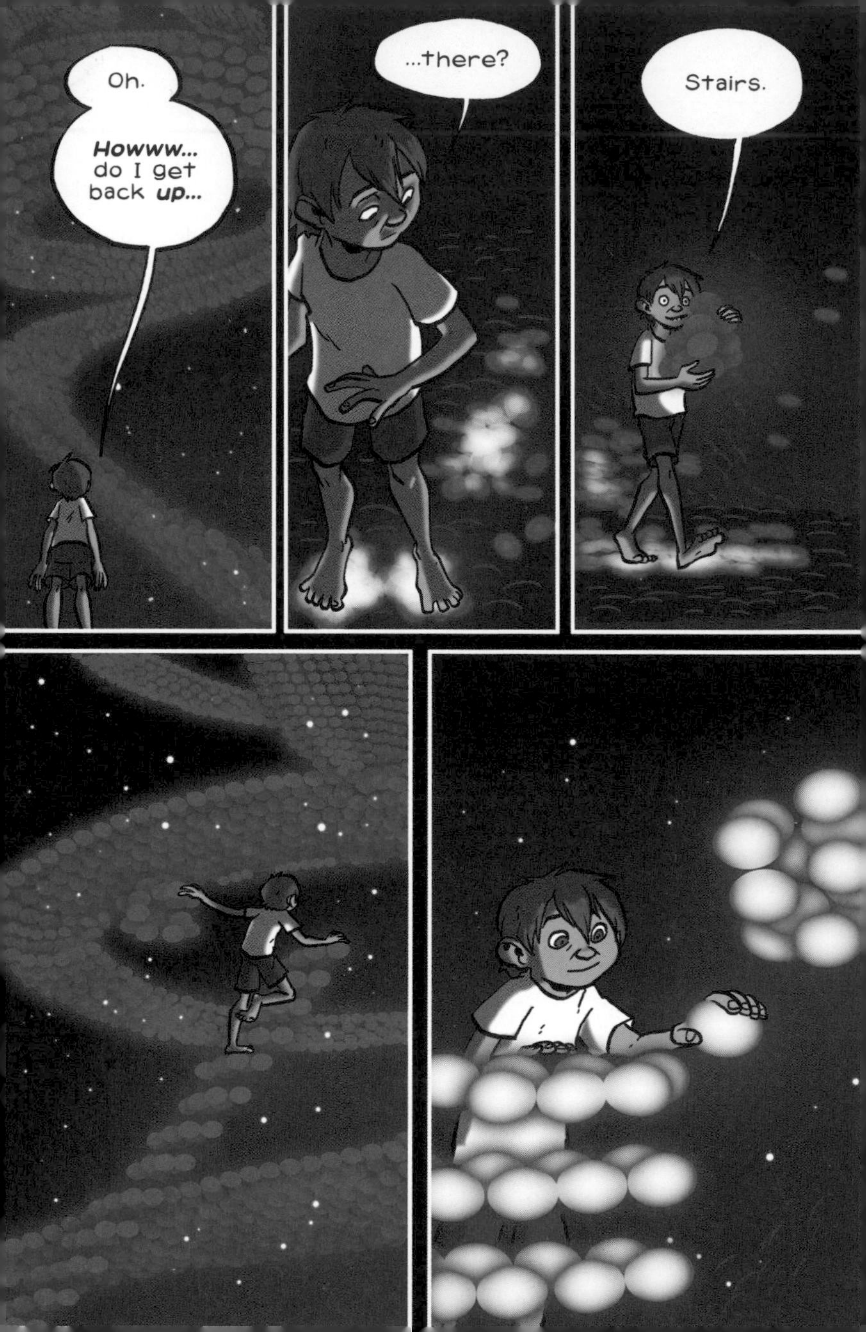
Oh.
**Howww...** do I get back **up**...
...there?
Stairs.

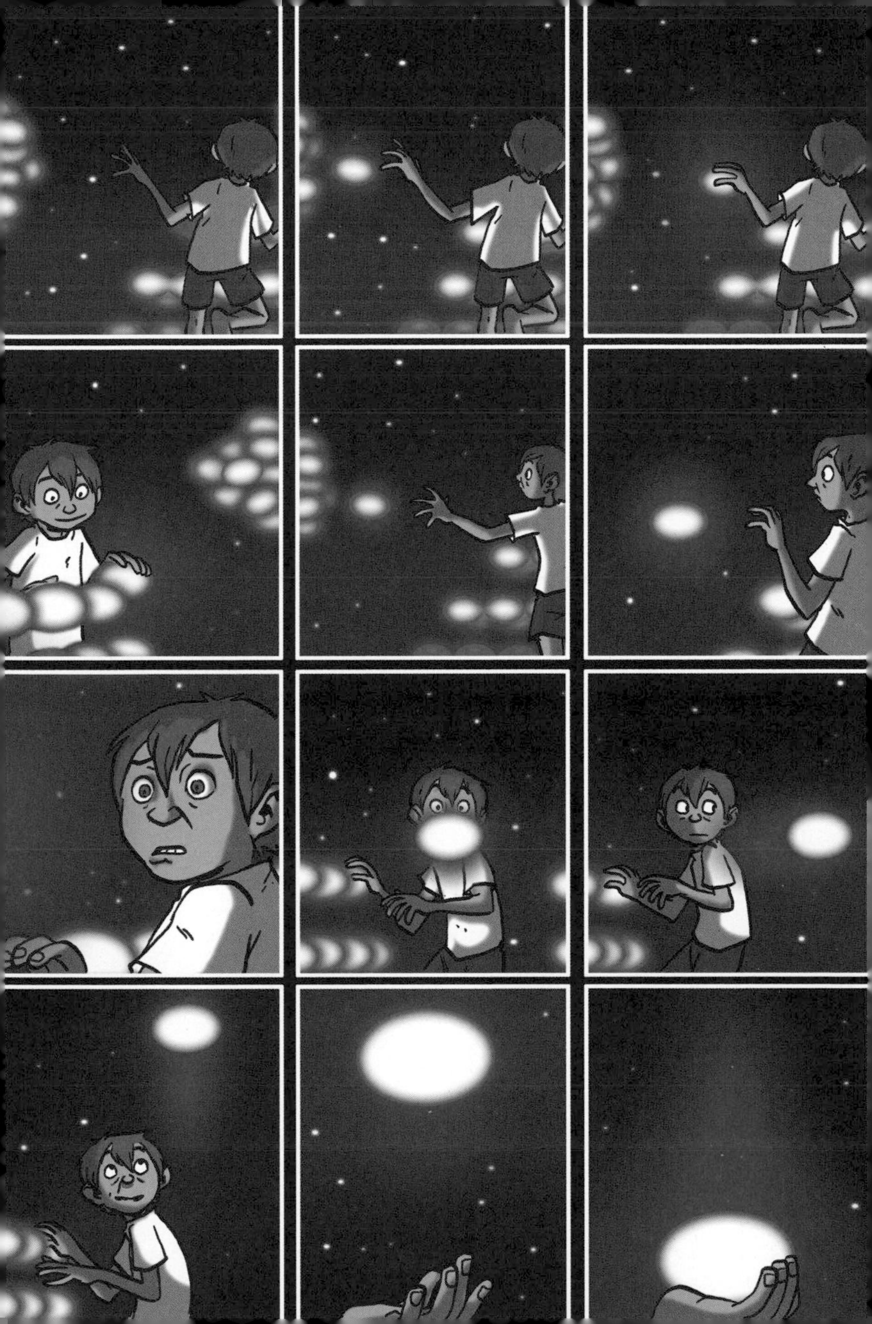

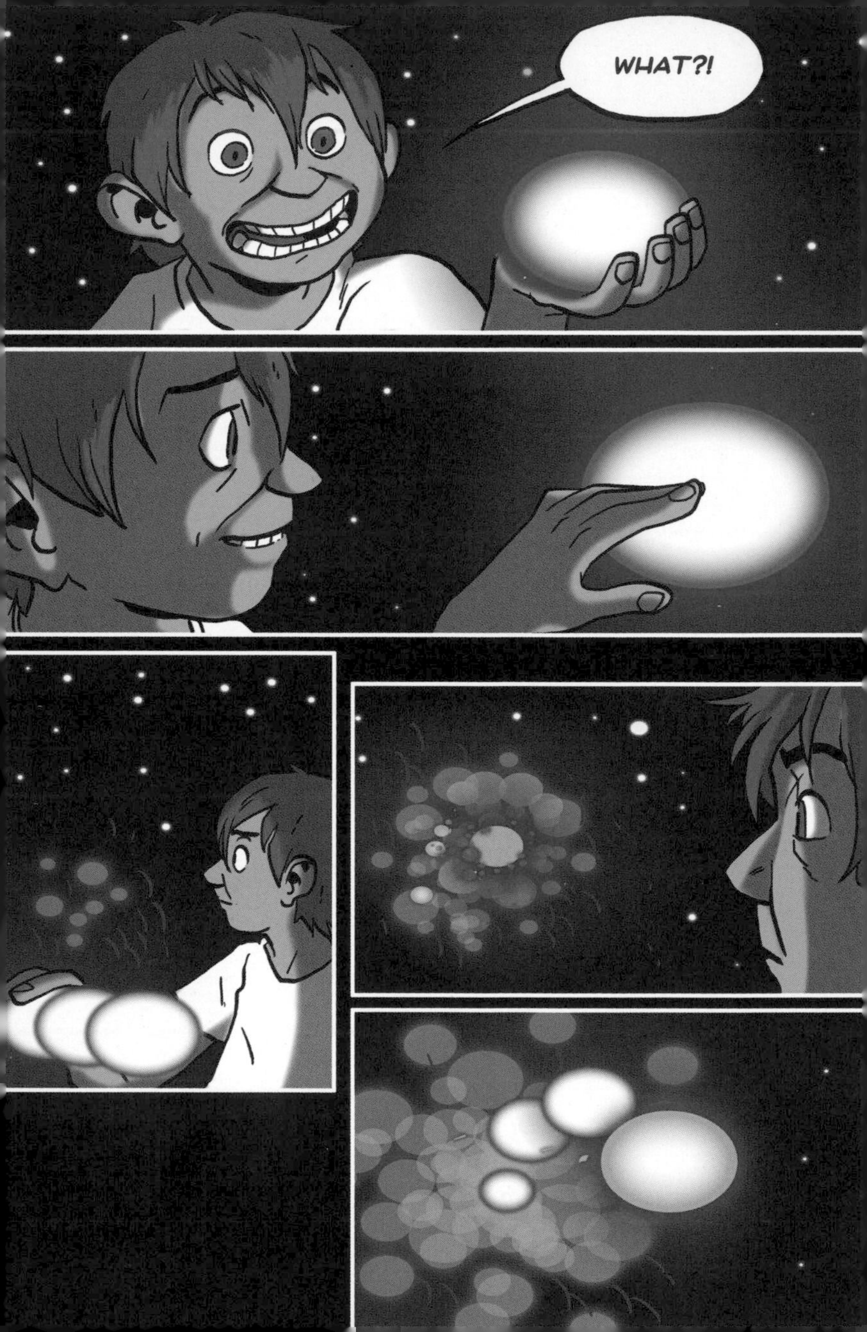
WHAT?!

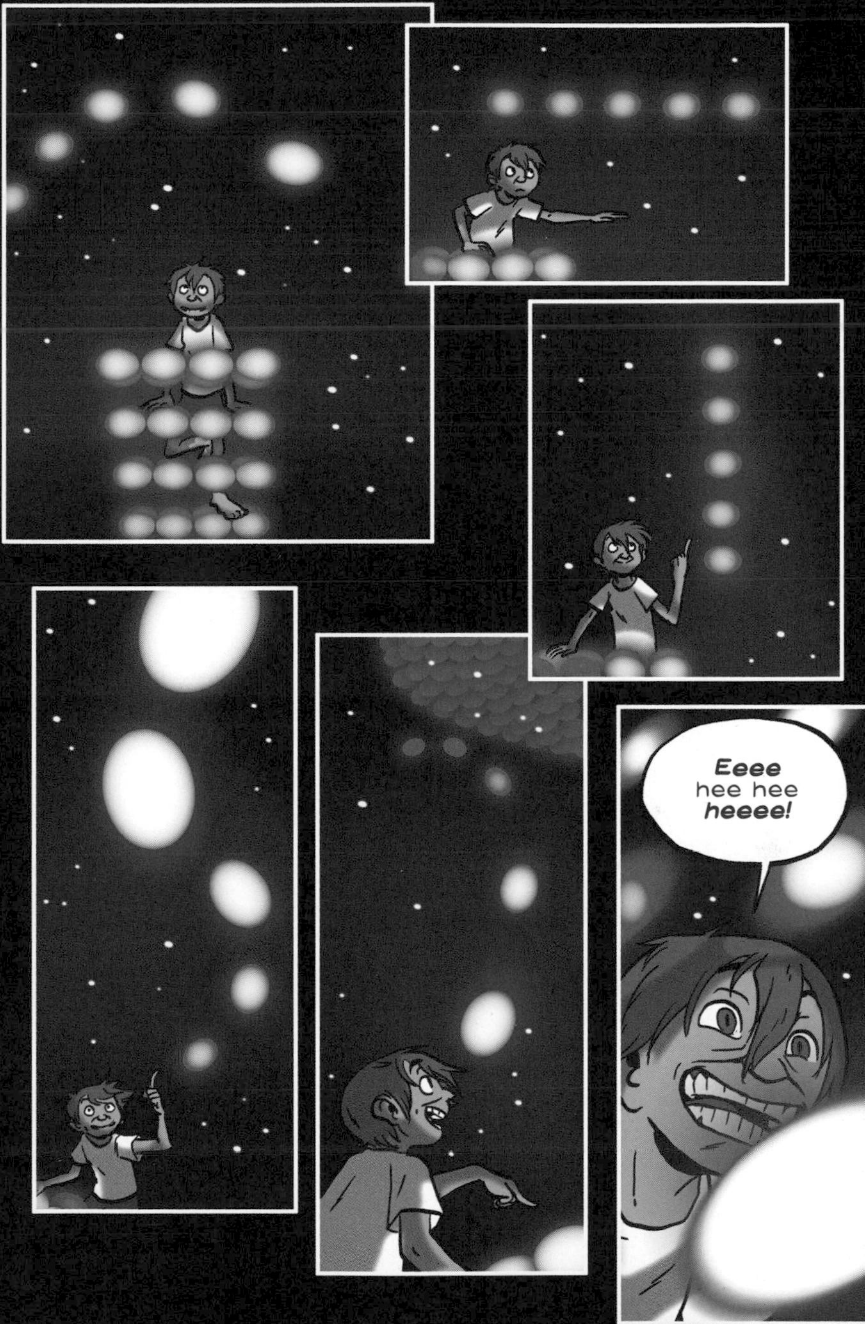
**Eeee** hee hee ***heeee!***

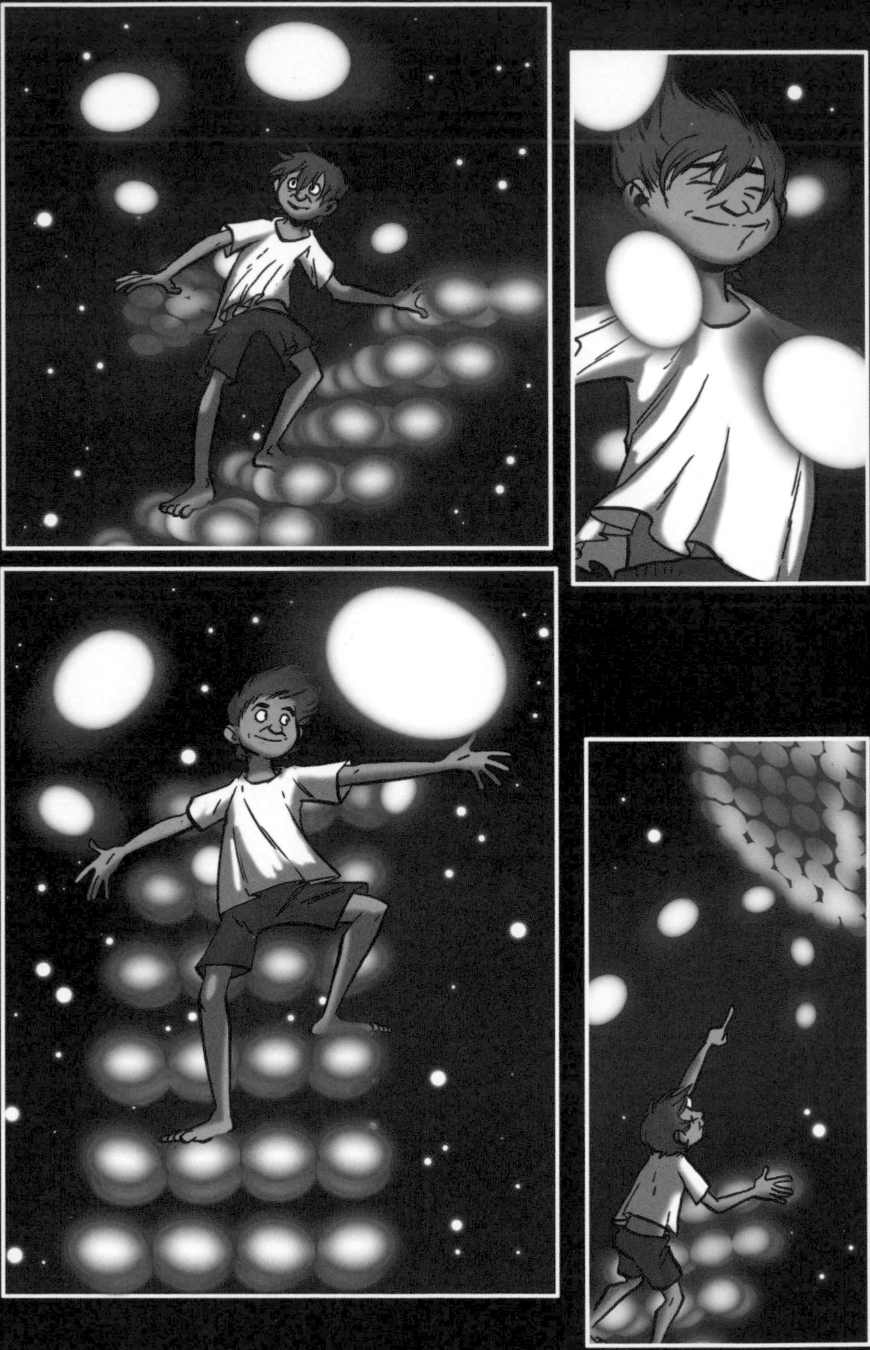

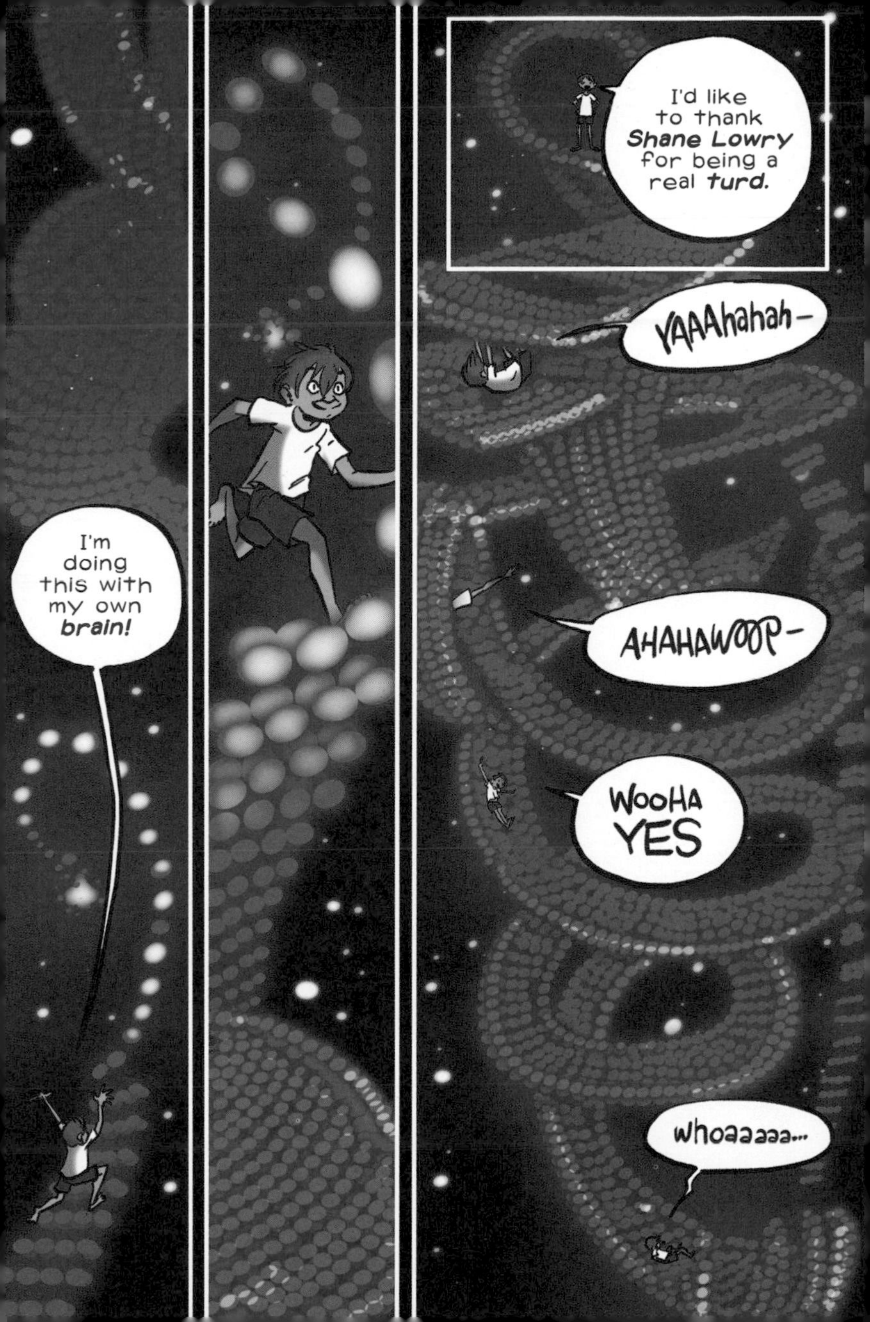
I'm doing this with my own brain!
I'd like to thank Shane Lowry for being a real turd.
YAAAhahah-
AHAHAWOOP-
WOOHA YES
whoaaaaa...

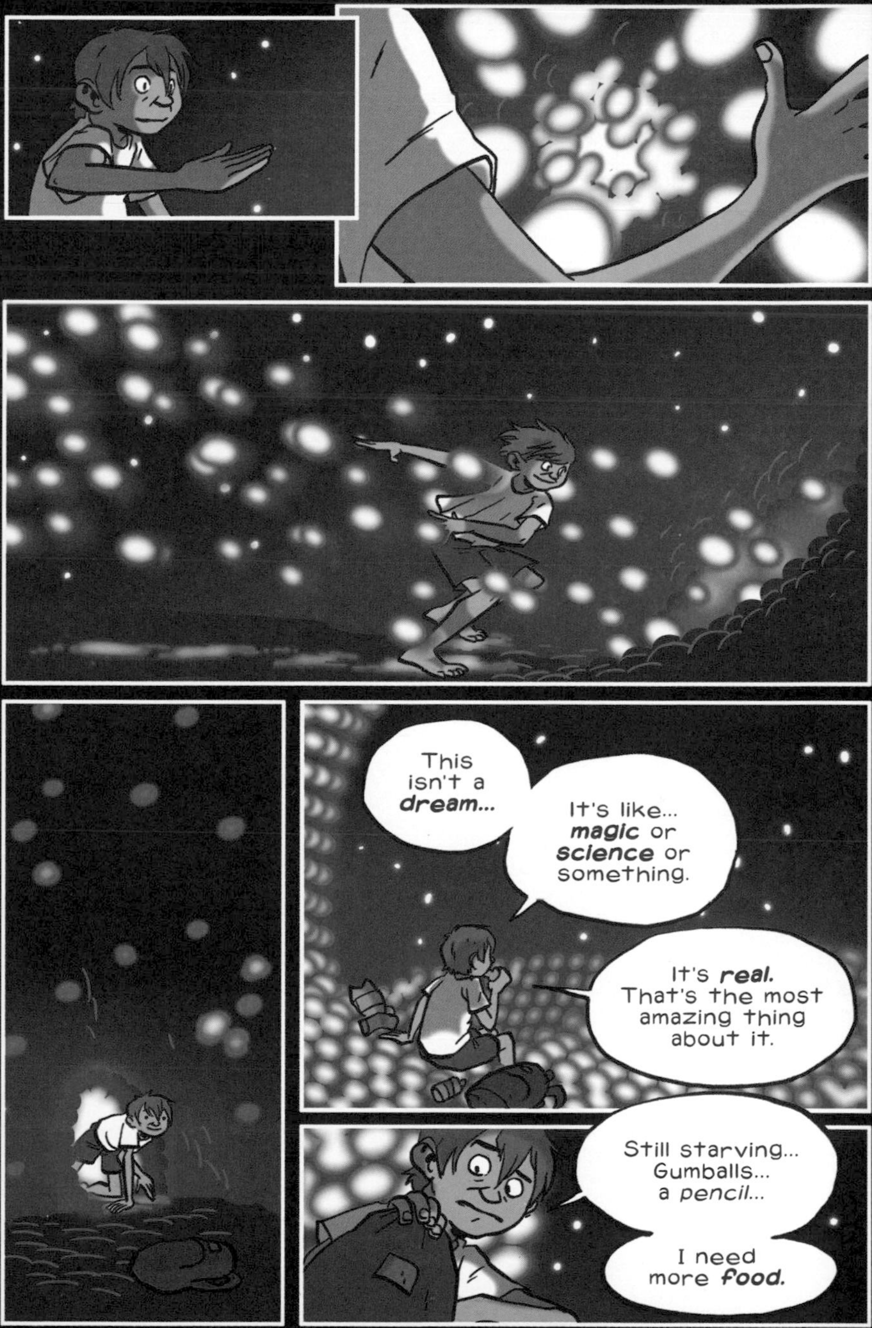
This isn't a *dream...*
It's like... *magic* or *science* or something.
It's *real.* That's the most amazing thing about it.
Still starving... Gumballs... a *pencil...*
I need more *food.*

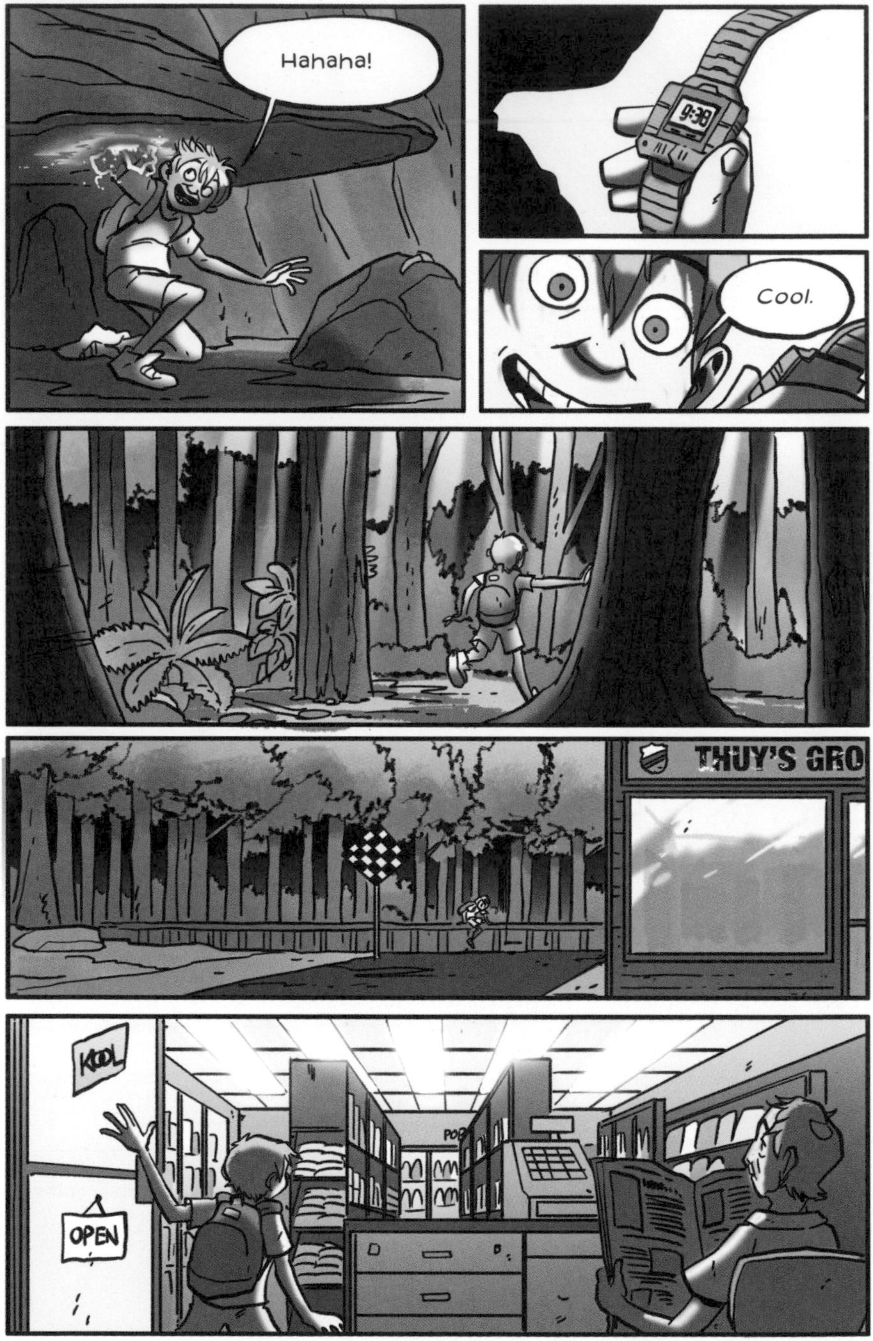
Hahaha!
9:38
Cool.
THUY'S GRO
KOOL
POP
OPEN

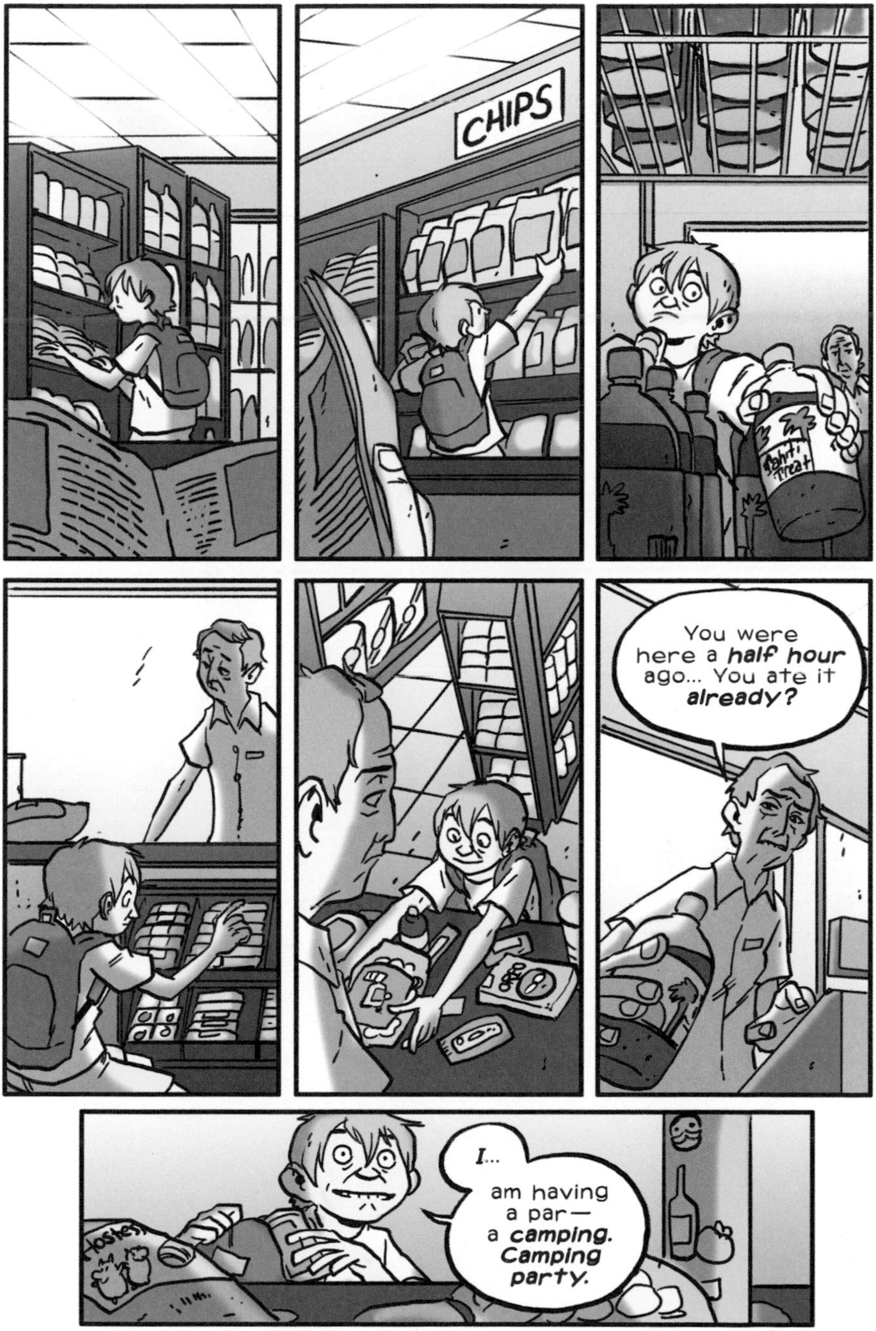
CHIPS
Tahiti Treat
You were here a ***half hour*** ago... You ate it ***already?***
*I...*
am having a par—
a ***camping. Camping party.***
Hostess

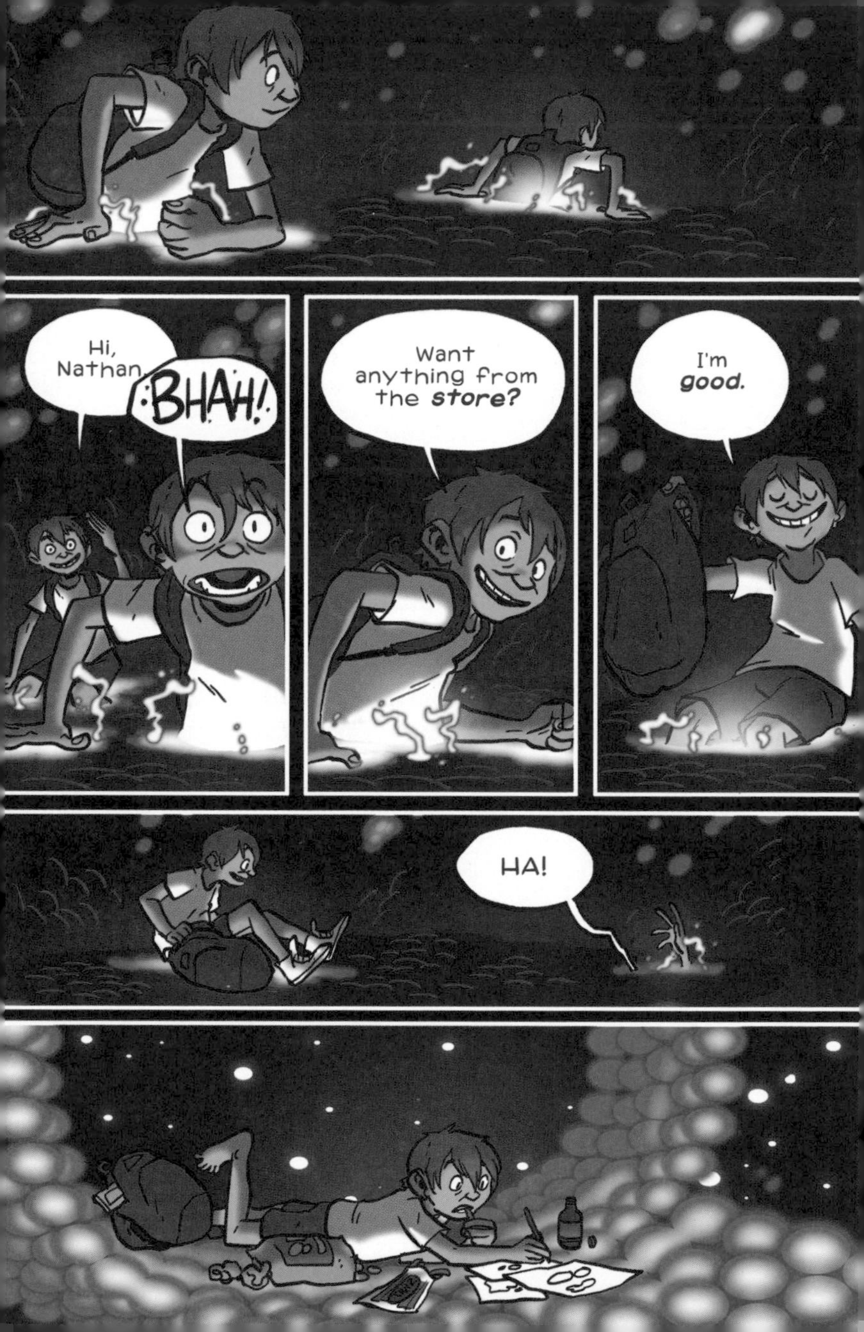
Hi, Nathan.
BHAH!
Want anything from the store?
I'm good.
HA!

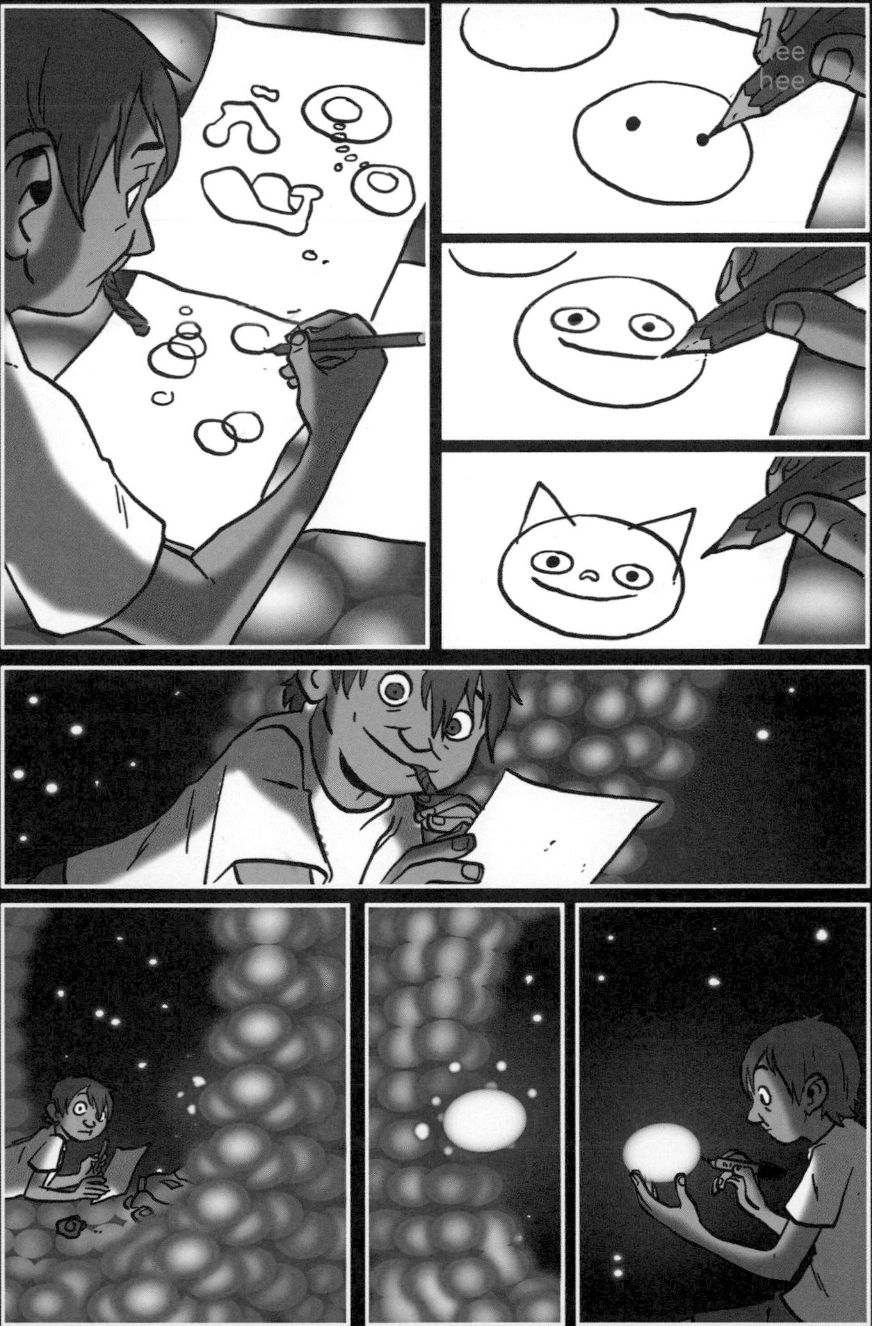
ee
hee

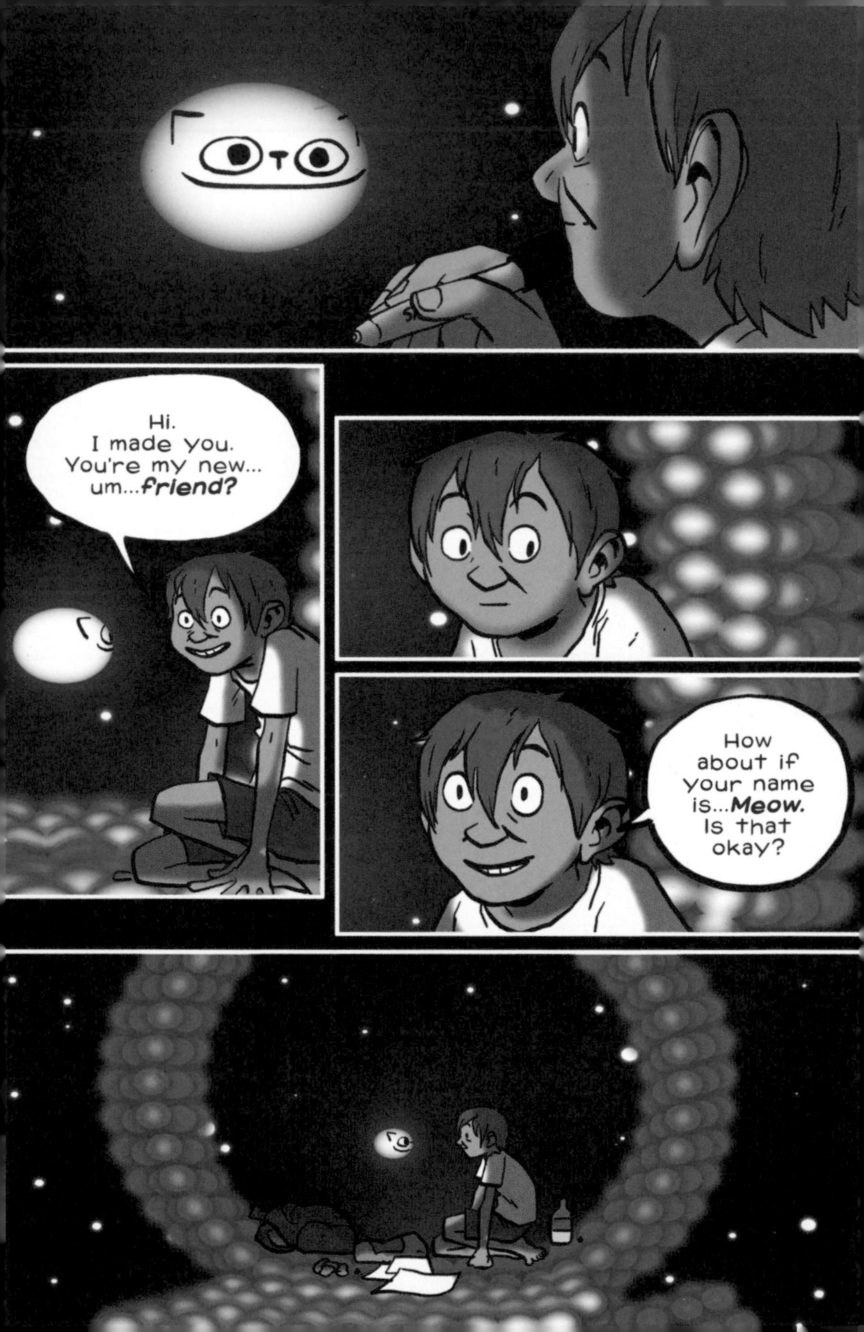
Hi.
I made you.
You're my new...
um...*friend?*
How about if your name is...*Meow.* Is that okay?

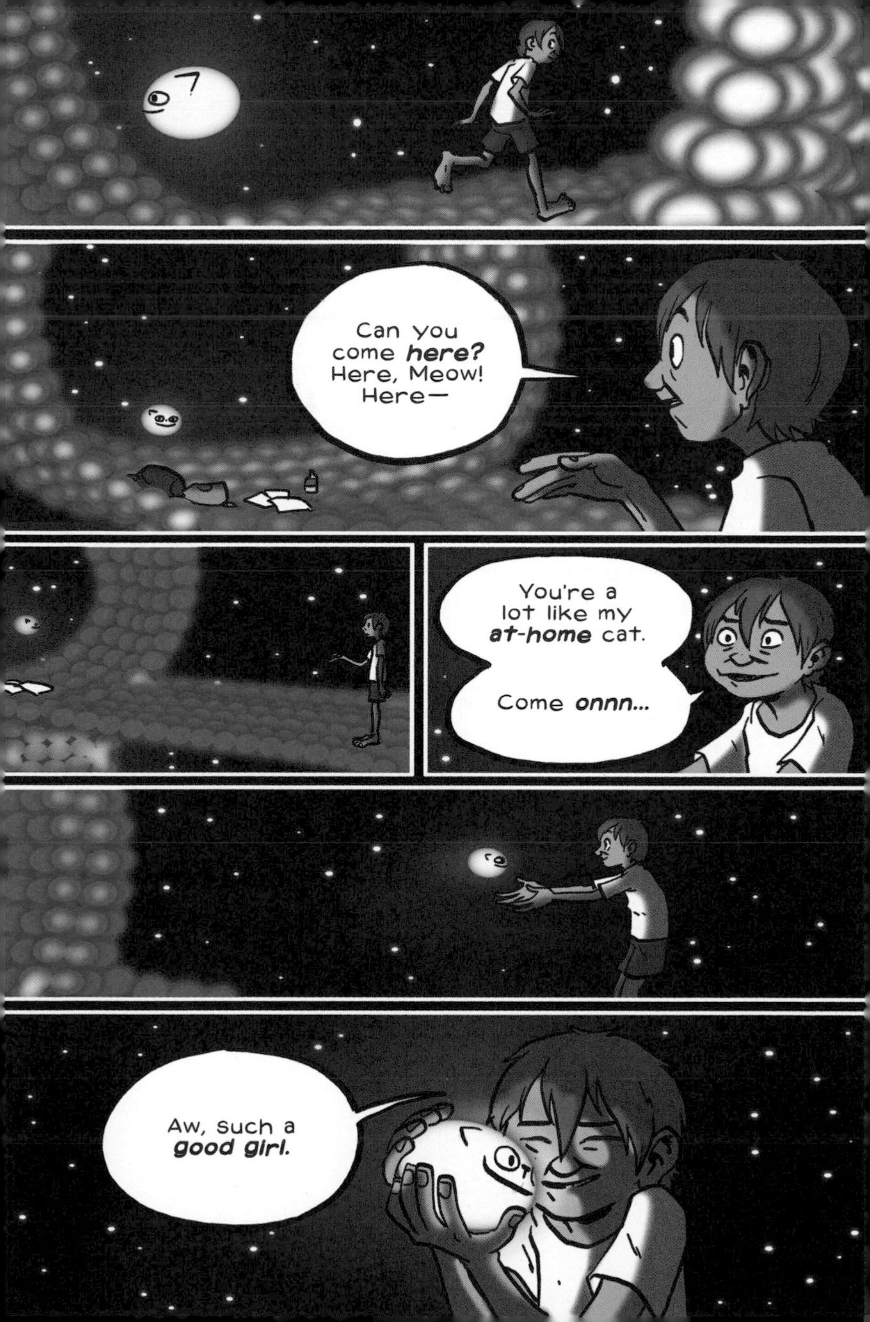
Can you come here? Here, Meow! Here—
You're a lot like my at-home cat.
Come onnn...
Aw, such a good girl.

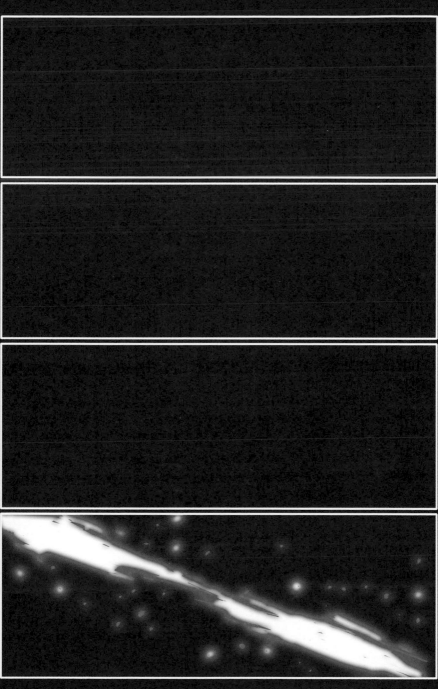

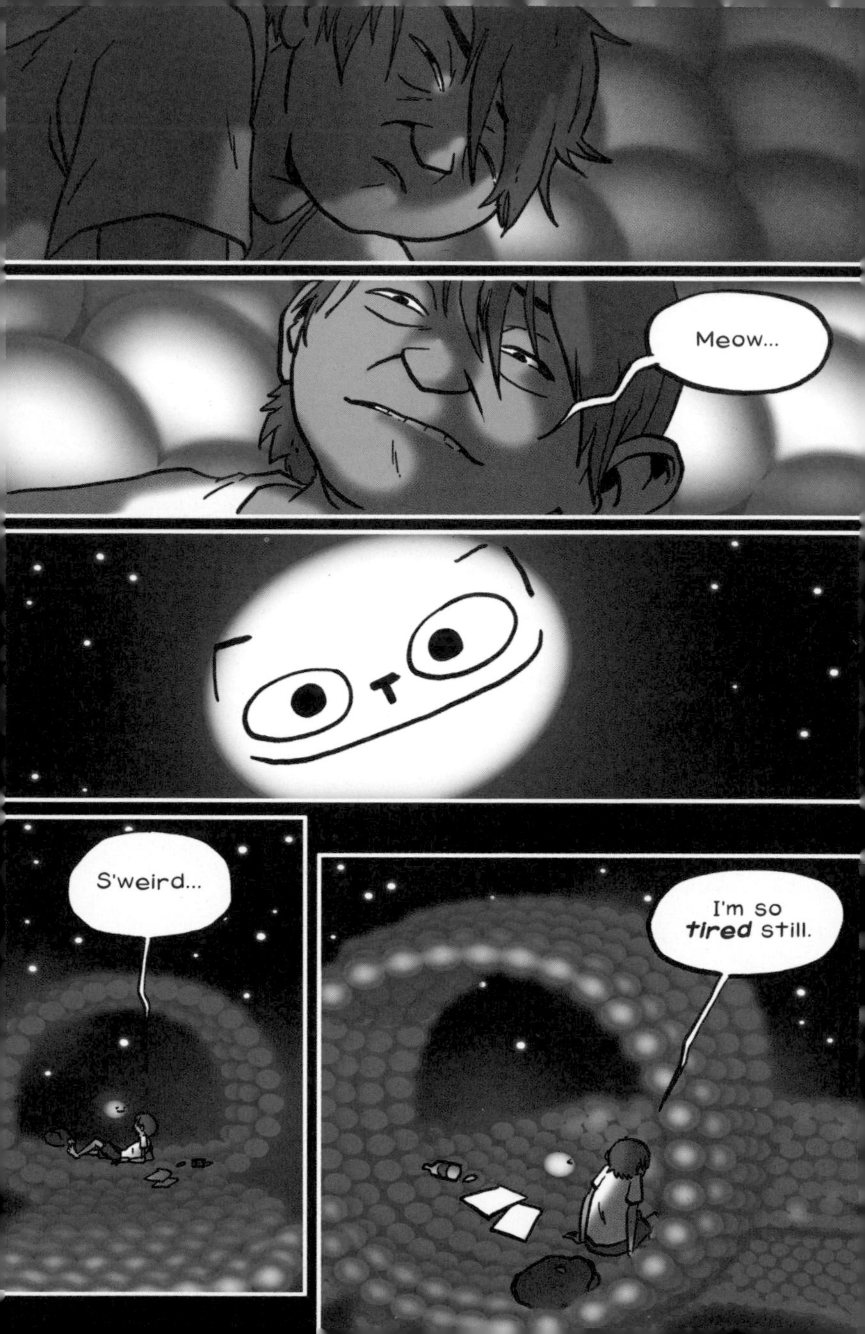
Meow...
S'weird...
I'm so *tired* still.

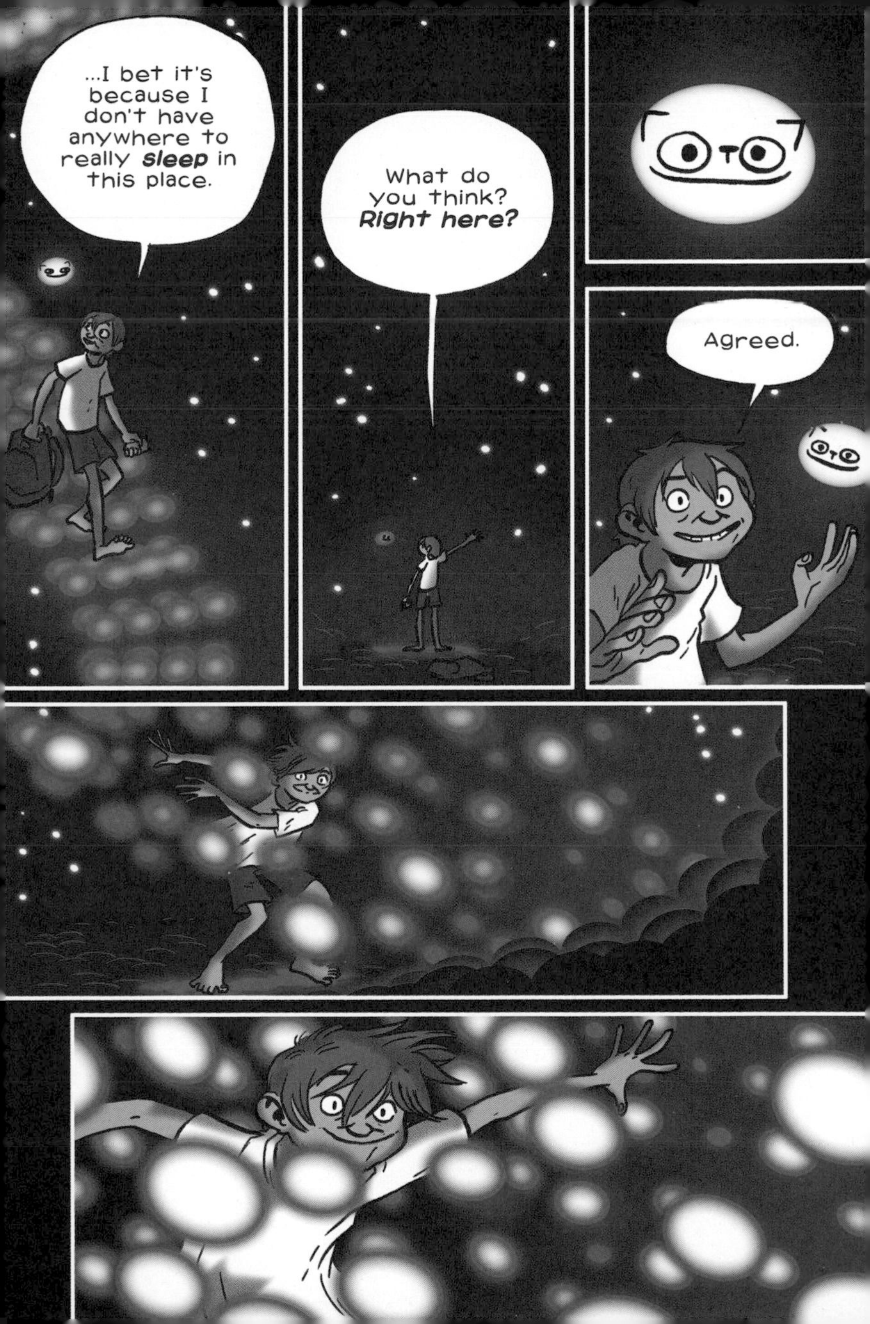
...I bet it's because I don't have anywhere to really *sleep* in this place.
What do you think? ***Right here?***
Agreed.

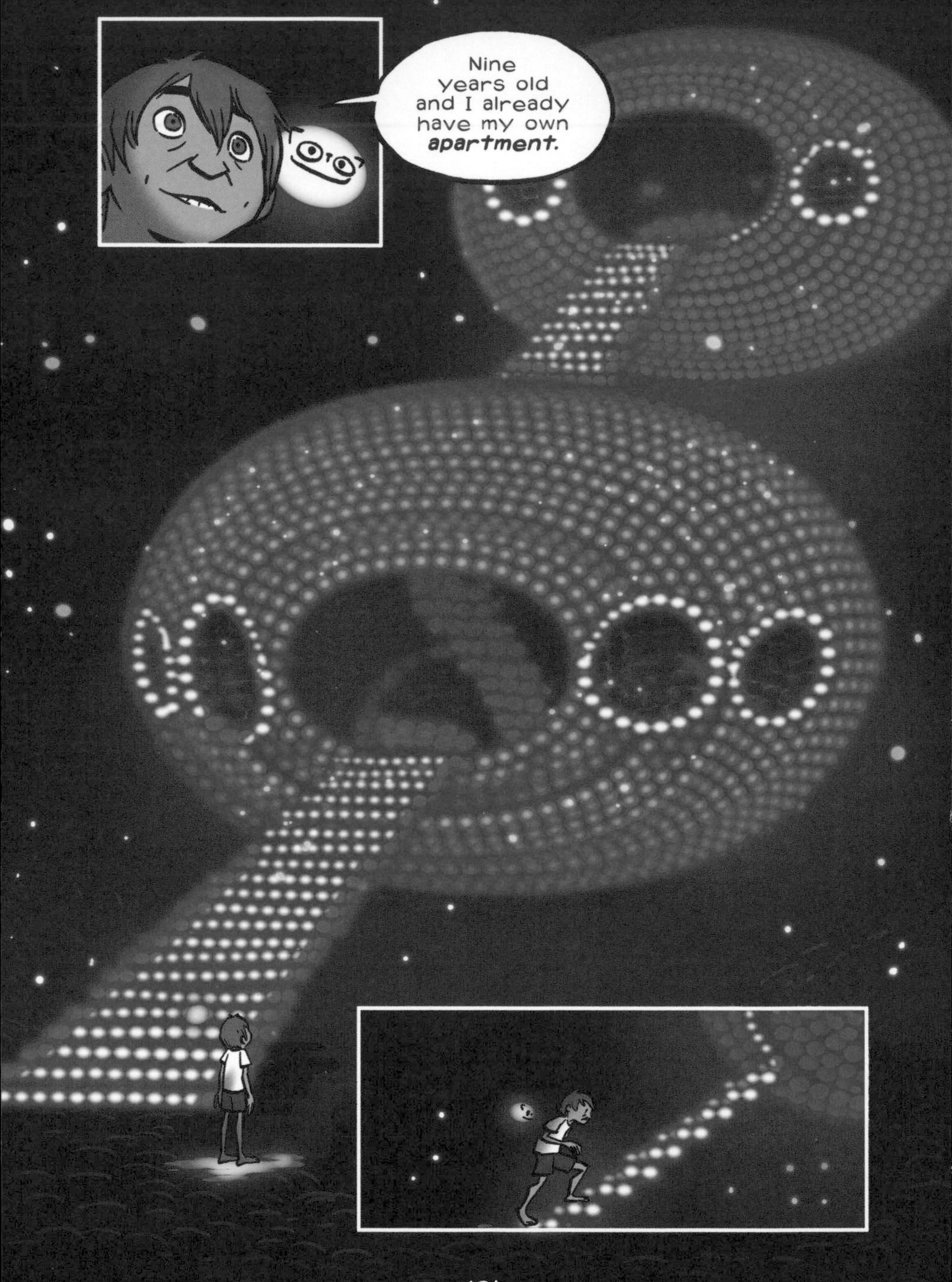
Nine years old and I already have my own *apartment.*

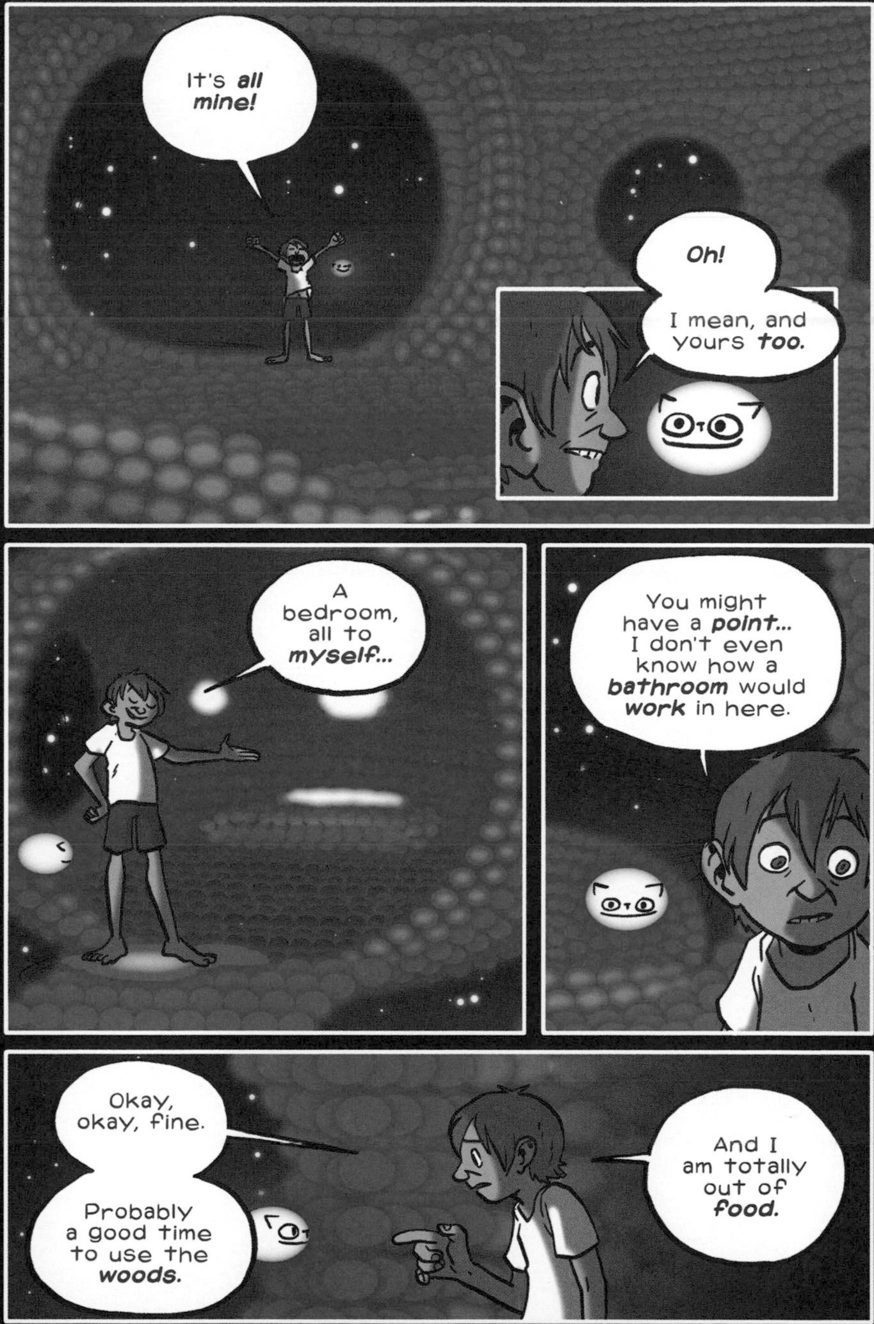

It's *all* *mine!*
*Oh!*
I mean, and yours *too.*
A bedroom, all to *myself...*
You might have a *point...* I don't even know how a *bathroom* would *work* in here.
Okay, okay, fine.
Probably a good time to use the *woods.*
And I am totally out of *food.*

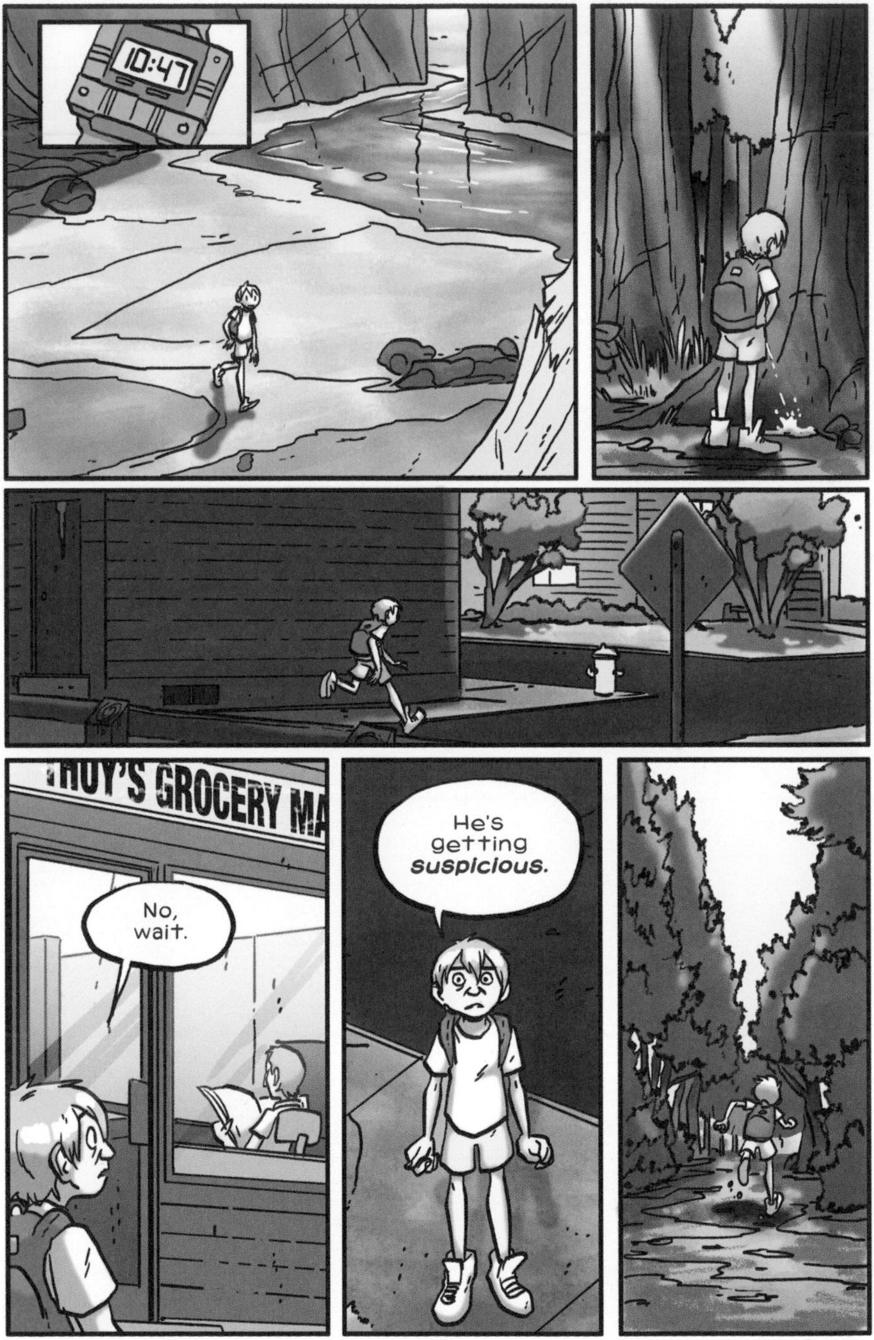
10:47
HOY'S GROCERY MA
No, wait.
He's getting *suspicious.*

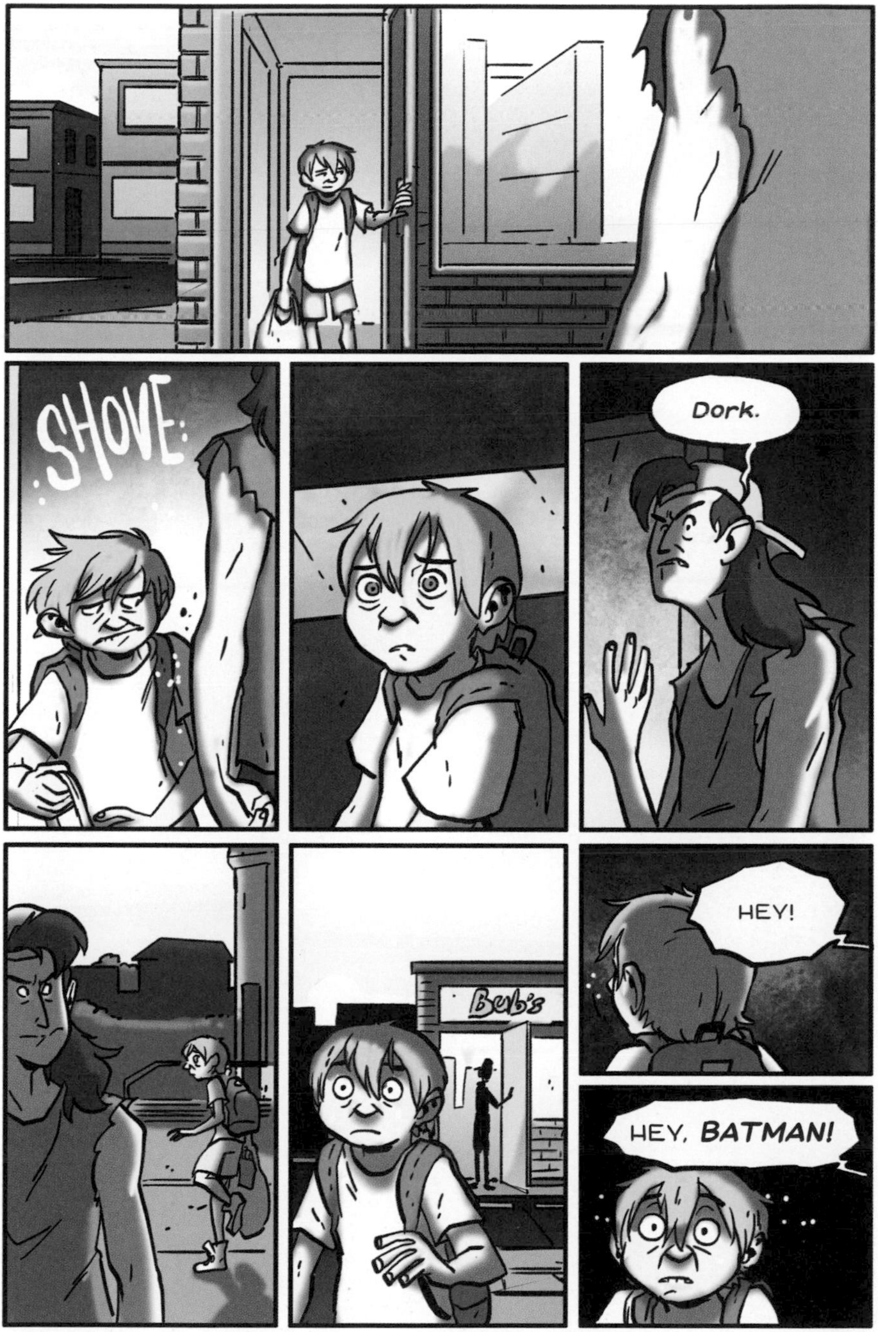
SHOVE
Dork.
Bub's
HEY!
HEY, BATMAN!

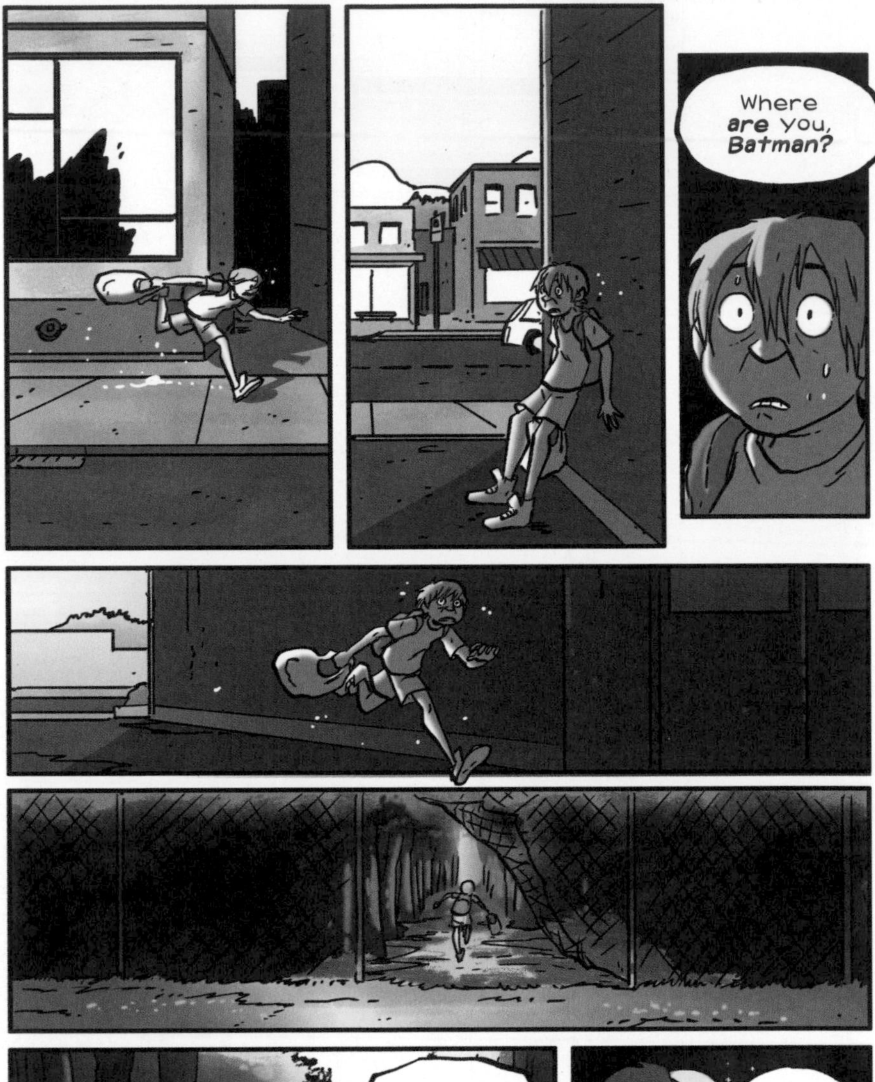
Where are you, Batman?
HEY!
You little...
HEY! KID!

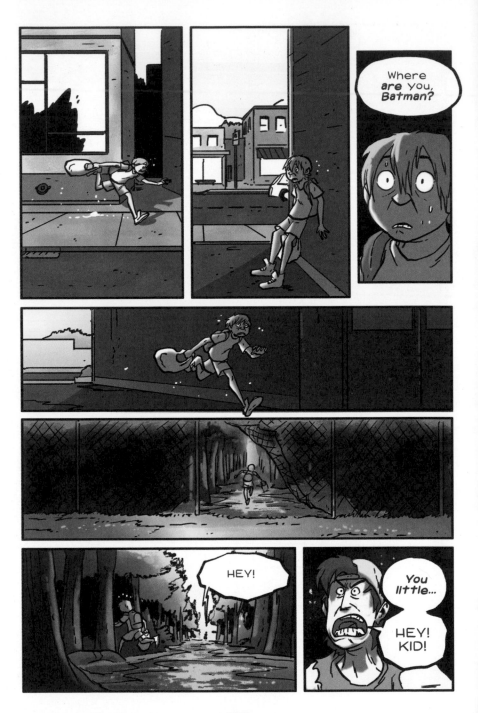

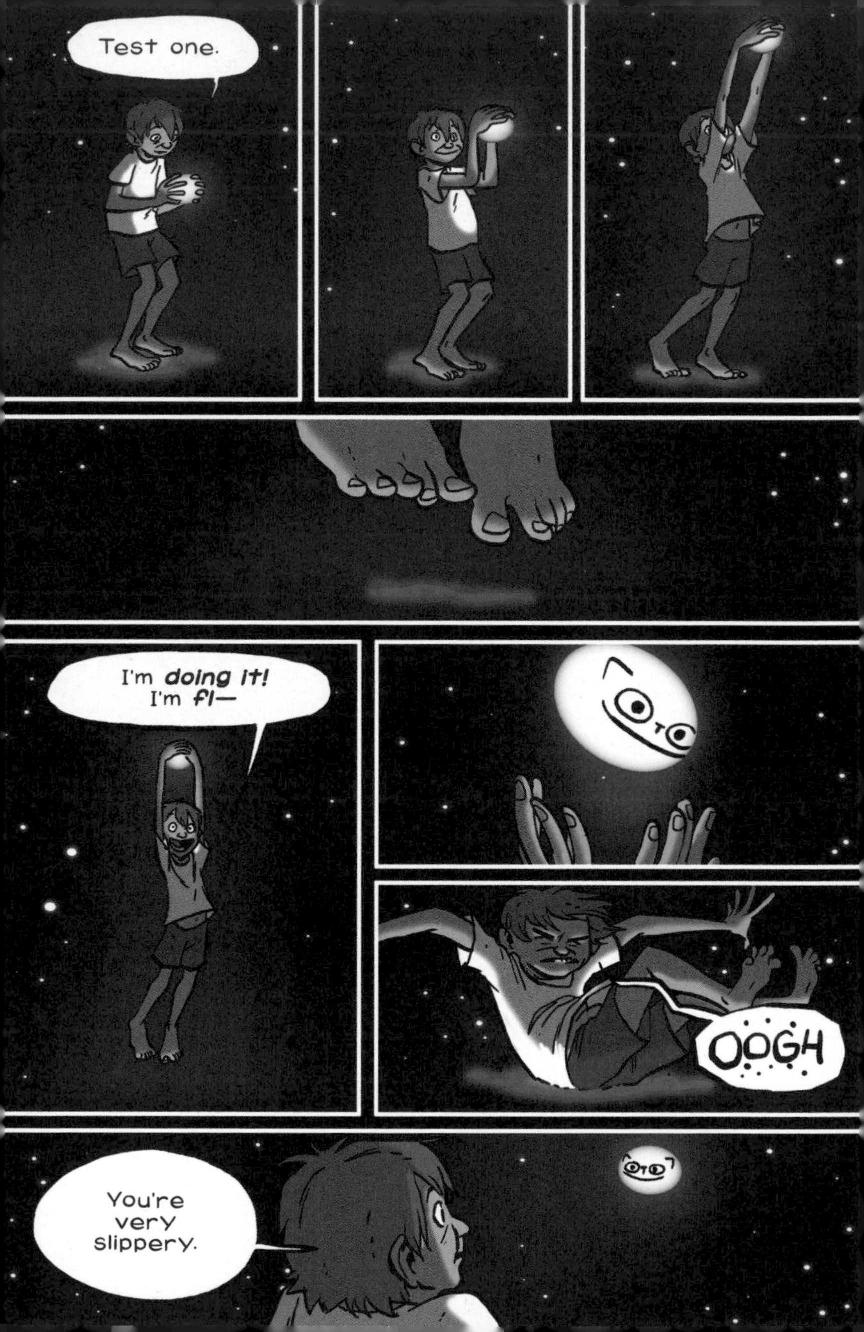
Test one.
I'm *doing it!* I'm *fl—*
OOGH
You're very slippery.

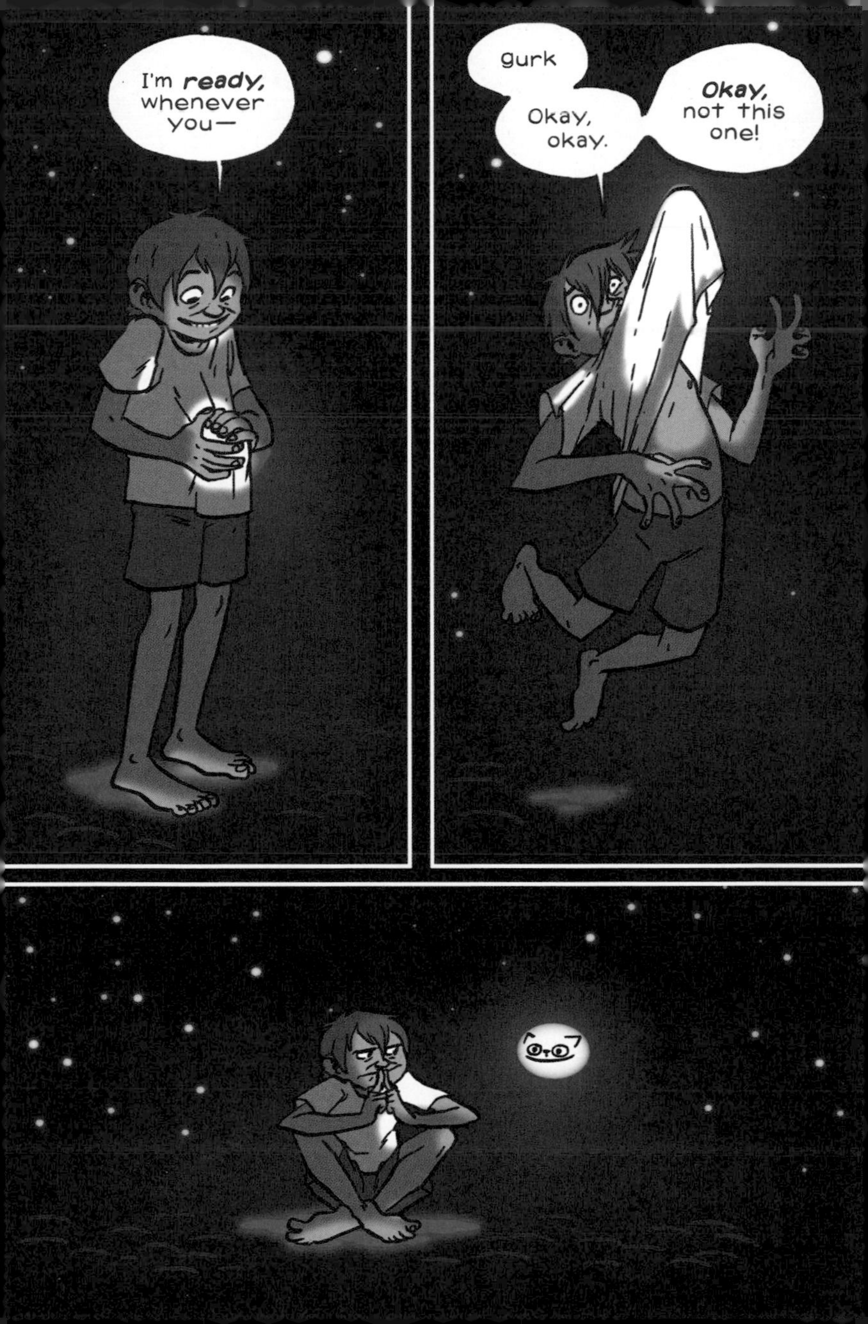
I'm ready, whenever you—
gurk
Okay, okay.
Okay, not this one!

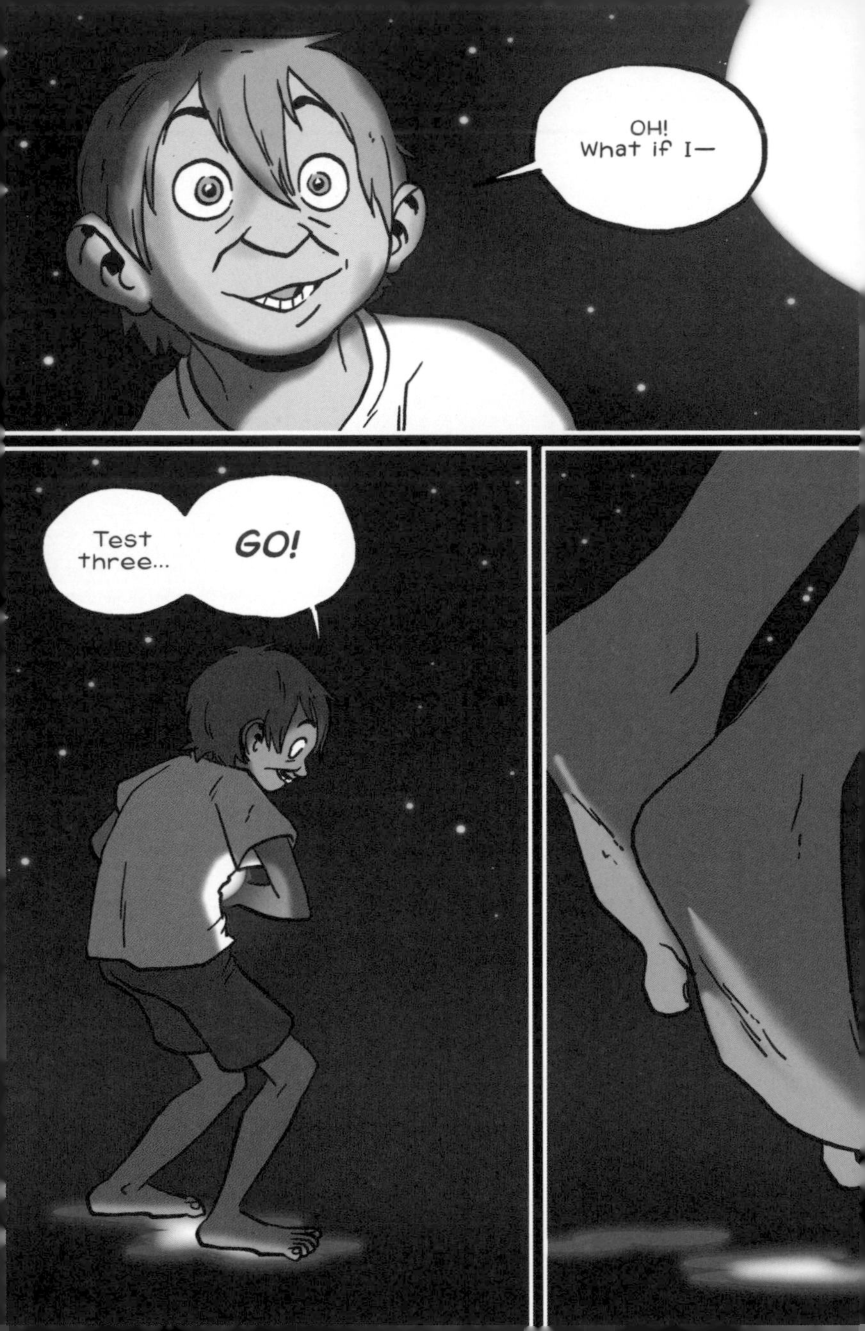
OH!
What if I—
Test three...
GO!

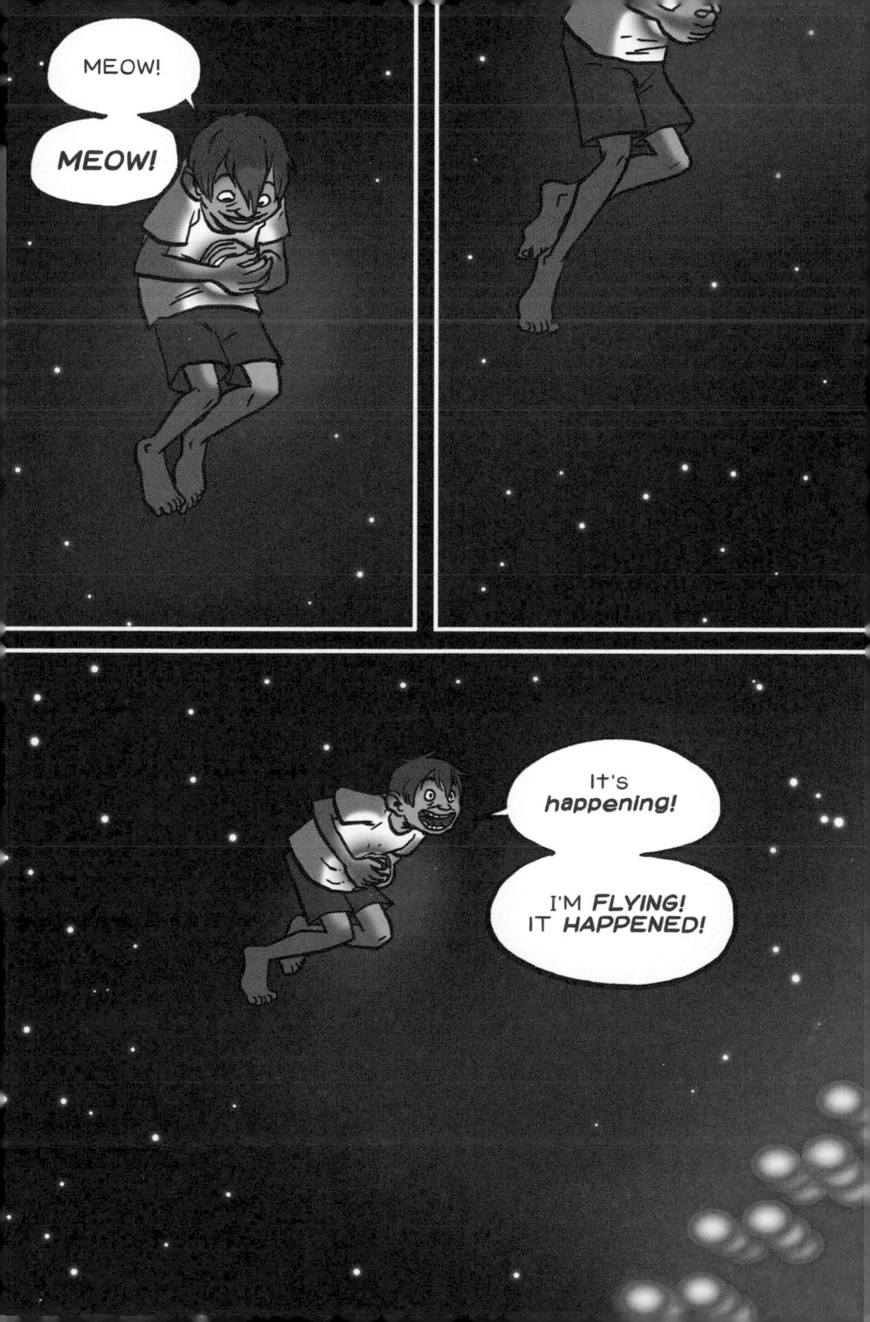
MEOW!
MEOW!
It's happening!
I'M FLYING! IT HAPPENED!

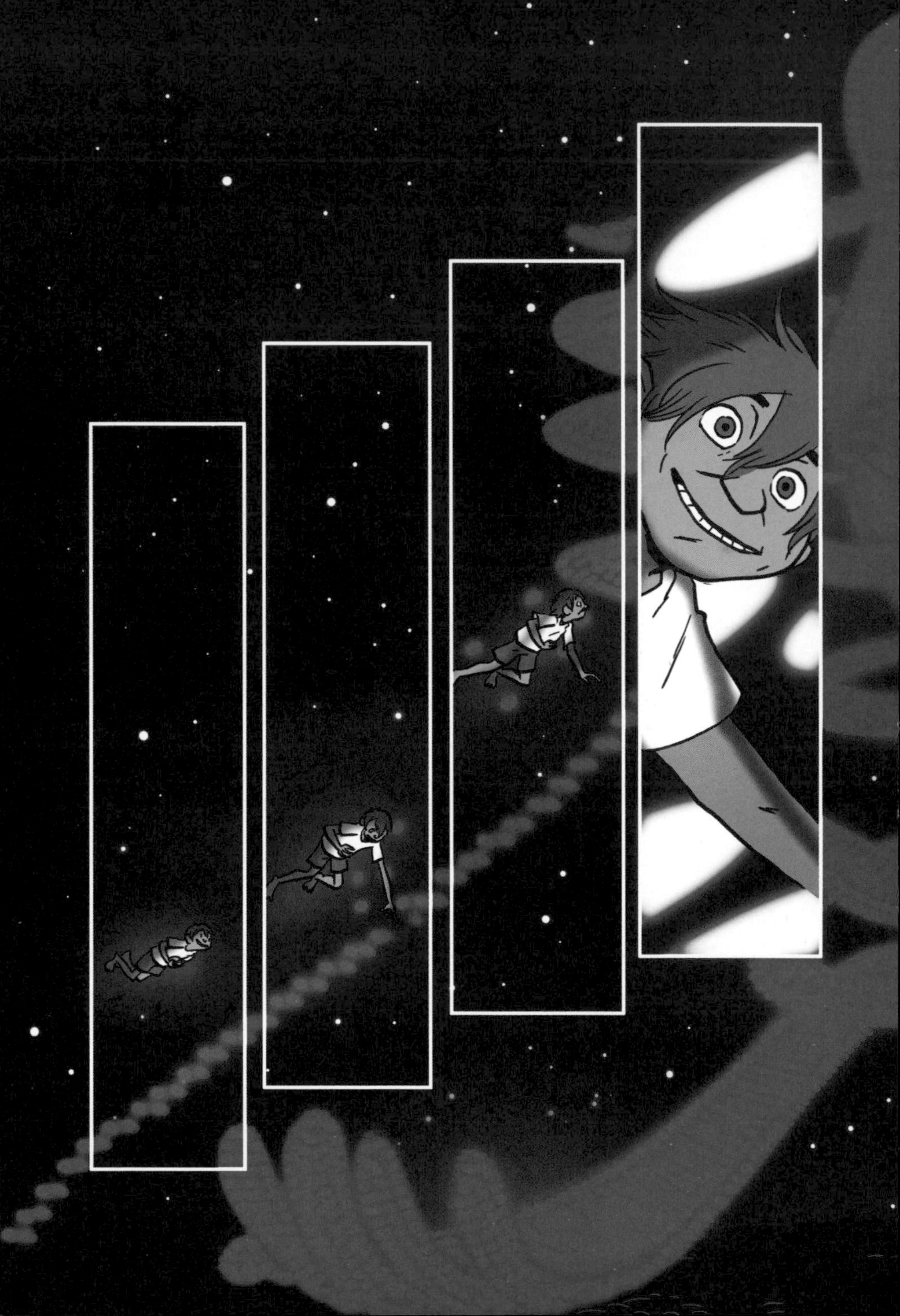

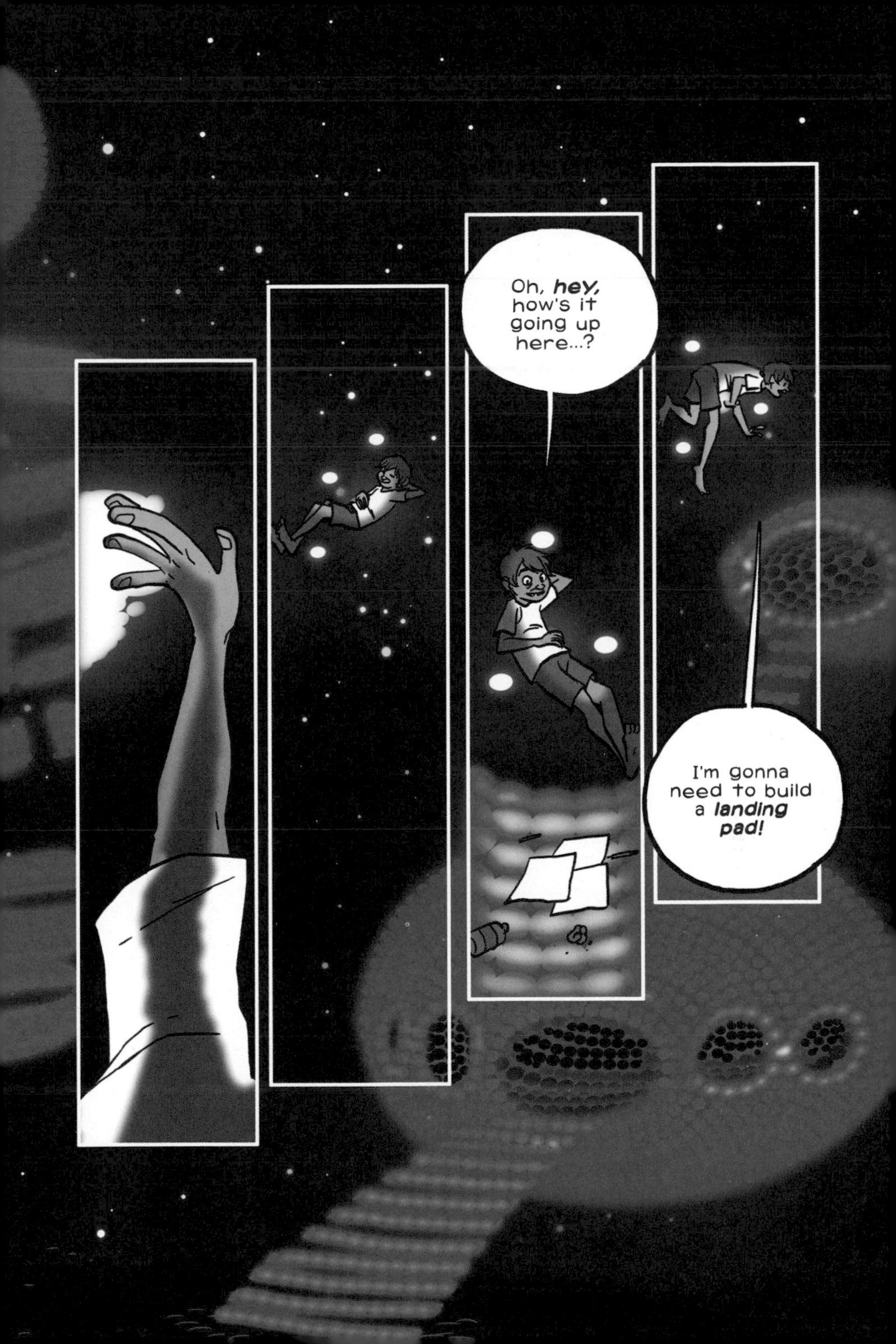
Oh, **hey,** how's it going up here...?
I'm gonna need to build a ***landing pad!***

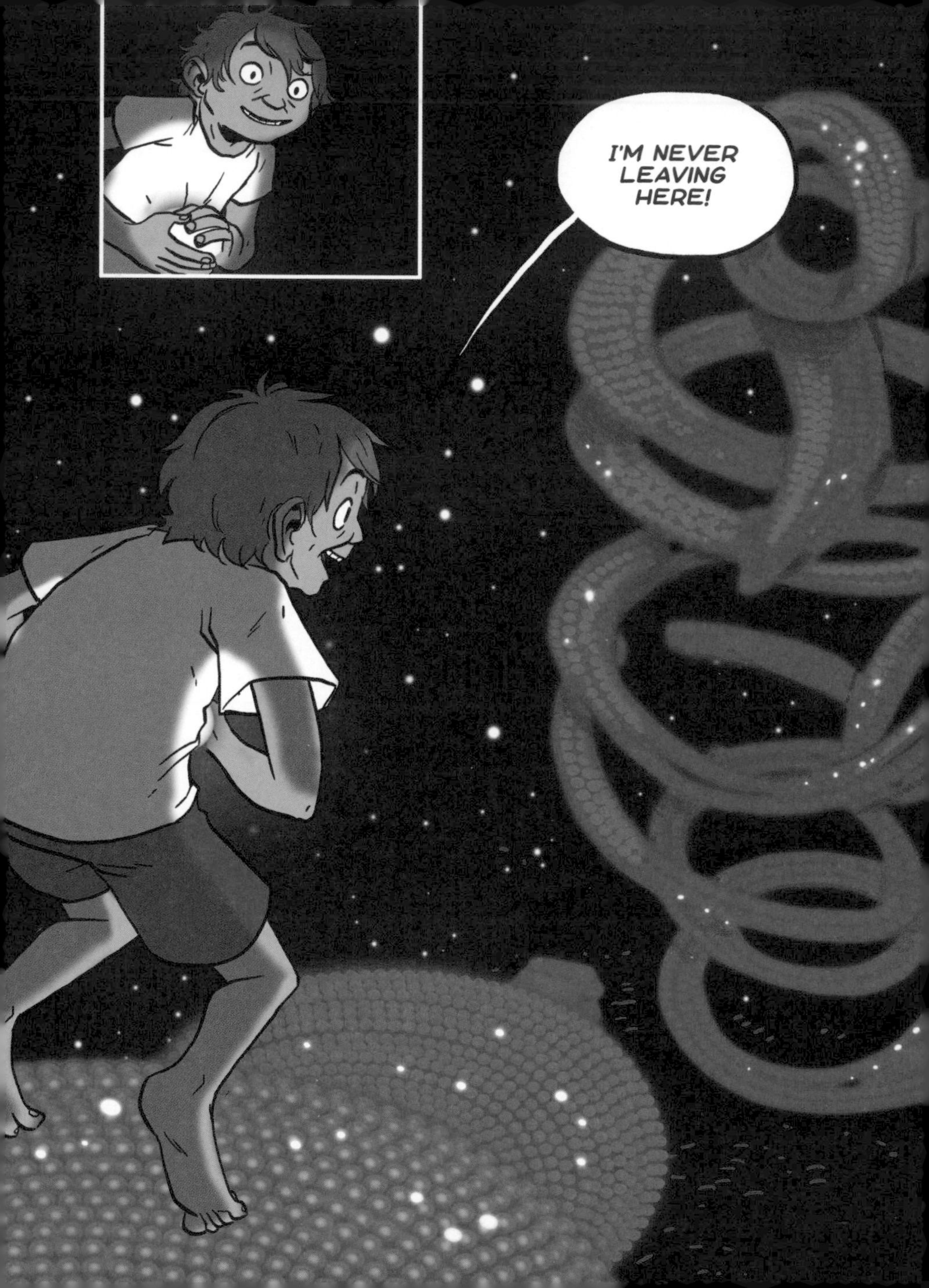
I'M NEVER LEAVING HERE!

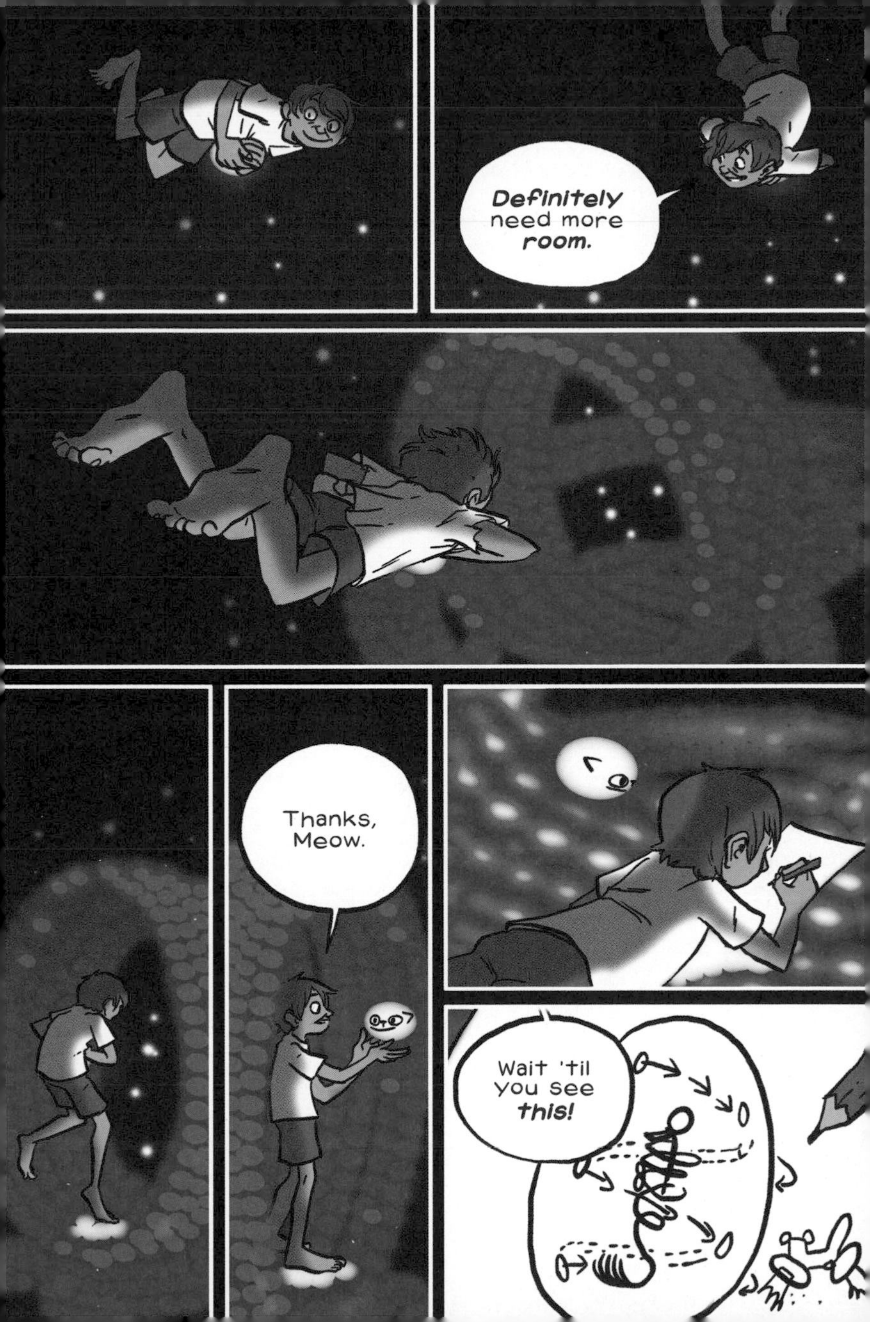
Definitely need more room.
Thanks, Meow.
Wait 'til you see this!

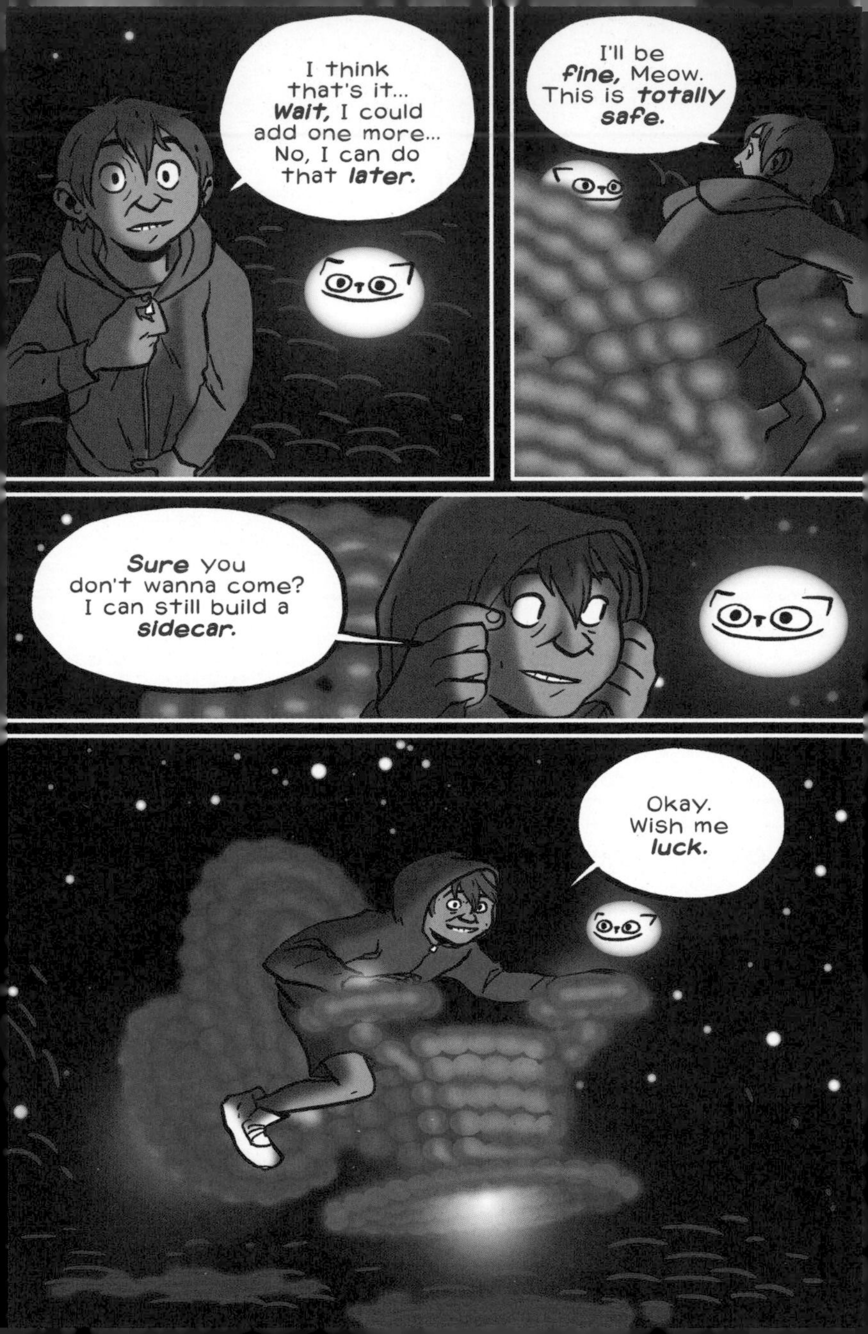
I think that's it... Wait, I could add one more... No, I can do that later.
I'll be fine, Meow. This is totally safe.
Sure you don't wanna come? I can still build a sidecar.
Okay. Wish me luck.

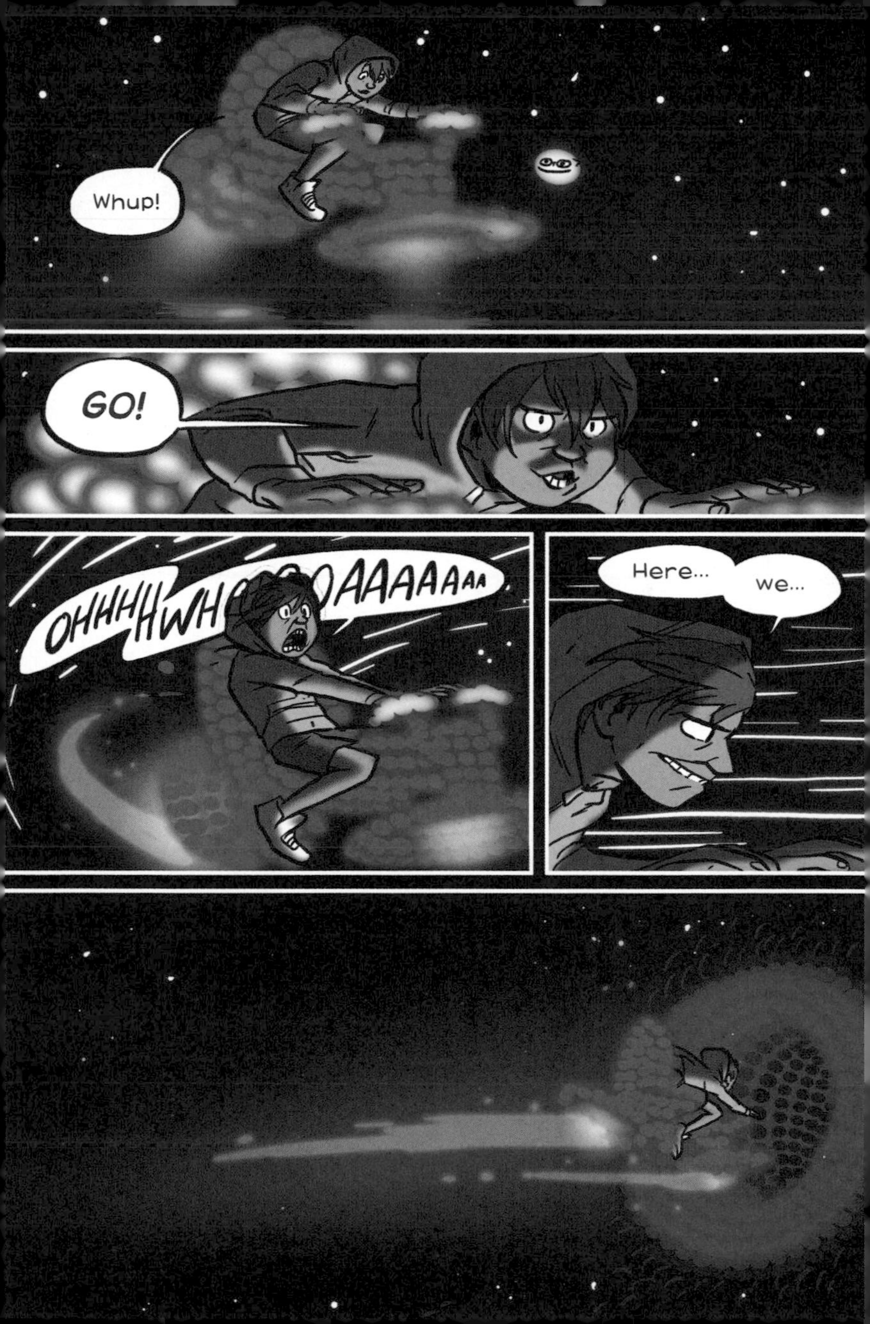
Whup!
GO!
OHHHHWH...OAAAAAAA
Here...
we...

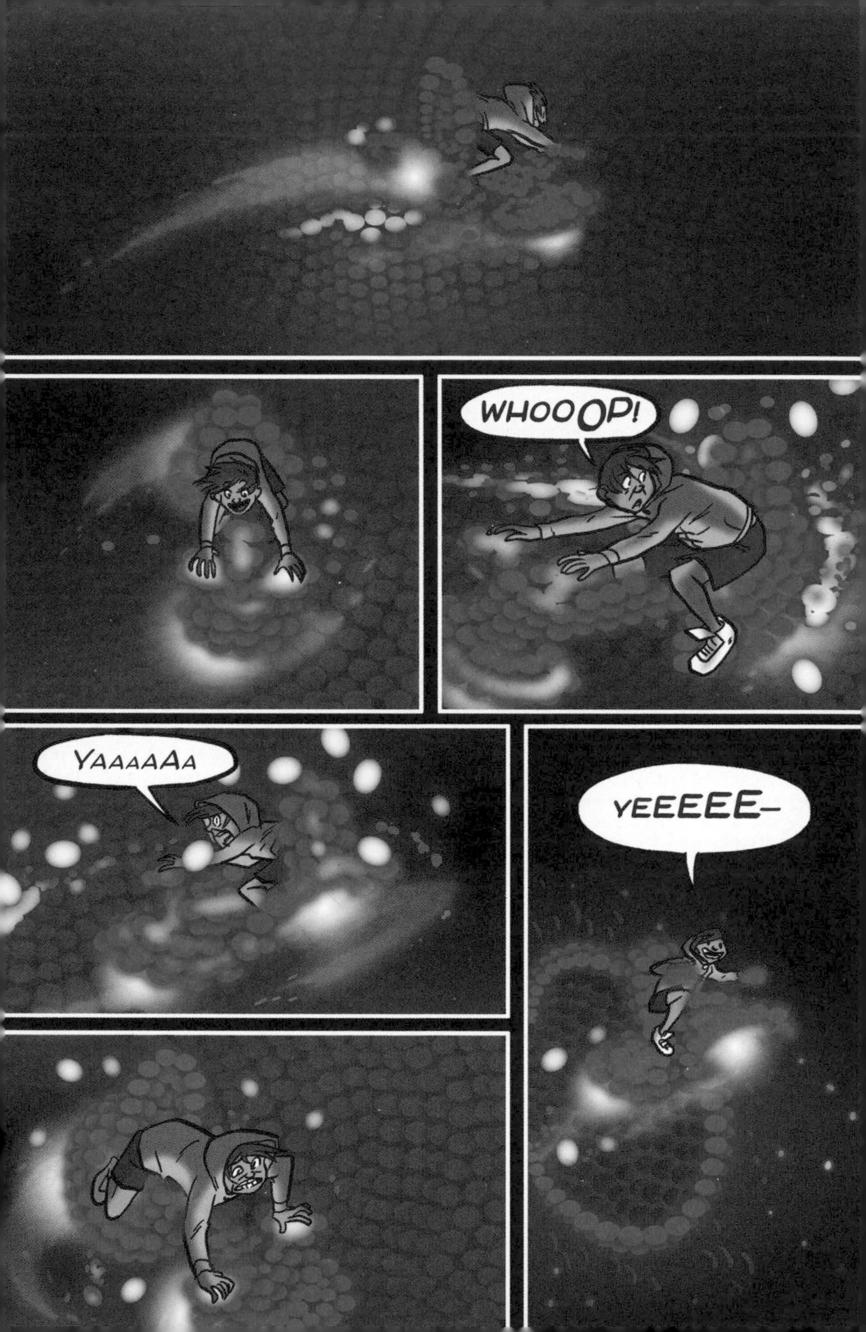
WHOOOP!
YAAAAAA
YEEEEE–

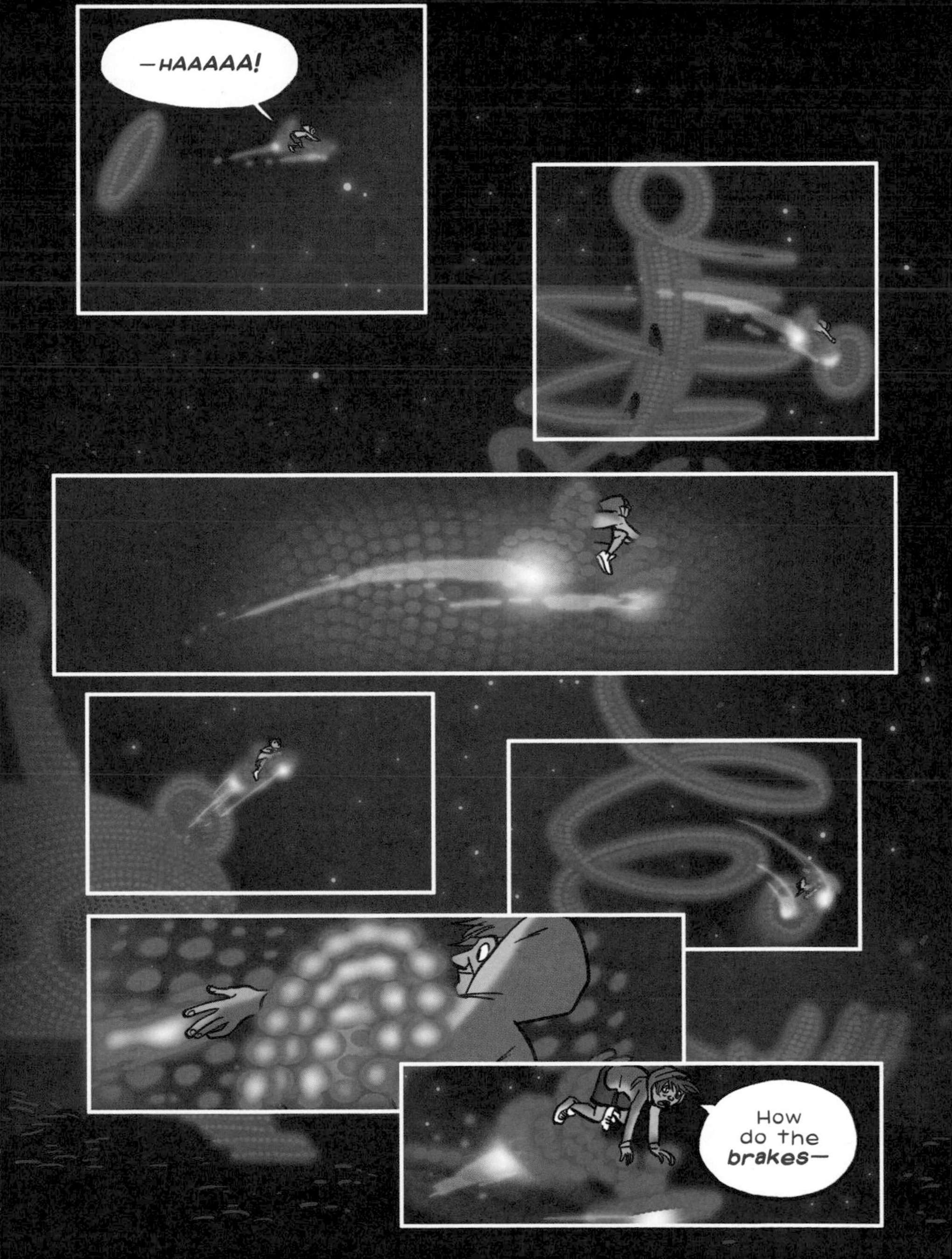
—HAAAAAA!
How do the brakes—

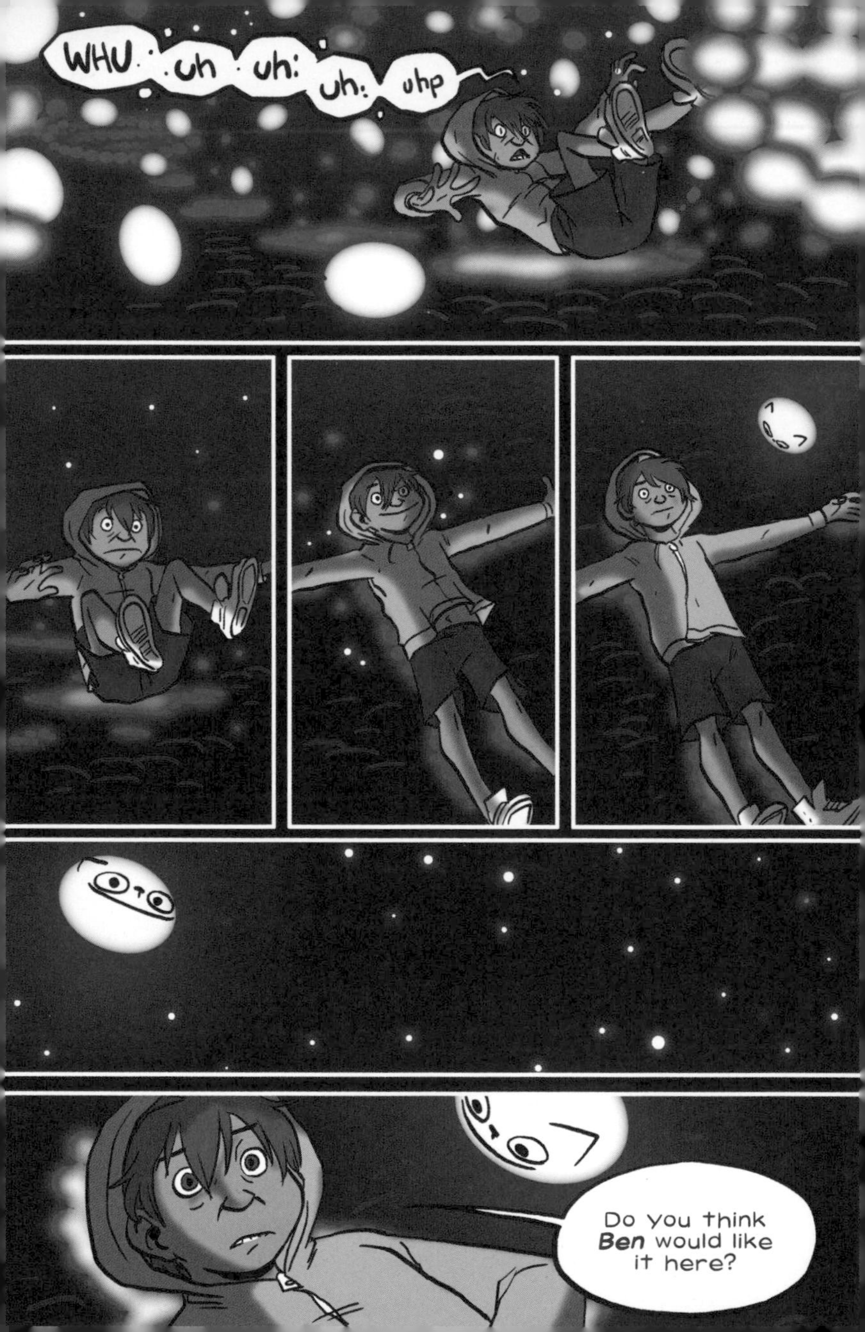
WHU. .uh .uh: uh: uhp
Do you think
**Ben** would like
it here?

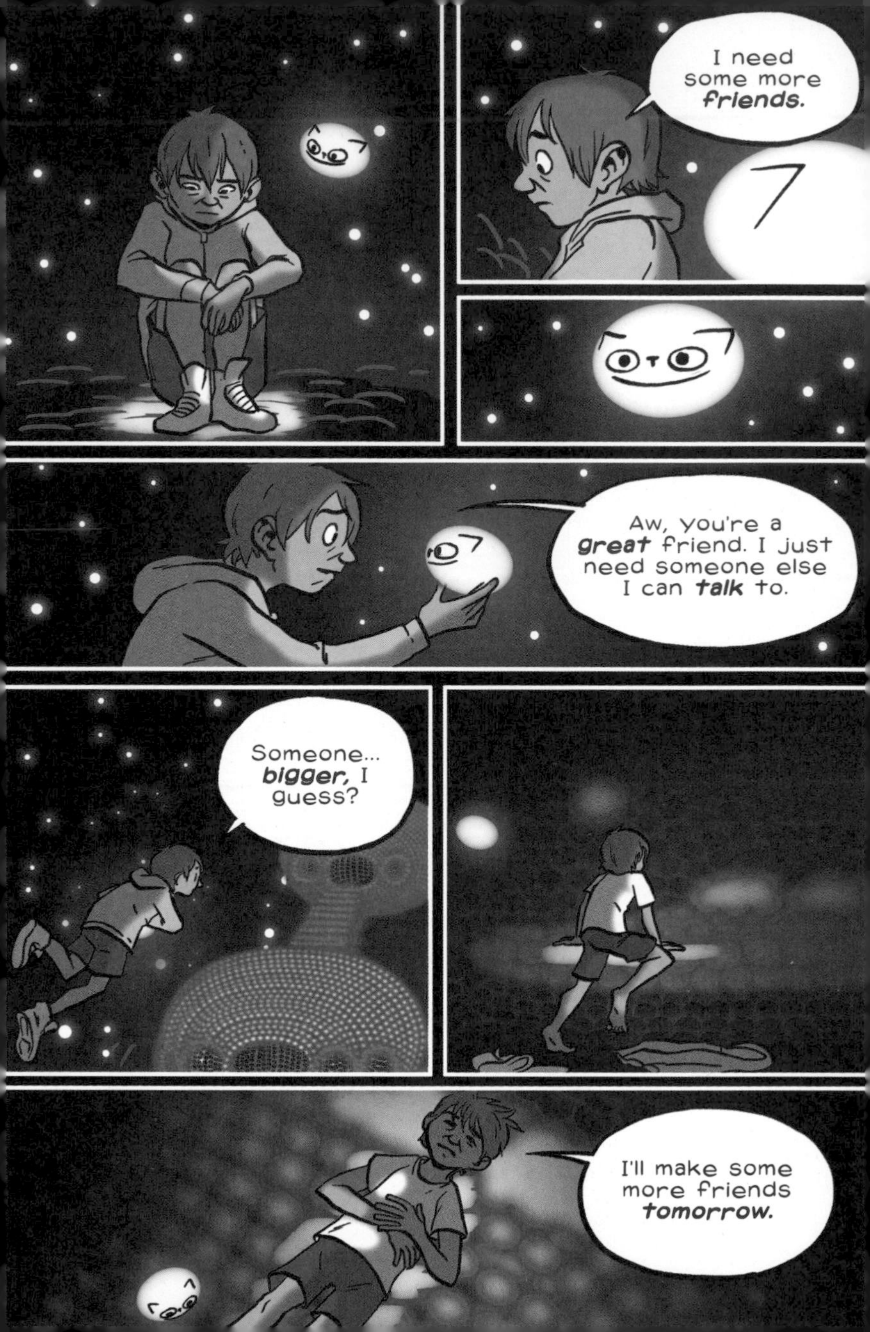
I need some more friends.
Aw, you're a great friend. I just need someone else I can talk to.
Someone... bigger, I guess?
I'll make some more friends tomorrow.

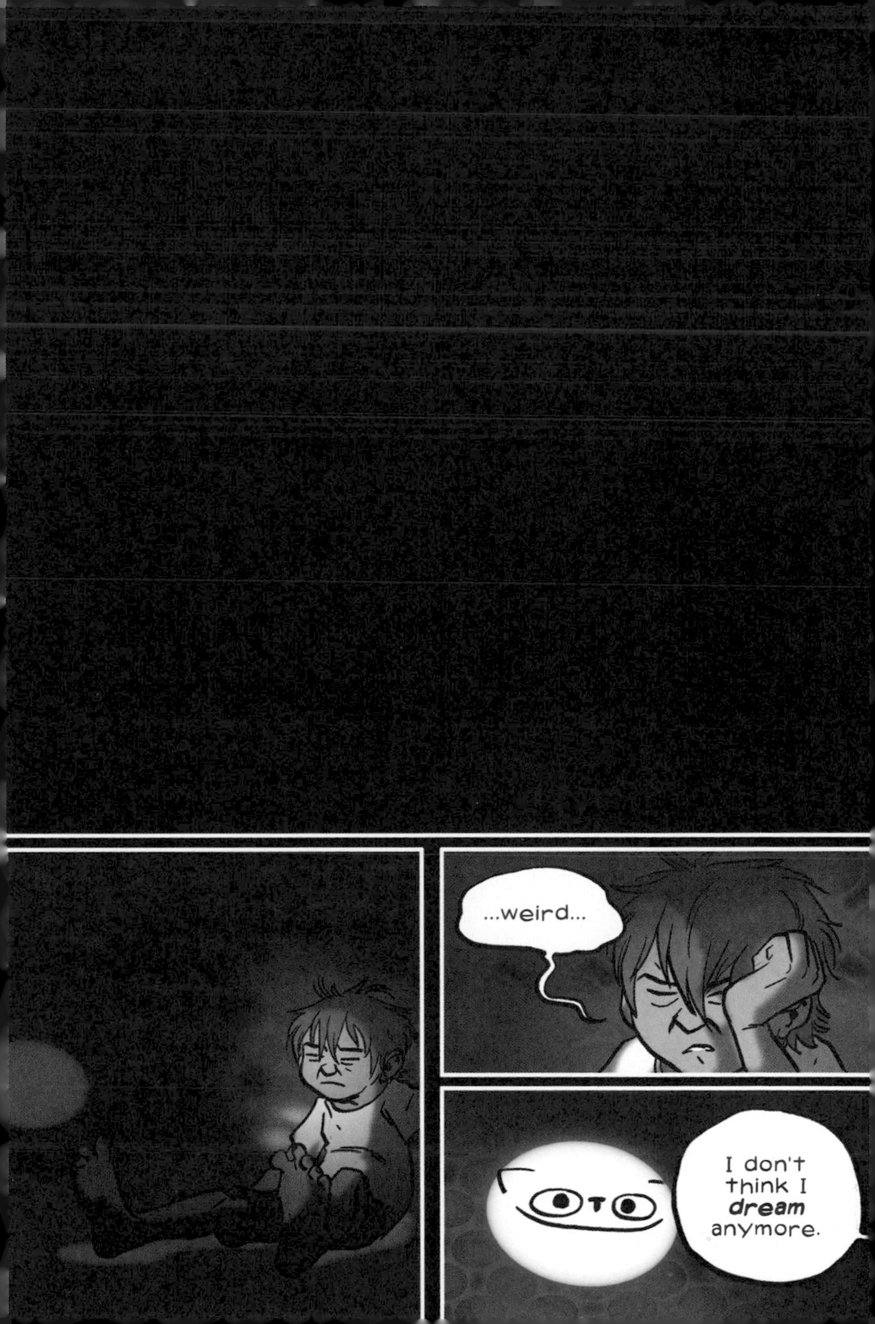
...weird...
I don't think I ***dream*** anymore.

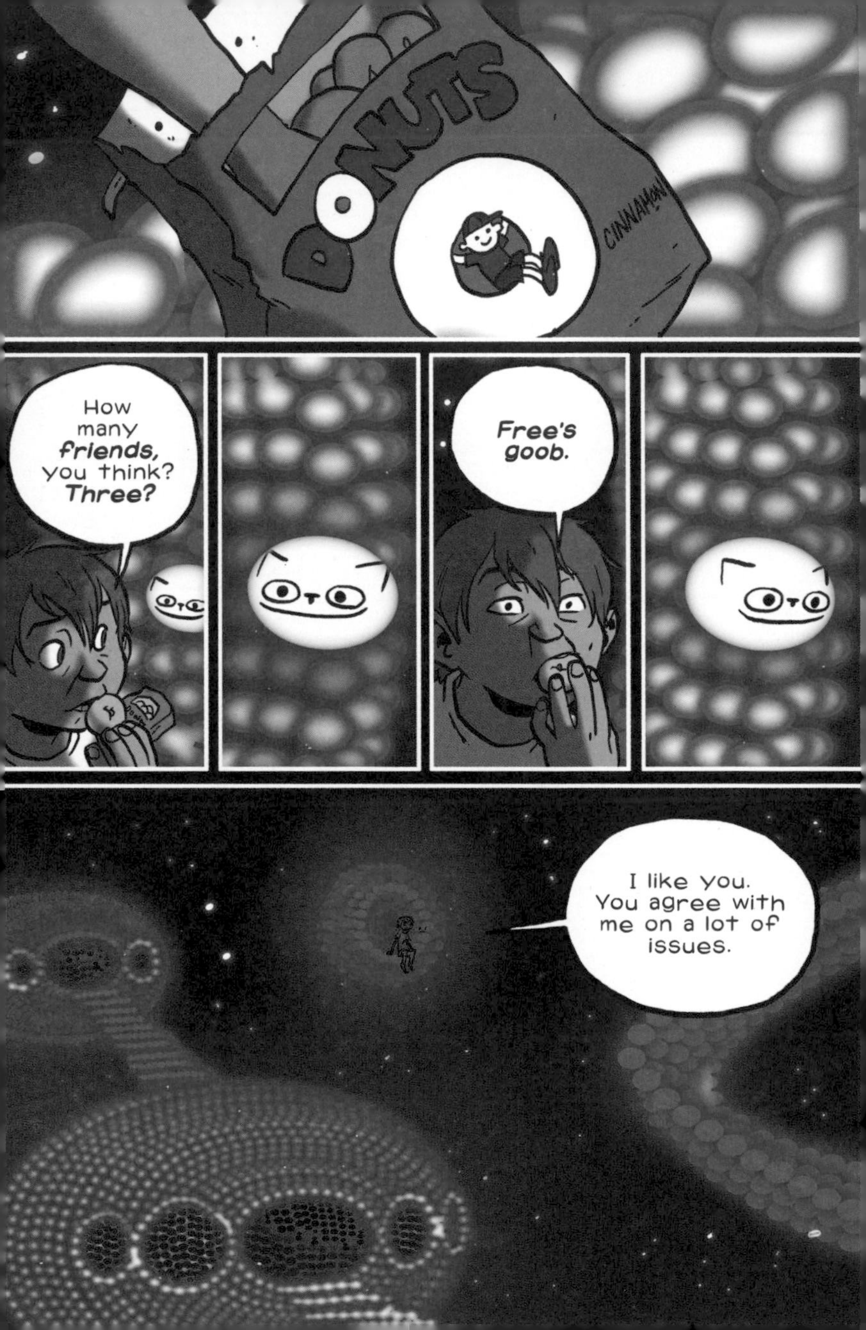
DONUTS
CINNAMON
How many friends, you think? Three?
Free's goob.
I like you. You agree with me on a lot of issues.

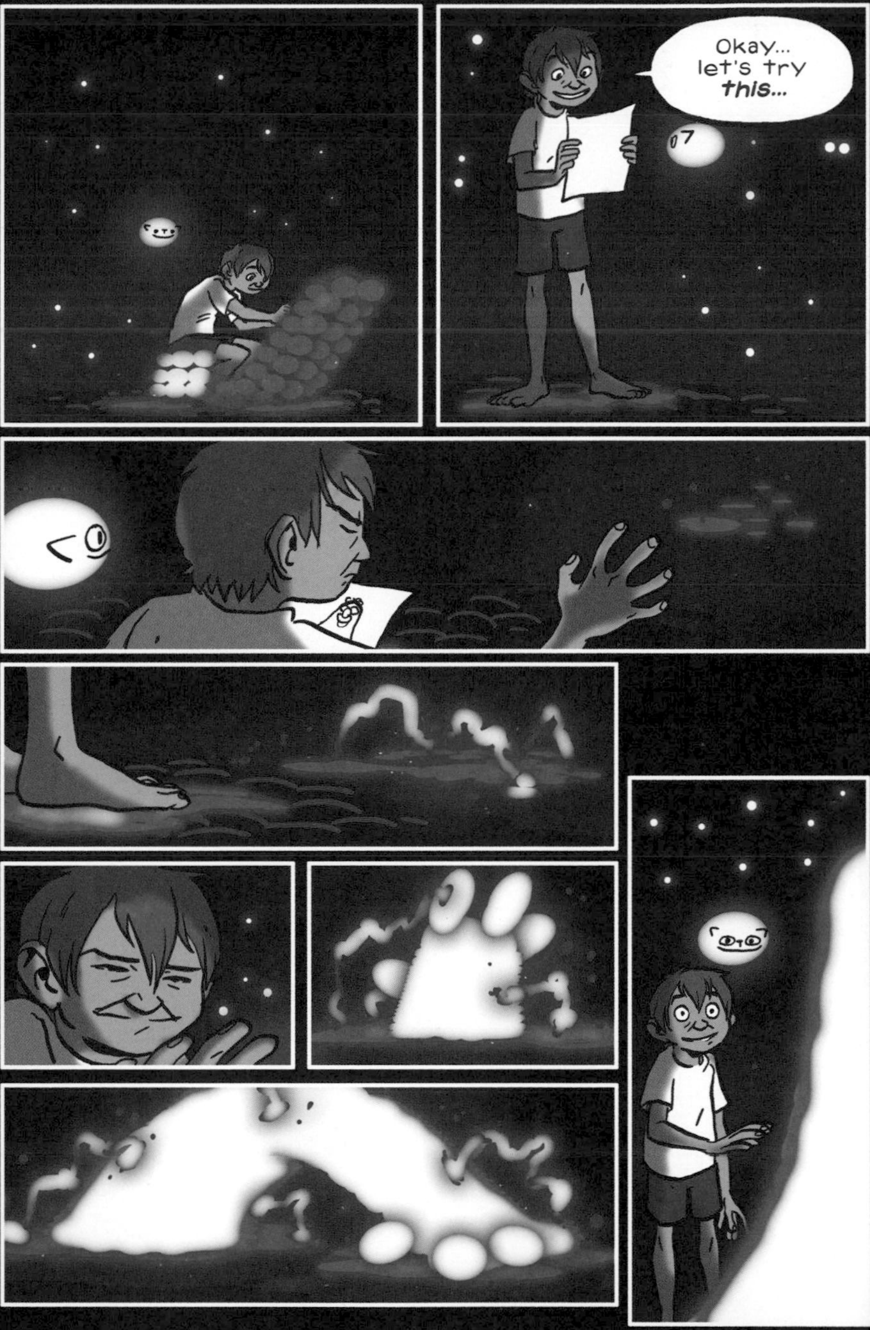
Okay...
let's try
*this...*

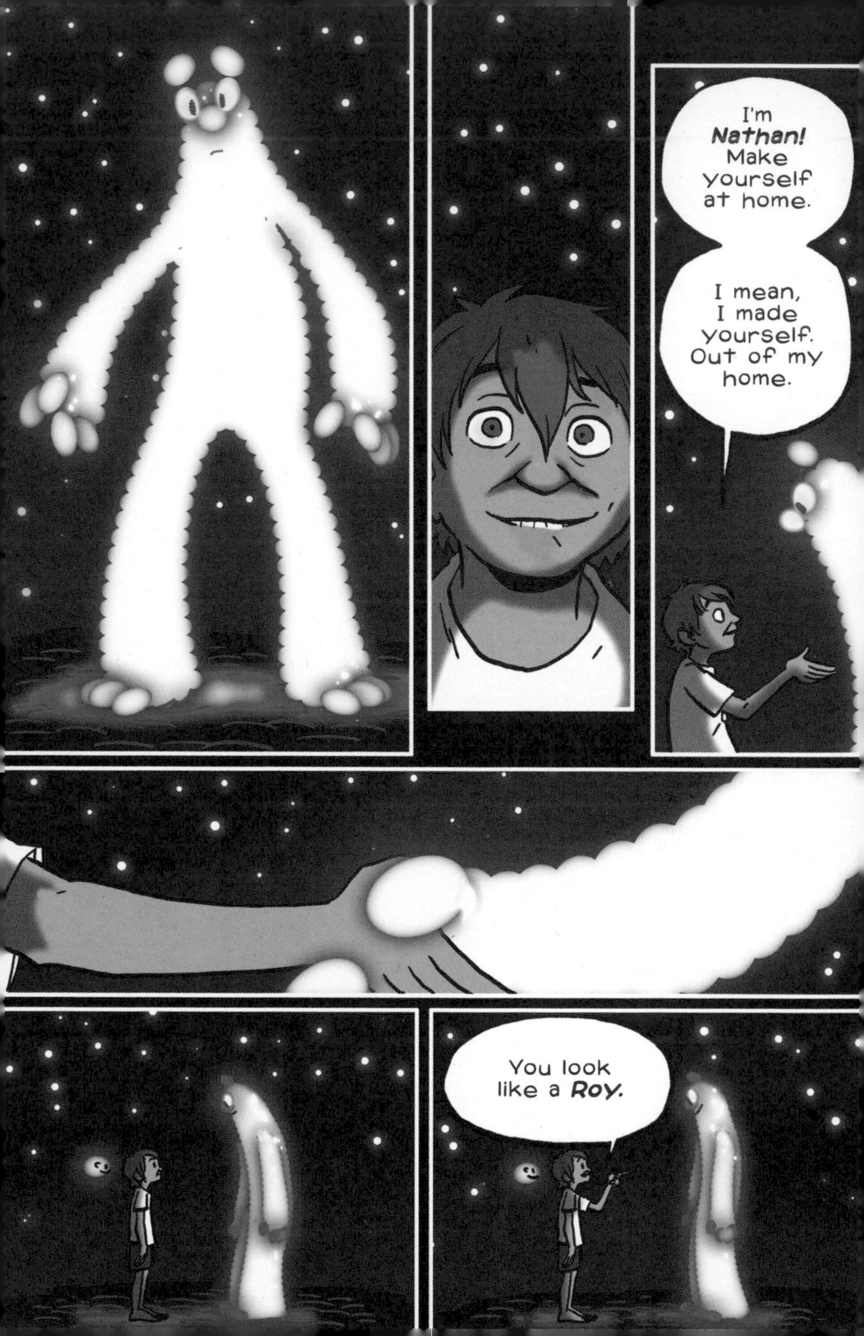
I'm Nathan! Make yourself at home.
I mean, I made yourself. Out of my home.
You look like a Roy.

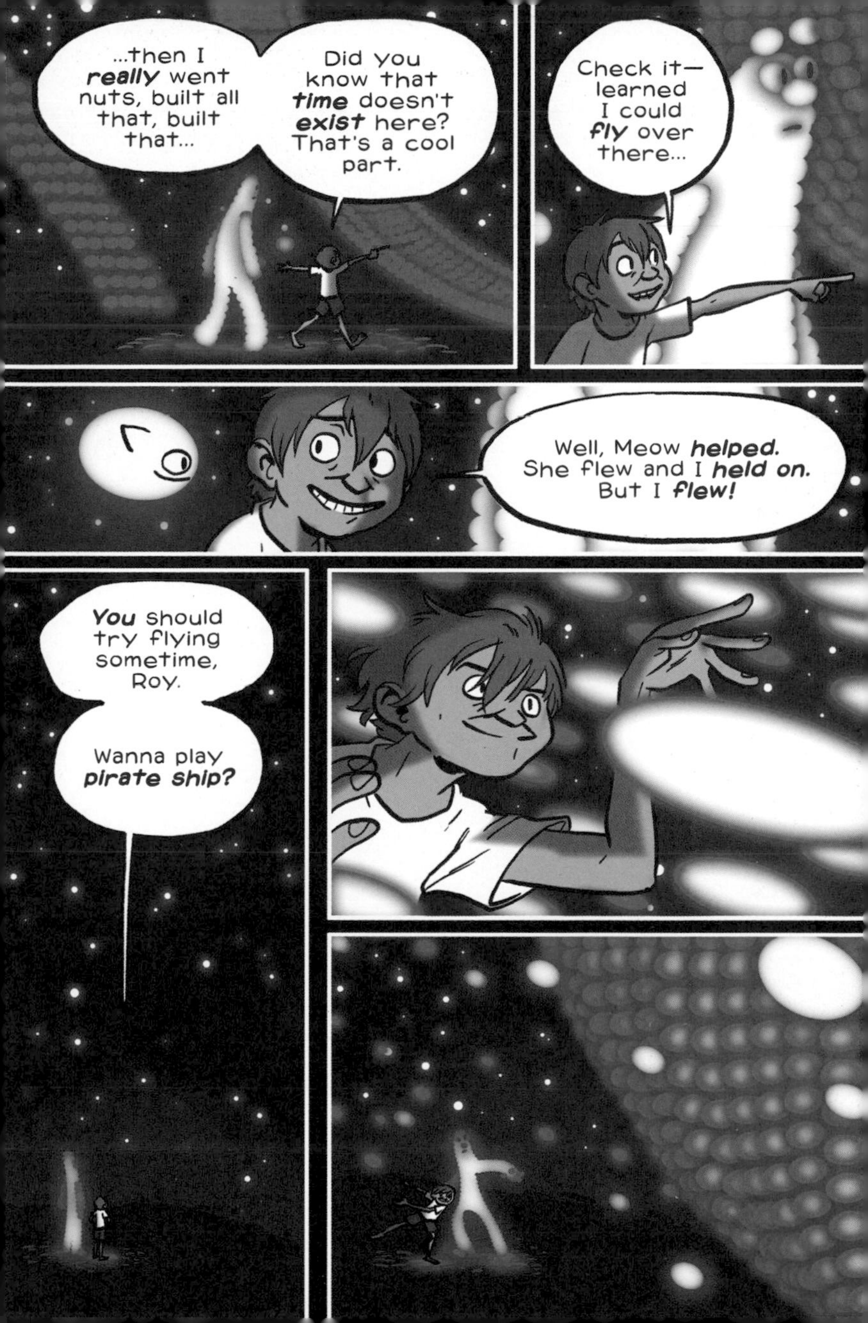
...then I **really** went nuts, built all that, built that...
Did you know that **time** doesn't **exist** here? That's a cool part.
Check it— learned I could **fly** over there...
Well, Meow **helped.** She flew and I **held on.** But I **flew!**
**You** should try flying sometime, Roy.
Wanna play **pirate ship?**

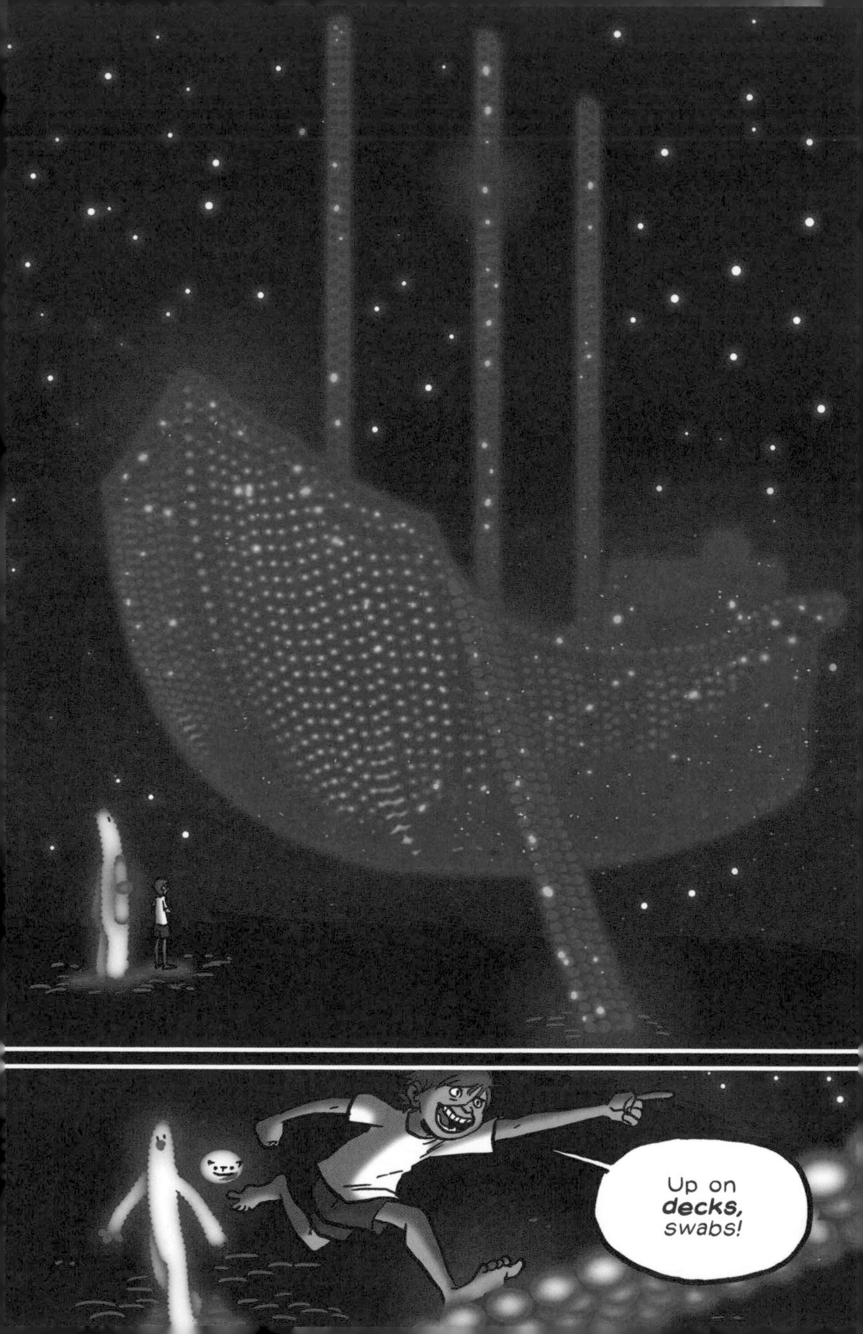
Up on **decks,** swabs!

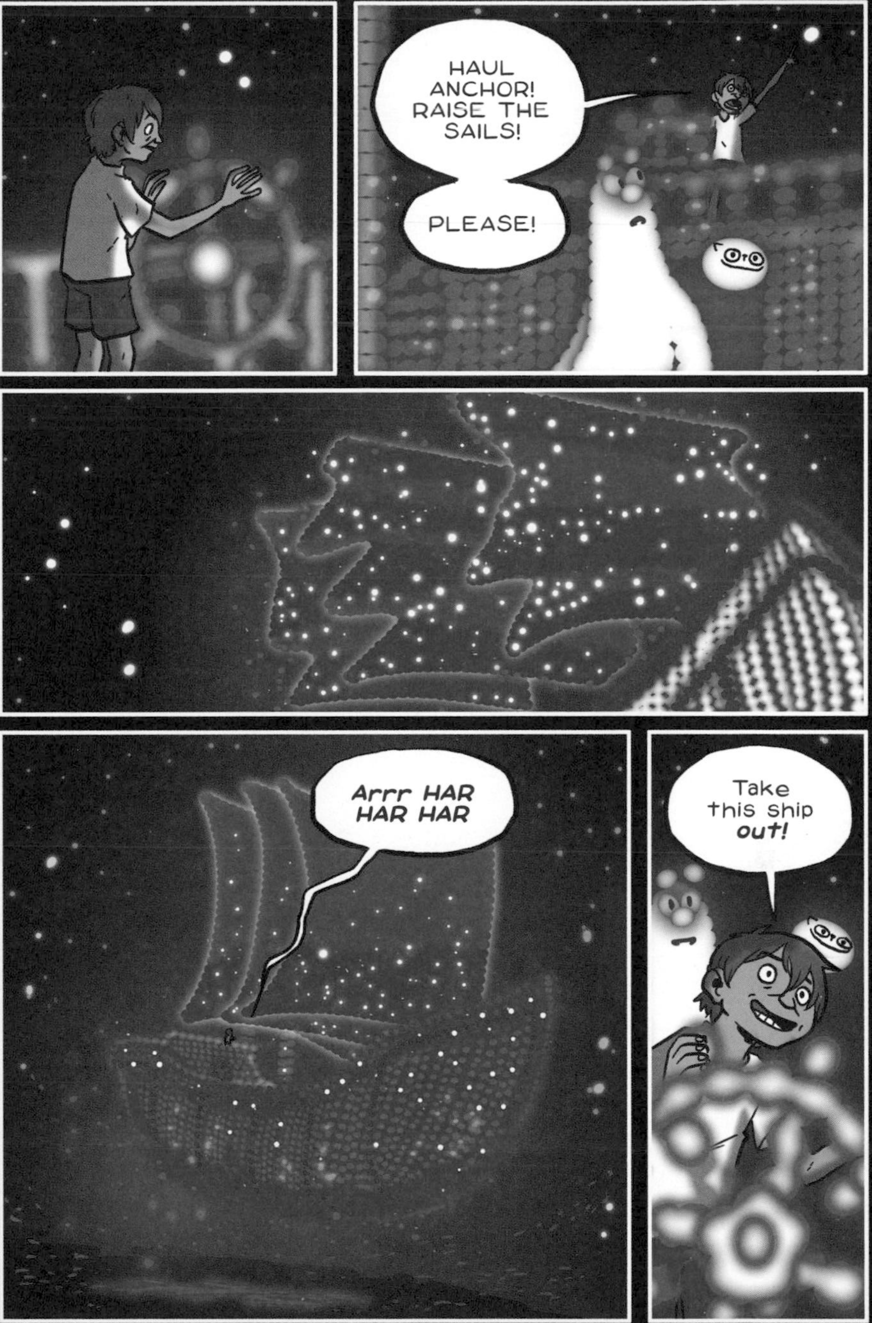
HAUL ANCHOR! RAISE THE SAILS!
PLEASE!
Arrr HAR HAR HAR
Take this ship ***out!***

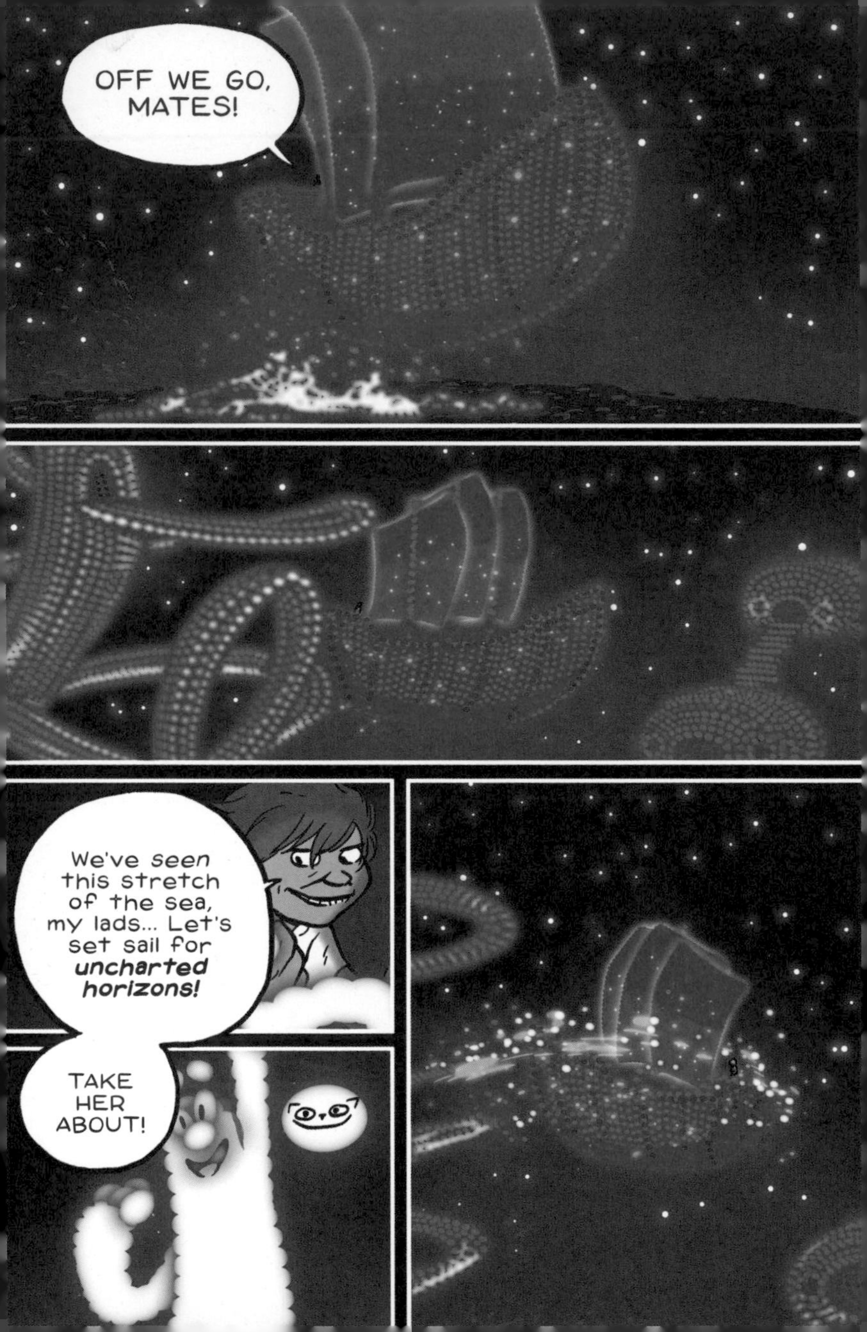
OFF WE GO, MATES!
We've *seen* this stretch of the sea, my lads... Let's set sail for ***uncharted horizons!***
TAKE HER ABOUT!

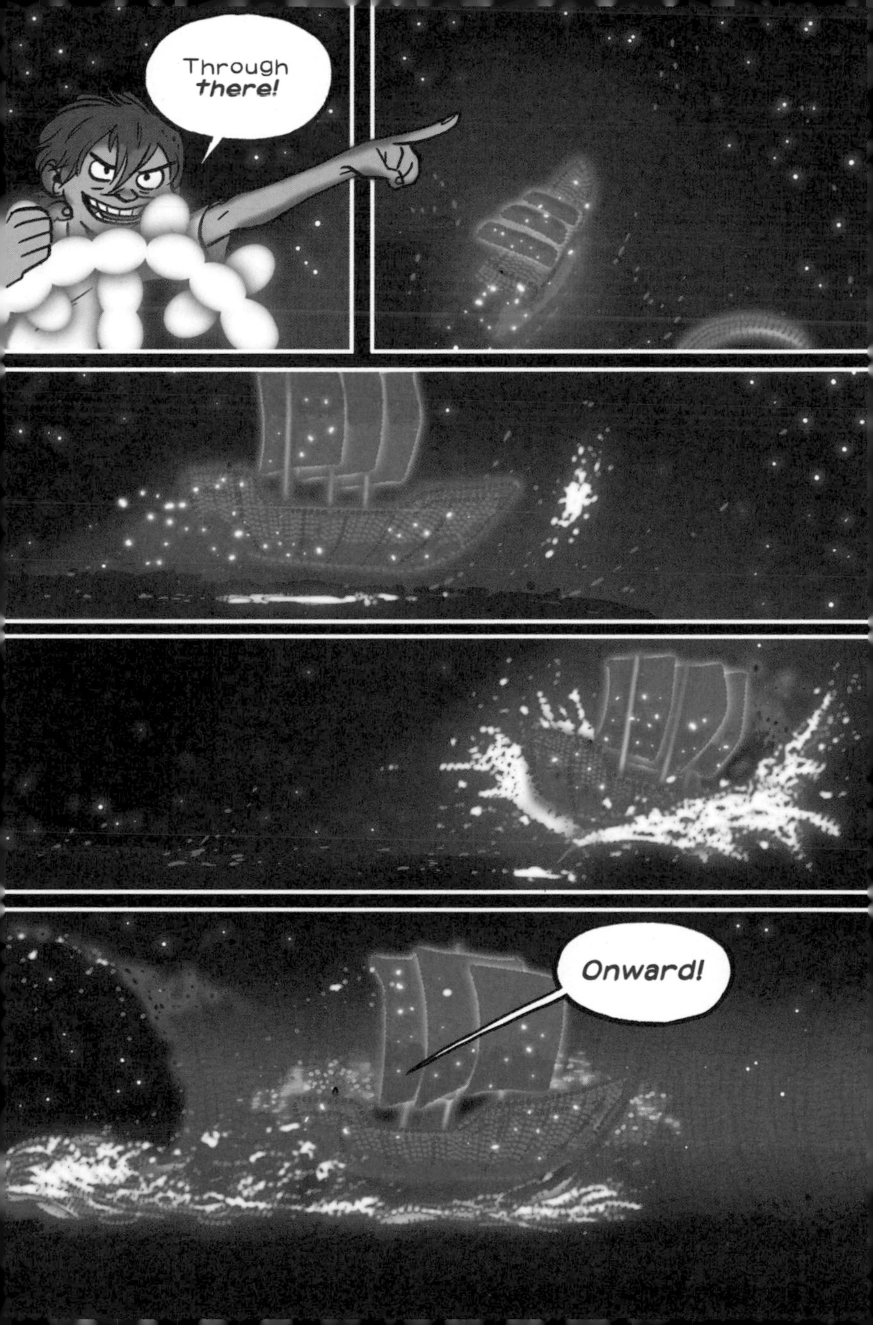
Through there!
Onward!

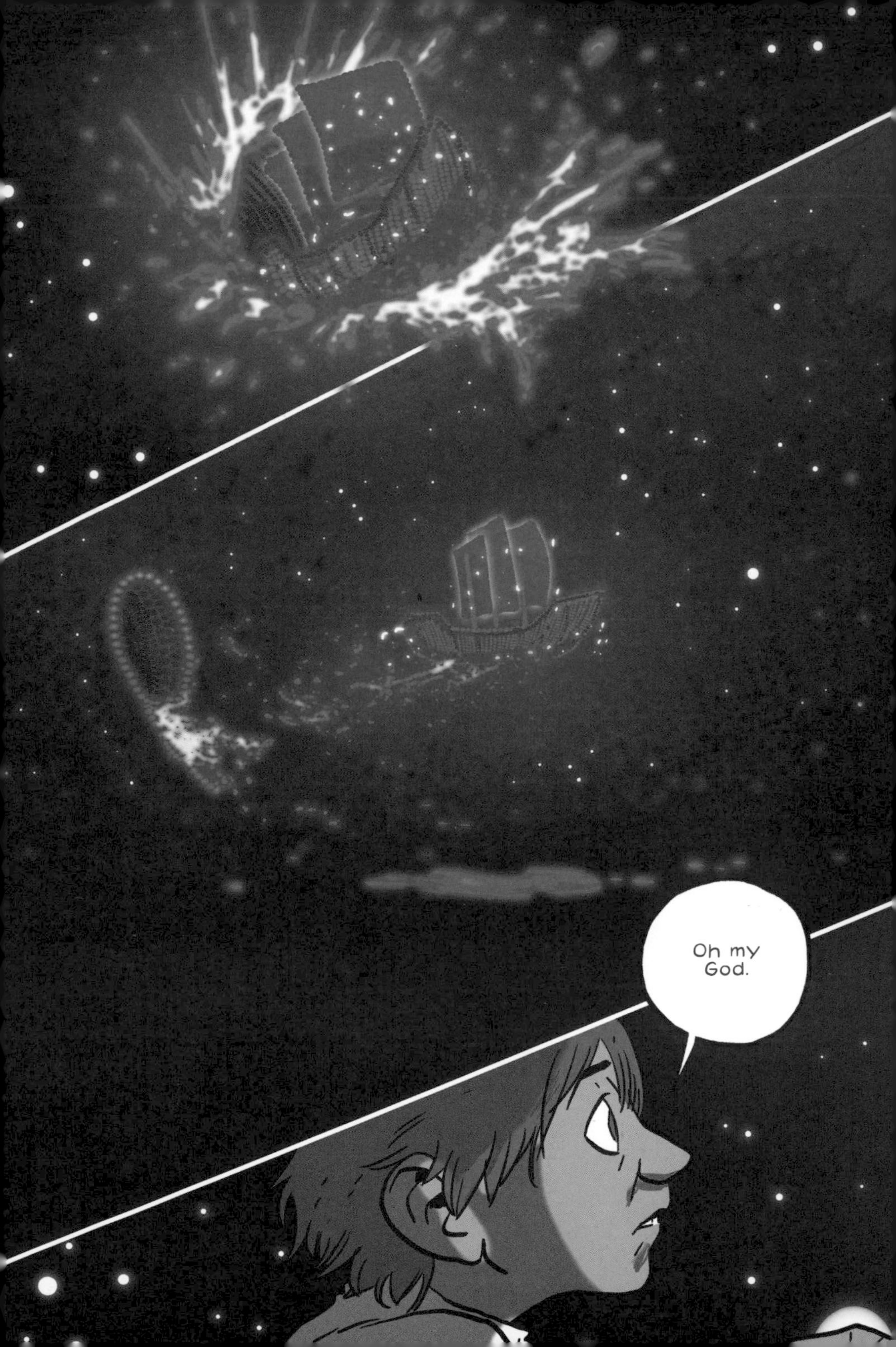
Oh my God.

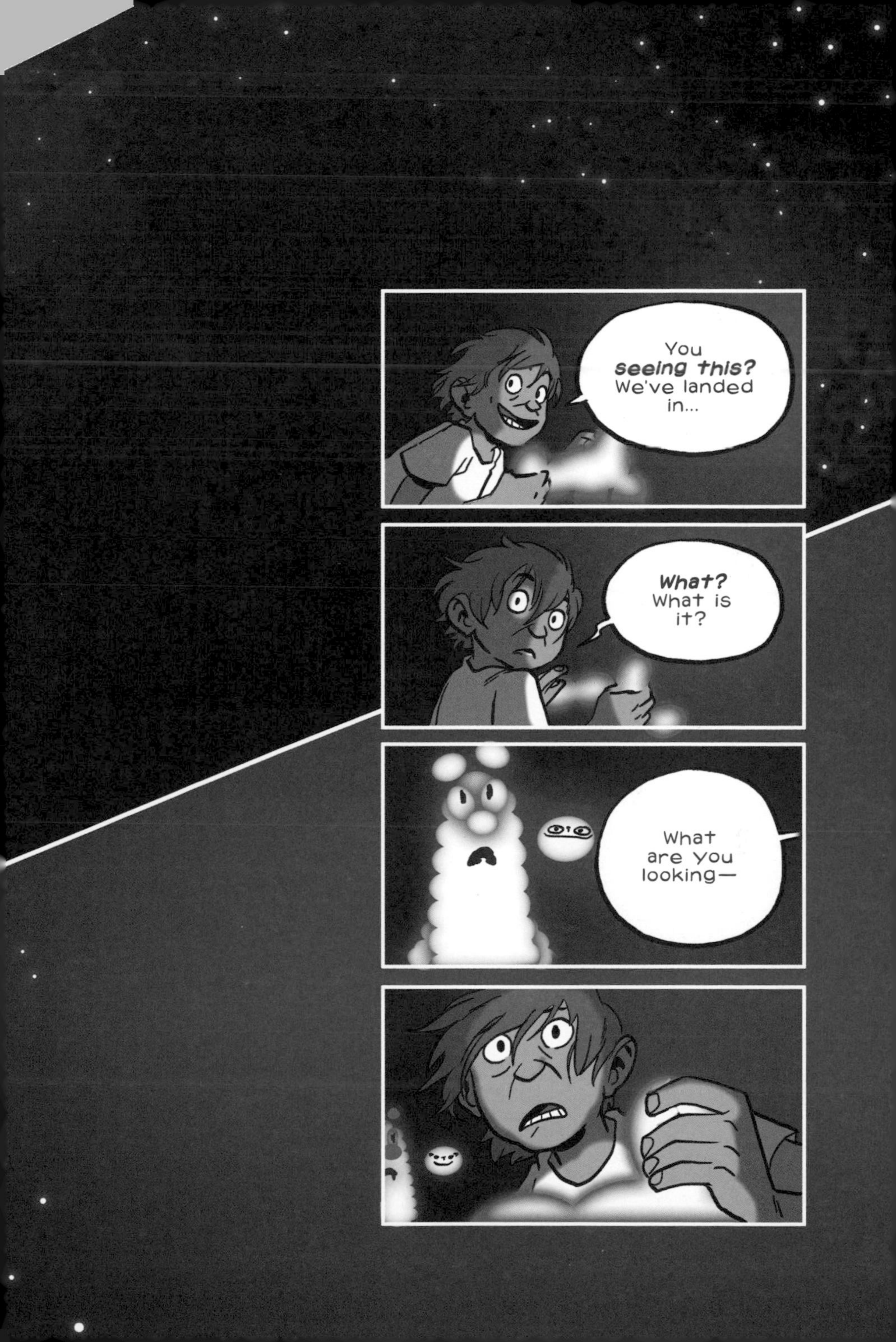
You seeing this? We've landed in...
What? What is it?
What are you looking—

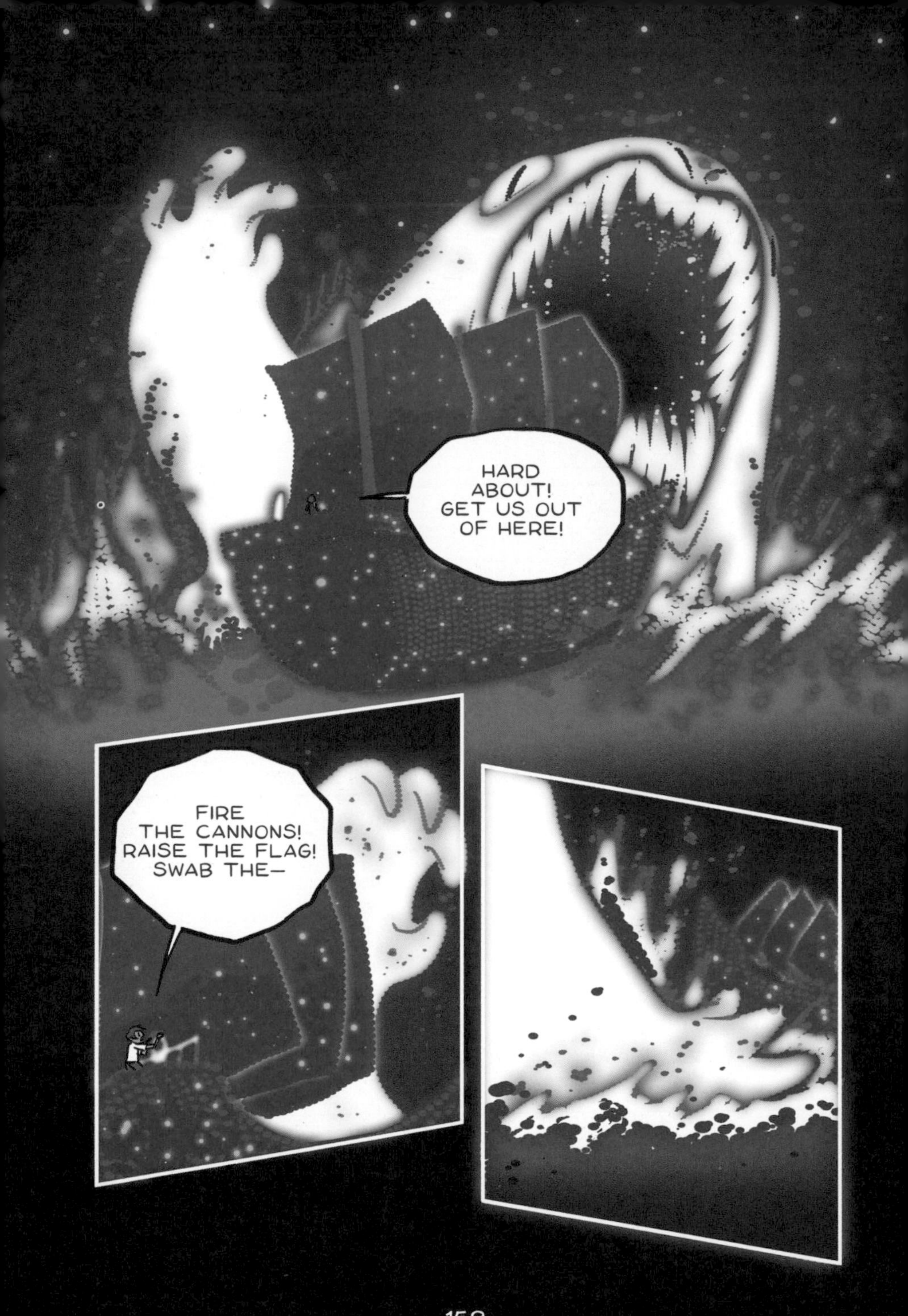
HARD ABOUT! GET US OUT OF HERE!
FIRE THE CANNONS! RAISE THE FLAG! SWAB THE–

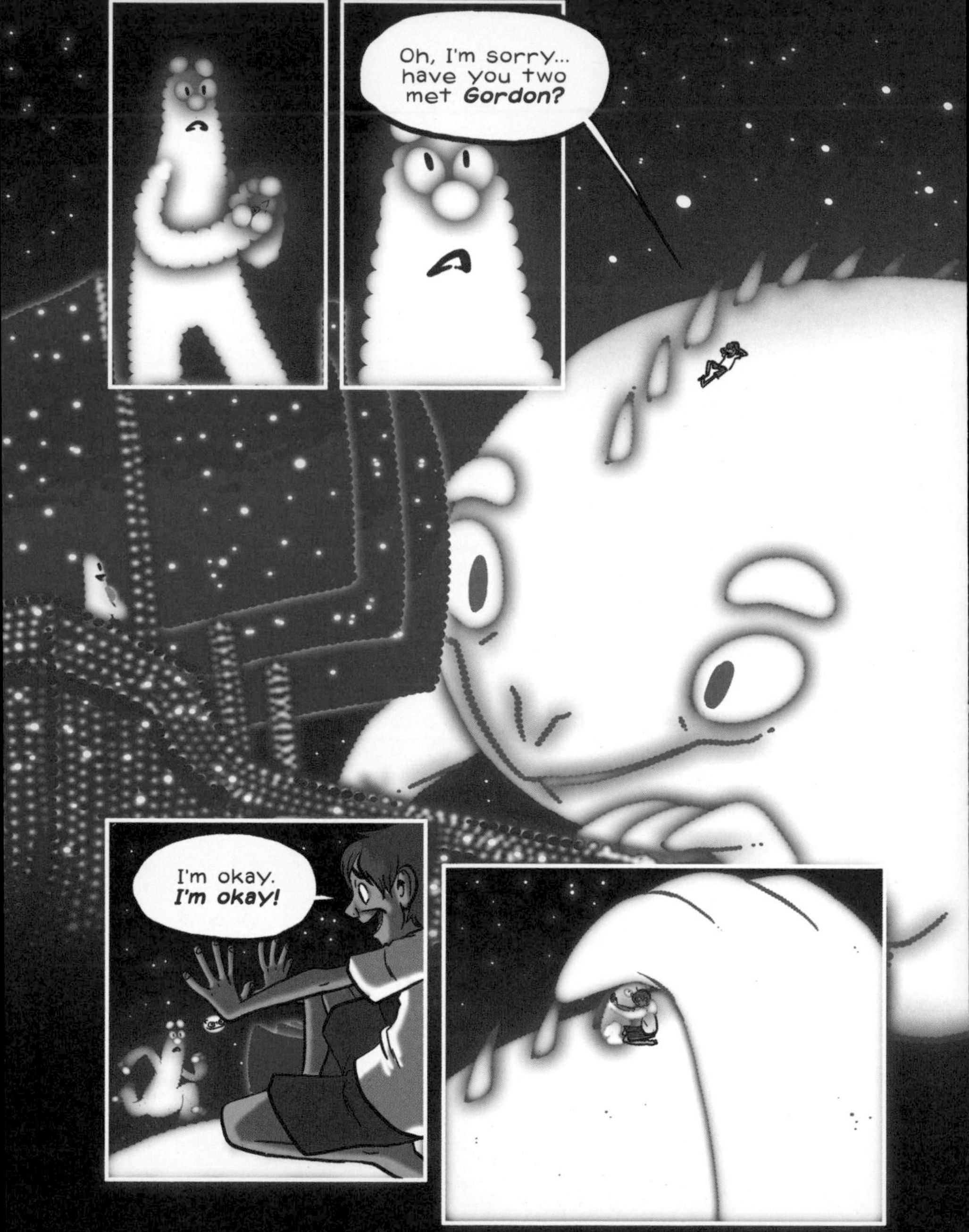
Oh, I'm sorry... have you two met *Gordon?*
I'm okay. *I'm okay!*

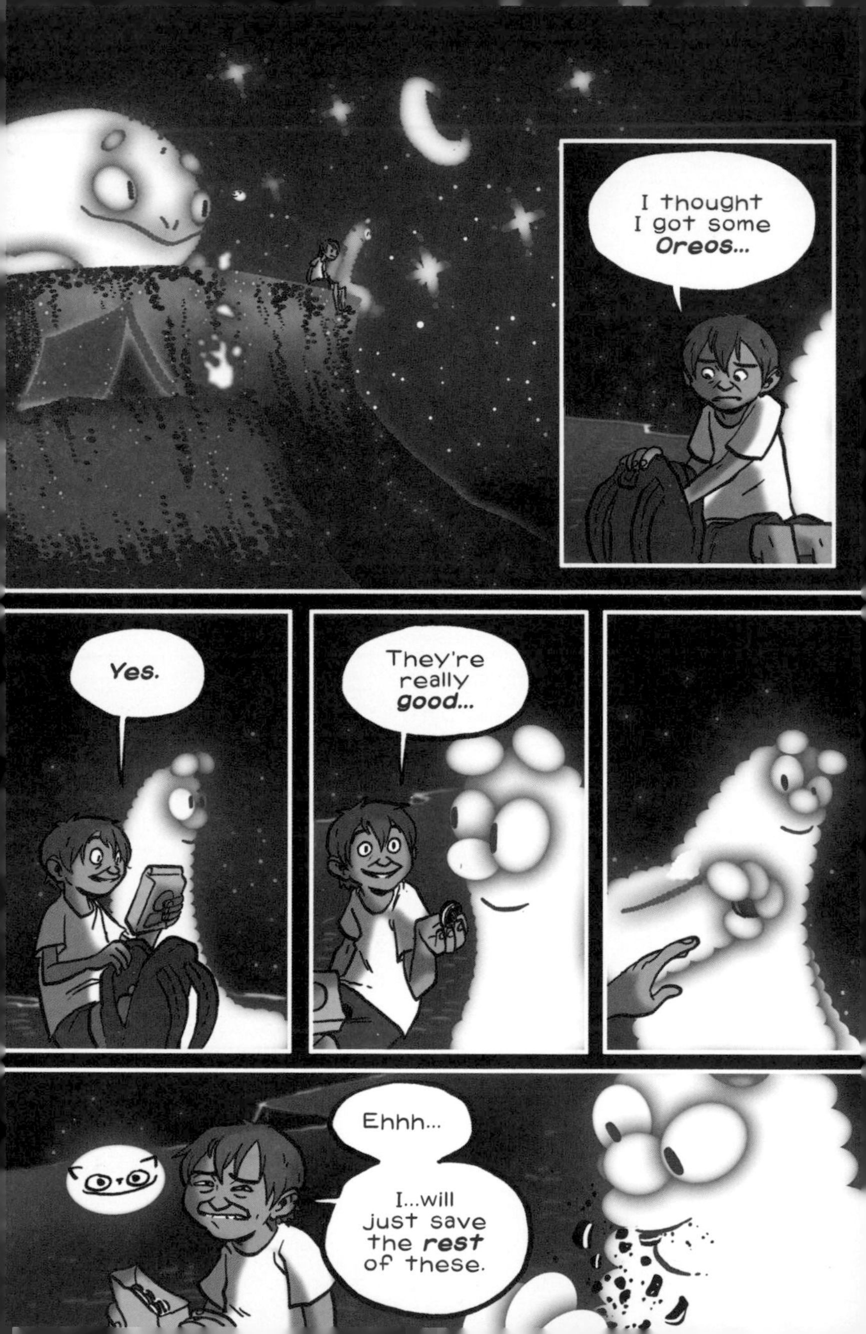
I thought I got some Oreos...
Yes.
They're really good...
Ehhh...
I...will just save the rest of these.

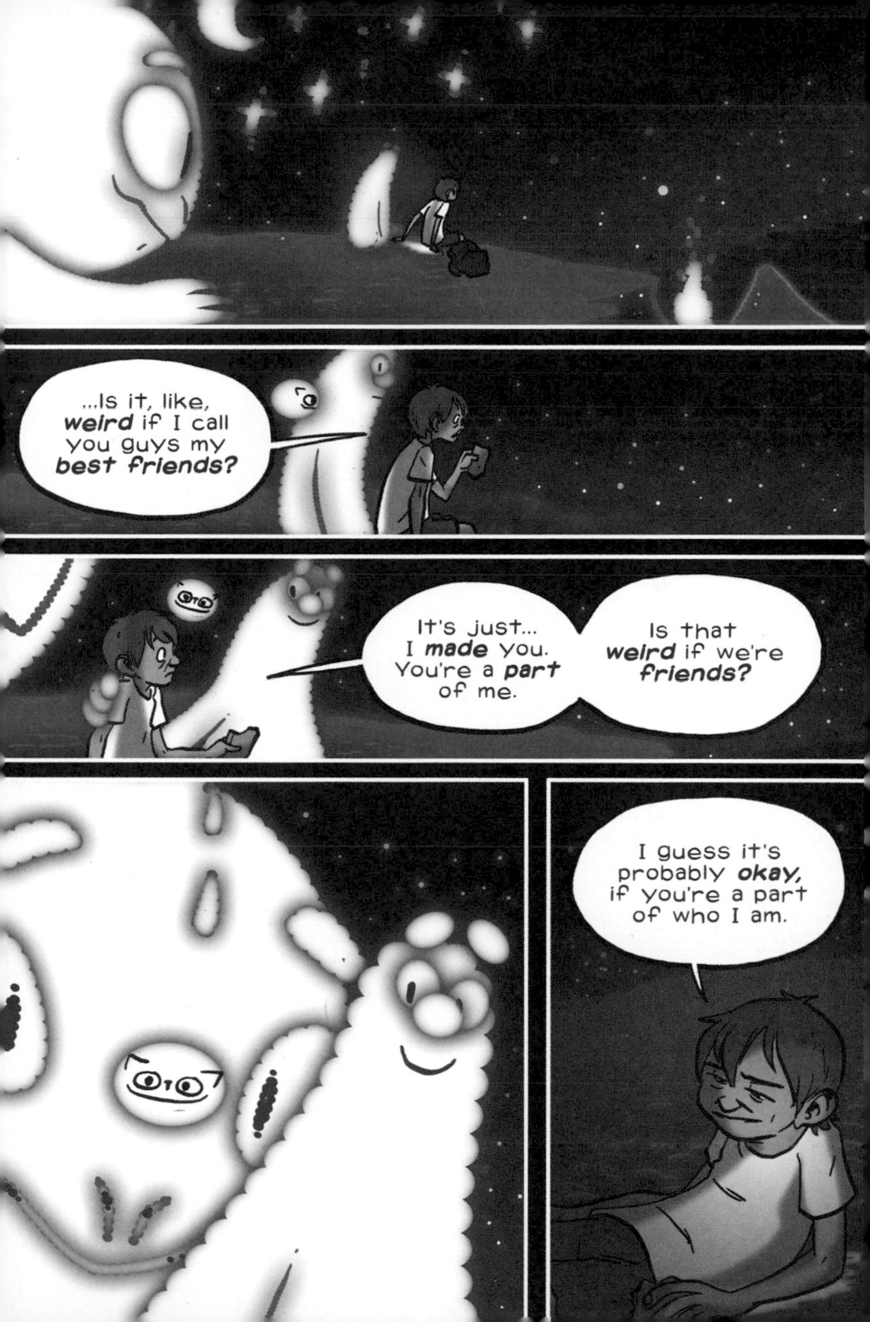

...Is it, like, **weird** if I call you guys my **best friends?**
It's just... I **made** you. You're a **part** of me.
Is that **weird** if we're **friends?**
I guess it's probably **okay,** if you're a part of who I am.

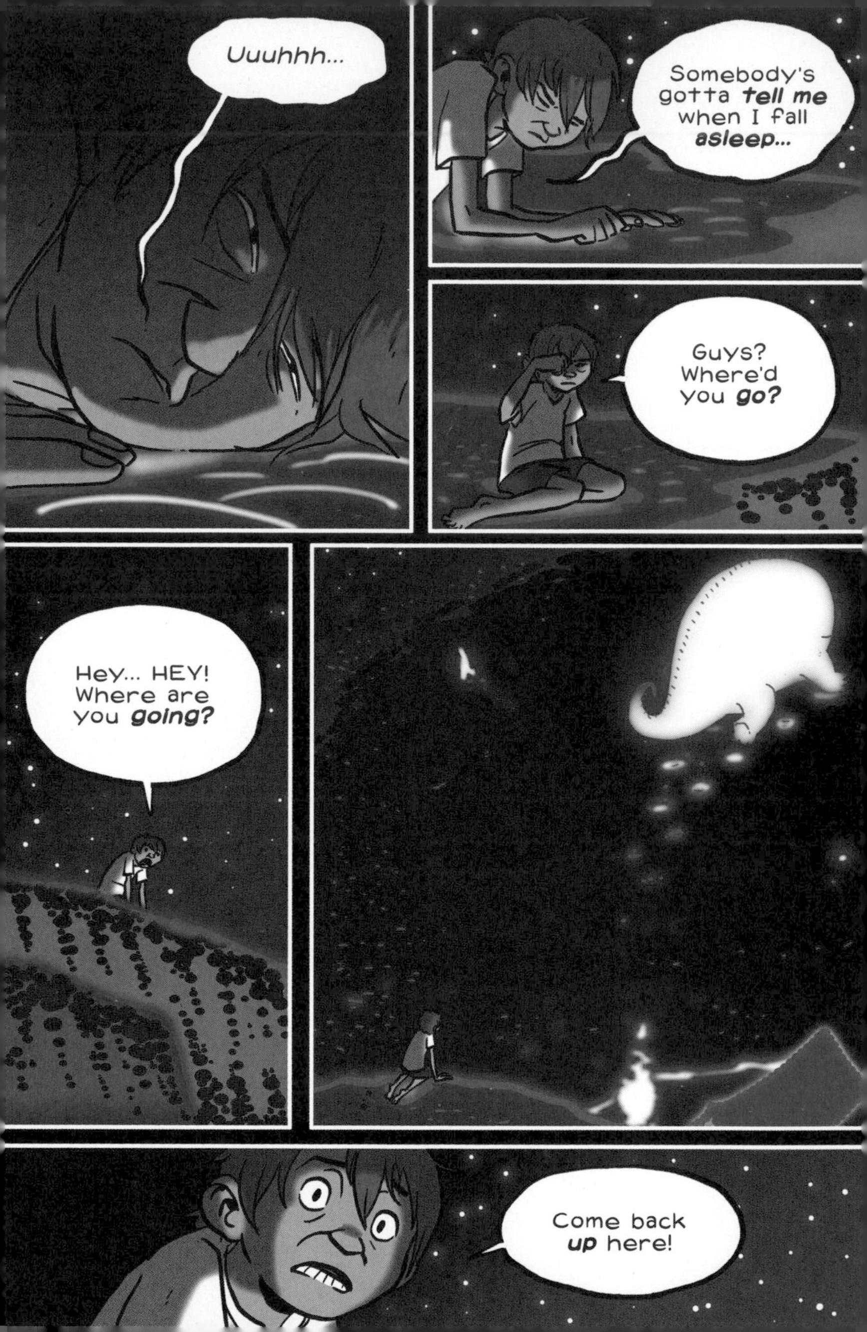
Uuuhhh...
Somebody's gotta **tell me** when I fall **asleep...**
Guys? Where'd you **go?**
Hey... HEY! Where are you **going?**
Come back **up** here!

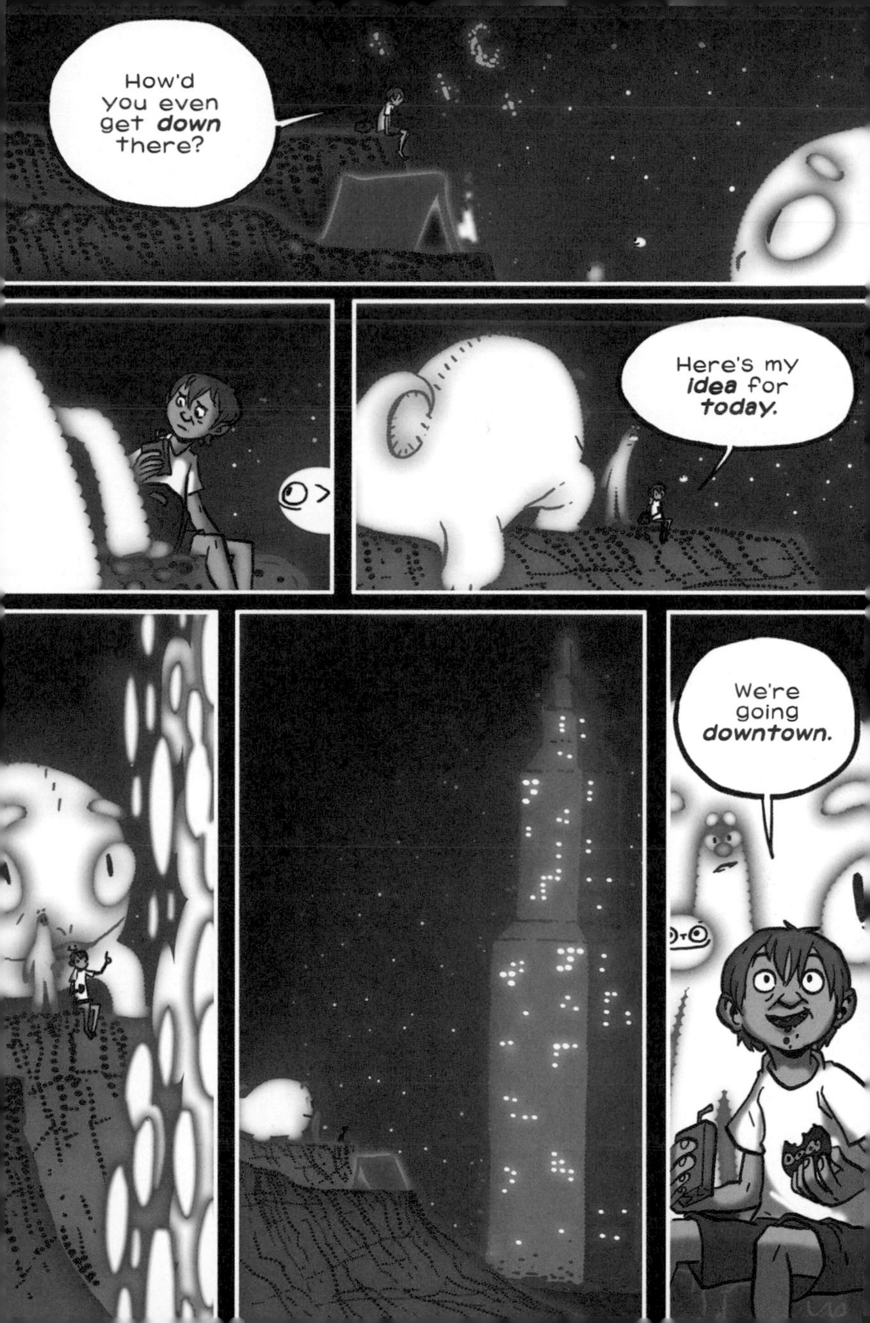
How'd you even get ***down*** there?
Here's my ***idea*** for ***today.***
We're going ***downtown.***

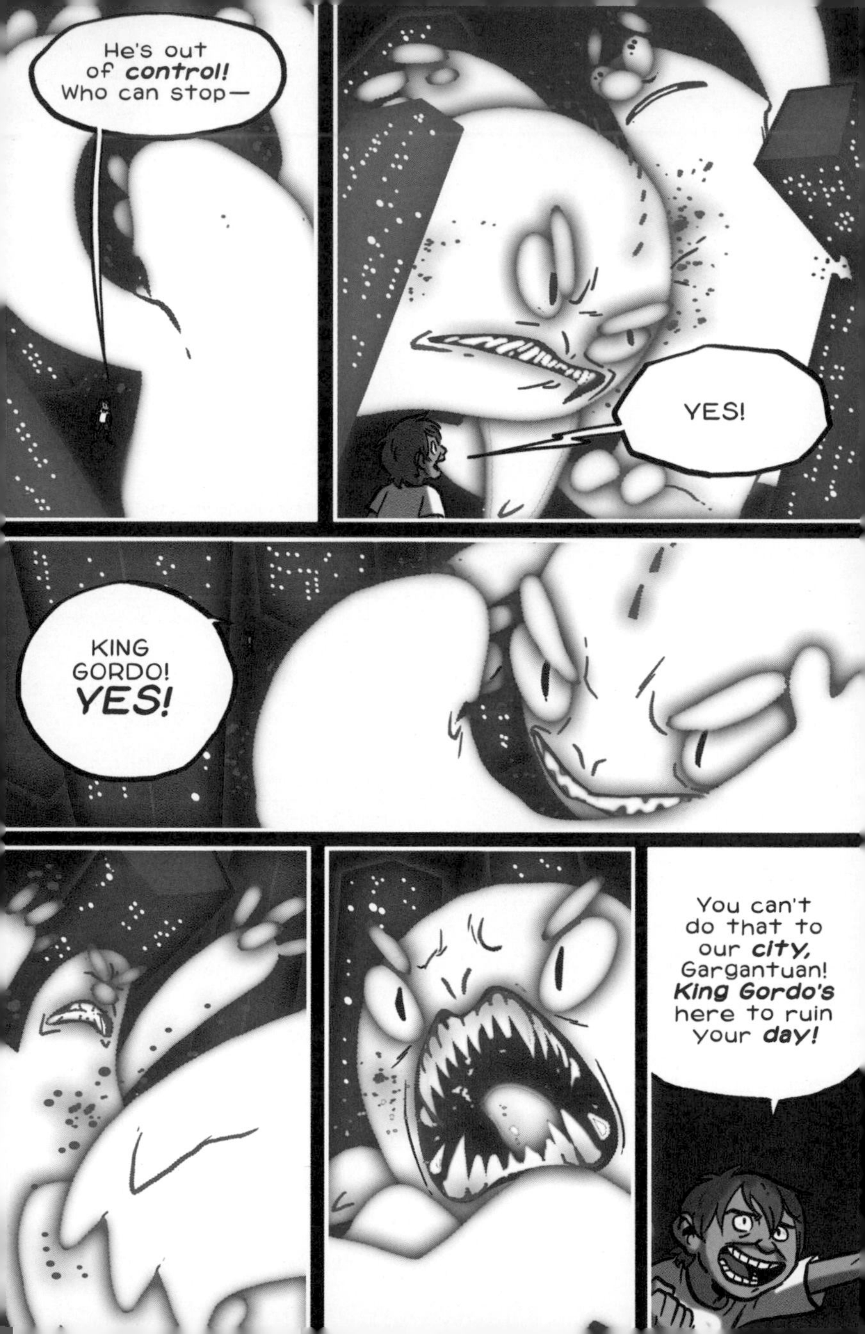
He's out of **control!** Who can stop—
YES!
KING GORDO! **YES!**
You can't do that to our ***city,*** Gargantuan! ***King Gordo's*** here to ruin your ***day!***

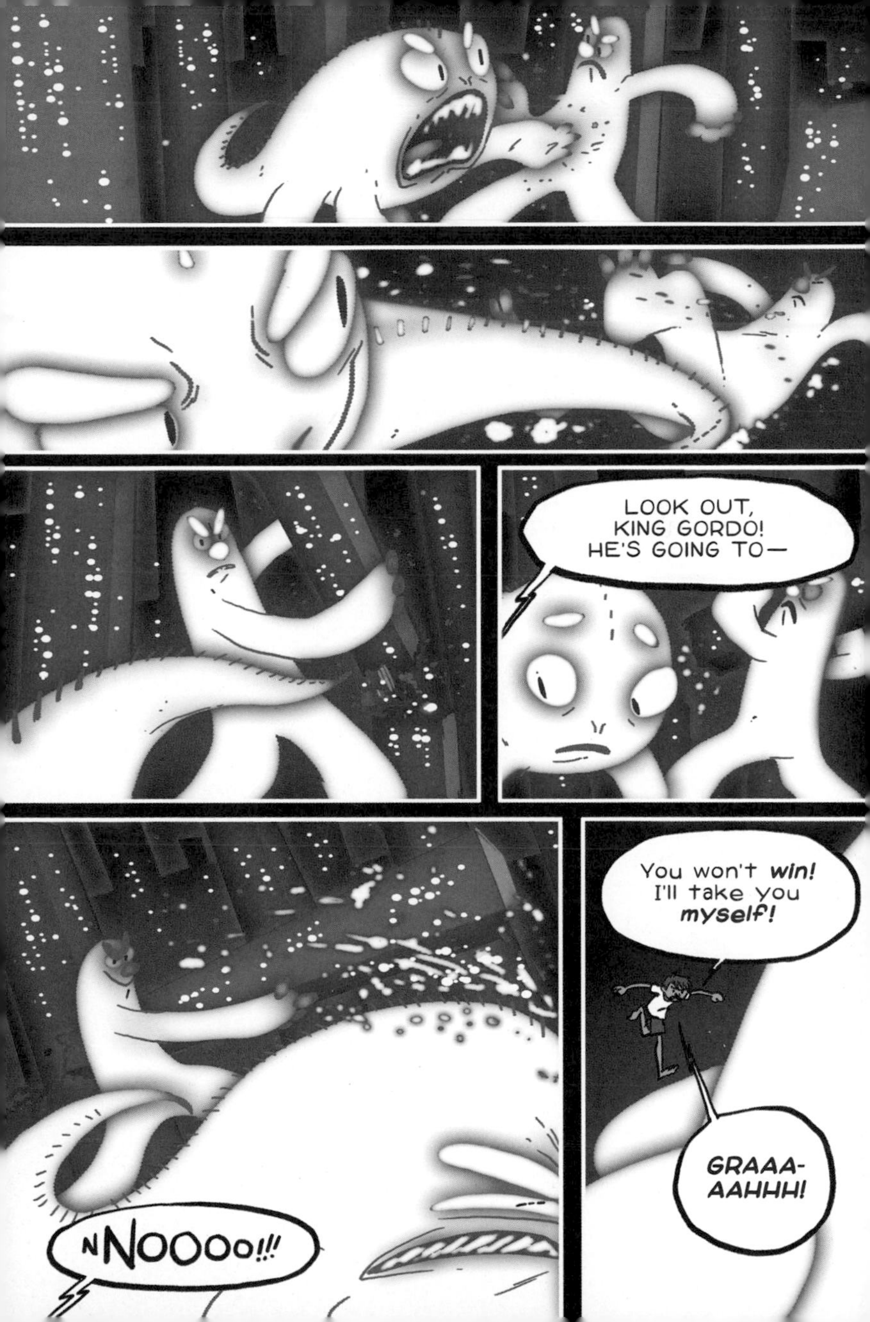
LOOK OUT, KING GORDO! HE'S GOING TO—
You won't *win!* I'll take you *myself!*
NNOOOO!!!
GRAAA-AAHHH!

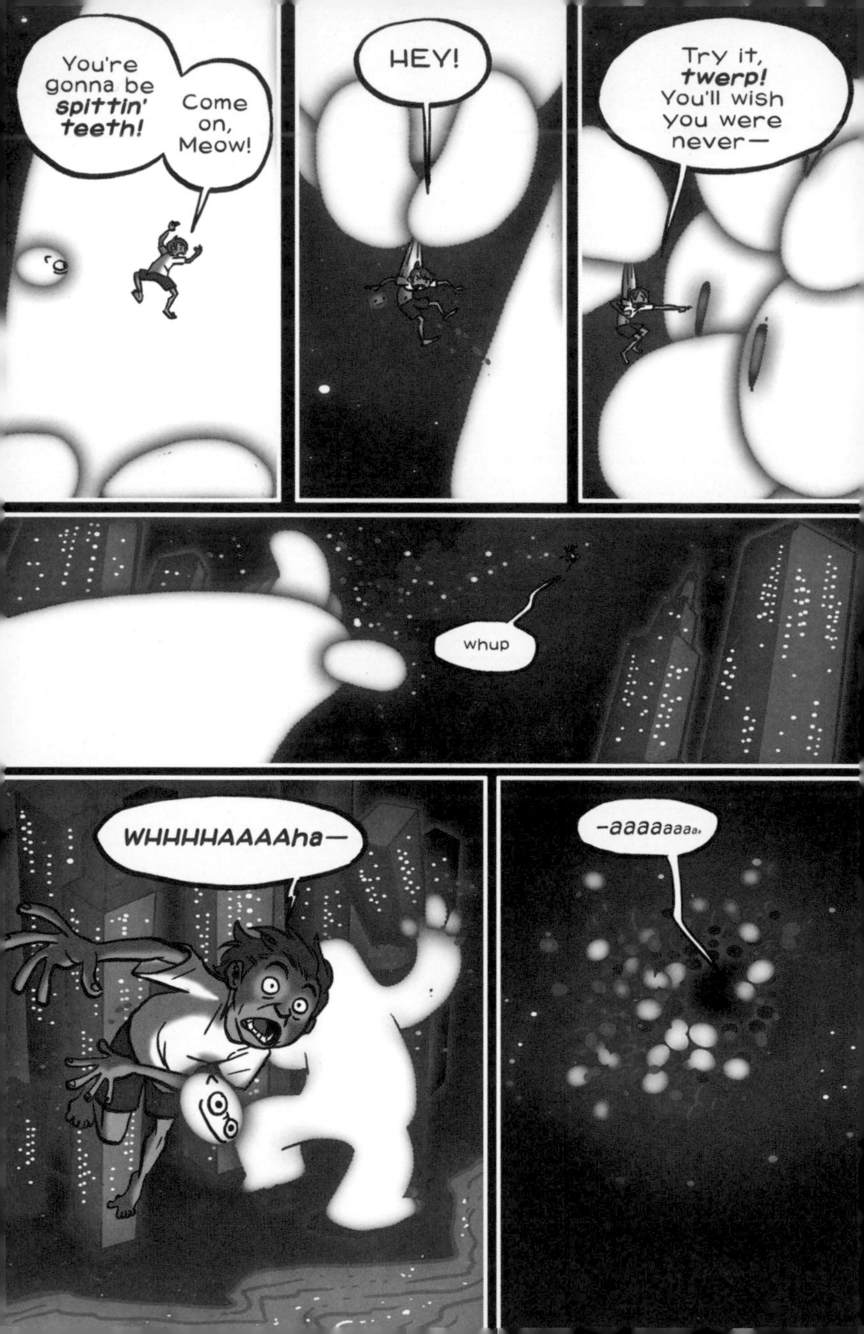
You're gonna be *spittin' teeth!*
Come on, Meow!
HEY!
Try it, *twerp!* You'll wish you were never—
whup
WHHHHAAAAha—
-aaaaaaaa.

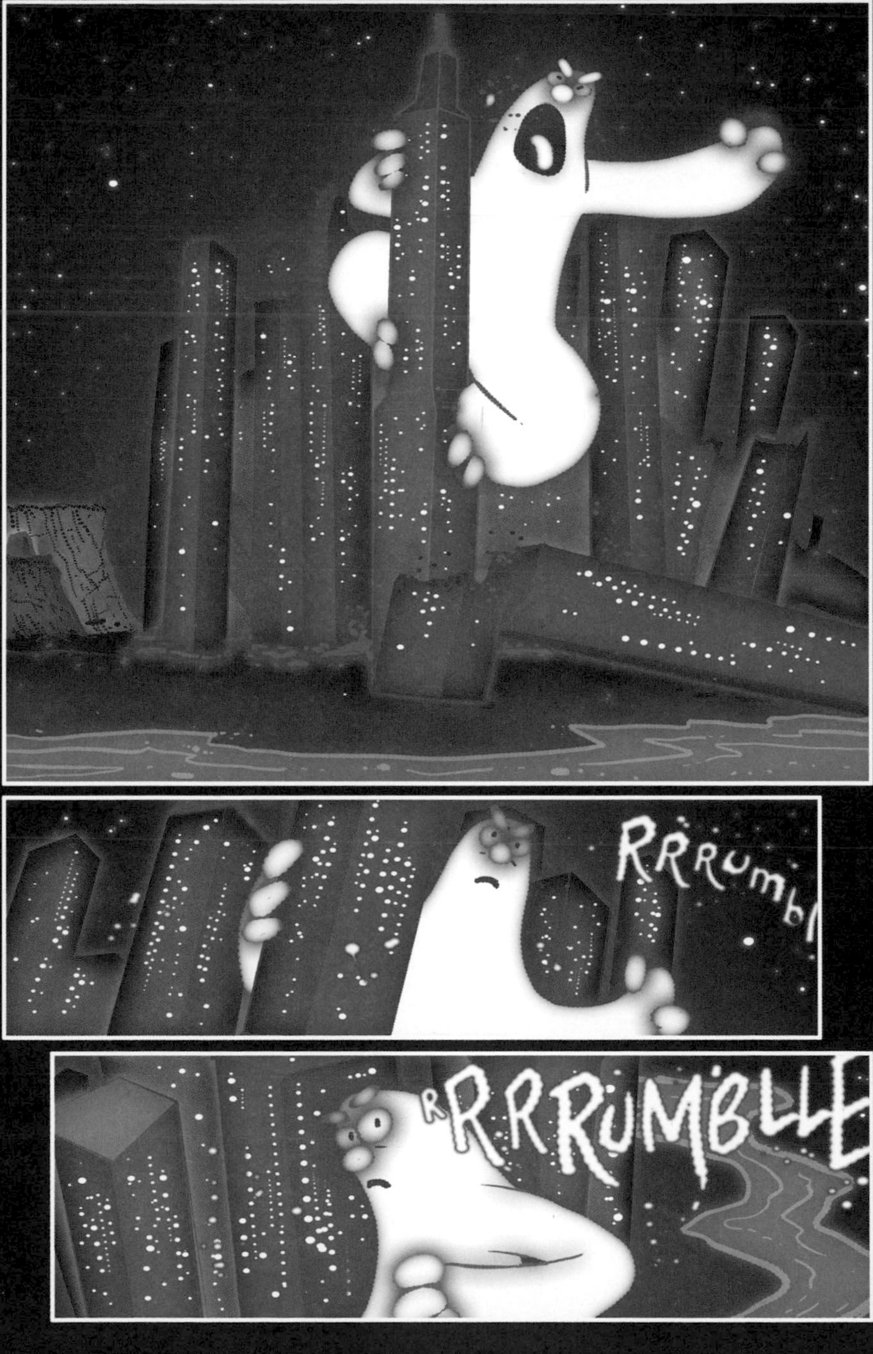
RRRUMBL
RRRRUMBLLE

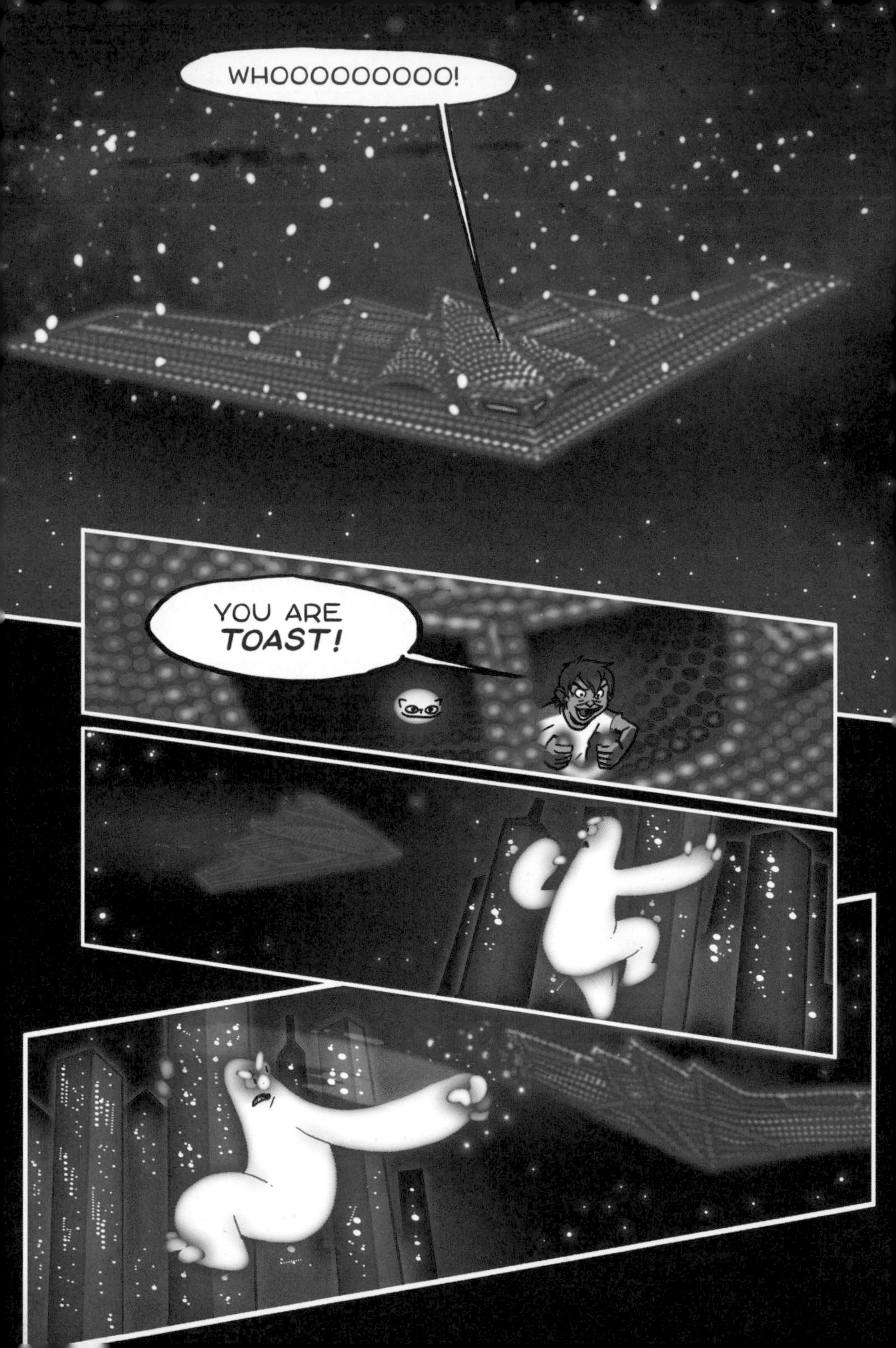
WHOOOOOOOOO!
YOU ARE *TOAST!*

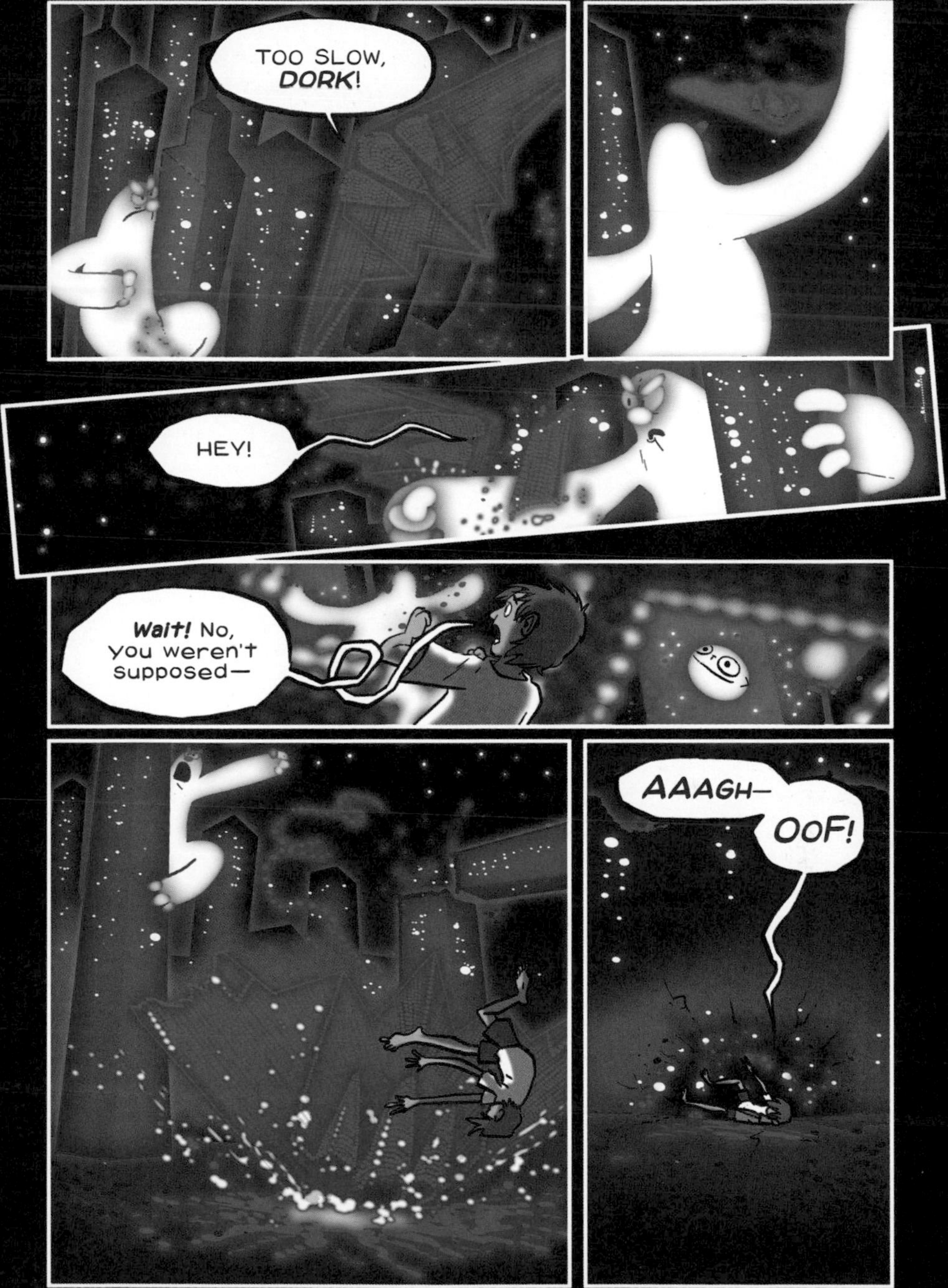
TOO SLOW, DORK!
HEY!
Wait! No, you weren't supposed—
AAAGH—
OOF!

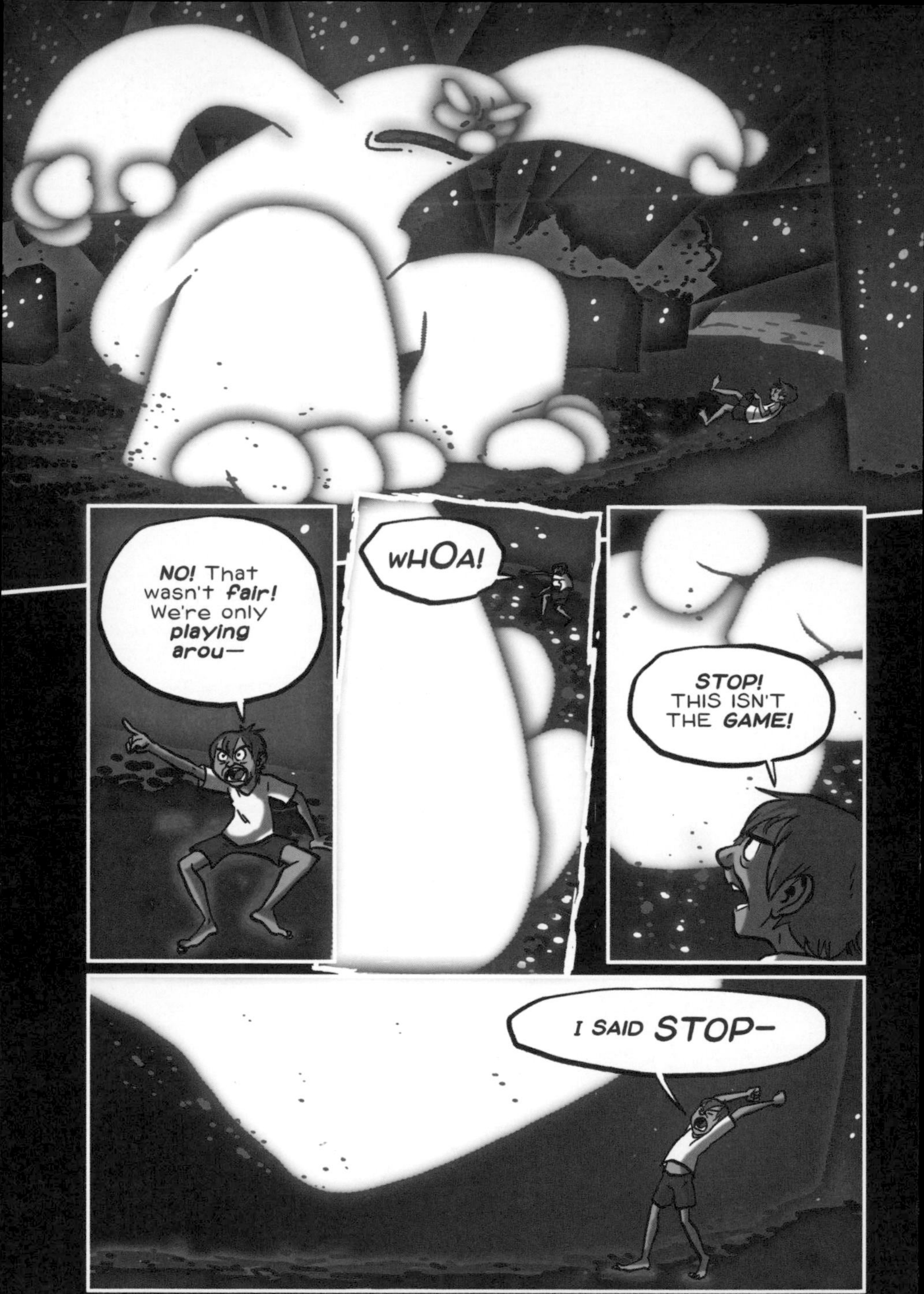
NO! That wasn't fair! We're only playing arou—
WHOA!
STOP! THIS ISN'T THE GAME!
I SAID STOP—

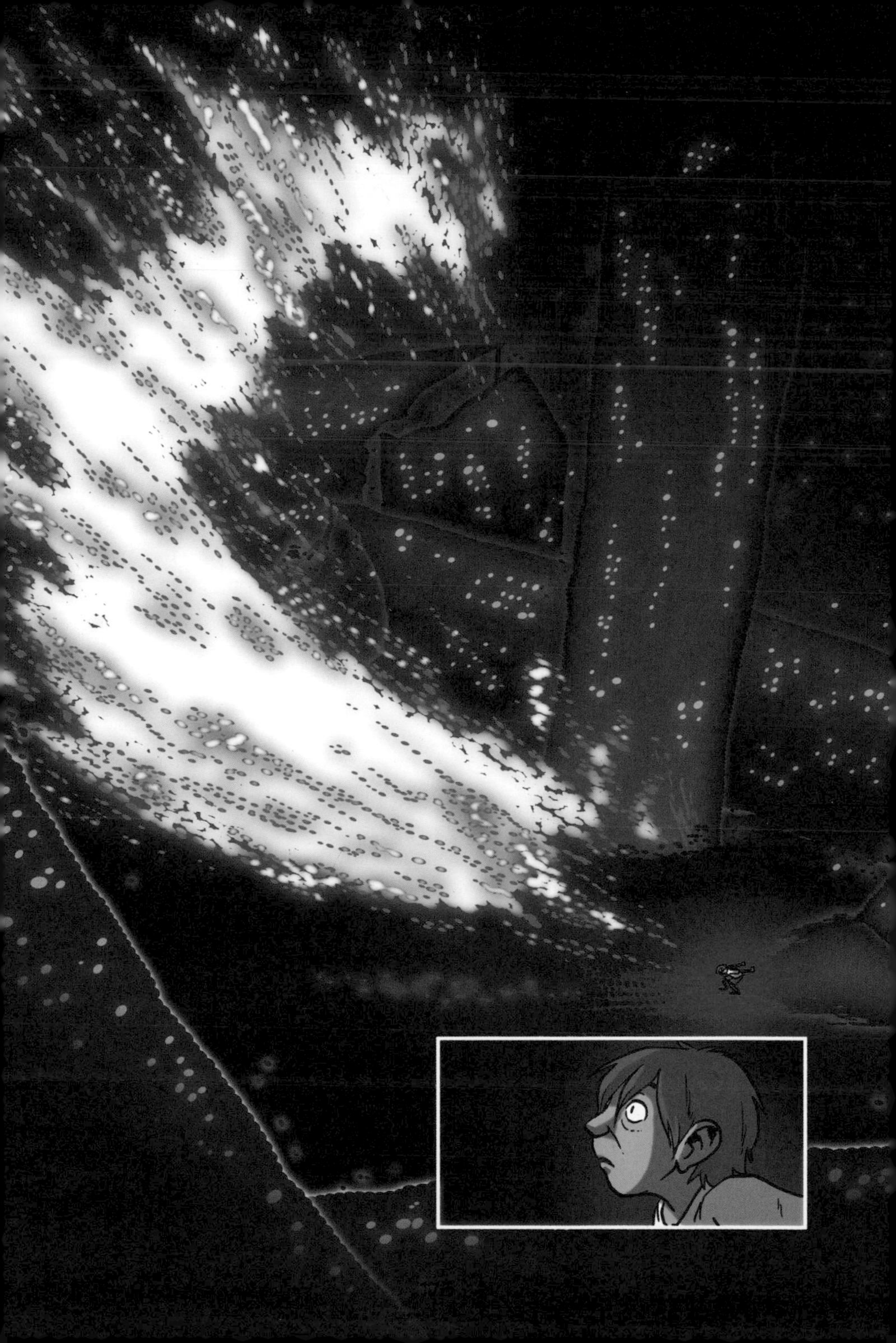

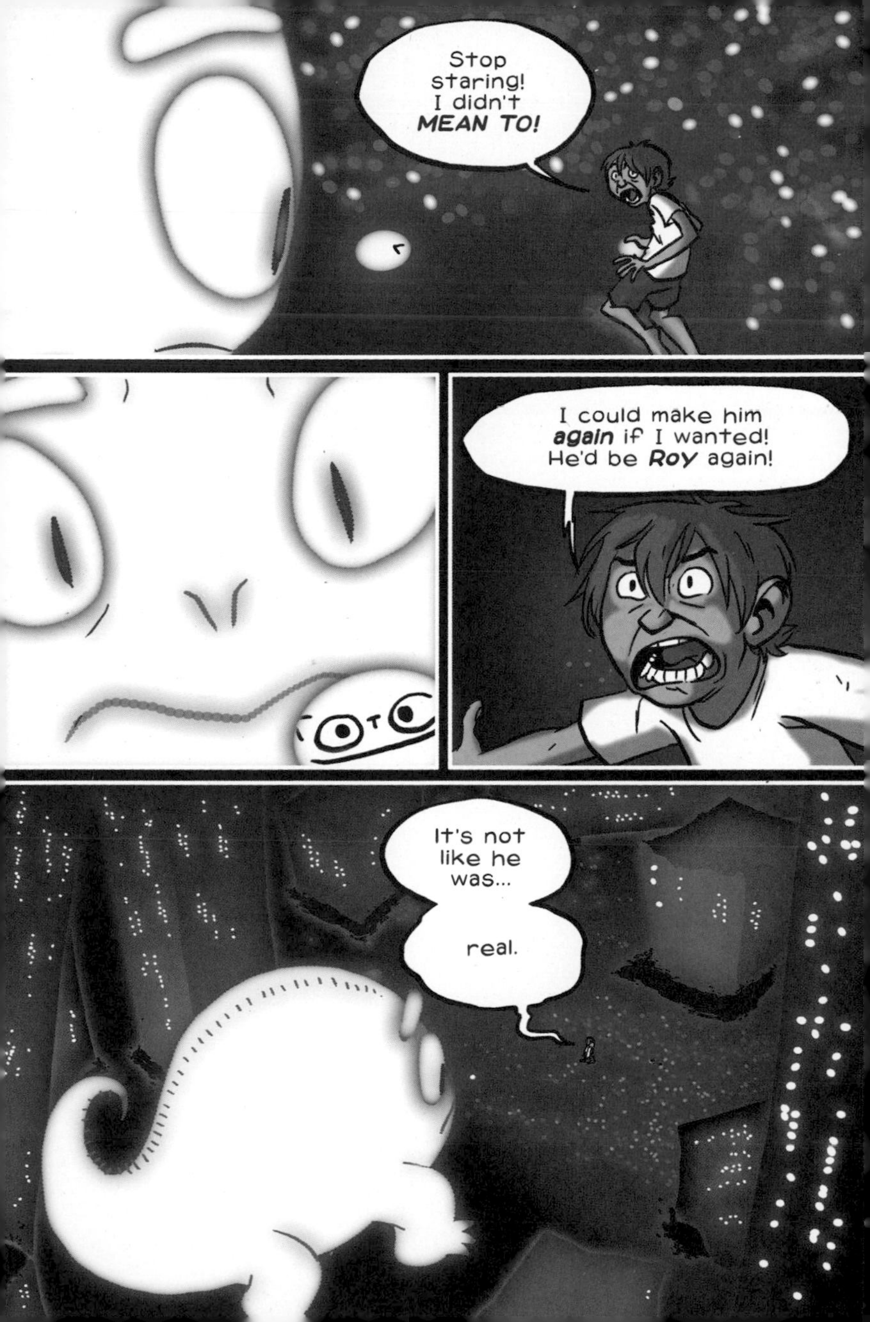
Stop staring! I didn't **MEAN TO!**
I could make him ***again*** if I wanted! He'd be ***Roy*** again!
It's not like he was...
real.

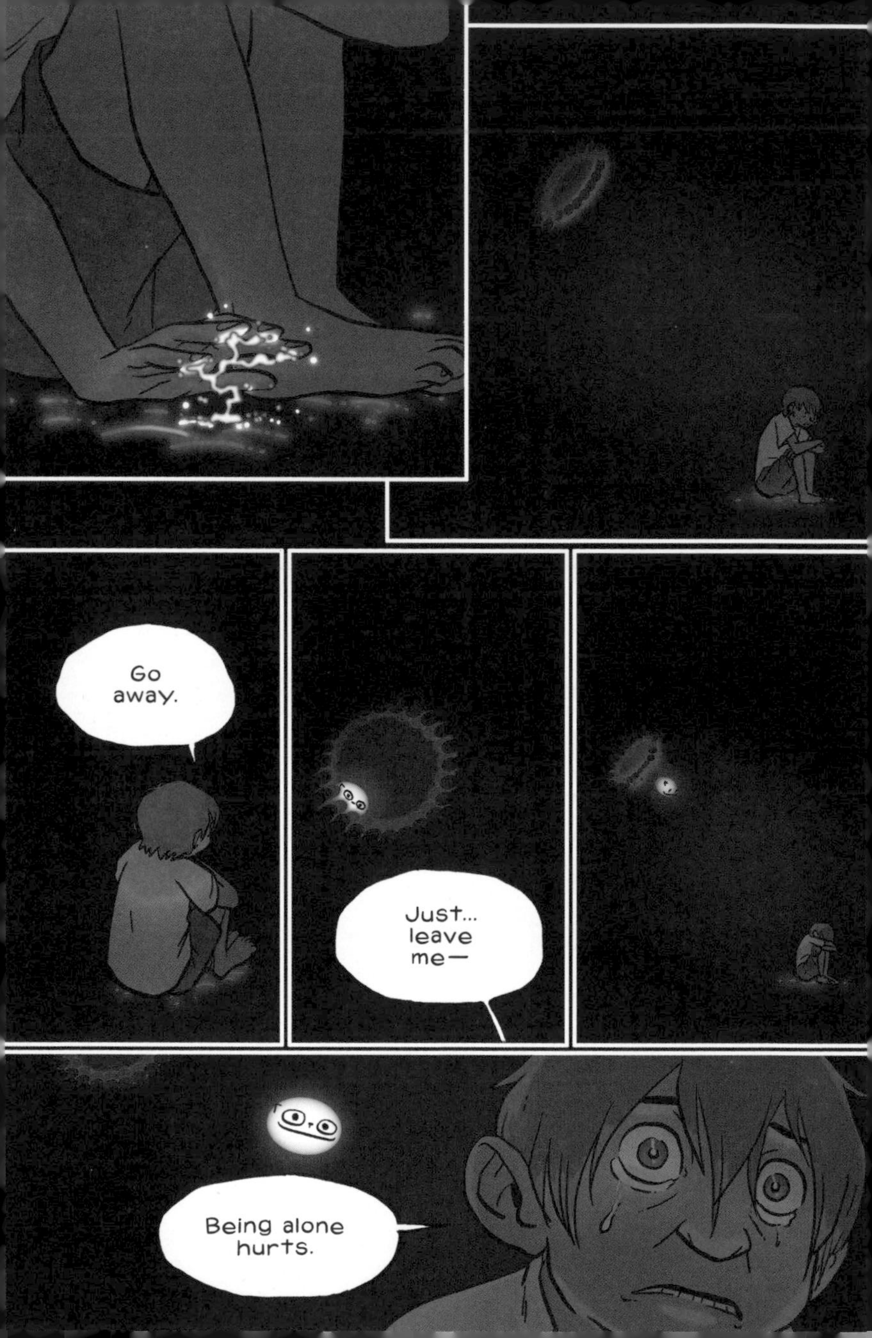
Go away.
Just... leave me—
Being alone hurts.

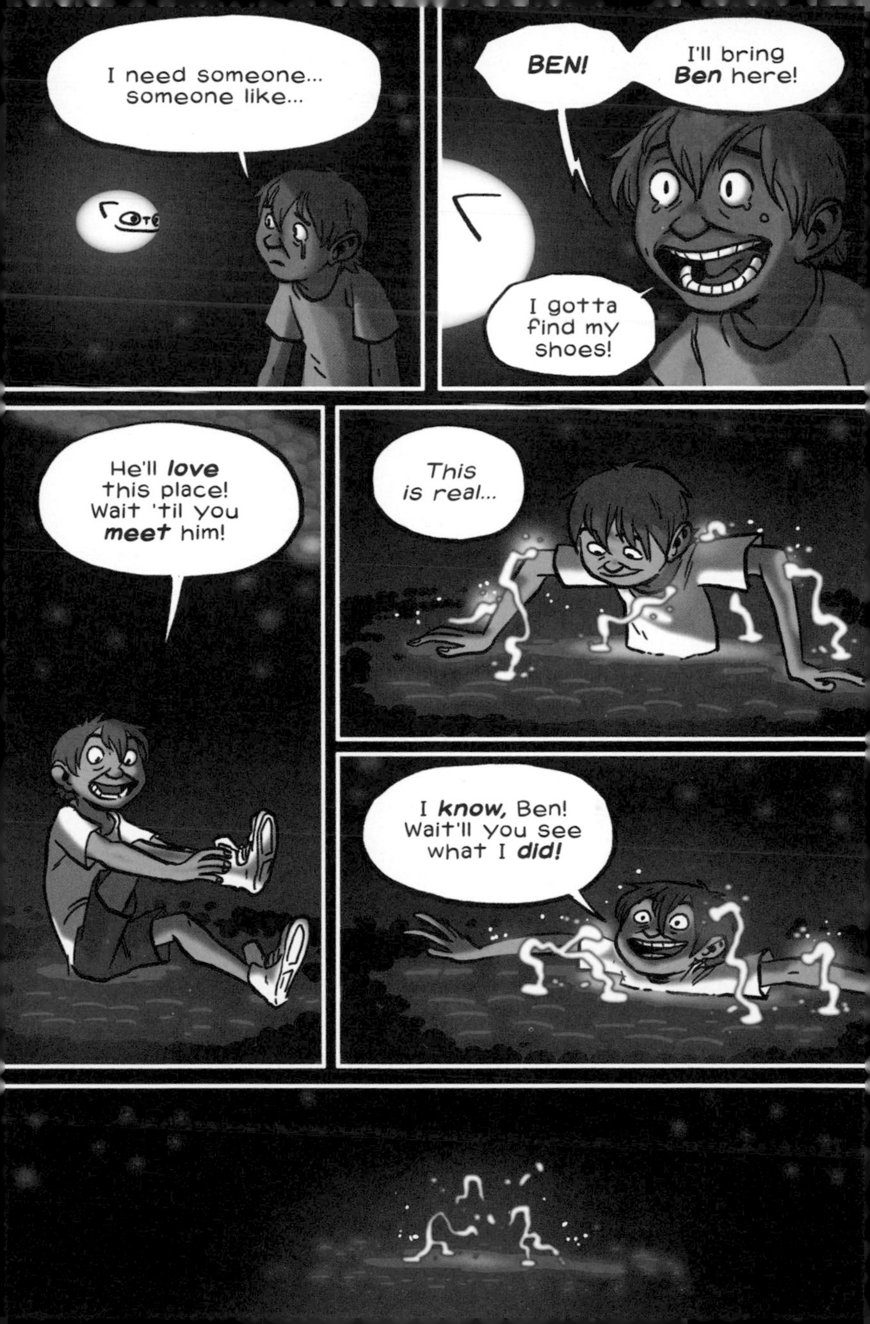
I need someone... someone like...
BEN!
I'll bring **Ben** here!
I gotta find my shoes!
He'll **love** this place! Wait 'til you **meet** him!
*This is real...*
I **know,** Ben! Wait'll you see what I **did!**

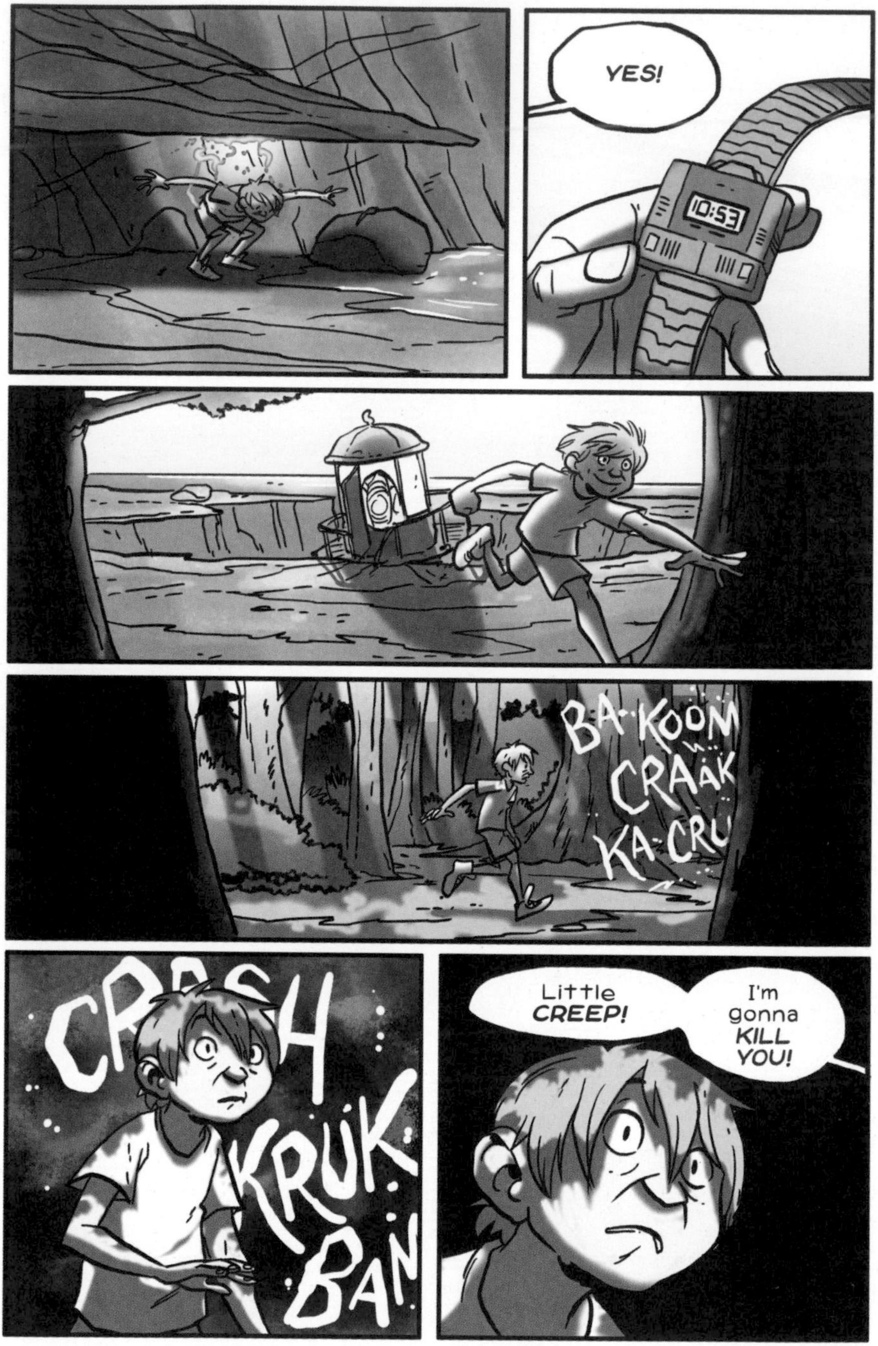
YES!
10:53
BA-KOOM
CRAAK
KA-CRU
CRASH
KRUK
BAN
Little CREEP!
I'm gonna KILL YOU!

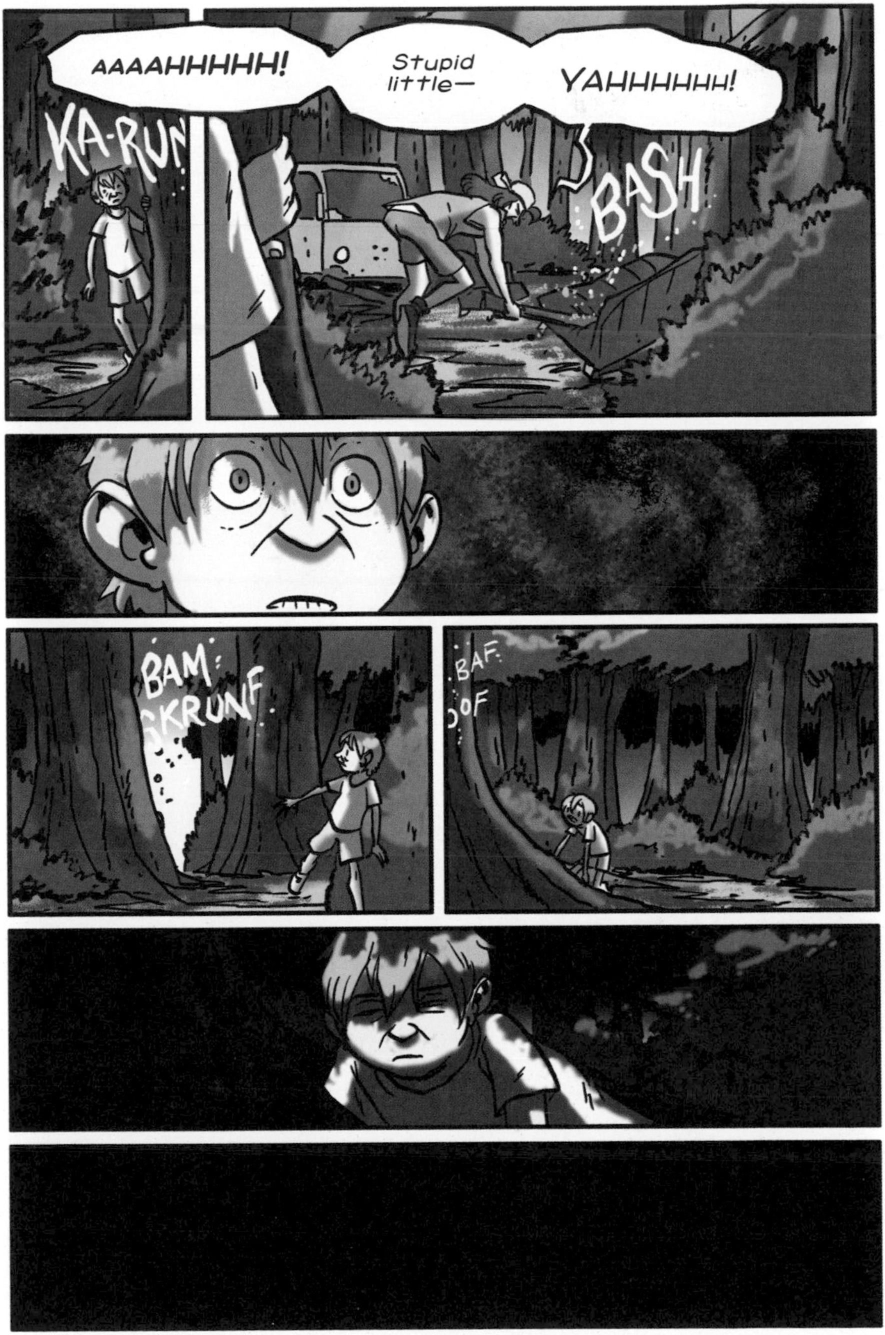
AAAAHHHHH!
KA-RUN
Stupid little—
YAHHHHHH!
BASH
BAM
SKRUNF
BAF
OOF

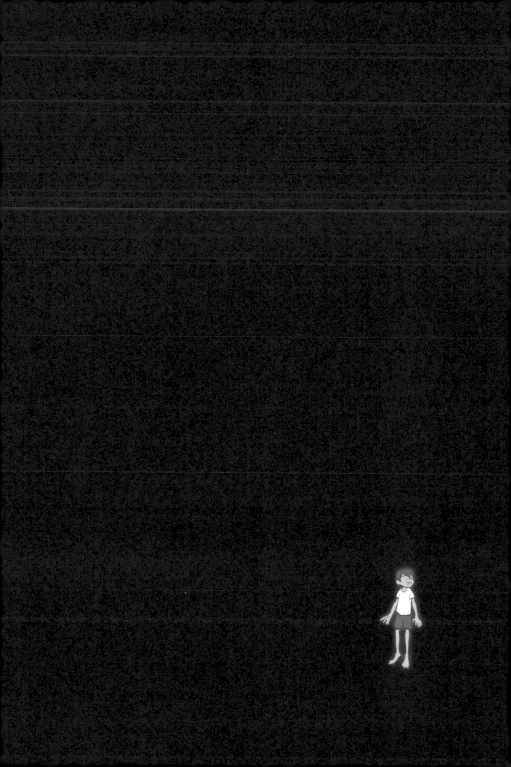

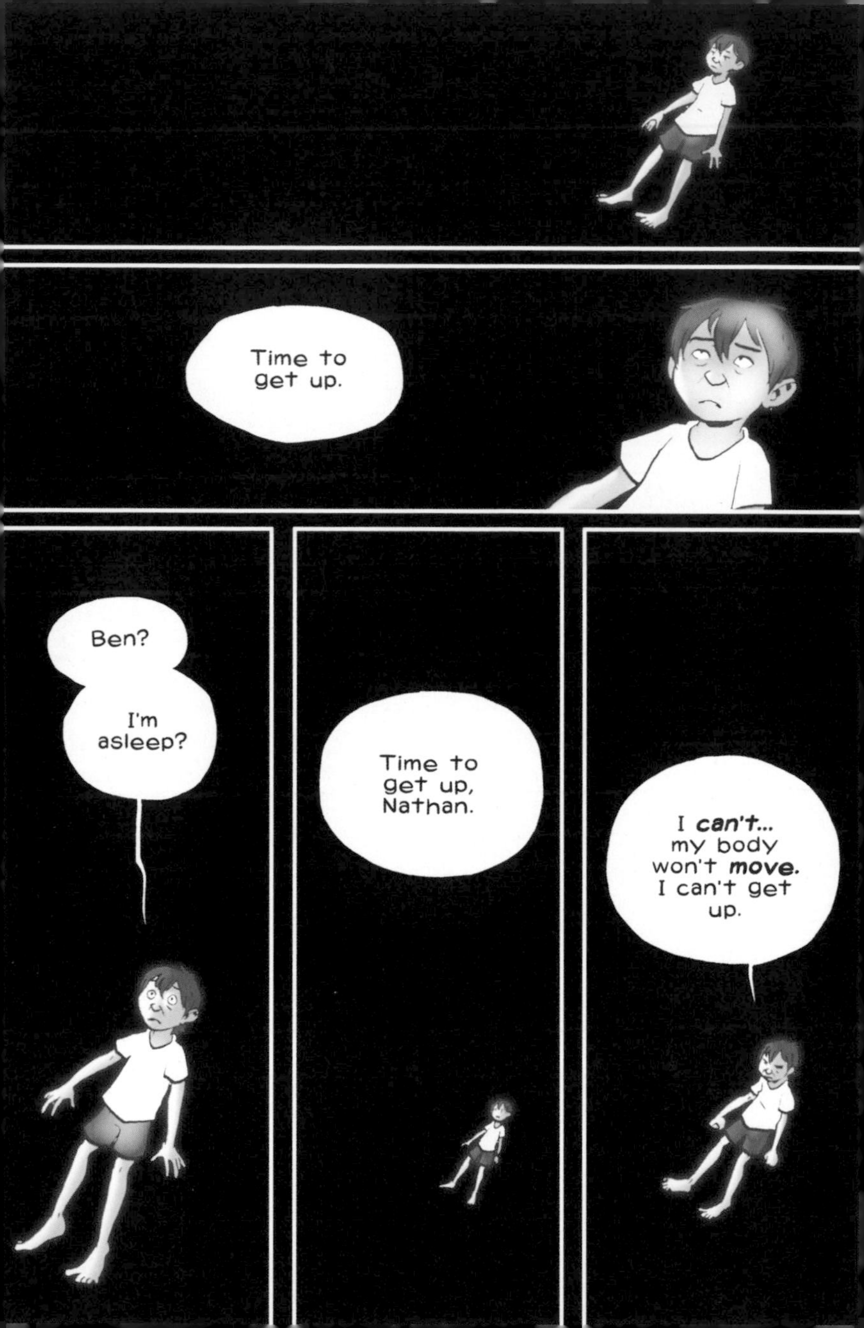
Time to get up.
Ben?
I'm asleep?
Time to get up, Nathan.
I *can't*... my body won't **move.** I can't get up.

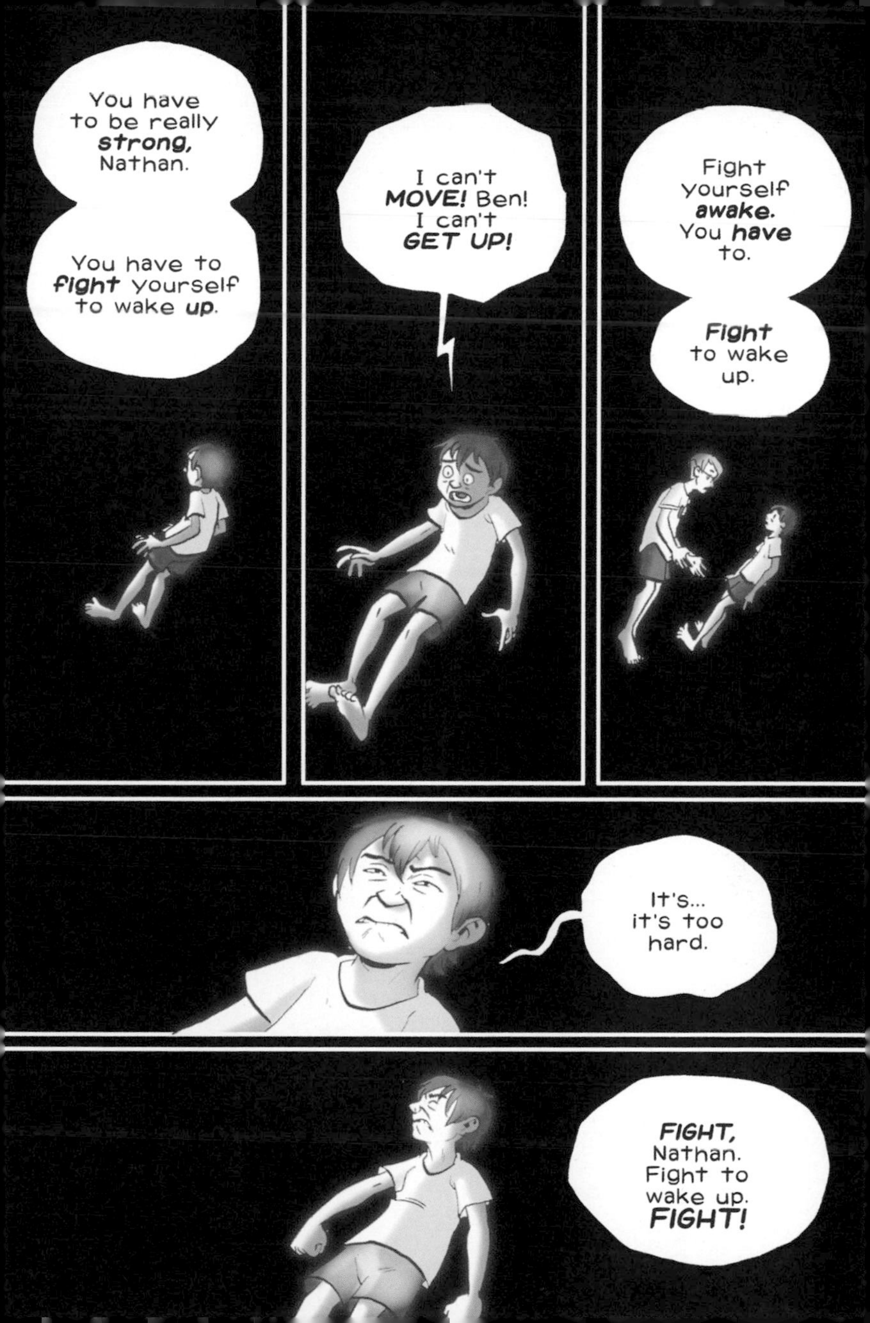
You have to be really **strong,** Nathan.
You have to **fight** yourself to wake **up**.
I can't **MOVE!** Ben! I can't **GET UP!**
Fight yourself **awake.** You **have** to.
**Fight** to wake up.
It's... it's too hard.
**FIGHT,** Nathan. Fight to wake up. **FIGHT!**

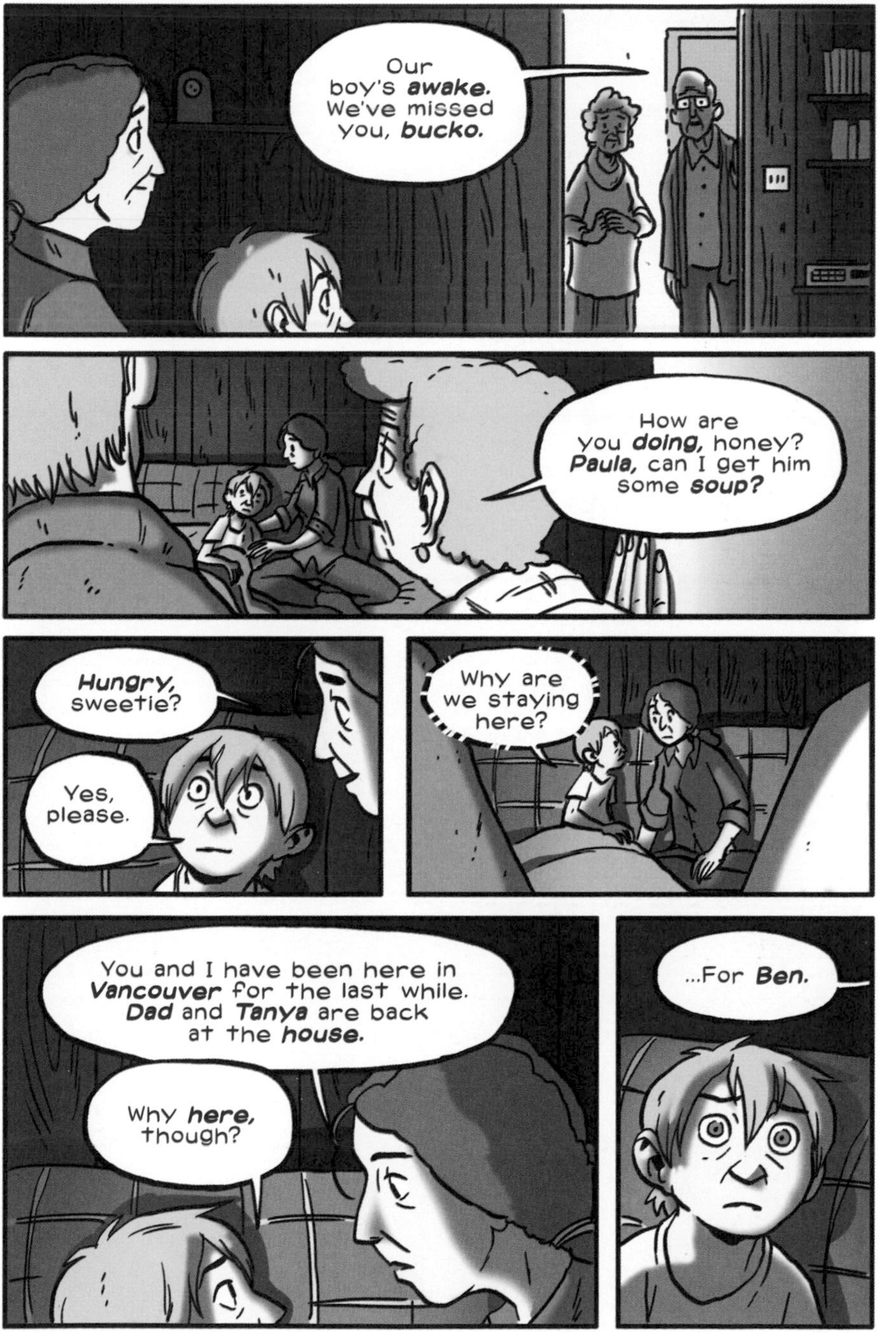
Our boy's **awake.** We've missed you, **bucko.**
How are you **doing,** honey? **Paula,** can I get him some **soup?**
**Hungry,** sweetie?
Yes, please.
Why are we staying here?
You and I have been here in **Vancouver** for the last while. **Dad** and **Tanya** are back at the **house.**
Why **here,** though?
...For **Ben.**

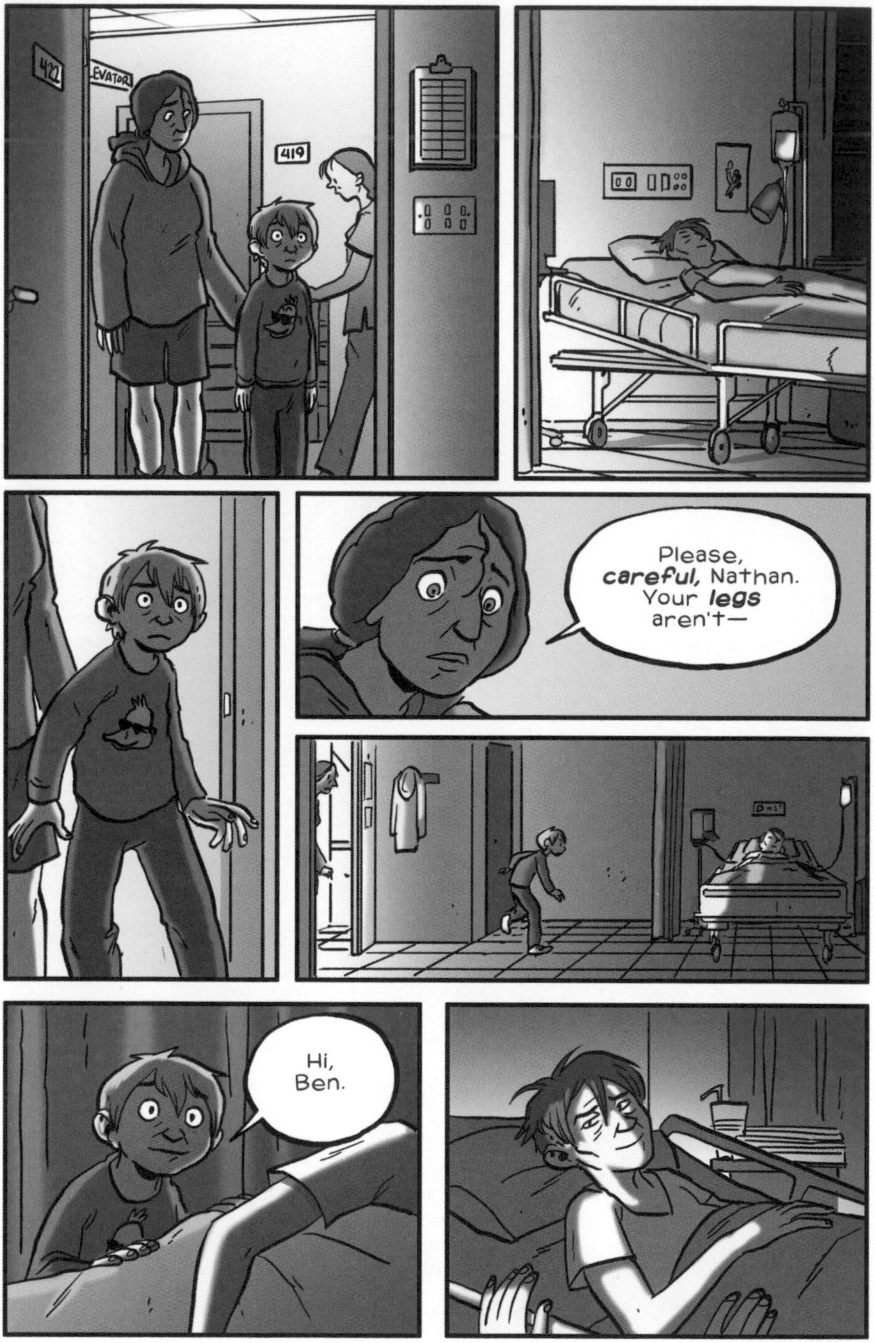
422
EVATOR
419
Please, **careful,** Nathan. Your **legs** aren't—
Hi, Ben.

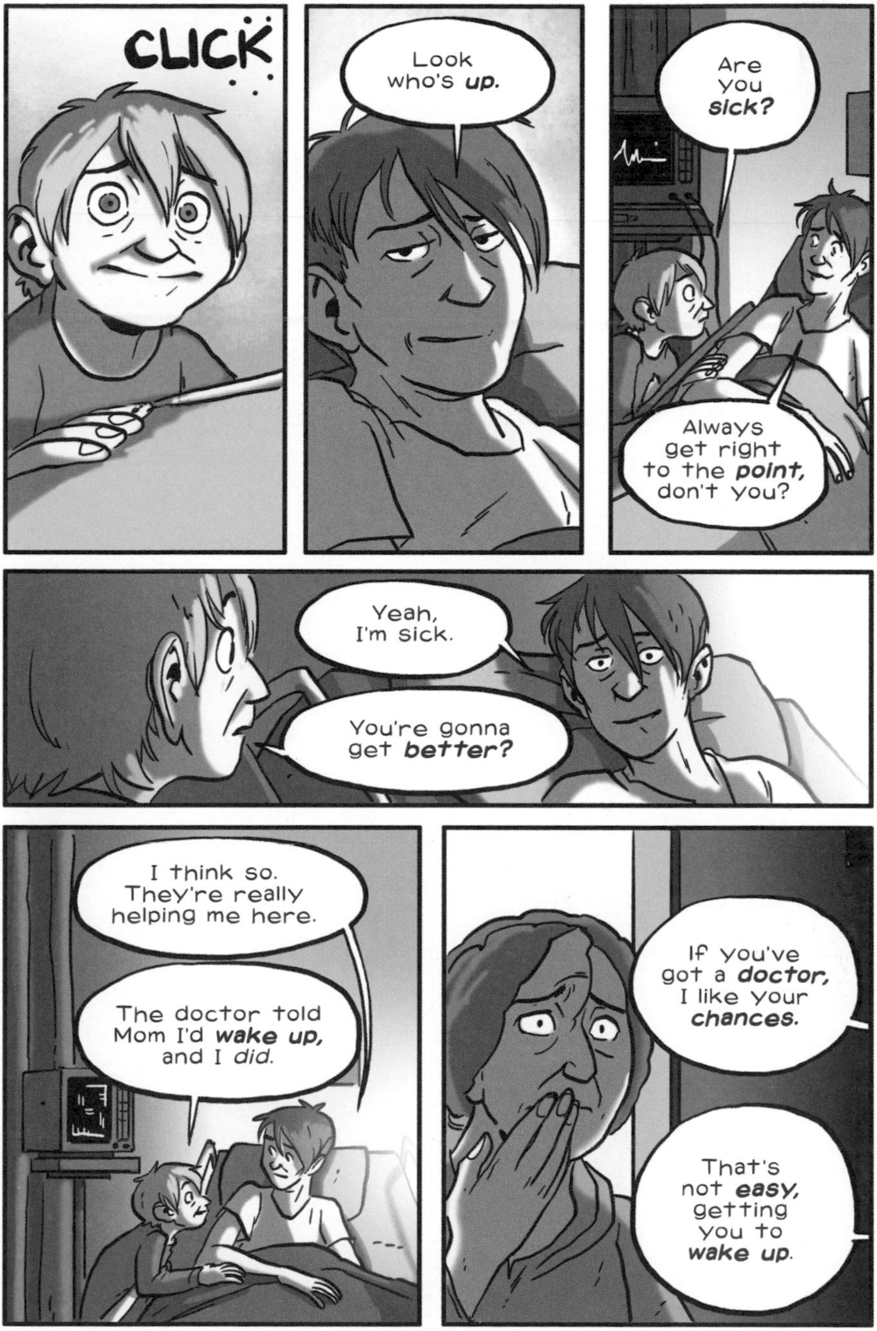
CLICK
Look who's **up.**
Are you **sick?**
Always get right to the **point,** don't you?
Yeah, I'm sick.
You're gonna get **better?**
I think so. They're really helping me here.
The doctor told Mom I'd **wake up,** and I *did.*
If you've got a **doctor,** I like your **chances.**
That's not **easy,** getting you to **wake up.**

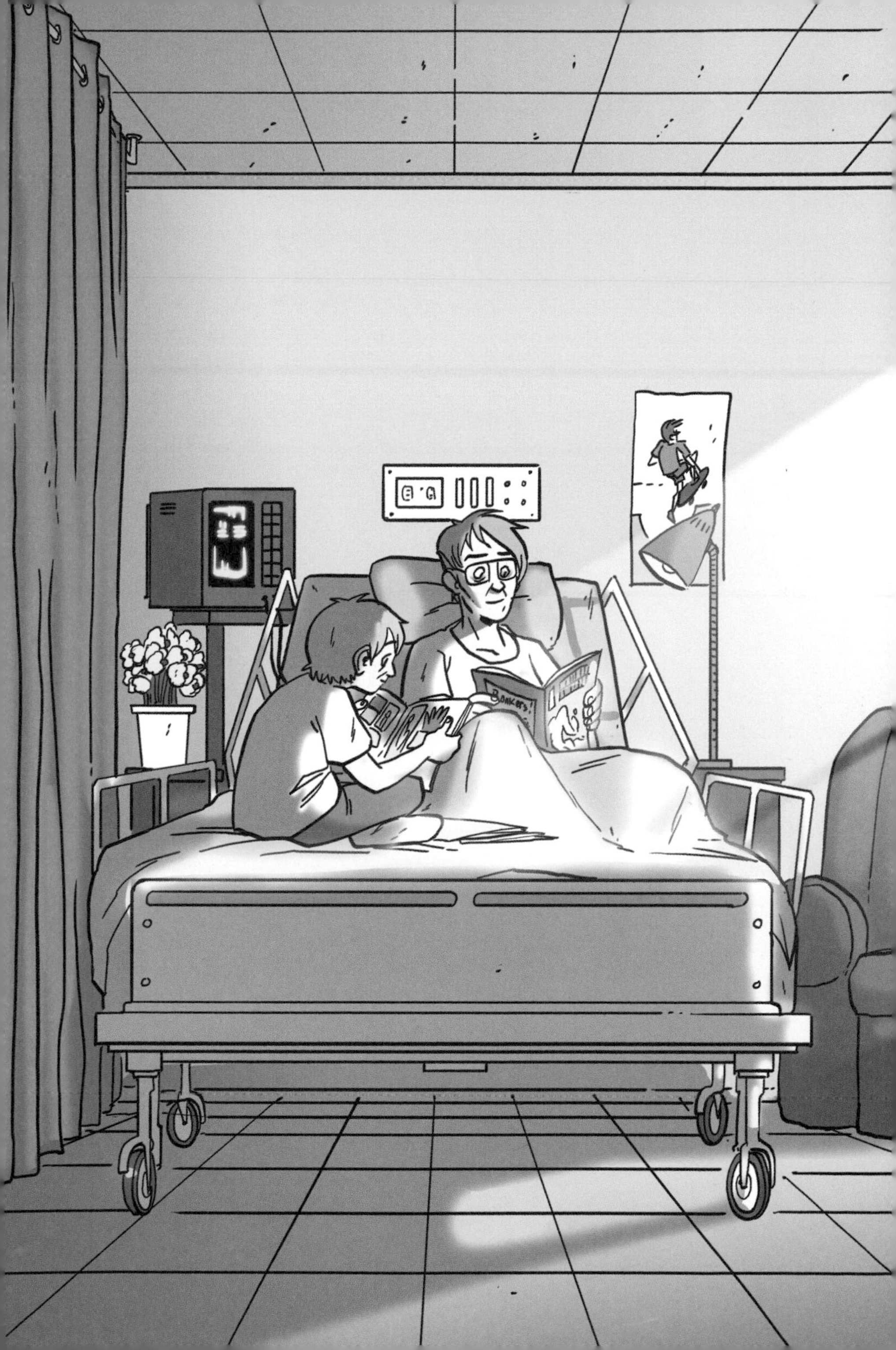
Bonkers!

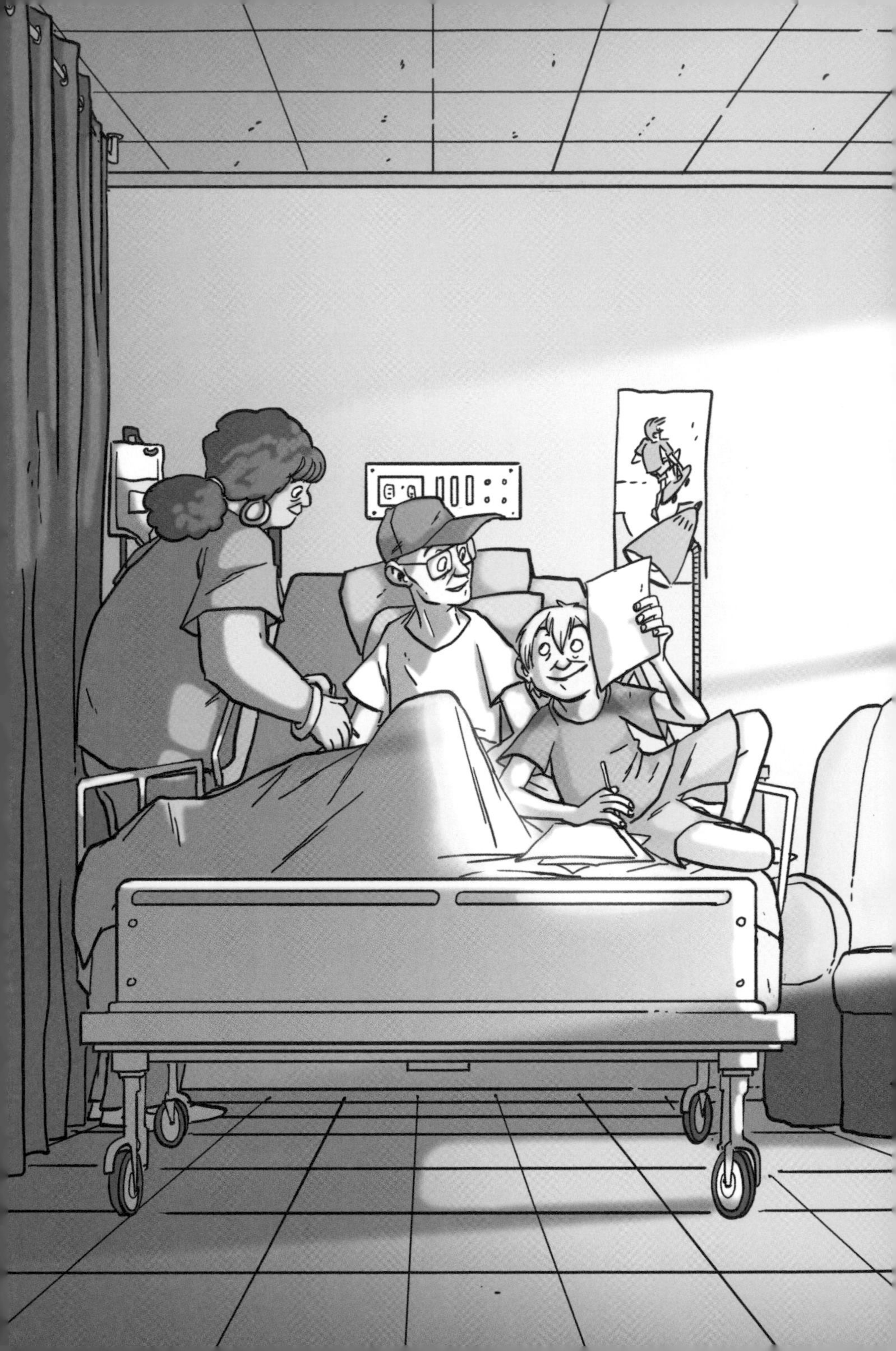

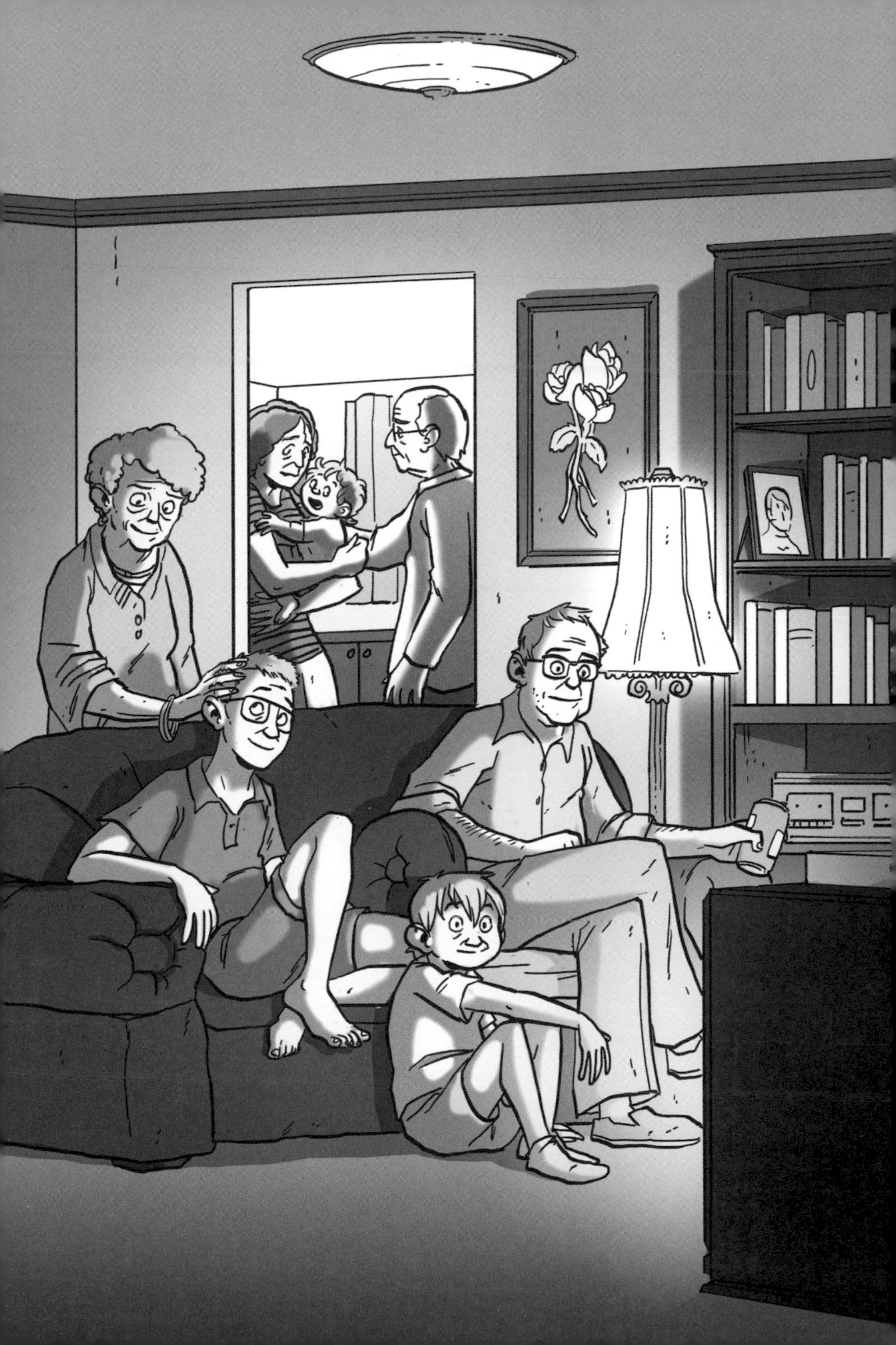

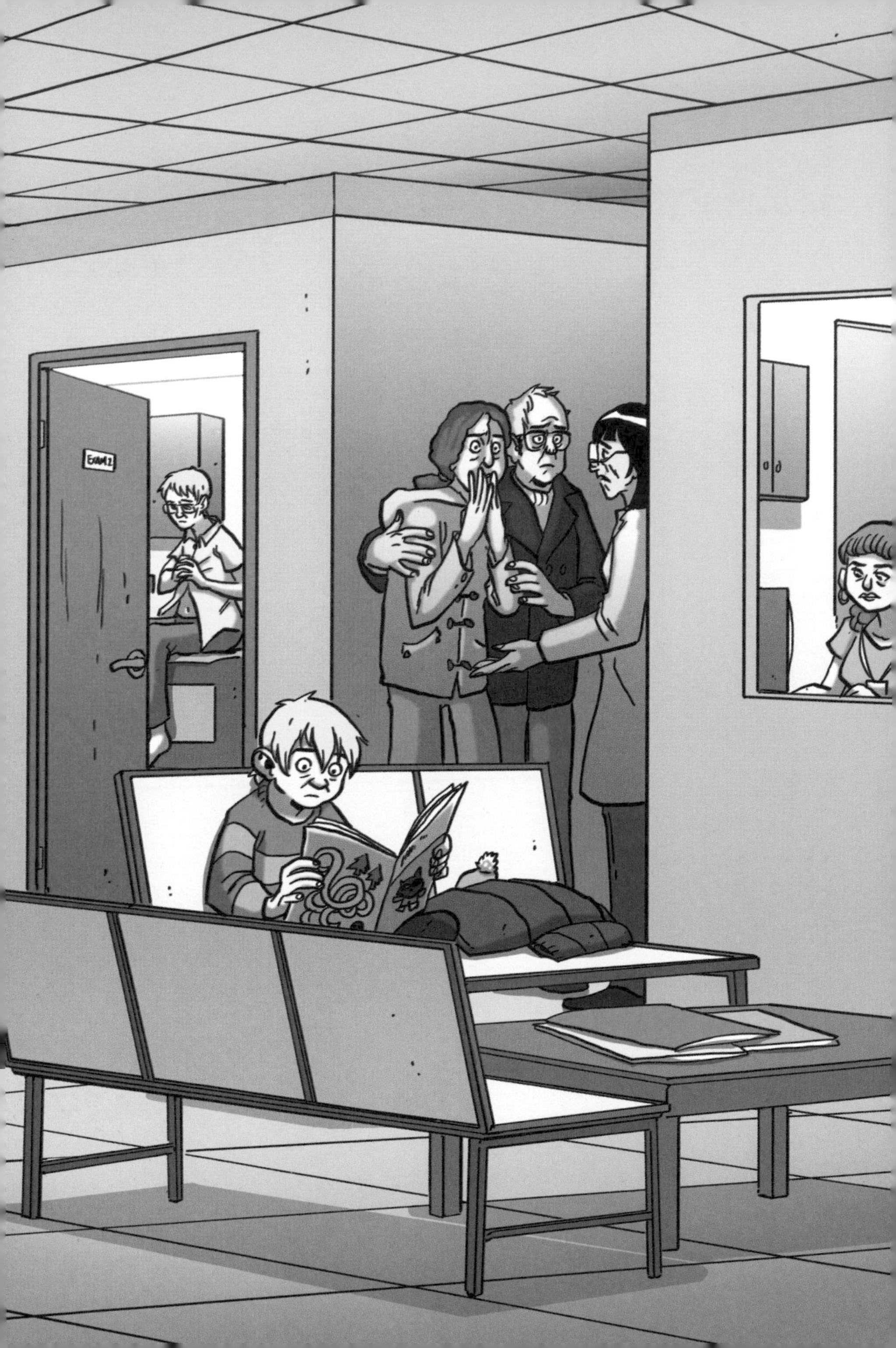

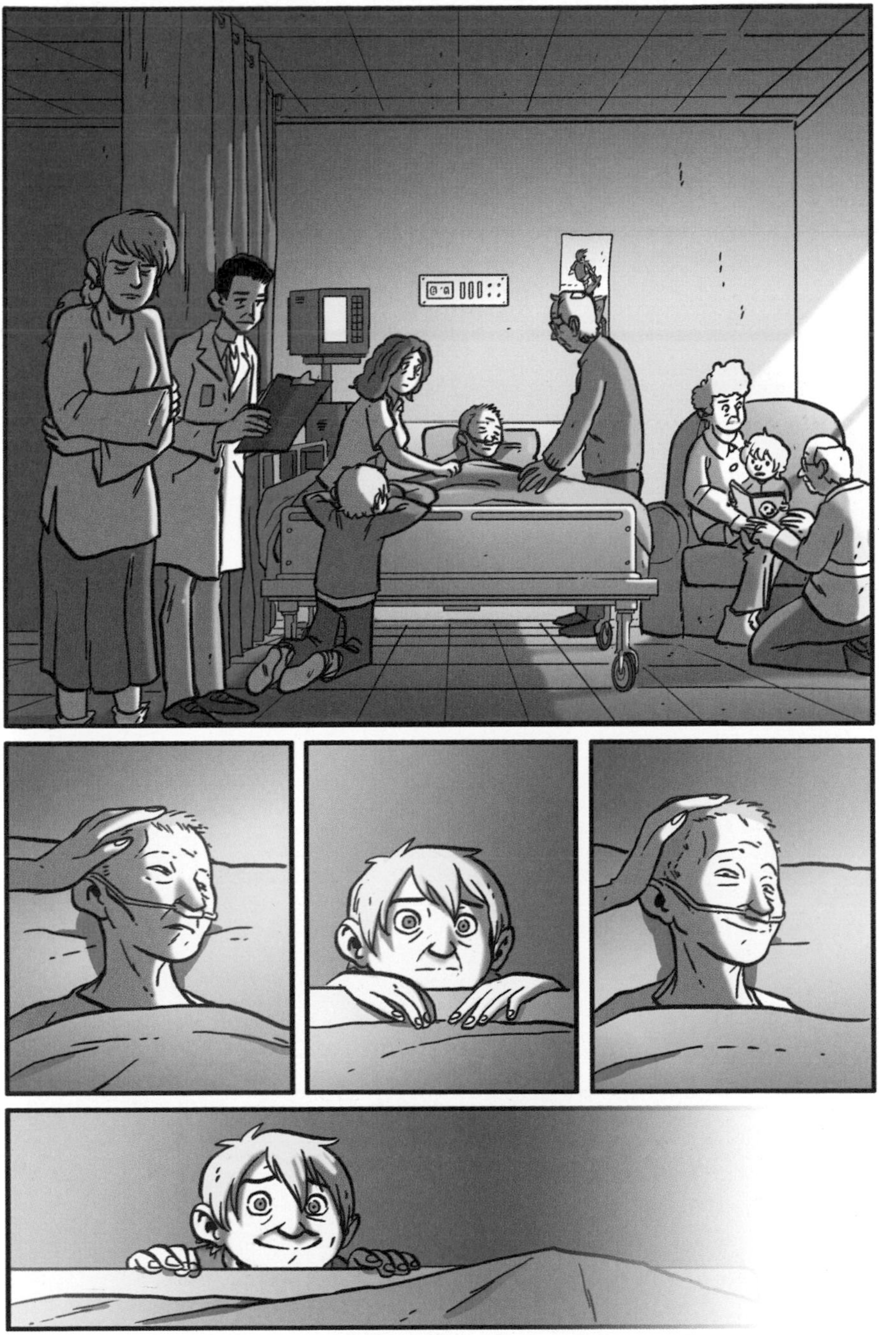

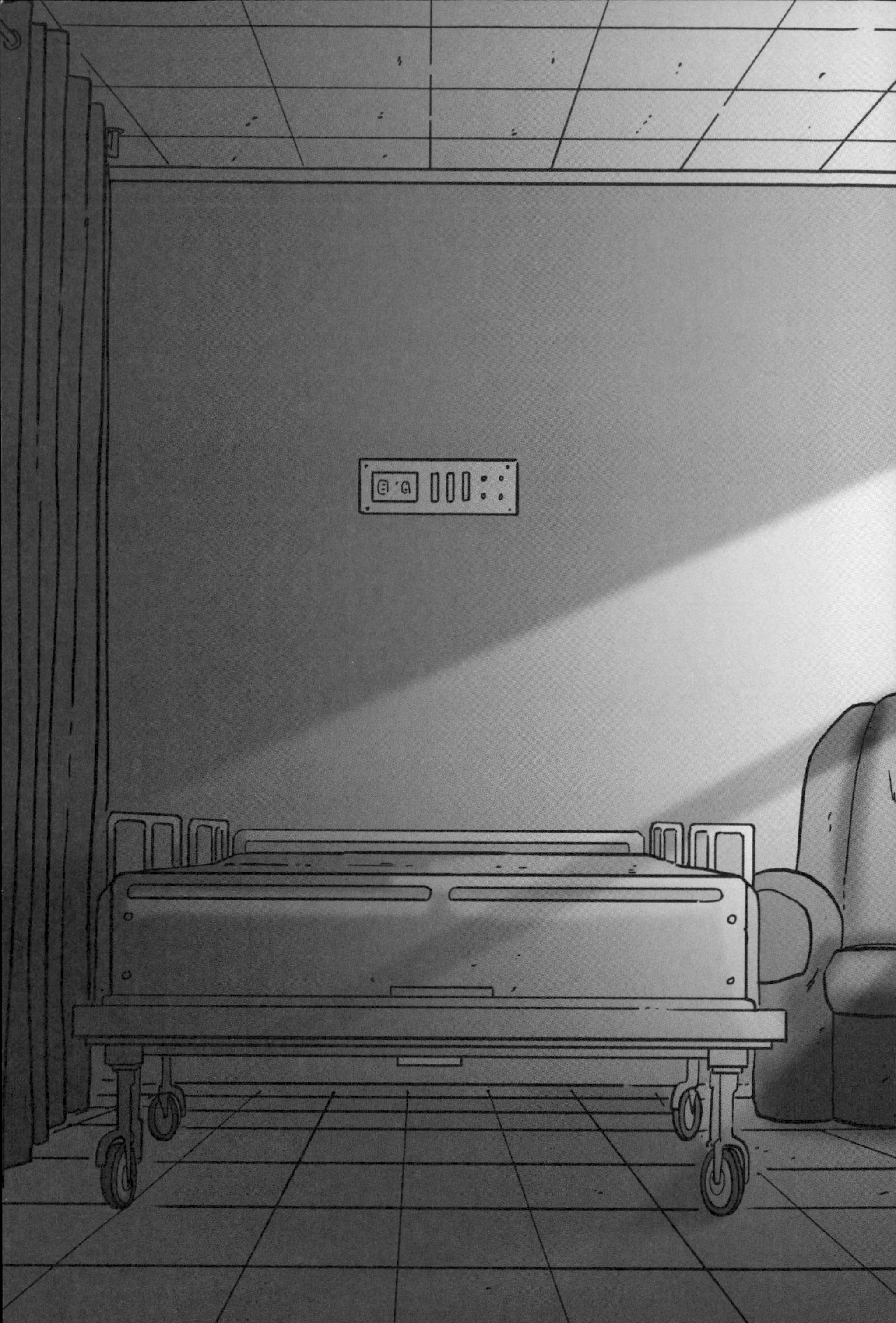

1995

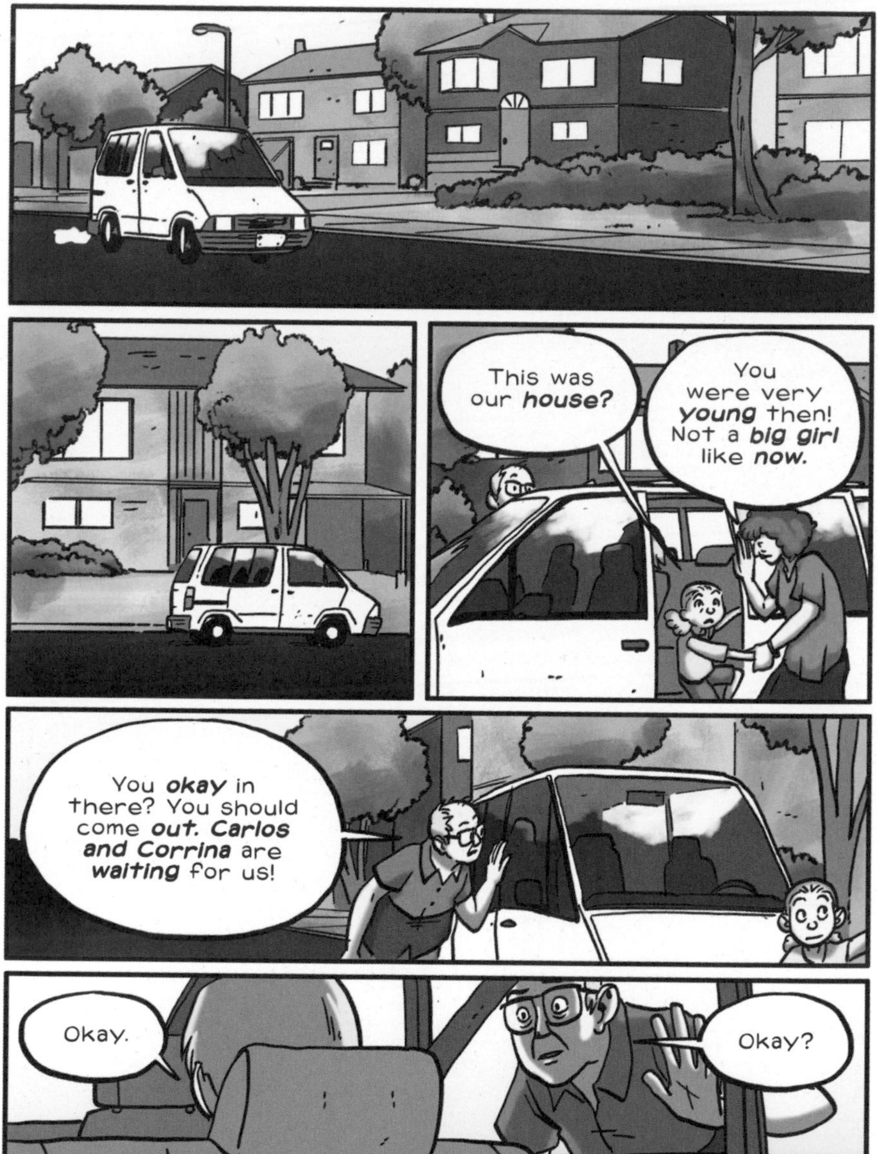

This was our house?
You were very young then! Not a big girl like now.
You okay in there? You should come out. Carlos and Corrina are waiting for us!
Okay.
Okay?

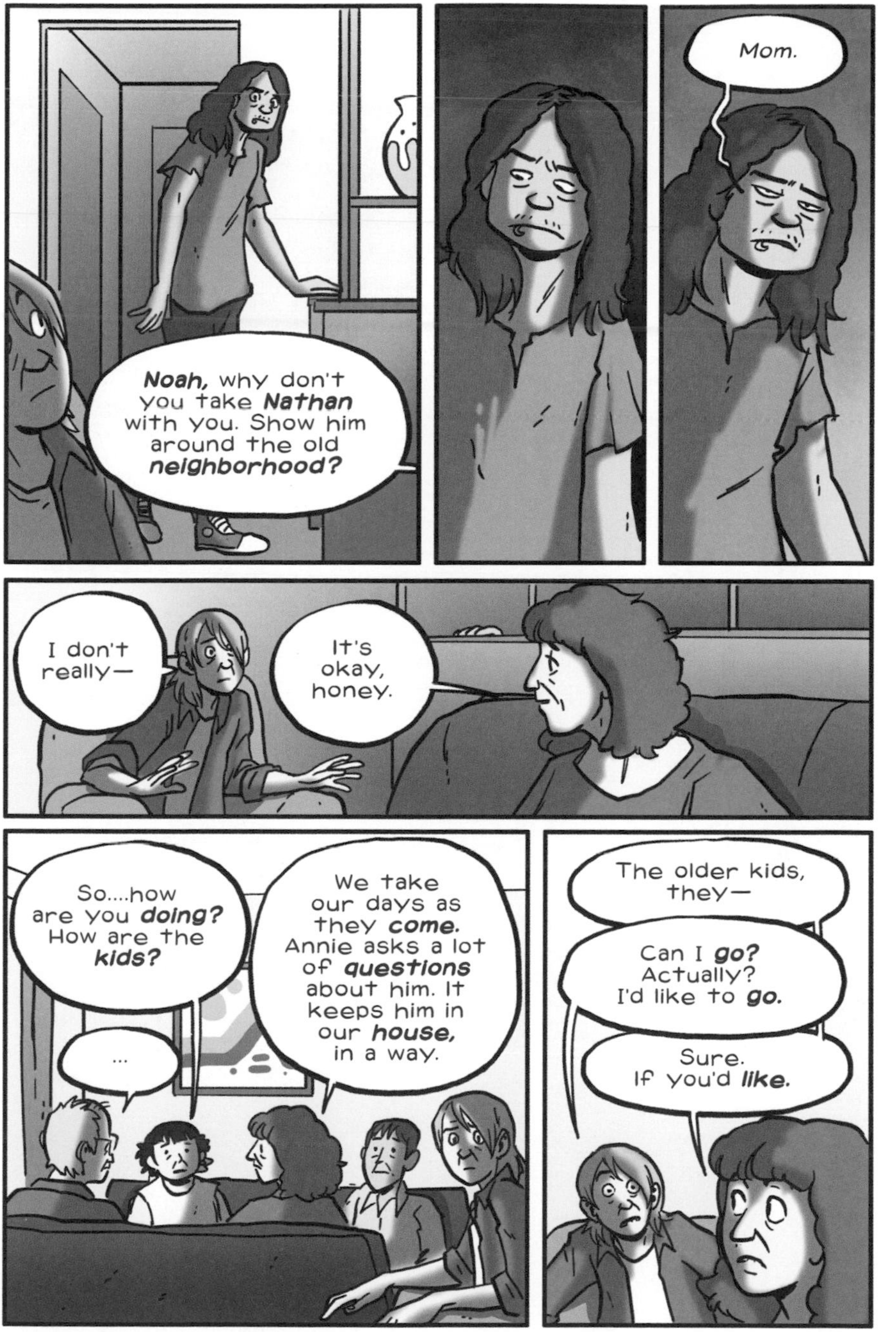

**Noah,** why don't you take **Nathan** with you. Show him around the old **neighborhood?**
Mom.
I don't really—
It's okay, honey.
So....how are you **doing?** How are the **kids?**
...
We take our days as they **come.** Annie asks a lot of **questions** about him. It keeps him in our **house,** in a way.
The older kids, they—
Can I **go?** Actually? I'd like to **go.**
Sure. If you'd **like.**

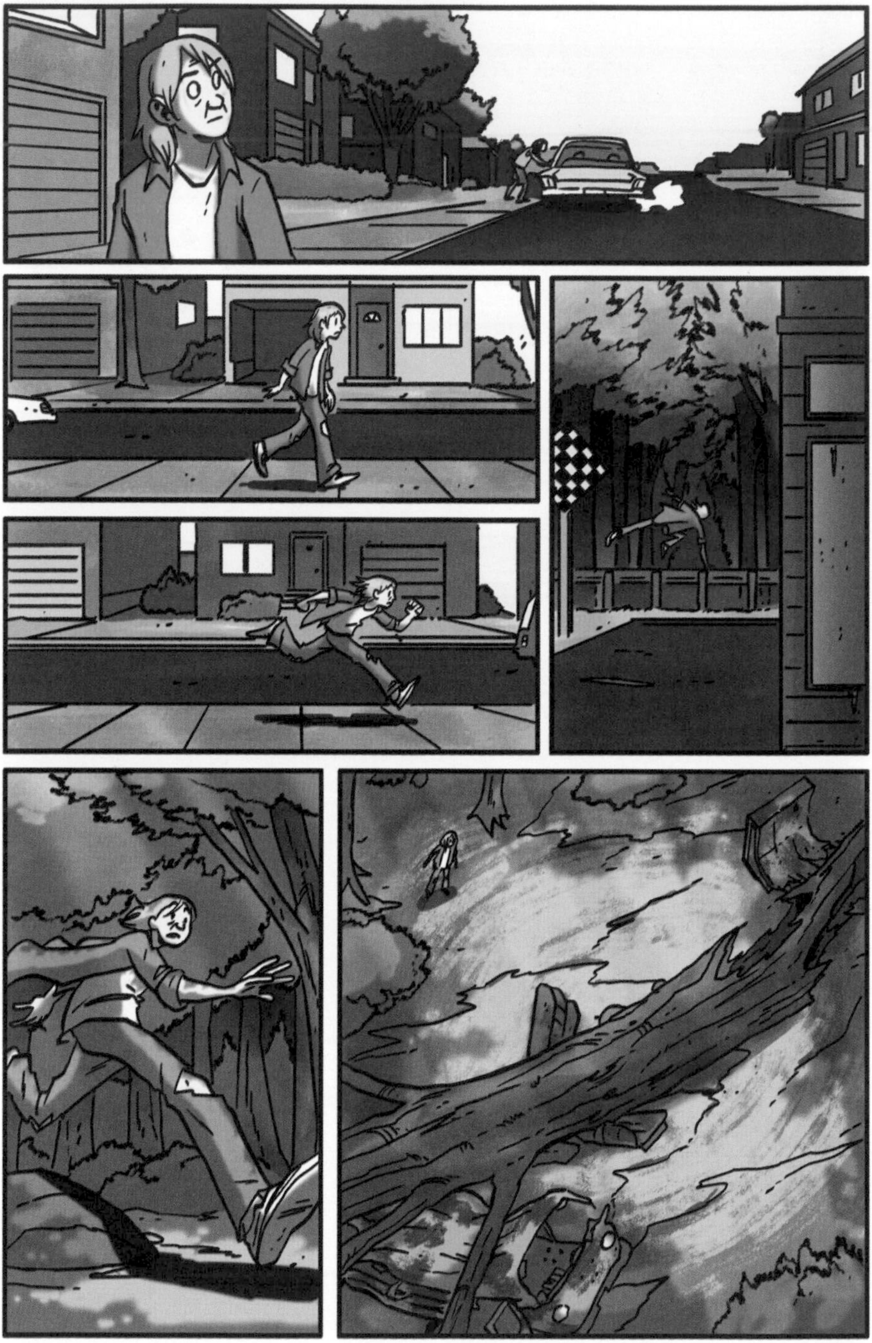

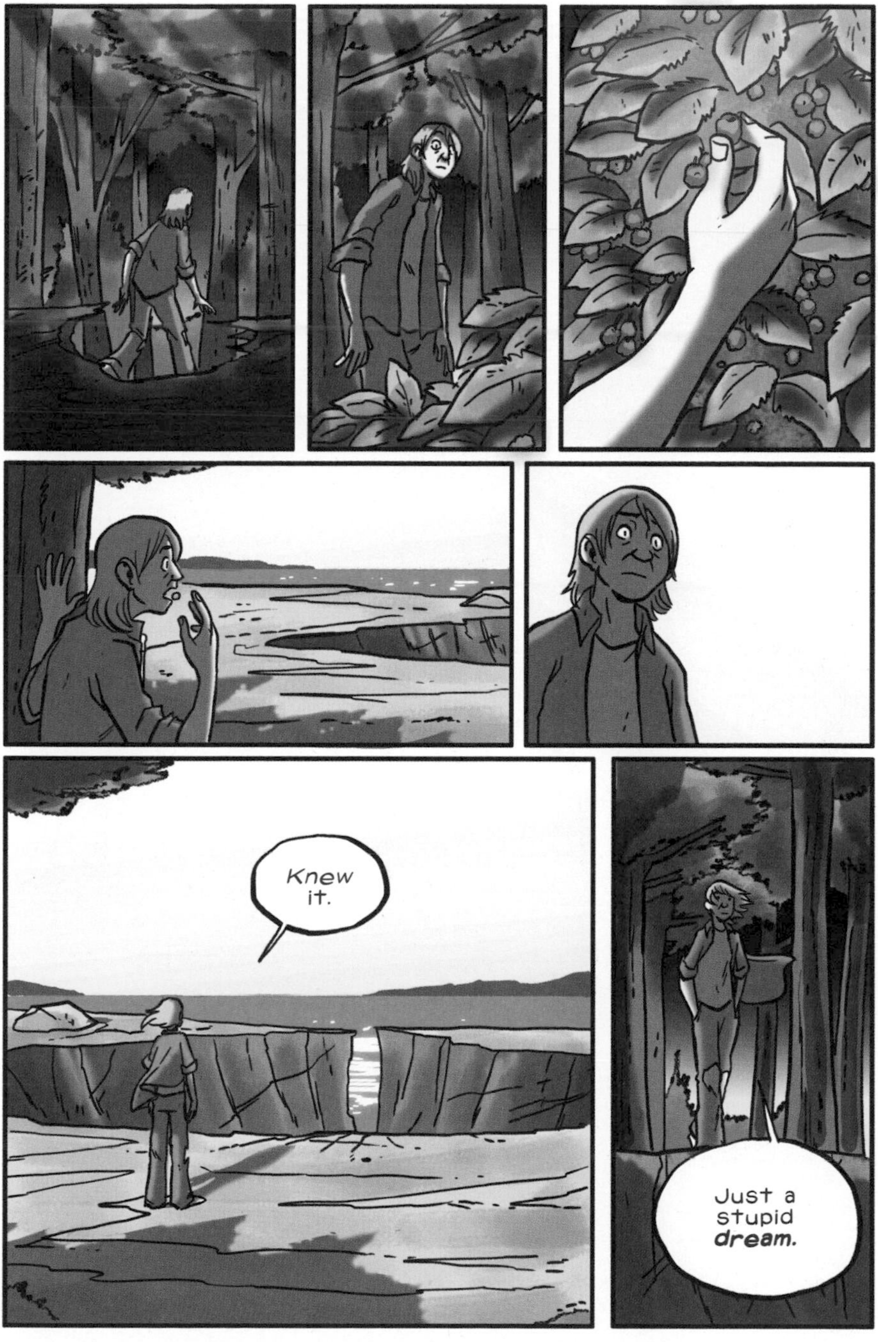
Knew it.
Just a stupid dream.

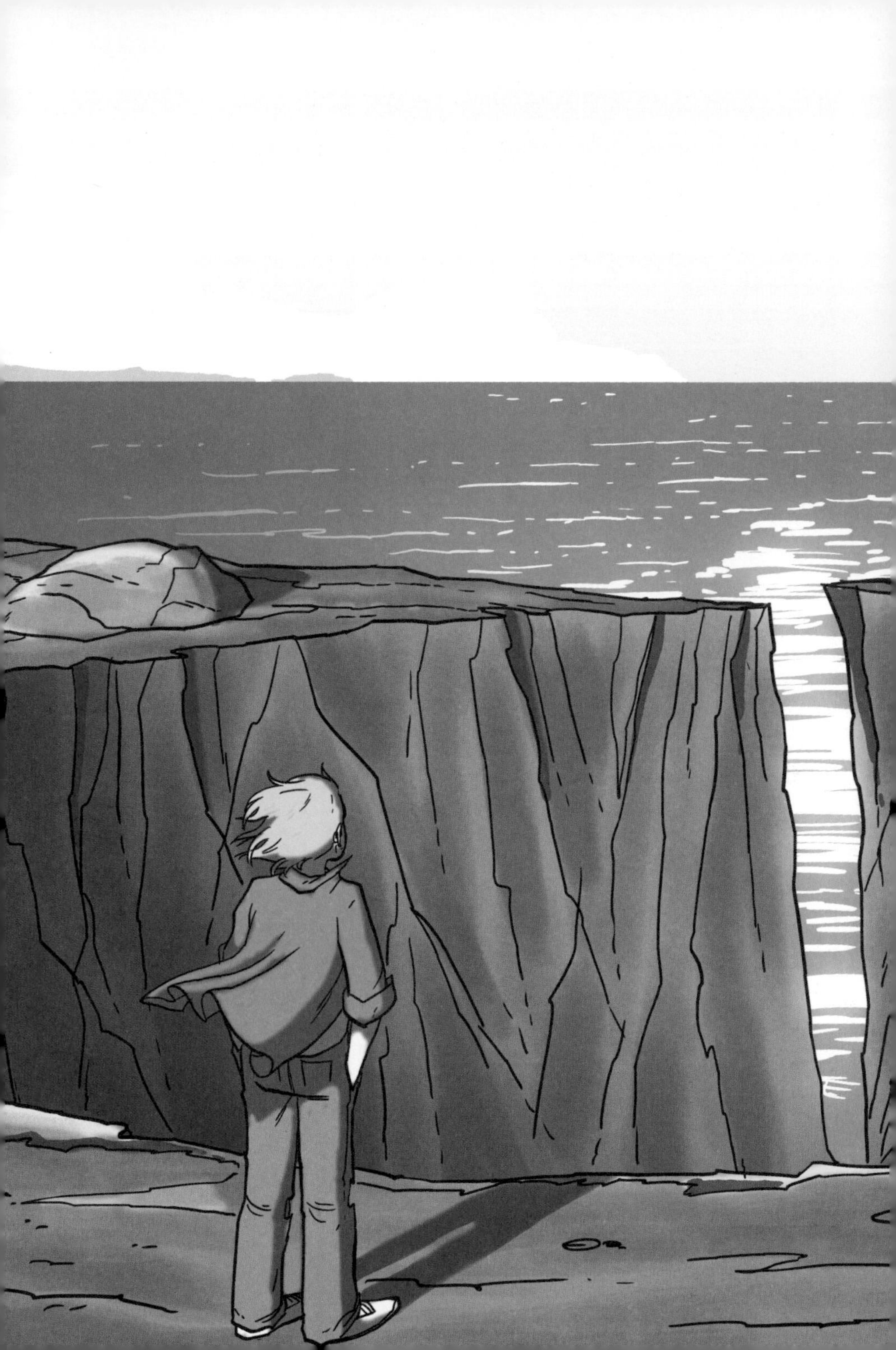

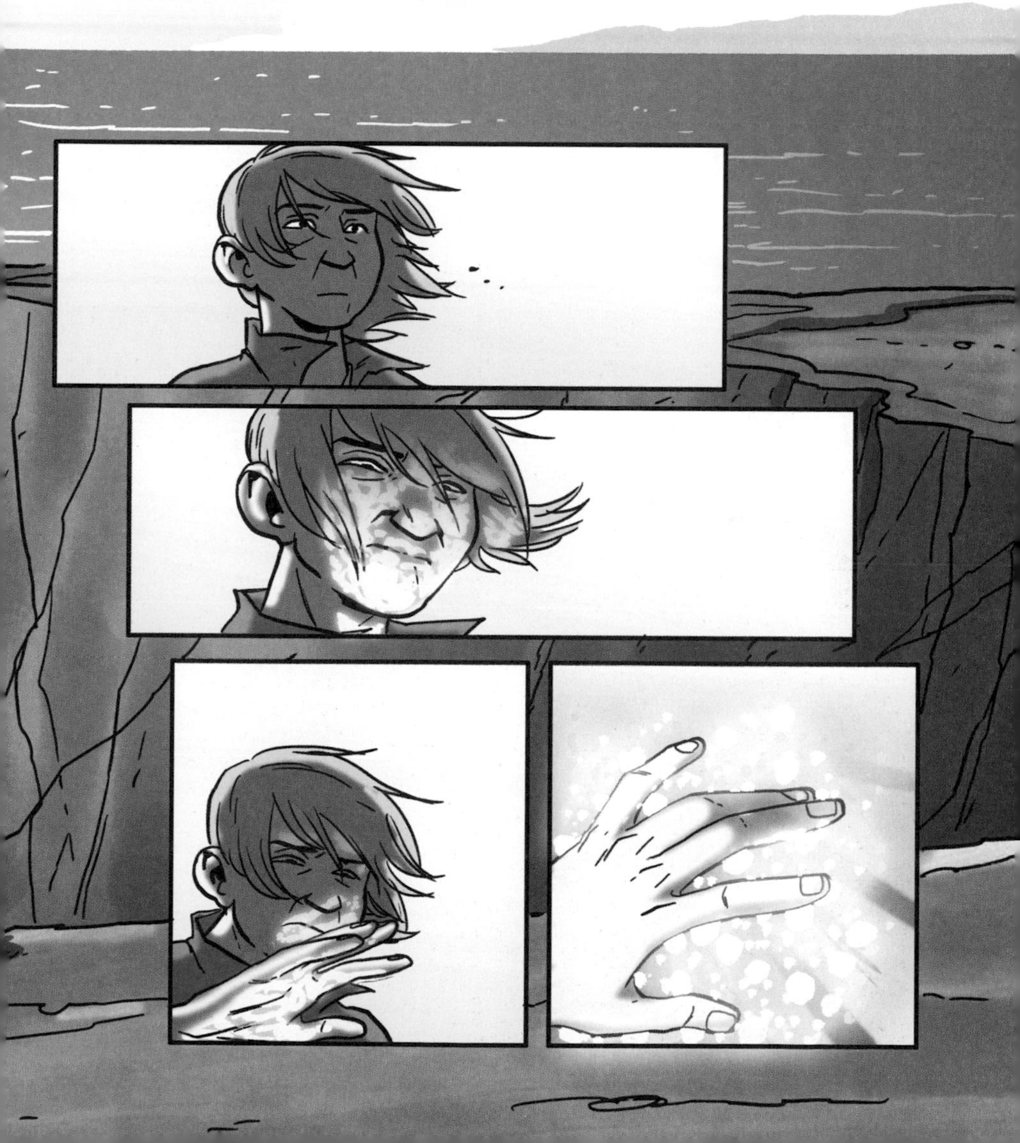

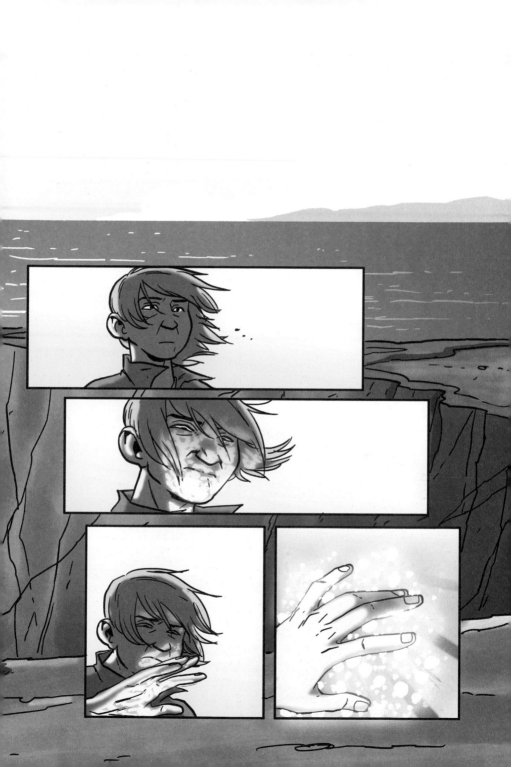

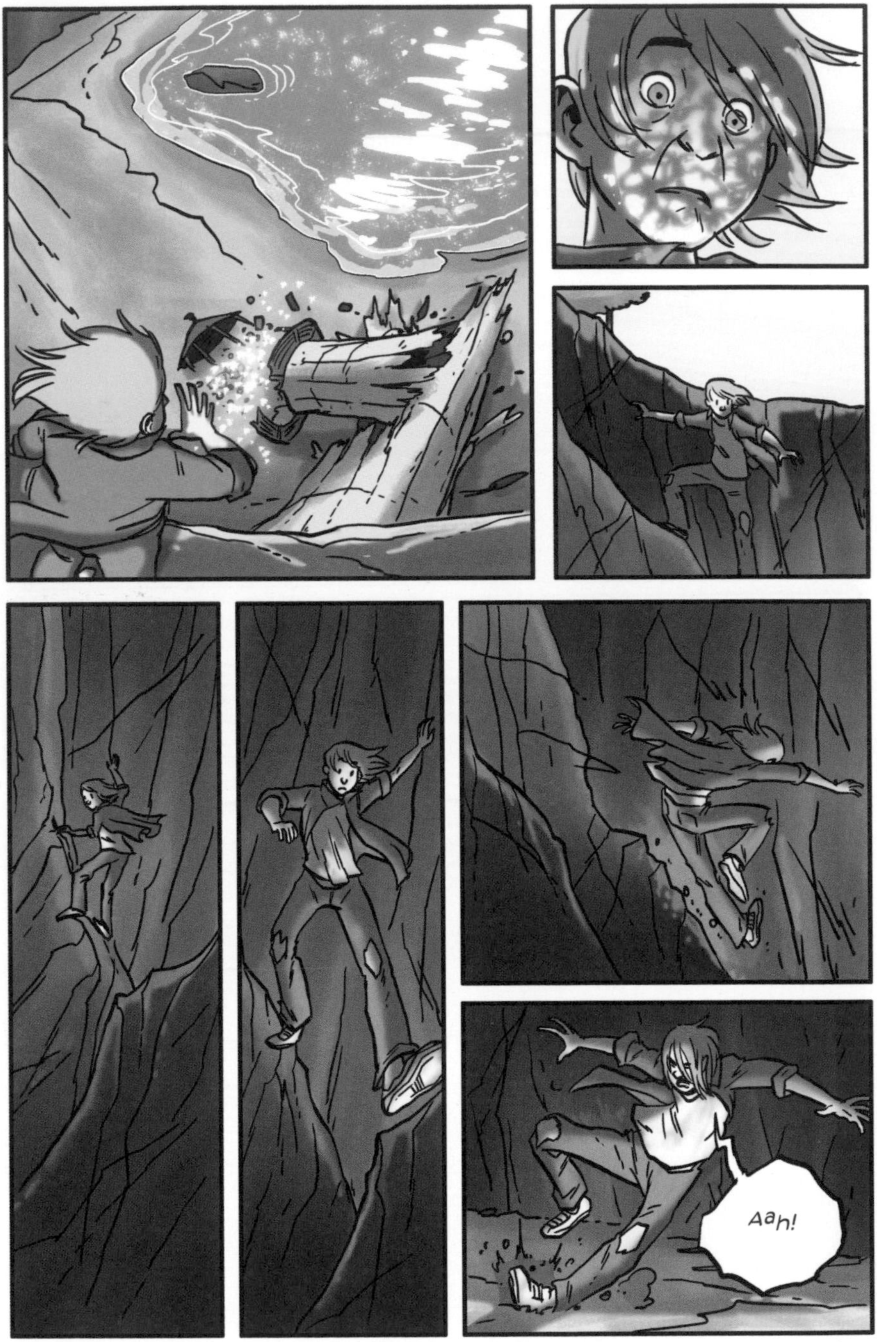
Aah!

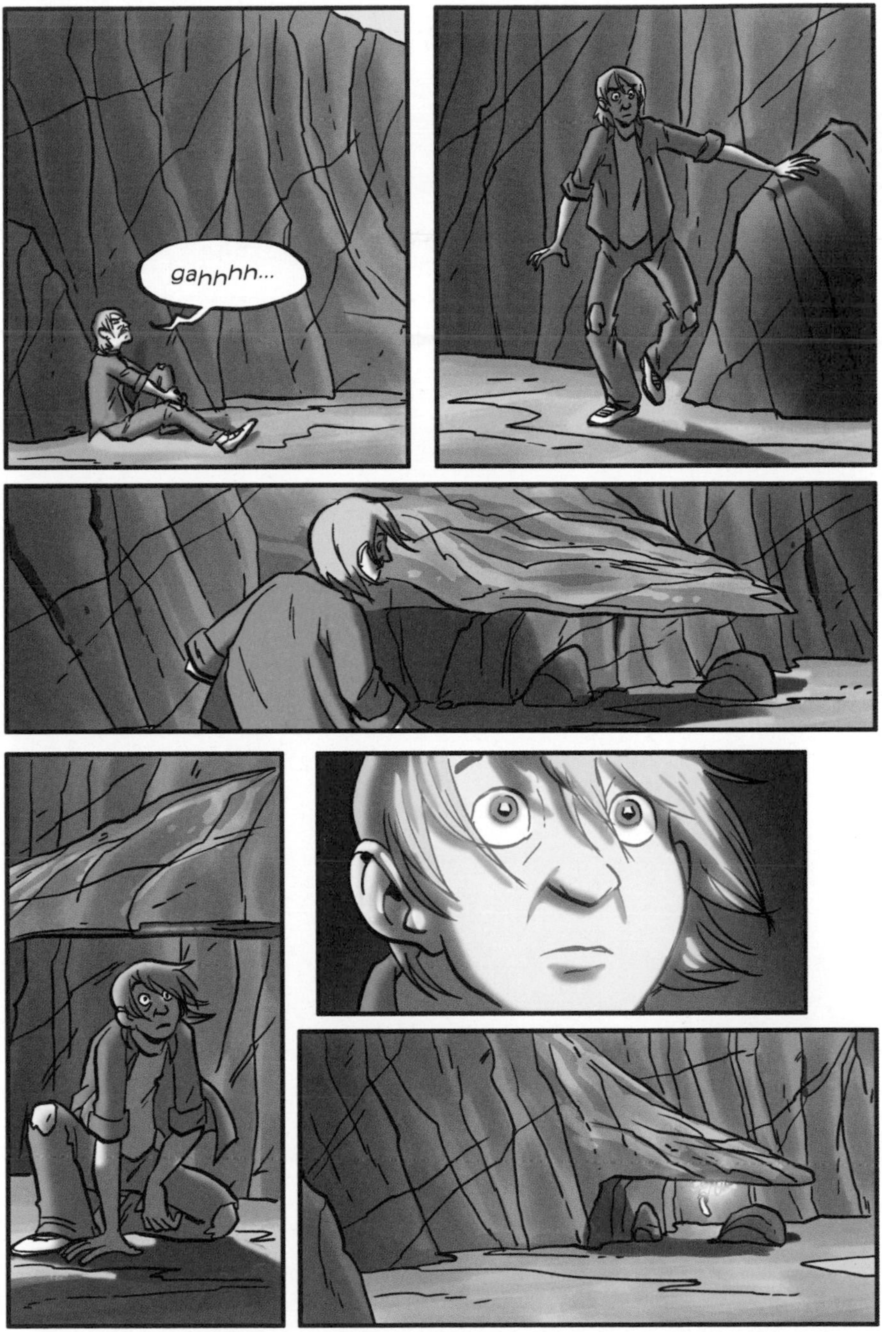
gahhhh...

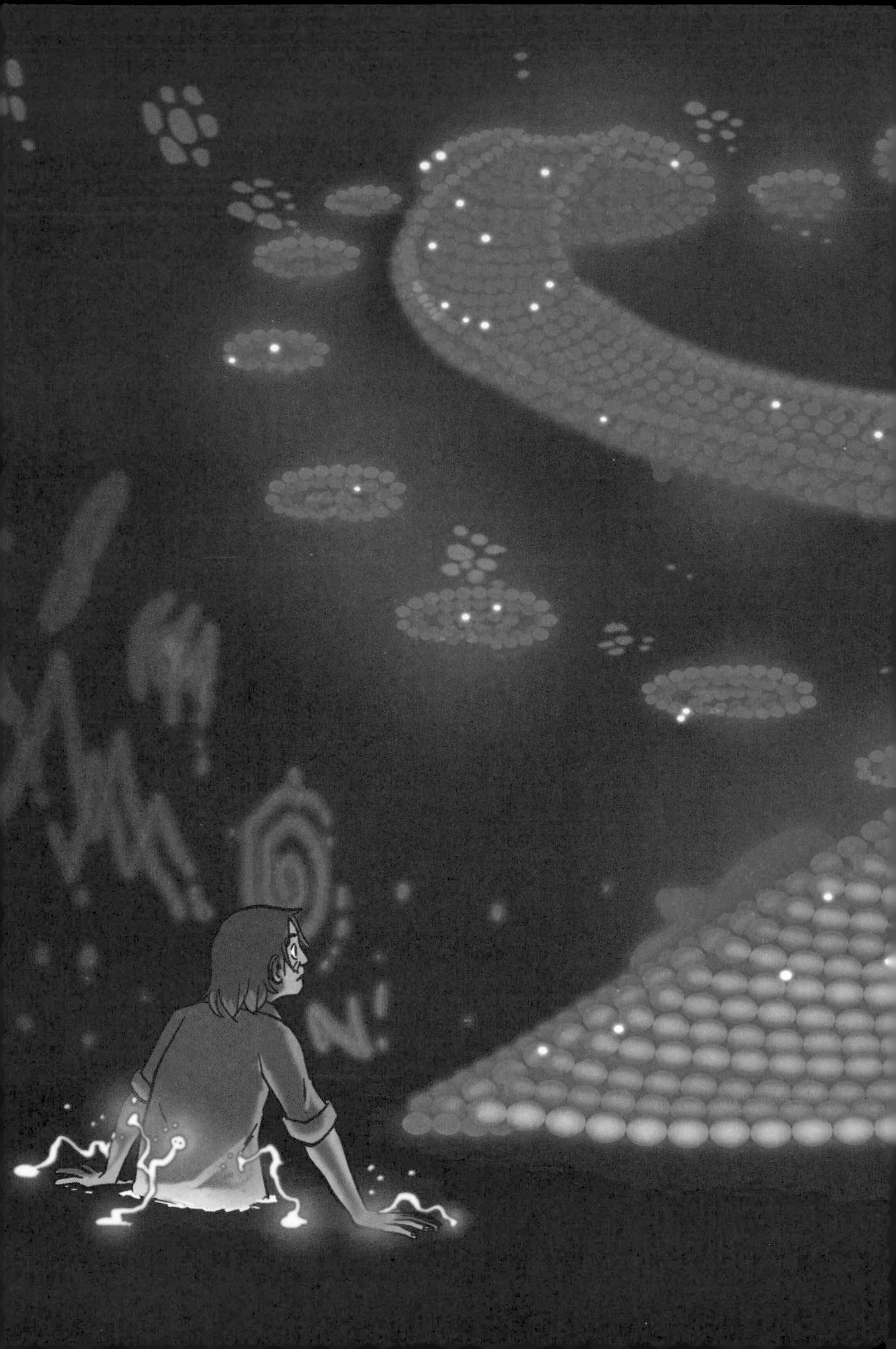

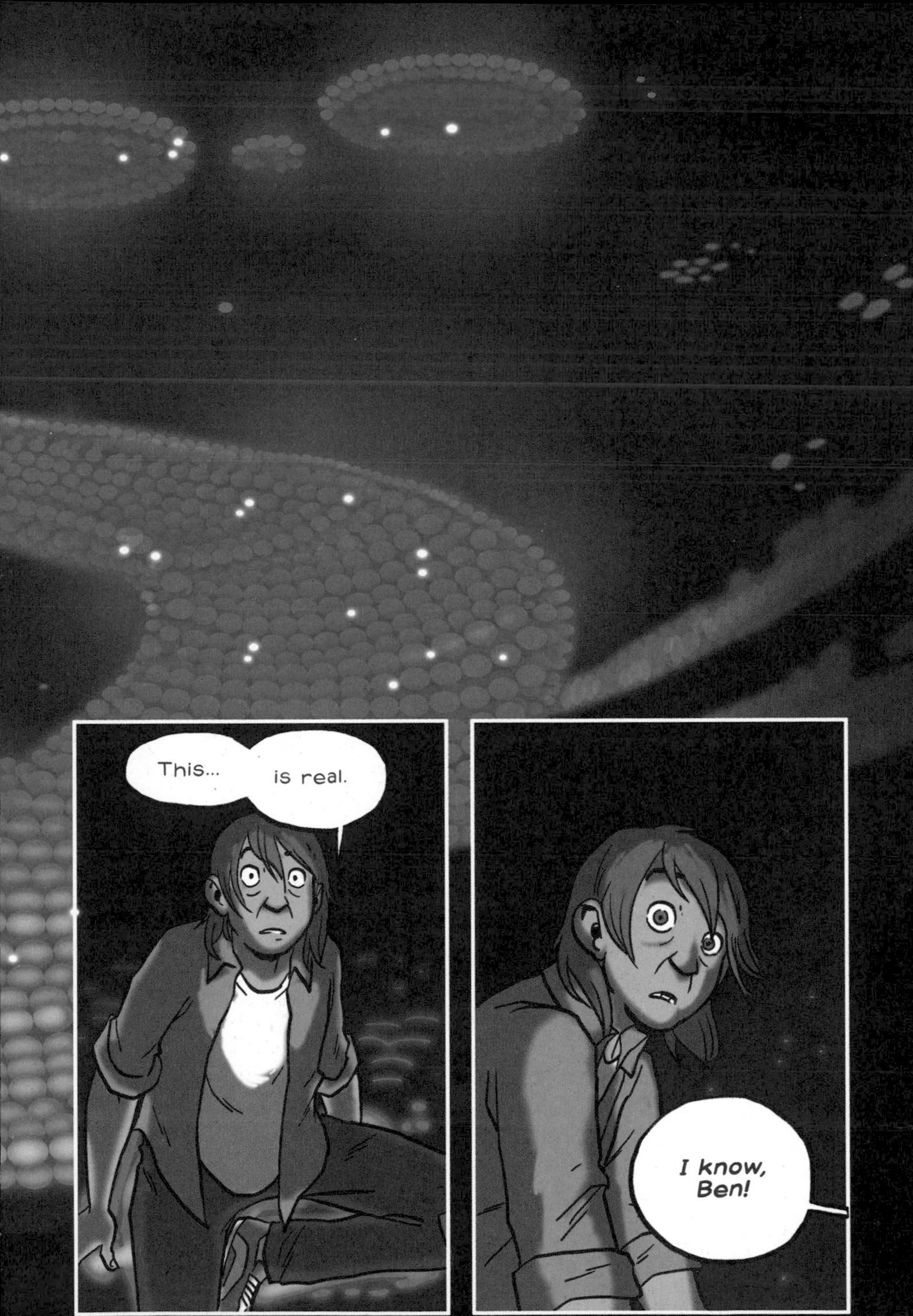
This...
is real.
I know, Ben!

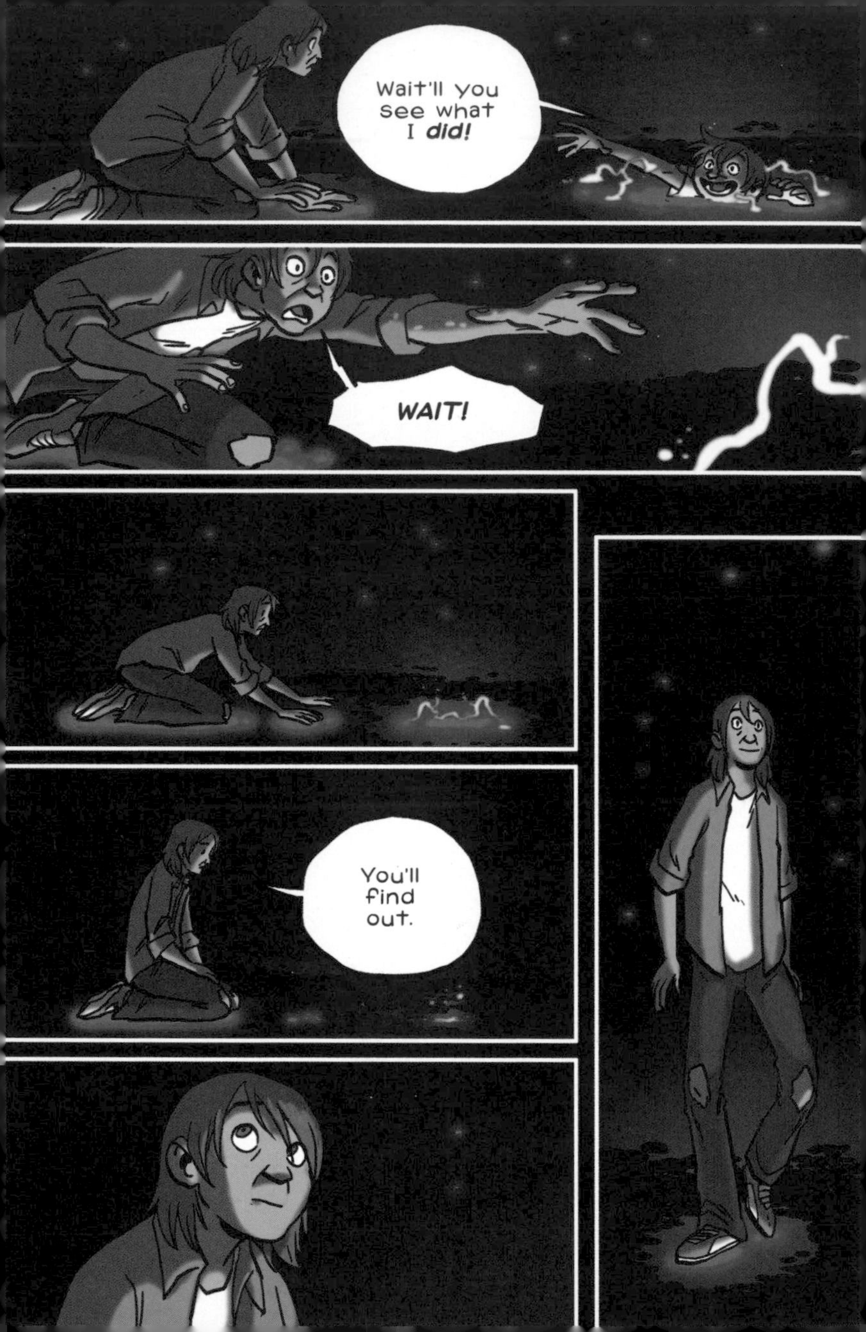
Wait'll you see what I *did!*
***WAIT!***
You'll find out.

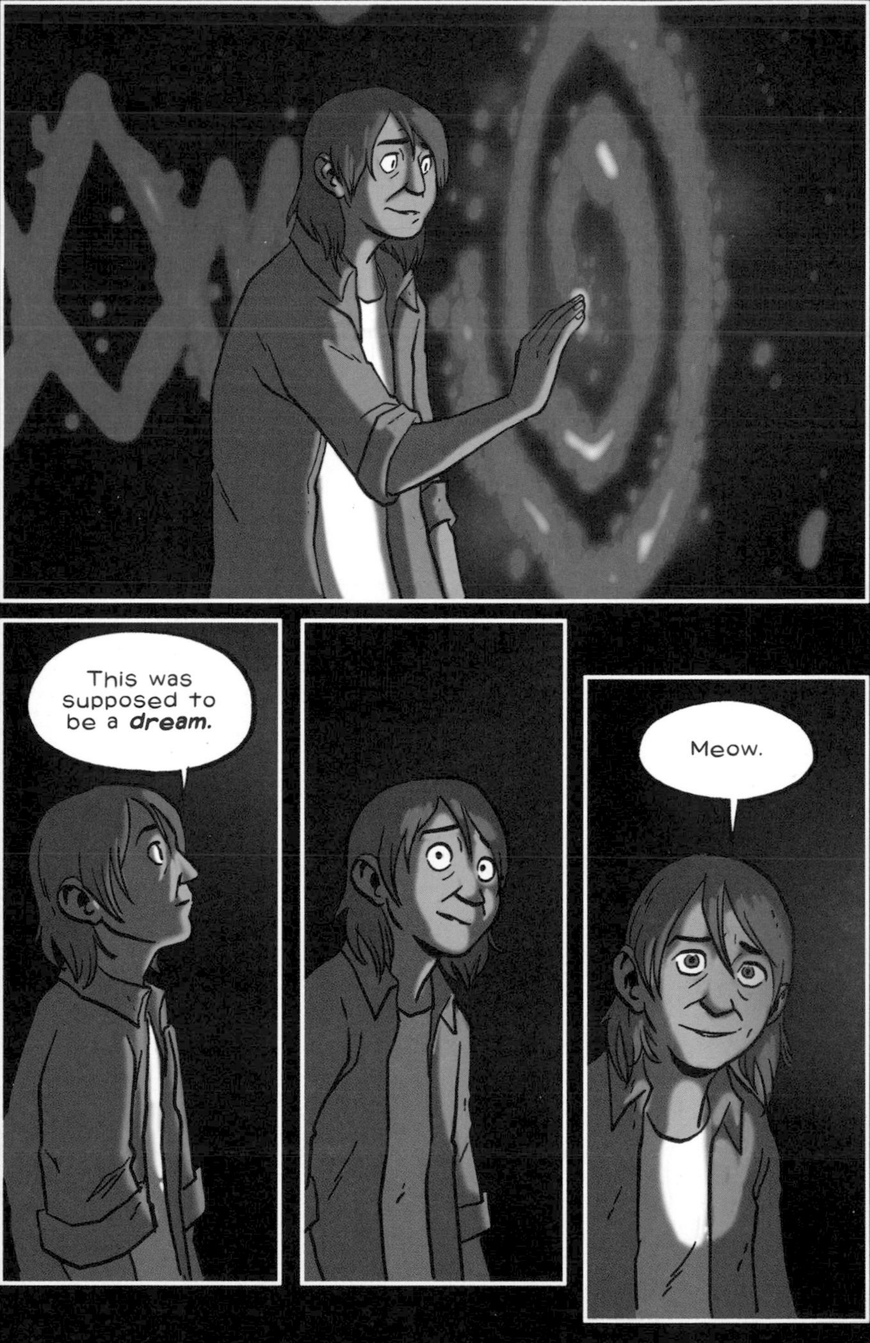
This was supposed to be a *dream.*
Meow.

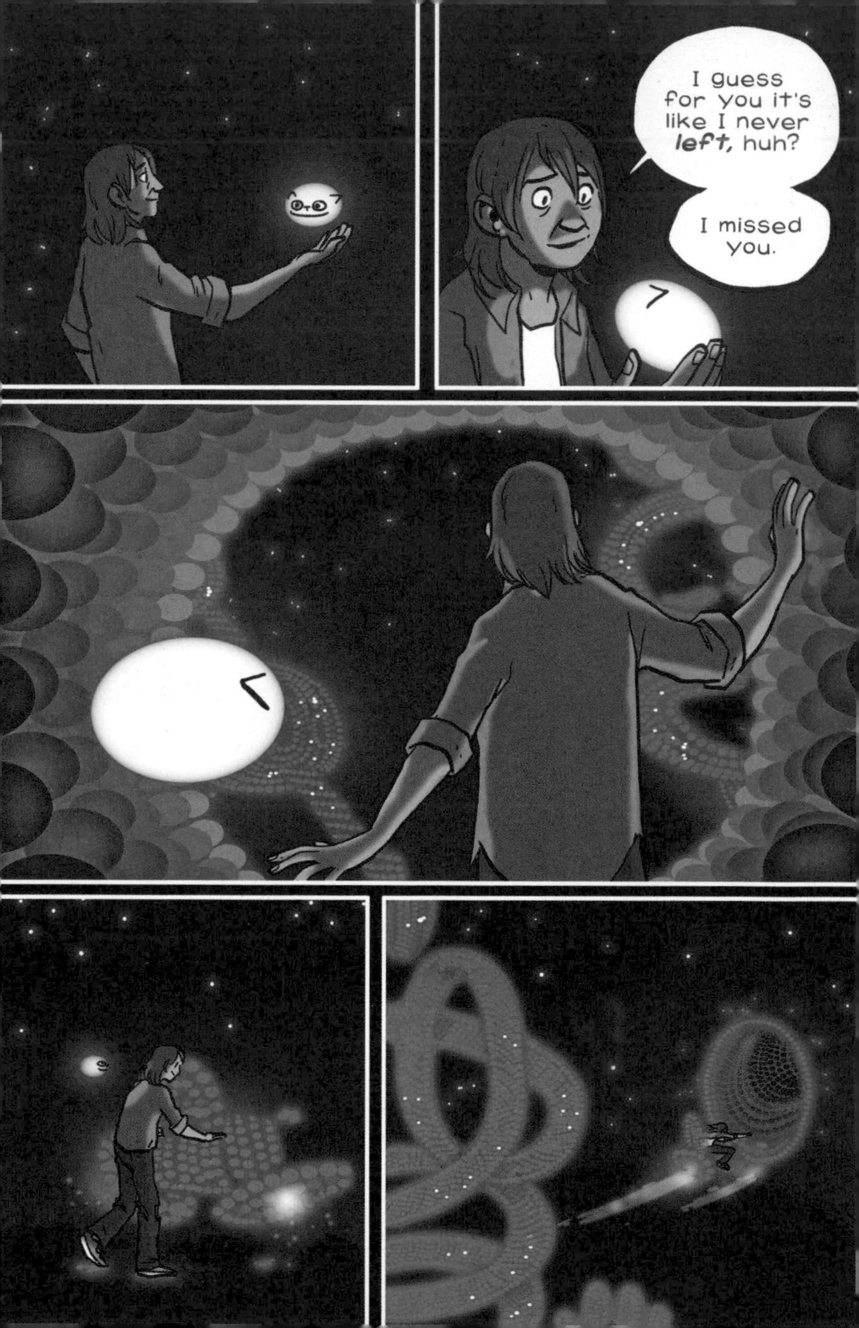
I guess for you it's like I never *left,* huh?
I missed you.

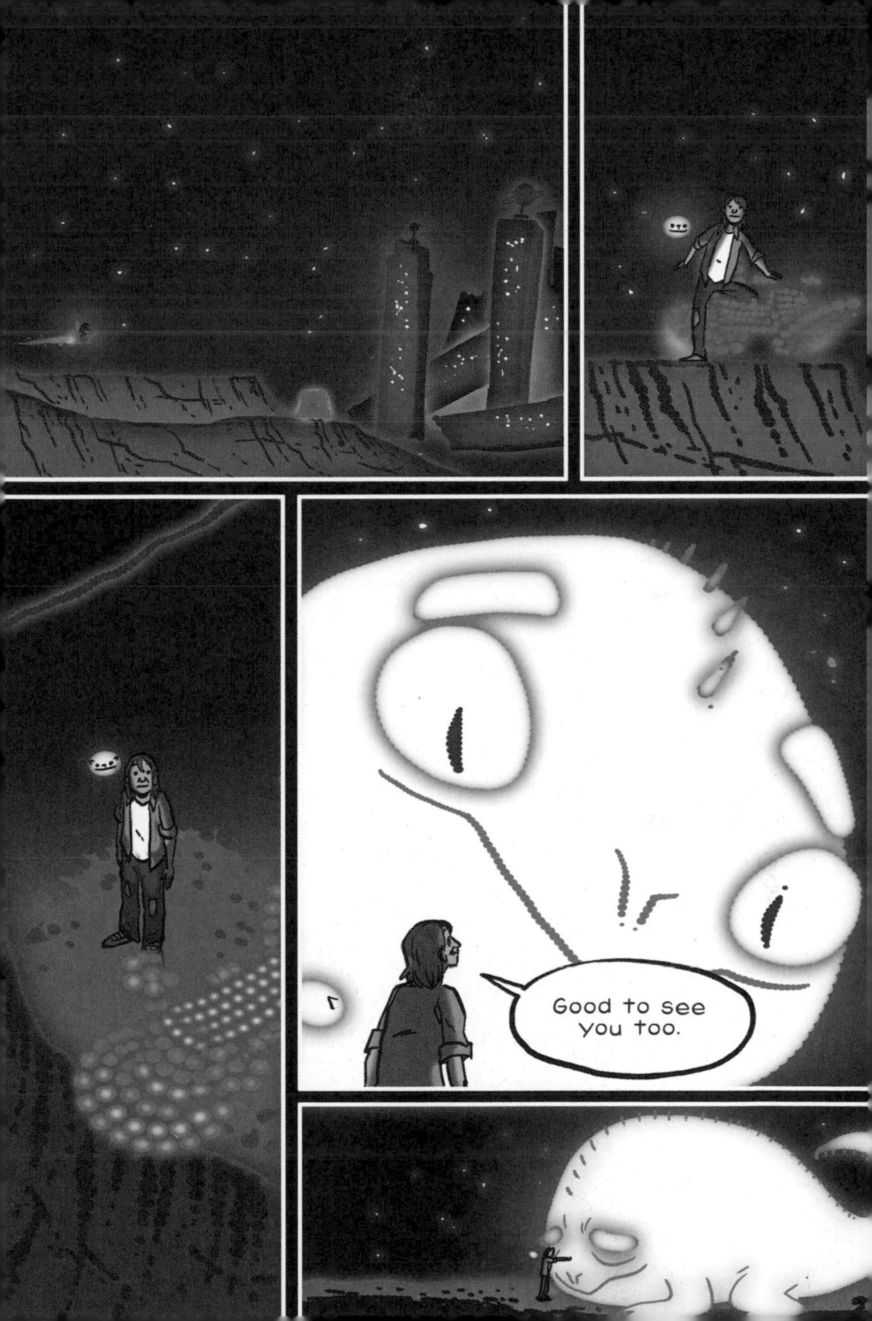
Good to see
you too.

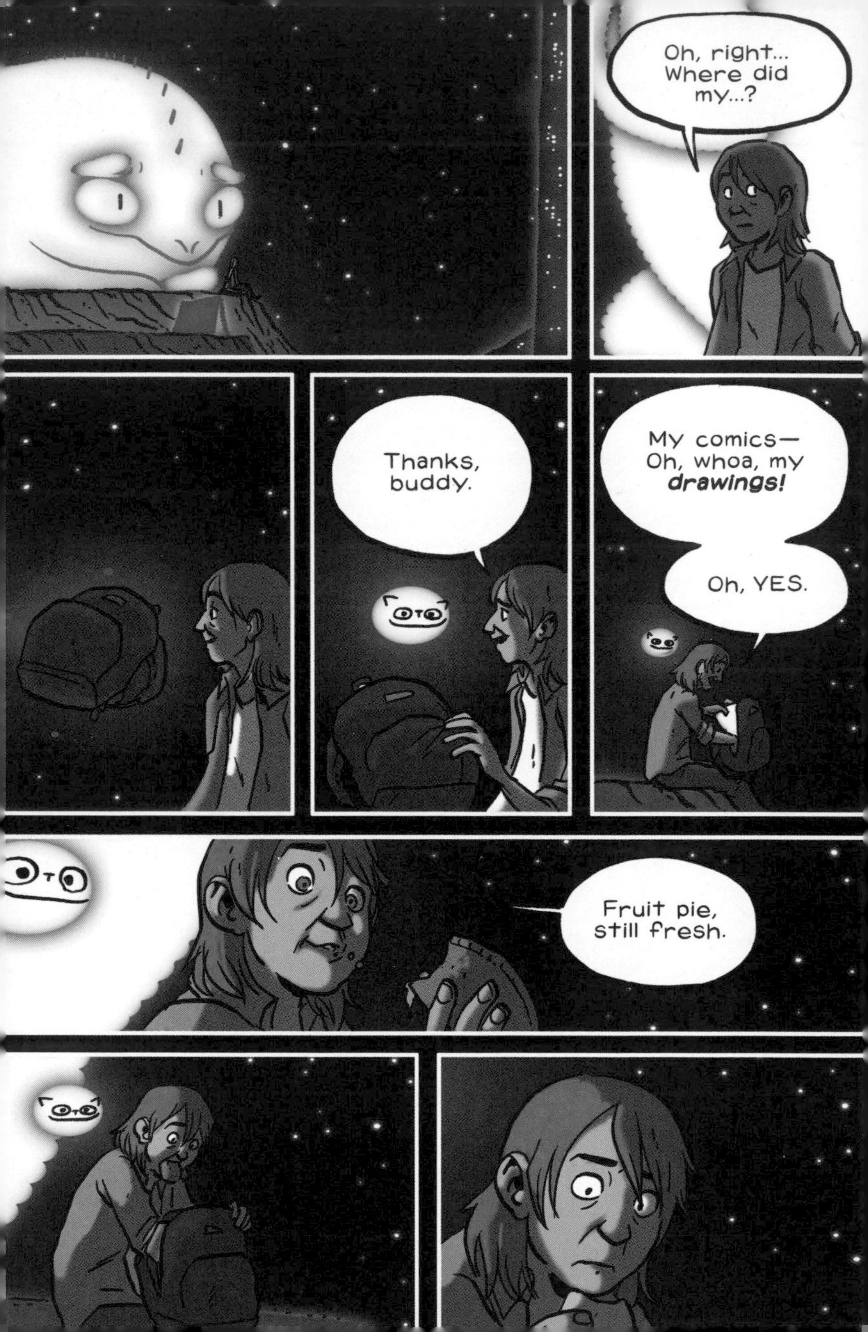
Oh, right... Where did my...?
Thanks, buddy.
My comics— Oh, whoa, my *drawings!*
Oh, YES.
Fruit pie, still fresh.

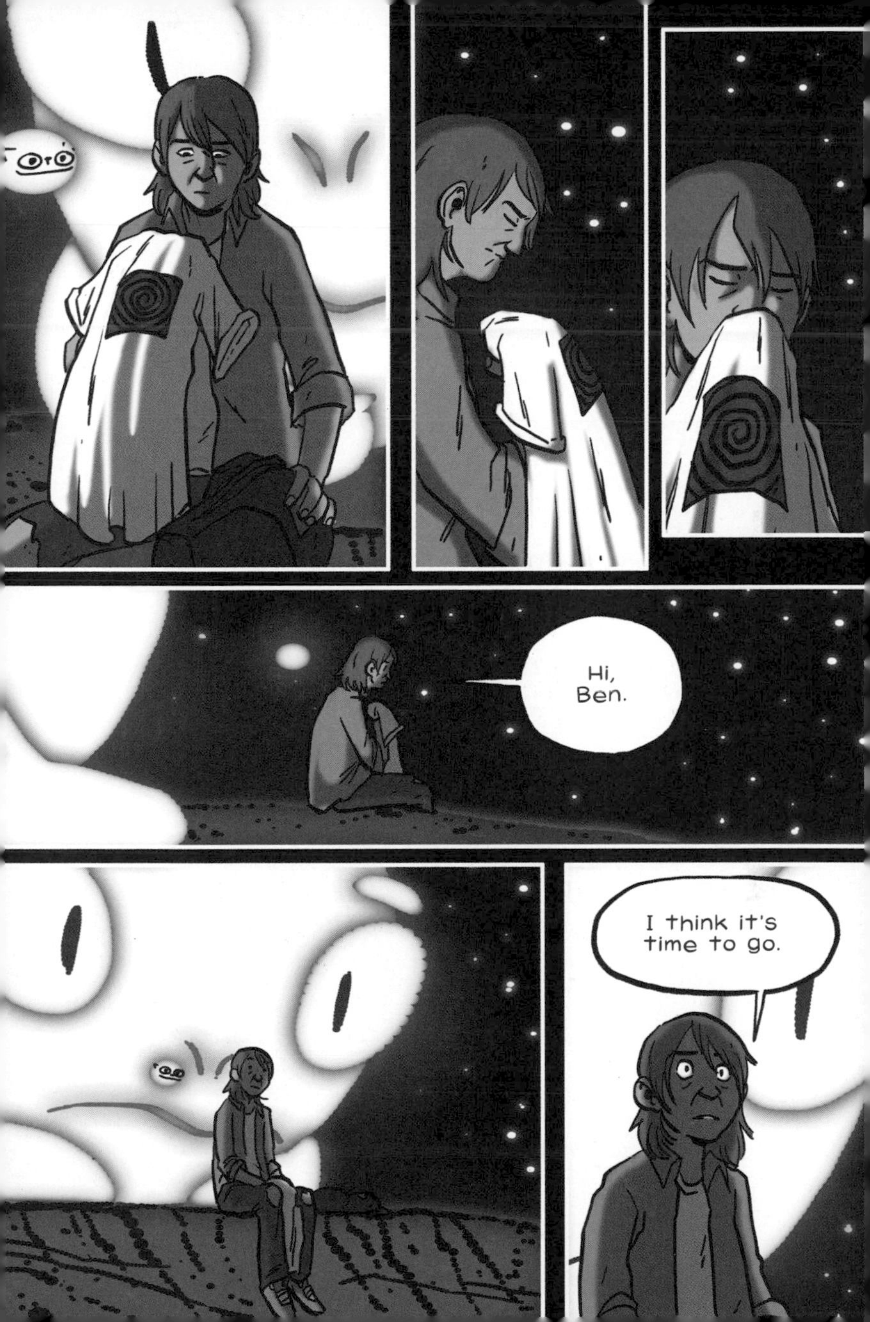
Hi,
Ben.
I think it's
time to go.

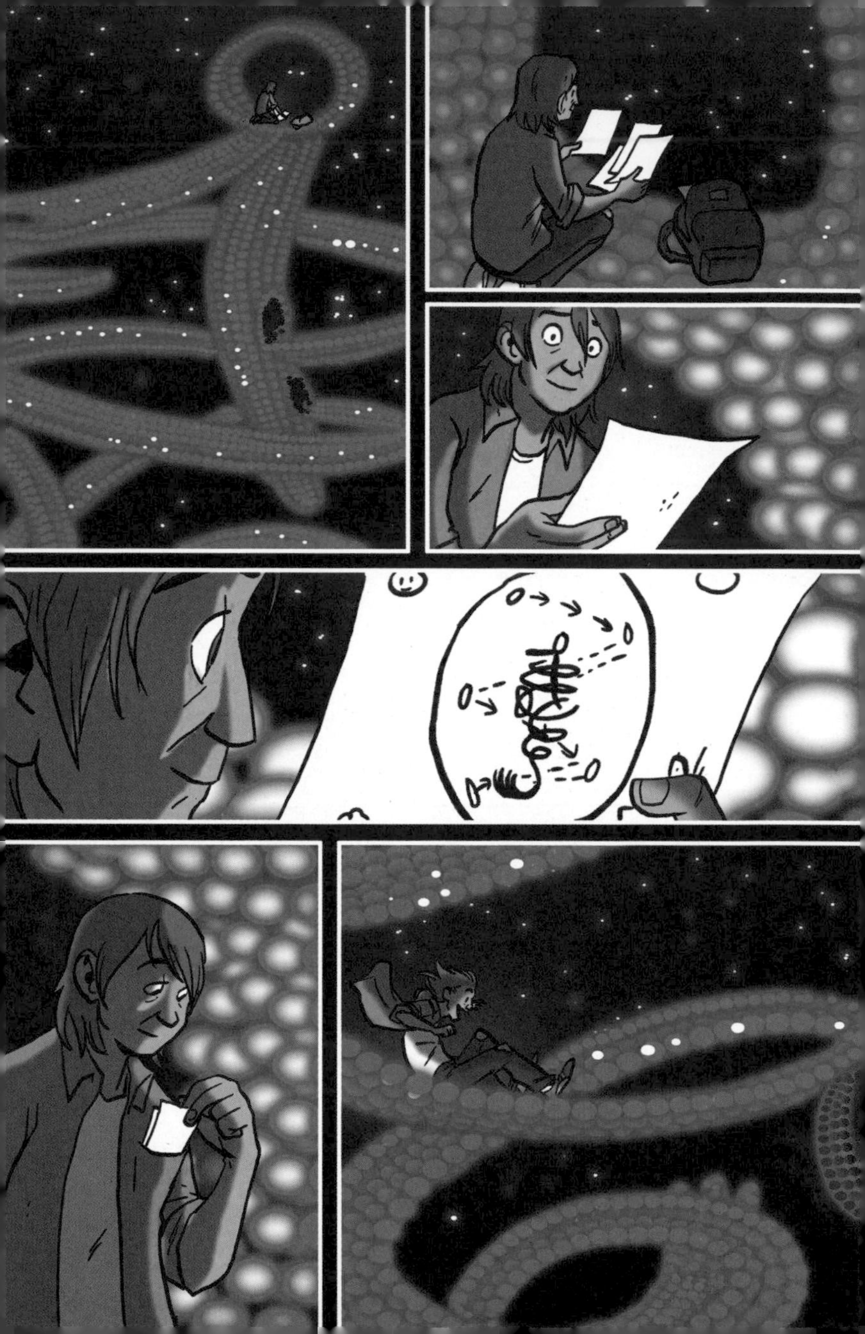

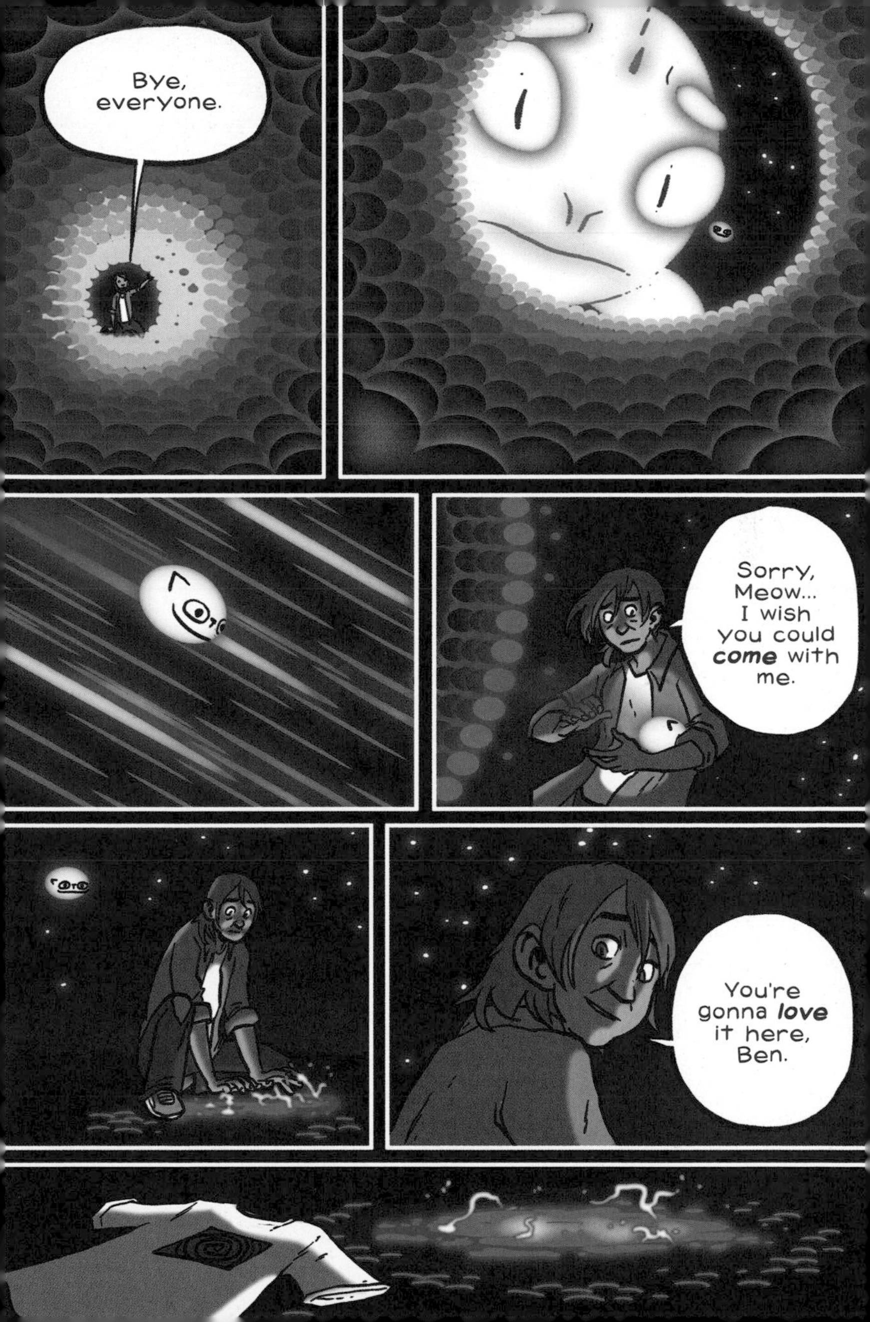
Bye, everyone.
Sorry, Meow... I wish you could *come* with me.
You're gonna *love* it here, Ben.

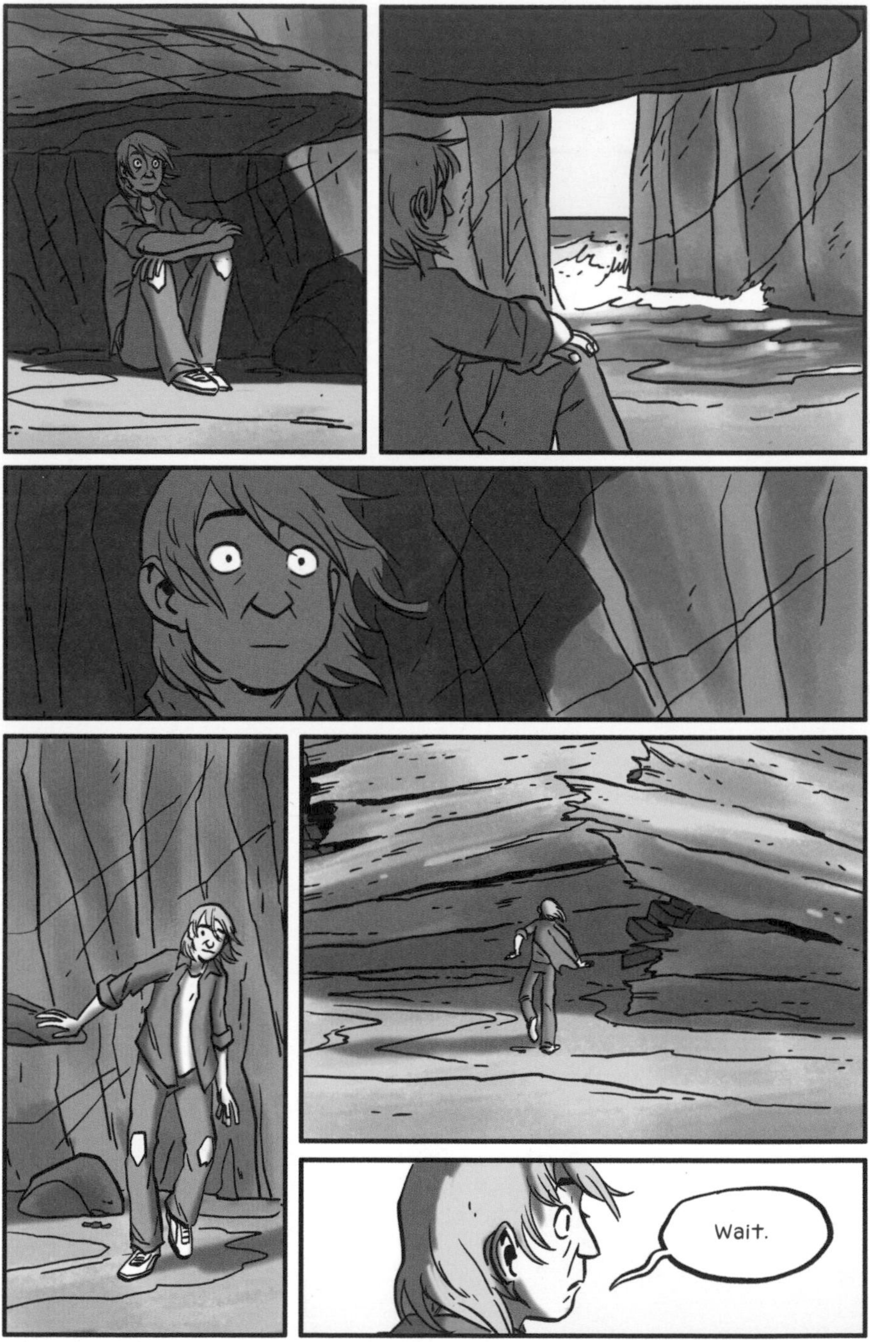
Wait.

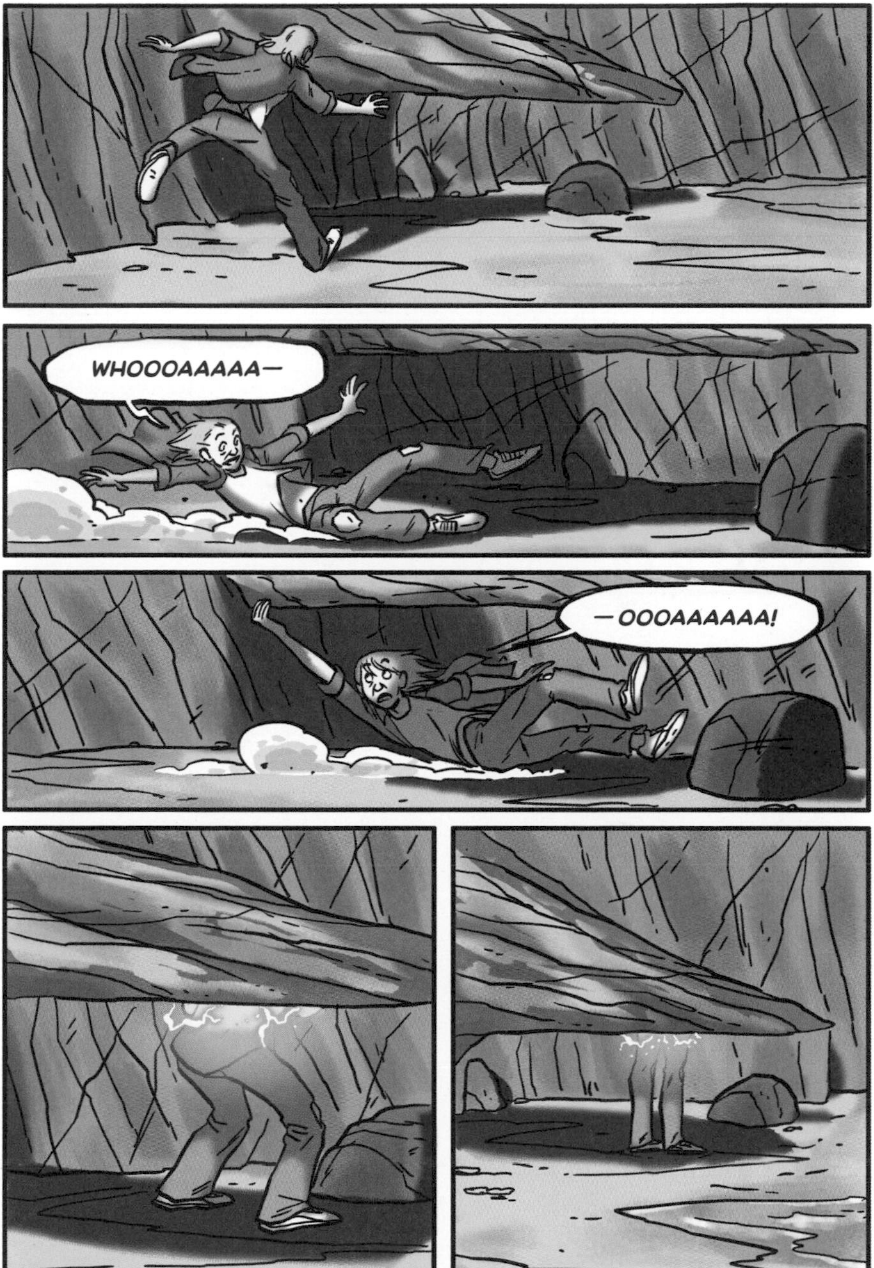
WHOOOAAAAA—
—OOOAAAAAA!

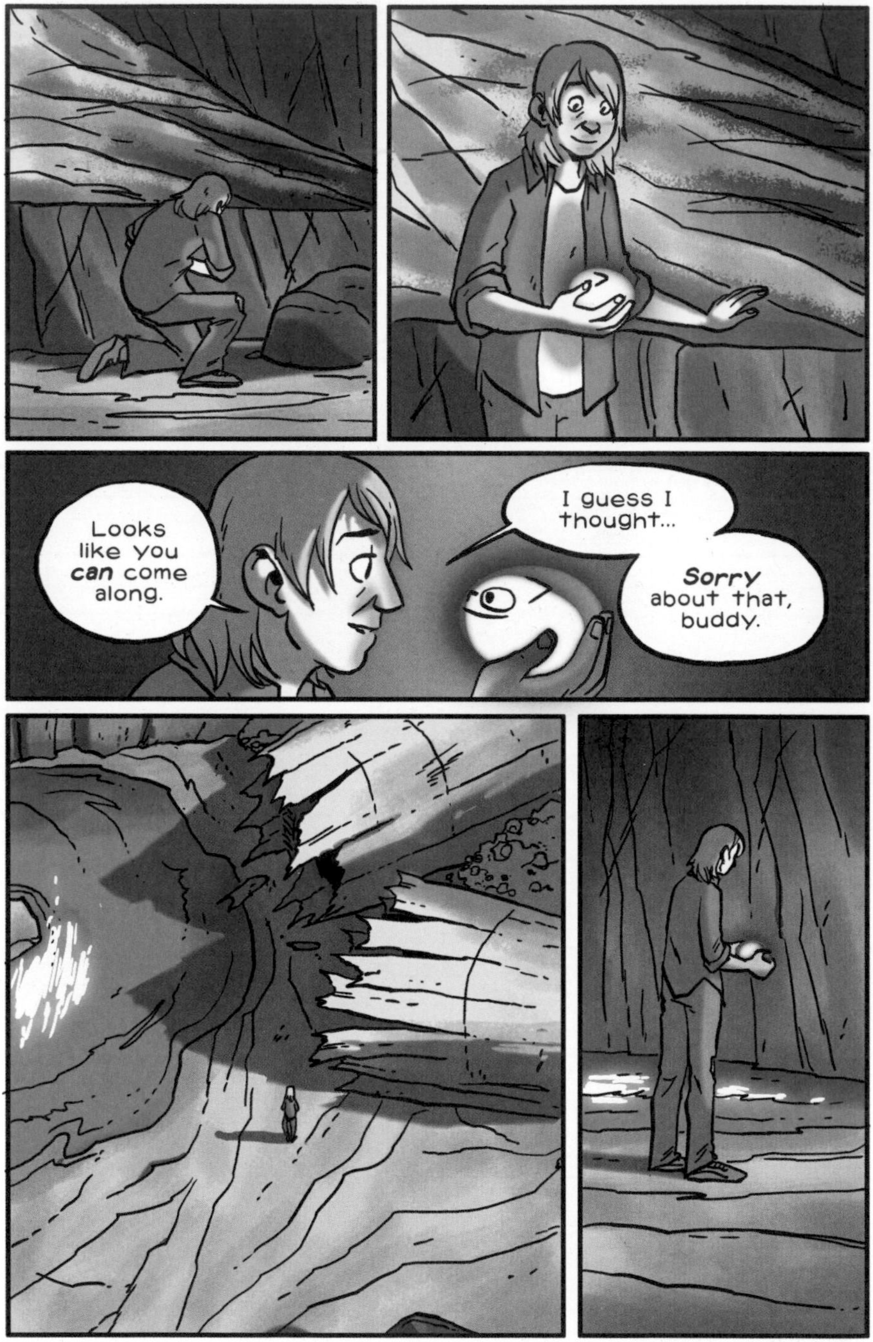
Looks like you **can** come along.
I guess I thought...
***Sorry*** about that, buddy.

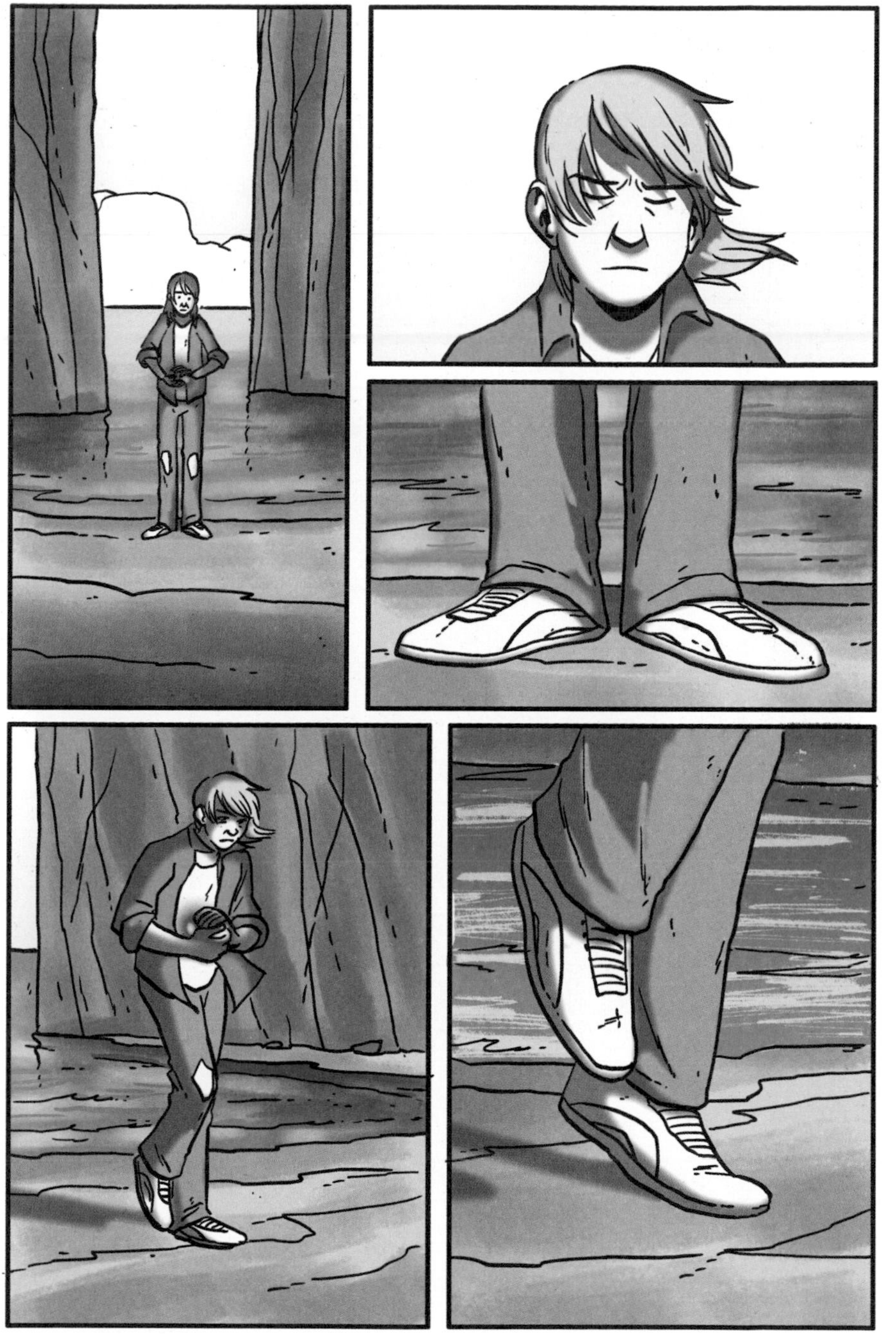

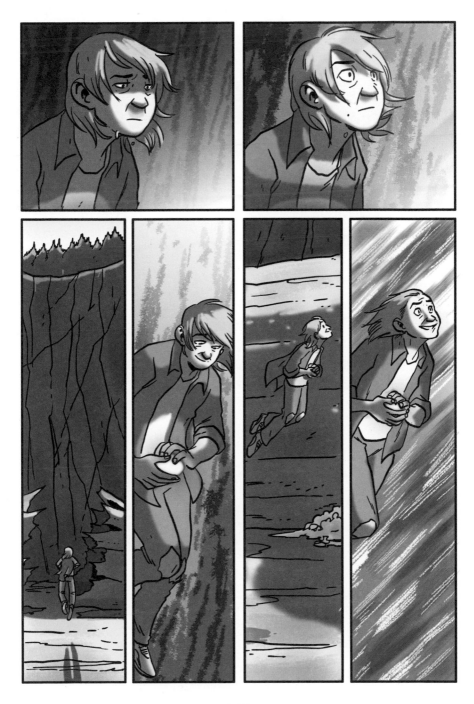

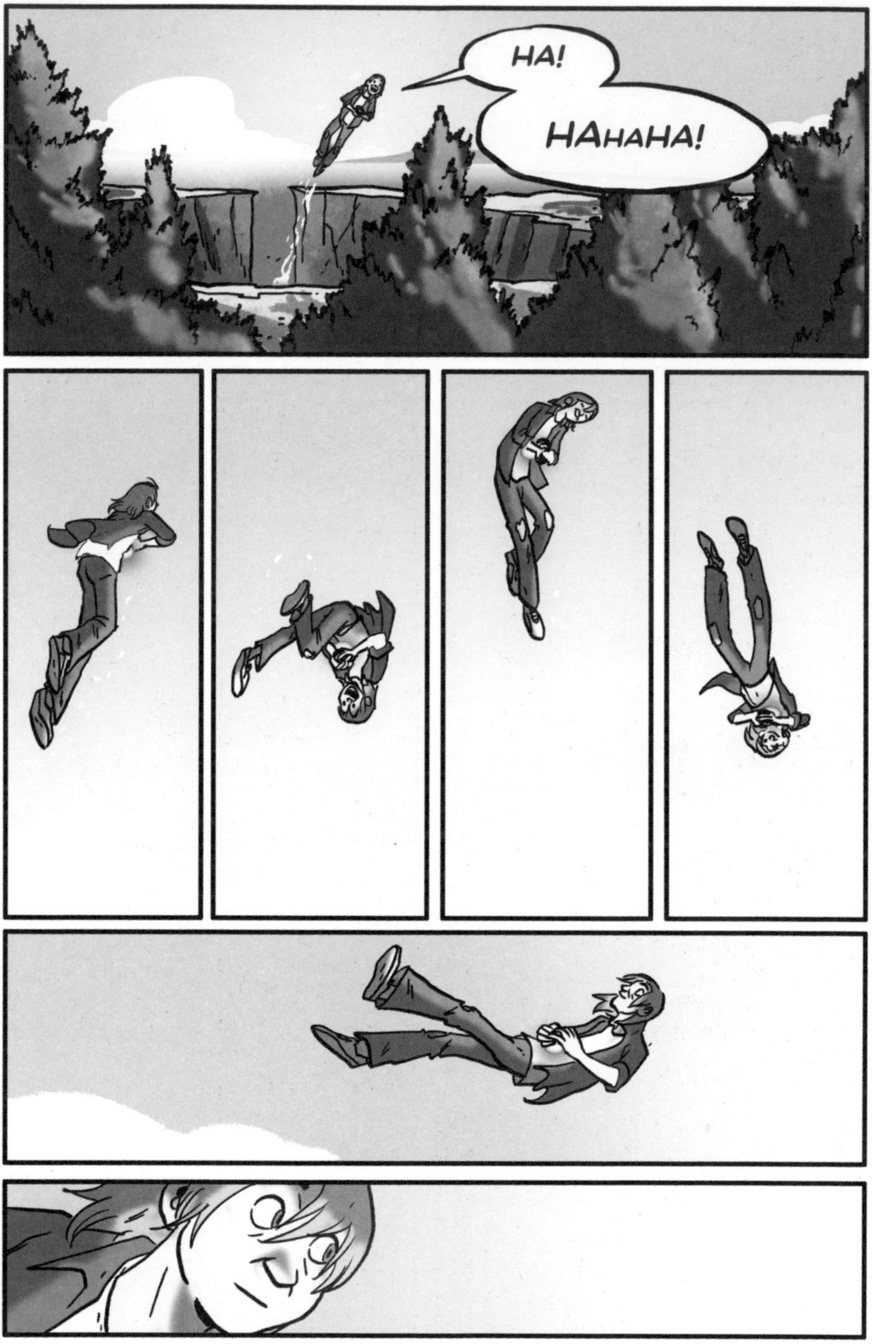
HA!
HAHAHA!

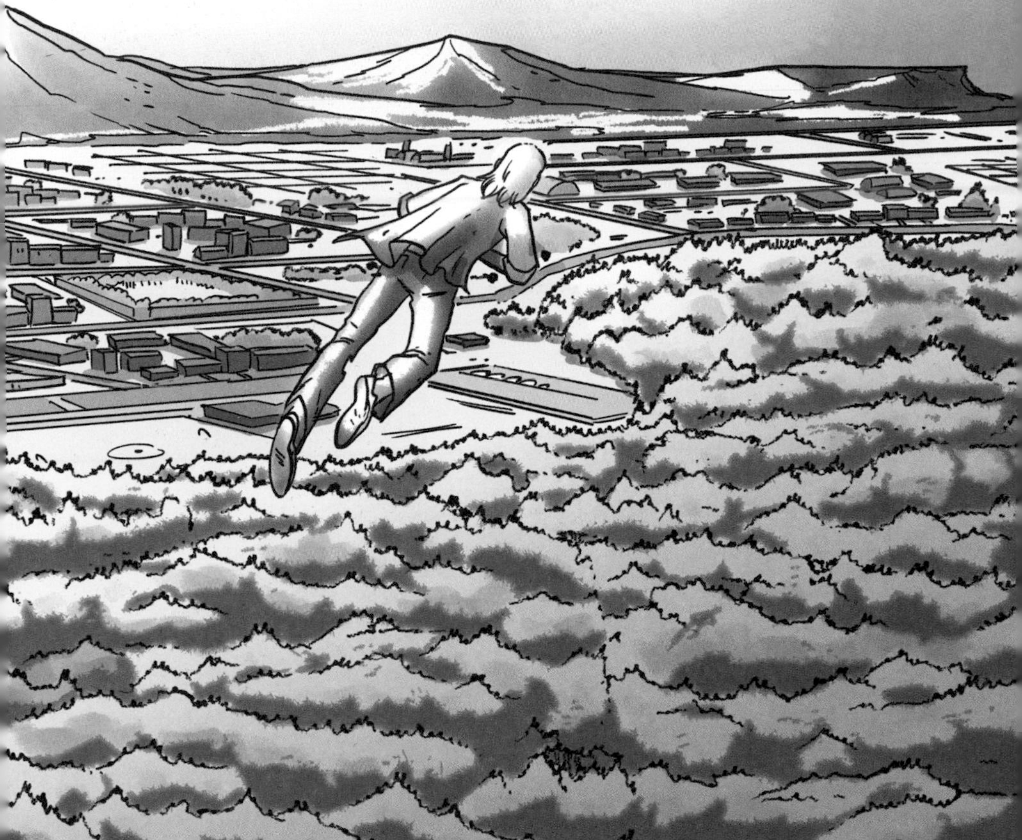

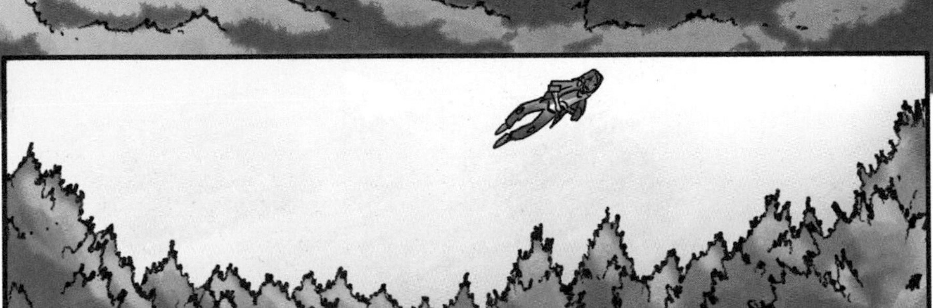

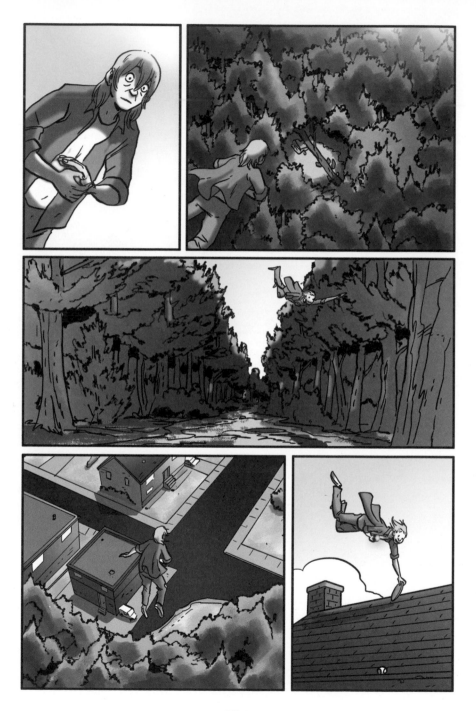

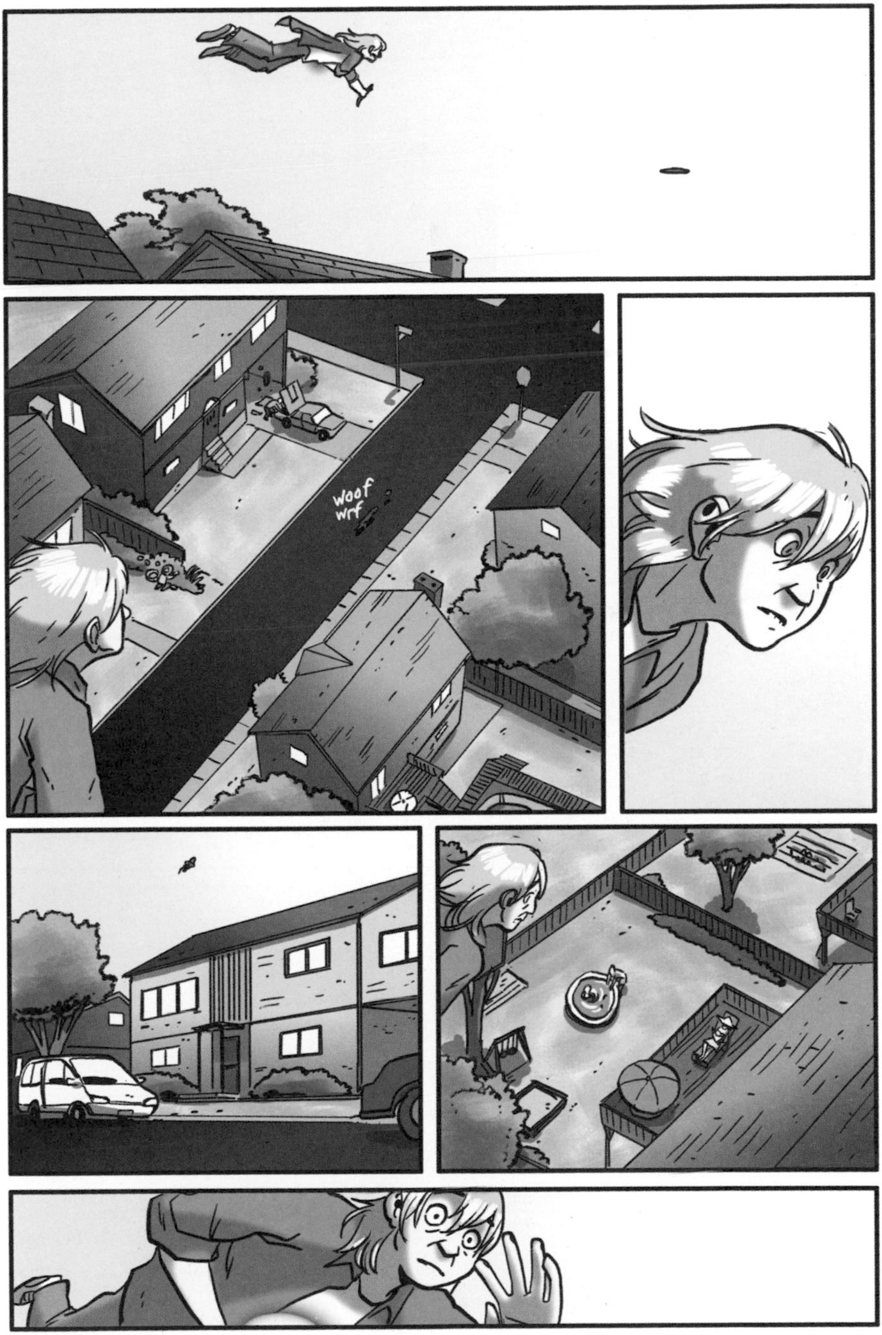
woof
wrf

Bub's
CONVENIENCE
CINEMAS 6

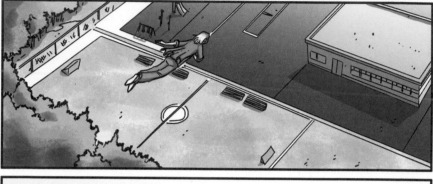

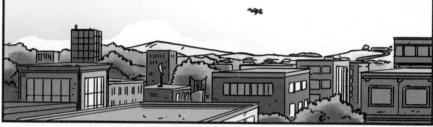

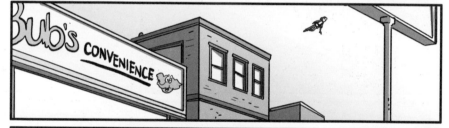

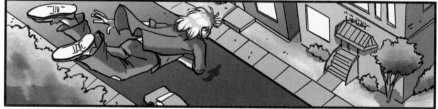

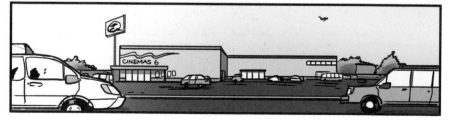

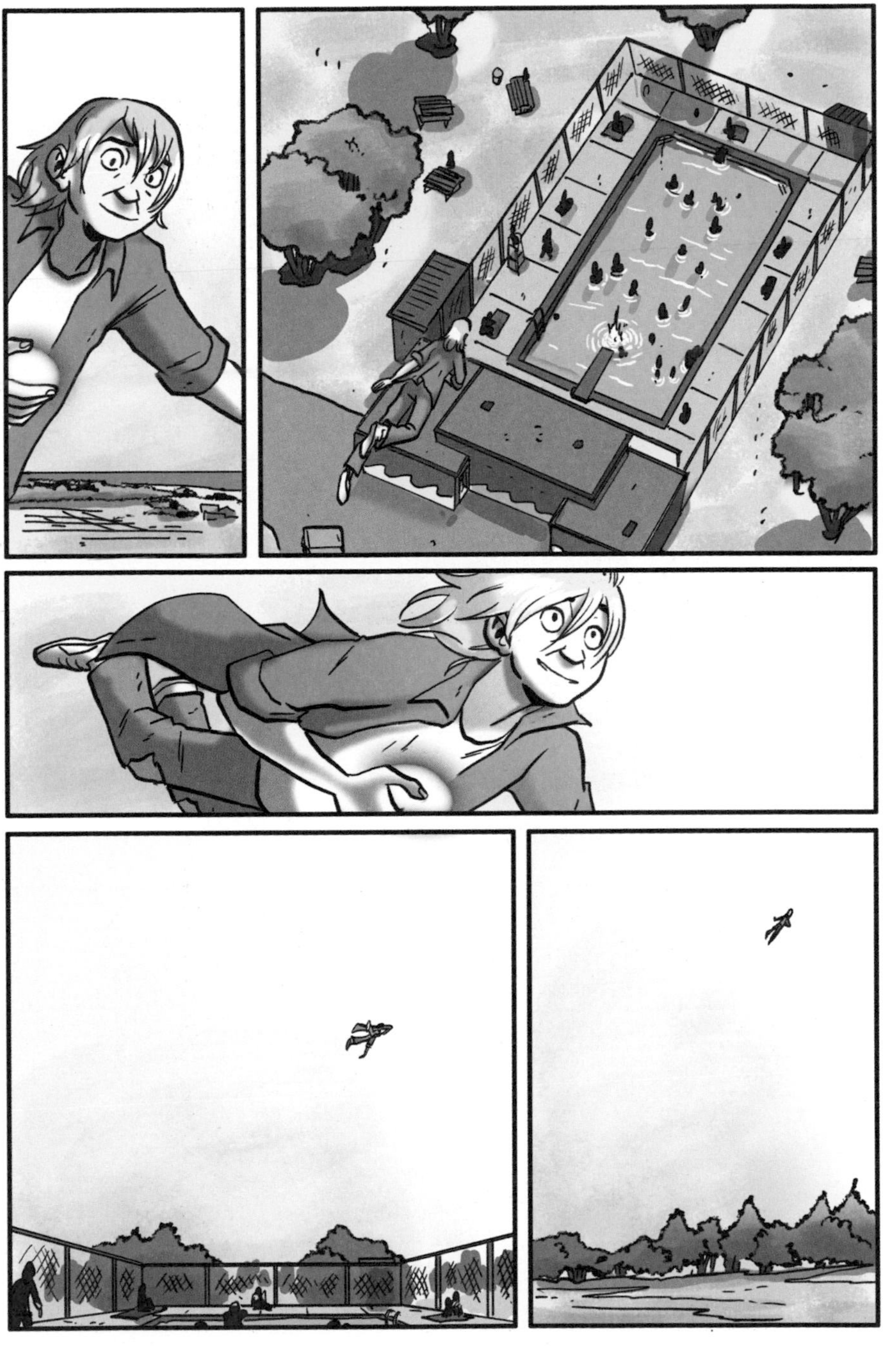

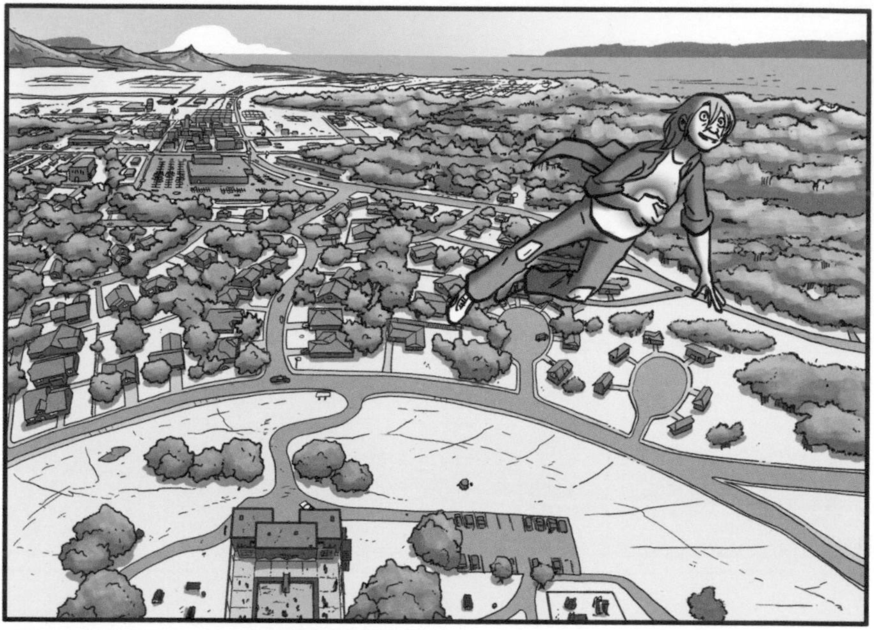

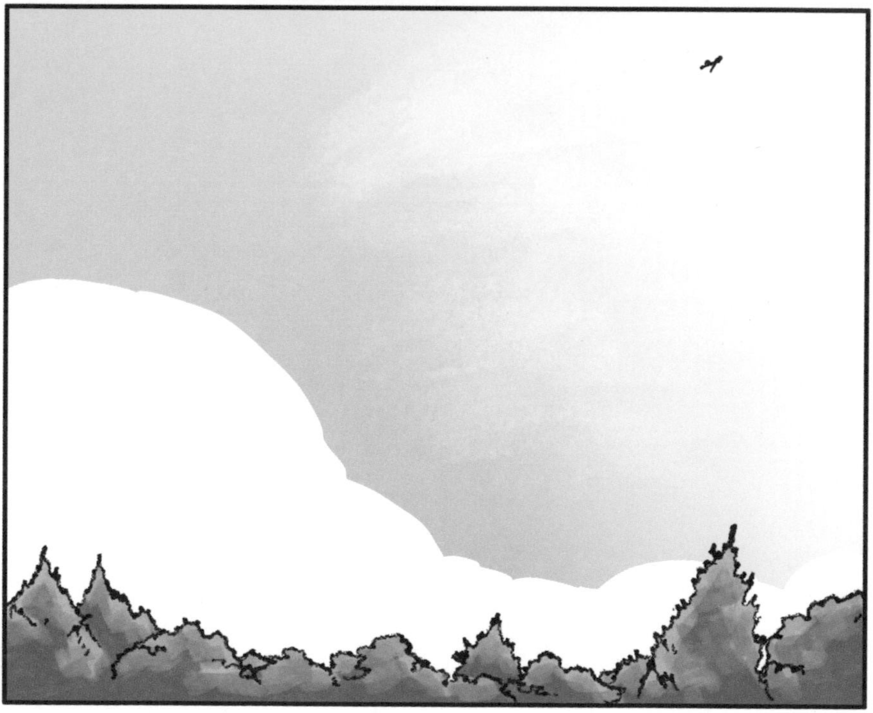

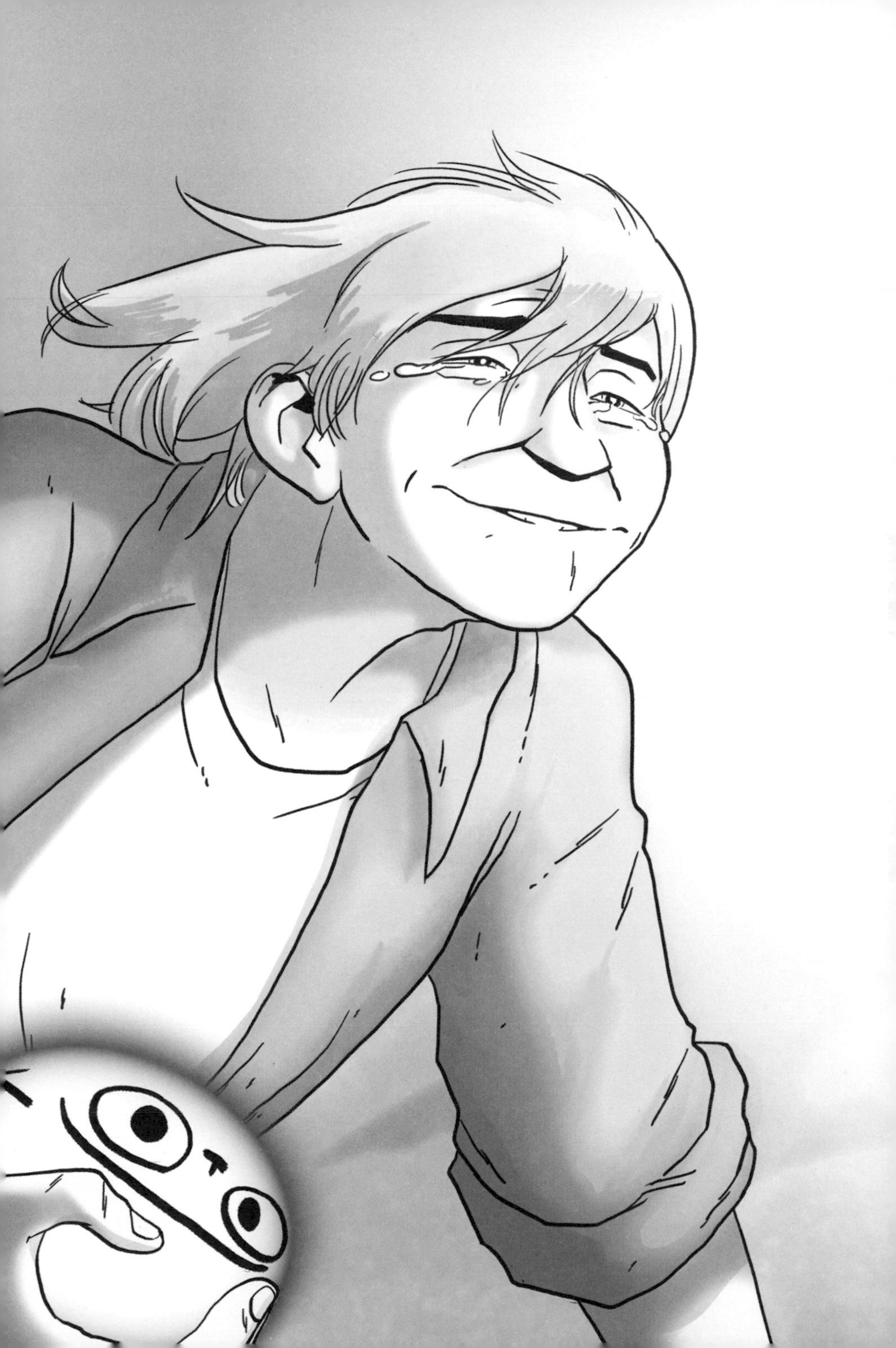

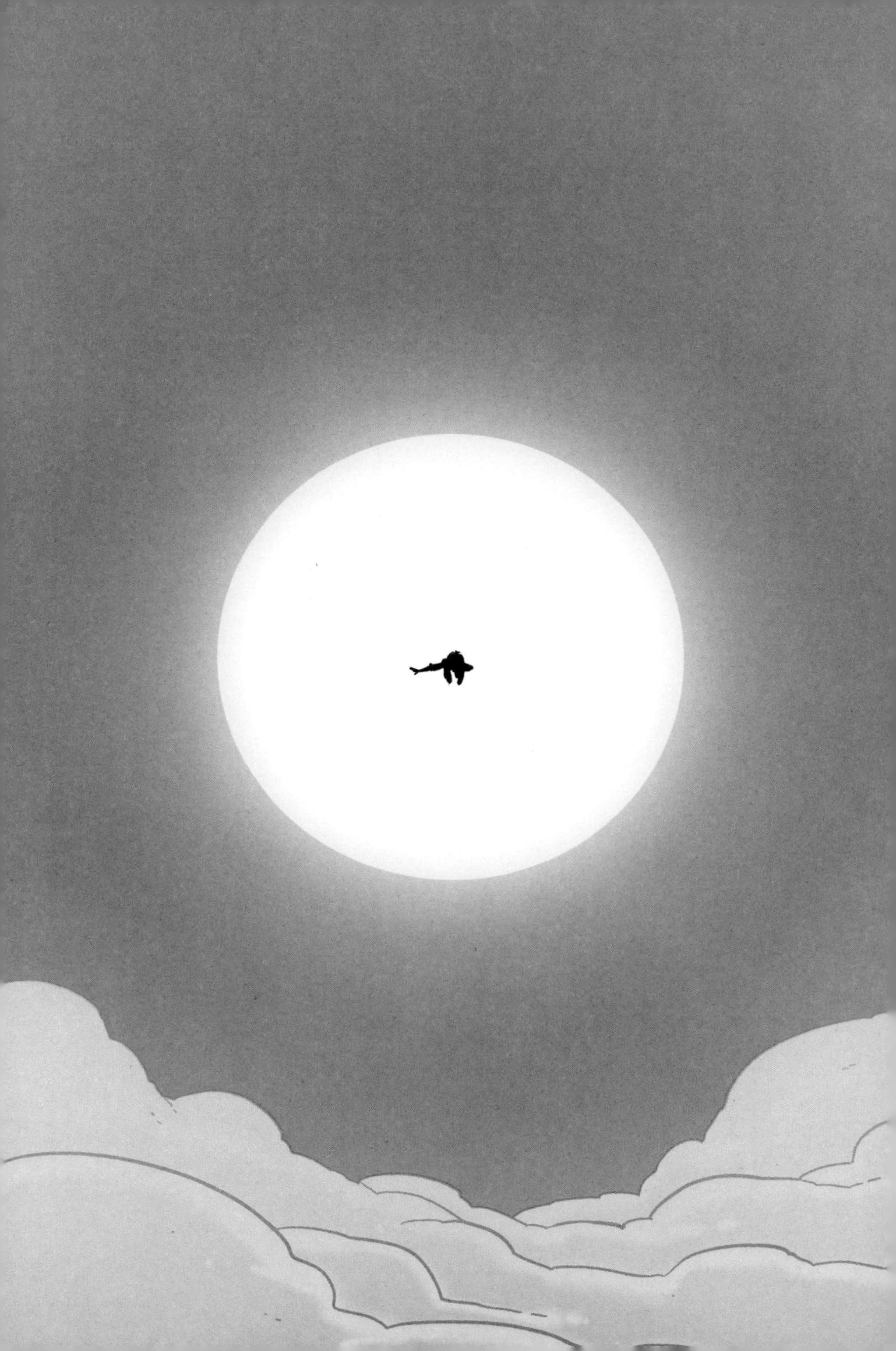

For Joseph

&

for Darwyn,

who left.

And for Oscar,

who showed up.

# Acknowledgments

Meredith, stop me if you've heard this before: You're the best of people. A truly excellent example of a human being, and my greatest friend.

Oscar, you're moving up the list with lightning speed. If you don't end up liking comics all that much, it's totally cool. I have other interests, too—I'm confident we'll find common ground. I love you like no one else in the universe.

To my family—Barbara, Tom, Jeremy, Sarah, Steven, Jodi, Ruby, Gabby—thank you for being my family, for loving me and fighting with me and letting me wander off to figure out what I wanted to do. There are fewer of us than there were, but there're more of us, too, and I take an odd comfort in that. To my extended family, the Grans, I've felt welcome and like one of the clan from day one, and you're very kind for creating that feeling.

Thanks to Jason Fischer, Judy Hansen, Mark Siegel, Robyn Chapman, and Samia Fakih for helping to see this book through.

Thanks always to my friends: Rusty, Vicki, Ken, Penelope, Lee, Evan, Geoff, Tessa, David, Kate D., Kate B., Frank, Becky, Bryan, Steve, Leslie, Lacey, Philip, Dave, Jim, Ian, Ben, Cal, Will, SJ, Alex, Randeep, Anne, Liz, Damian, and the cities of Philadelphia and Halifax.